"Please hold me."

...ms.

...d in his bed.

...ax didn't push her away, though. She was falling apart right in front of him, and he felt his arms close around her before he could talk himself out of it.

"I'm sorry," she said.

The latest apology put his teeth on edge. No way could an apology erase what she'd done. For nearly a year, he'd grieved for her. Cursed her. Because he'd believed she had caused her own death. Now he was cursing her for lying to him. Cursing her because of this blasted attraction that just wouldn't die.

SIX-GUN SHOWDOWN

BY
DELORES FOSSEN

First Published in Great Britain 2016
By Mills & Boon, an imprint of HarperCollins*Publishers*
1 London Bridge Street, London, SE1 9GF

© 2016 Delores Fossen

ISBN: 978-0-263-91912-7

46-0816

1 2 0595453 1

Delores Fossen, a *USA TODAY* bestselling author, has sold over fifty novels with millions of copies of her books in print worldwide. She's received a Booksellers' Best Award and an RT Reviewers' Choice Best Book Award. She was also a finalist for a prestigious RITA® Award. You can contact the author through her website at www.deloresfossen.com.

Chapter One

I'm not dead.

The voice mail message caused Deputy Jax Crockett to freeze. He stabbed the replay button on his phone and listened to it again. Three words. That was it.

But it felt as if a stick of dynamite had just gone off in his chest.

Paige.

Oh, mercy. It was his ex-wife, Paige.

That was her voice, all right. He was sure of it. But it couldn't be her because he'd buried her a year ago.

Jax listened to the message again. And again. Then, he checked the name and number of the caller.

Unknown.

Which meant the person might have blocked him from seeing it. But it'd come in a half hour earlier when he'd been on the back part of his ranch looking for a calf that'd strayed from the herd. No phone reception was back there, so the call had gone straight to voice mail.

Was that fear he'd heard in her voice?

Or maybe fear that someone else was pretending to feel?

This had to be some kind of sick prank. That was it. Maybe someone who sounded like Paige.

But his gut didn't go along with that notion.

He knew his ex-wife's voice, and that'd been her on the other end of the line. Of course, that didn't mean someone hadn't used an old recording of her voice, perhaps piecing together words from other conversations to come up with that one sentence.

I'm not dead.

"You okay, boss?" he heard someone ask.

Jax dragged his thoughts back to reality and noticed that one of his ranch hands, Buddy Martindale, was looking at him as if he'd lost his mind.

Heck, maybe he had.

After all, he was standing in the barn while he repeatedly punched the voice mail button on his phone.

"Did anybody call the ranch in the past hour or so?" Jax asked him.

Buddy lifted his cowboy hat enough to scratch his head, giving that some thought. "Not that I know of. Maybe you oughta check with Belinda, though."

Yes, Belinda Darby would know. His son's nanny was inside the house, and since it was coming up on dinnertime, Belinda would be close to not only Jax's son, Matthew, but also near the house phone. She would have been able to hear the line ringing in Jax's home office, too, if someone had tried to reach him there.

Someone like a dead woman.

Get a grip.

Paige had been murdered by the serial killer known as the Moonlight Strangler. And there had to be some reasonable explanation for the call.

Jax handed off his horse's reins to Buddy, something he wouldn't normally do. Tending the horses was a task he enjoyed. Not today, though. Not after that message.

There were a good thirty yards between the barn and the back porch, so while he made his way to the house,

Jax listened to the recording again. Hearing it for the fifth time didn't lessen the impact.

The memories came, slamming into him.

Nightmares of the violence Paige had suffered. Folks often reminded him that she'd only died once. That she wasn't suffering now, that she was at peace. And while that was true, Jax couldn't stop himself from reliving every last horrifying moment of Paige's life.

Their marriage had fallen apart several months before she was killed, but it didn't matter that their divorce had been finalized only days before that fateful night. Paige sure hadn't deserved to die, and their son hadn't deserved to lose his mother.

Before Jax reached the back porch, the door opened, and Belinda stuck out her head. Even though the sunset wasn't far off, it was still hot, the August air more humid than cooling, and the breeze took a swipe at her long blond hair.

"You look like you saw a ghost," she said, smiling, but that smile quickly vanished. "Is everything all right?"

Heck, he must have been wearing his emotions on his face and every other part of him. A rarity for him since, to the best of his knowledge, no one had ever called him the emotional type.

"Have there been any calls since I've been out?" he asked.

"No." Unlike Buddy, Belinda didn't even hesitate. "Why? What's wrong?"

Jax waved her off. No need to worry her. And she would be worried if he told her about the voice mail. Belinda took care of Matthew as if he were her own and would have done the same for Jax if he'd let her. Anything that bothered the two of them would bother her.

"Can you stay late tonight? I need to go back to the sheriff's office and look over some reports," he lied.

Well, it was sort of a lie, anyway. He was a deputy after all, and there were always reports to read, write or look over. He'd maybe work on a few while he was there.

But what he really wanted was to have the voice mail analyzed.

He'd saved the old answering machine with Paige's recorded message on it. Jax had figured when Matthew got older, he might want to hear his mommy's voice.

Or at least that's what Jax had told himself.

But now, the recording could be compared to the one on his voice mail, and he'd have the proof he needed that this was some kind of a sick hoax. Maybe then the knot in his stomach would ease up.

"No problem. I can stay as late as you need," Belinda assured him.

He hadn't expected her to say anything different. "Thanks. And don't hold dinner for me. I'll be back before Matthew's bedtime, though."

Belinda nodded and went back inside. But not before giving him another concerned look. She would believe his lie because she wanted to believe it, but she knew something was wrong.

Jax was within a few steps of the back porch when he caught some movement from the corner of his eye. Just a blur of motion in the open doorway of the detached garage. Since Buddy was still in the main barn, Jax knew it wasn't him, and none of the hands from his family's ranch had come to help him work today. Still, that didn't mean his sister or brothers hadn't sent someone over to get a vehicle or something.

Except it didn't feel like anything that ordinary.

Probably because of that voice mail.

He was armed, his Glock in his waist holster, and Jax slid his hand over it and started toward the garage.

There.

He saw the movement again.

Someone was definitely inside.

He'd made some enemies over the years. That came with the territory of being a lawman. But if someone had decided to bring a fight to his ranch, then the person could have already ambushed him.

Not exactly a thought to steady his nerves.

"Who's there?" he asked. Not a shout.

Jax kept his voice low enough so that Belinda or anyone in the house wouldn't necessarily hear him. But a person in the garage should.

He got no answer, and he glanced back at his house to make sure Belinda was still inside. She was. Jax considered firing off a text to warn her to get Matthew and herself away from the windows, but it might be overkill.

Or not.

He got another glimpse of the shadowy figure and decided to confront this head-on. Literally. Jax drew his gun and hurried to the entry. It was dark inside, but not so dark that he didn't see the person lurking behind the back end of one of the trucks.

"Paige?" Jax whispered.

He could have sworn everything stopped. His heartbeat. His breath. Maybe even time. But that standstill didn't last.

Because the person stepped out, not enough for him to fully see her, but Jax knew it was a woman.

"You got my message," she said. "I'm so sorry."

Paige. It was her. In the flesh.

Jax had a thousand emotions hit him at once. Relief.

Mercy, there was a ton of relief, but it didn't last but a second or two before the other emotions took over: shock, disbelief and, yeah, anger.

Lots and lots of anger.

"Why?" he managed to say, though he wasn't sure how he could even speak with his throat clamped shut.

Paige cleared her throat, too. "Because it was necessary."

As answers went, it sucked, and he let her know that with the scowl he aimed at her. "Why?" he repeated.

She stepped from the shadows but didn't come closer to him. Still, it was close enough for him to confirm what he already knew.

This was Paige.

She was back from the grave. Or else, back from a lie that she'd apparently let him believe.

For a *dead* woman, she didn't look bad, but she had changed. No more blond hair. It was dark brown now and cut short and choppy. She'd also lost some of those curves that'd always caught his eye and every other man's in town.

"I know you have a thousand questions," she said, rubbing her hands along the outside legs of her jeans. She also glanced around. Behind him.

Behind her.

"Just one question. Why the hell did you let me believe you were dead?" But Jax couldn't even wait for the answer. He cursed. "I saw pictures of you after the Moonlight Strangler had gotten his hands on you. There's no reason you should have let me believe that'd happened to you."

"It *did* happen." She stepped even closer, and thanks to the sunlight spearing through the door, he saw the scar on her cheek.

The crescent-shaped knife cut that the Moonlight Strangler had given all his victims.

There were marks on her throat, too. Scars from the piano wire that had sliced into her skin when the killer strangled her.

"Yes." Paige touched her fingers to her neck. "It's healed now. For the most part."

She was wrong. It would never heal. Never go away. Not in his mind, anyway.

"But clearly you're not dead," he snapped. And he didn't want her to be, but he damn sure wanted some answers. "I've been through hell for the past year. *Hell*," Jax emphasized. "You didn't just put me through this, either. Matthew went through it, too."

Even though his son had been only a year old when Paige died, it'd broken Jax's heart to hear his son call out for his ma-ma.

"Matthew." Her breath hitched, and tears sprang to her eyes. "I did this for him. For you."

"You didn't do anything for me." There was no way for him to rein in the anger in his voice or any other part of him. "You let me believe you'd been murdered."

She nodded, came even closer. So close that he caught her familiar scent. But she also glanced around again. "Because if I hadn't let you believe that, the Moonlight Strangler would have come after me again. And I was afraid he'd use Matthew and you to get to me."

He cursed again, dismissing that. "I'm a deputy sheriff."

"And that didn't stop him from getting to me," Paige reminded him just as quickly.

Good grief, she might as well have slugged him with a two-by-four. Because it was the truth. And it was a truth that Jax had struggled with for the past year.

He hadn't managed to save her.

But someone obviously had.

"What happened?" he demanded.

She paused, gathered her breath. Maybe her thoughts, too. "By the time the San Antonio cops got to the crime scene, I was barely alive. In fact, the first cop on the scene did report me as dead. That's the report that went out to you and everybody else. But the paramedics managed to revive me in the ambulance on the way to the hospital. I knew if word got out that I was alive, the killer would just come after me again."

He mentally went through all the details and saw one big question at the end of that explanation. "Who helped you come up with this stupid plan?"

"*I* came up with it." She glanced around again. "And I convinced a cop at SAPD who knew about me to go along with it."

Jax didn't miss the glancing around, nor the hesitation in her voice.

"Who helped you?" he pressed.

She dodged his gaze. "Other than the cop, Cord Granger helped."

Jax would have cursed again if he could have gotten his jaw unclenched. Cord Granger, a DEA agent. Also the biological brother to his adopted sister, Addie.

Cord and Addie's father was none other than the Moonlight Strangler himself. Though the law didn't have the actual identity of the vicious serial killer, they knew from DNA comparisons that both Cord and Addie were his biological children. Children the killer had abandoned when they were a little more than toddlers, and neither had any recollection of the man.

Too bad.

If they had a name, then they could find and arrest the piece of slime.

Something that Cord had made his top priority.

Jax had never cared much for Cord. And this wouldn't help. Because Cord was much more concerned about catching his birth father than he was with the safety of the people around him. Jax wouldn't have put it past the man to actually use Paige to draw the killer out. And now he'd apparently put Paige up to lying to him.

Not just any old lie, either.

But one that'd crushed Jax and the rest of his family.

"You were a fool to trust Cord," he finally managed to say. Jax shoved his thumb against his chest. "You should have trusted me instead."

She huffed. Not an angry sound, but more like stating the obvious. "We weren't exactly in a good place, Jax."

That was the wrong thing to say. A new wave of anger came. "You're sure you didn't *die* because you didn't want to face the divorce?" Or maybe because she hadn't wanted to face him?

Her eyes narrowed when their gazes connected again. "No. It was to save Matthew and you."

Jax didn't have time to figure out if he believed that or not. Because he heard something he didn't want to hear.

Belinda's voice.

"Jax, are you all right?" the nanny called out.

Belinda was on the back porch, peering into the garage. She could almost certainly see him, but probably not Paige. Paige kept it that way by stepping into the shadows.

"Tell her to go back inside," Paige insisted.

Jax opened his mouth to ask why, but because he

was watching Paige so closely, he saw the urgency slide across her face.

And the fear.

"I'm fine," he told Belinda. "Just checking a few things before I head to the office."

He waited to see if that'd be enough or if he truly would have to tell her to go inside. But thankfully, it worked. Belinda went back in and closed the door.

"What happened?" Jax asked Paige. And he didn't need his lawman's instincts to tell him that not only had something happened...

Something had gone wrong.

"What made you come back now?" he pressed.

The fear in her face went up a significant notch. "I think the Moonlight Strangler is on his way here to draw me out."

All right. That upped his concern, too. A lot. "And how exactly would he do that?"

Paige's mouth trembled. "The Moonlight Strangler is coming after Matthew and you...tonight."

Chapter Two

Paige stood there and waited for Jax to react to the news she'd just delivered.

And he reacted all right.

He turned, ready to bolt inside the house. To protect Matthew, no doubt. But Paige took hold of his arm to stop him.

"Just listen to what I have to say," she insisted. "I don't want to give the Moonlight Strangler a reason to fire shots into the house."

He slung off her grip. "Neither do I, but I'm not going to stand here while he goes after my son."

Our son, she nearly corrected, but Paige figured that was a different battle for a different time. They had to survive this one first.

"The killer likely knows I'm here," she explained, hoping it would get Jax to stay put. "I figure he's watching me. Somehow. Maybe with cameras. Maybe he's out there somewhere in the woods with infrared equipment. He's been watching me for the past three days, though I haven't spotted him yet."

Jax's eyes narrowed. "And even though you knew he was watching, you brought him here, to my doorstep?"

She had no trouble hearing the anger in his voice. Or seeing it on his face. "I didn't have a choice."

"There's always a choice," he snapped.

They weren't just talking about her being here now, but all the other things that'd happened between them. Again, another battle, another time.

Paige stopped him again when he tried to bolt. "The killer would have come here no matter what I did because he knew he'd be able to use Matthew and you to get to me."

He went still. Not in a good way. But in that calm, almost lethal way of a lawman who'd just heard something he didn't want to hear. "And how the heck do you know that?"

"Because he's sent me several texts. And, yes, I'm certain they're from the Moonlight Strangler because he knew details about my attack that hadn't been released to the press. In the last one he sent, he said if I didn't meet him tonight at 9:00 p.m., then he'd go after Matthew and you."

That was still nearly two hours away.

Not much time to pull off a miracle. But it might be enough time to bring all of this to an end. An end that would keep Matthew and Jax out of danger.

Jax stood there, obviously processing that, and cursed again. Glared at her, too.

She deserved the profanity and the glare. Deserved every drop of rage that he wanted to sling at her. Because he was right. She had turned his life upside down. Her precious little boy's, too.

"If you knew the killer was watching you, following you, then why hide here?" Jax asked.

She'd known that question was coming. Others would, too. "Because I didn't want to pull Belinda or your ranch hands into this. I'm not hiding from the killer. I'm hiding from them. That's why I parked by the creek and walked here."

Paige was thankful no one on the ranch had spotted her. Even though she'd altered her appearance, someone could have recognized her. Especially Belinda. They'd known each other since childhood, and a change of hairstyle wasn't going to fool anyone for long.

"At the time I faked my death," she continued, "I thought I was doing the right thing. I thought I was trusting the right people."

"You mean Cord," he snarled.

Paige hated that Jax was aiming his venom at Cord. Because Cord was the one person she was certain had kept his promise to make sure Jax and Matthew stayed out of harm's way.

But someone else had betrayed her.

Paige hoped she got a chance to discover who'd done that and deliver some payback. First, though, she had to protect Matthew—and Jax if he'd let her.

"After the attack, I went to a safe house in the Panhandle," she said. "Not an official safe house," Paige corrected, "but it was a place for me to recover and get back on my feet. Then, I moved to an apartment in Houston. That's where I've been, where I probably would have stayed, if I hadn't started getting those texts from the Moonlight Strangler three days ago."

"And those texts just appeared without any kind of warning or sign that the killer knew you were alive?" His voice stayed a snarl.

"Yes. I'm still trying to figure out how he learned that." She gave a heavy sigh. "Look, I know you have a lot of questions, but they have to wait. We have to put Matthew's safety first."

He couldn't argue with that, but mercy, she was

dreading those questions. Dreading even more that she didn't have the answers that Jax wanted to hear.

Jax cursed again before he glanced around the garage, the yard and the back of the house. "I don't want you inside. I don't want Matthew seeing you yet."

"Agreed." Though it broke her heart to say that.

Jax's eyebrow lifted, and he got that look, the one that condemned her as a mother.

"I want to see him and hold him more than I want my next breath," Paige clarified. "But if I go inside, it might give the killer a reason to try to get in there, too. He warned me not to try to hide behind my son."

As if she'd do that.

But she would have to draw Jax into the middle of this. Paige couldn't see a way around it.

"If I'd thought I could make Matthew safer by going inside with him, I would have already been in there," Paige added.

That stirred Jax's jaw muscles, but thankfully he didn't try to bolt toward the house again. However, he did take out his phone, and he moved into the shadows of the garage, his attention nailed to the house.

"I'm texting Belinda to tell her to lock the doors and set the security system," Jax relayed to her. "I'll tell her it's just a precaution, that a prisoner has escaped. And then I'm calling for backup."

Paige didn't stop him from sending the first text. She wanted the house locked down. But she did stop him from texting his brother Jericho. Jericho was the sheriff, and while he would ultimately get involved in this, now wasn't the time. Ditto for Jax's other two brothers, Chase and Levi. They were both lawmen, too, and having them here could make a bad situation worse.

"Hear me out before you involve your brothers in

this," she said. "After I got those messages from the Moonlight Strangler, I knew he wasn't going to back down until he had me. I'm the one who got away, and he wants me dead."

"I'm listening," Jax said when she hesitated.

Paige hadn't hesitated because she thought he wasn't listening, but rather because she wasn't sure how to say this. Best just to get it out there. "If I'd thought it would keep Matthew out of danger, I would have just surrendered to him. Would have let him finish what he started."

Jax cursed again. "Do you hear yourself? You're talking about suicide. What you should have done is gone to the cops. Or to me."

"I did come to you, tonight," she whispered. "You won't be thanking me for that, though, but it was the only way. I want this monster dead, and I want you to kill him for me."

He gave a crisp nod. "Tell me where he is, and I will," Jax said as if it were a done deal.

It was far from being a done deal, though.

"He wants me to meet him tonight at nine on the bridge at Appaloosa Creek. I'm sure he already had the area under some kind of surveillance before he told me it was the meeting place. He said if I show up with anyone but you, then he'll start a killing spree. One that will involve *our* son."

She gave him a moment to let that sink in. It didn't sink in well. The fire went through his already fiery blue eyes. Actually, plenty of things about Jax fell into the fiery category. All cowboy, even with that badge clipped to his belt. *Hot* cowboy, she mentally corrected.

Even now, after all this time and water under the bridge, Paige was still attracted to him. Something she shouldn't be remembering. Not when she had more important things to deal with.

"That's why you can't involve your brothers," she added. "If they go rushing to the area, he'll know."

"How?" he snapped.

"I'm not sure. Like I said, I suspect long-range cameras. Of course, that means he has the resources to set up something like that without being detected."

His stare drilled into her. "Who is he?"

A heavy sigh left her mouth. "I honestly don't know."

No one did. The Moonlight Strangler had murdered more than a dozen women before he'd finally made a mistake and left his DNA at a crime scene. There'd been no match for the DNA in the system, but there had been a match of a different kind.

To Jax's adopted sister, Addie.

"As you know, Addie doesn't remember her father," Paige said.

Of course, Addie had been just three when she'd been found wandering around the woods near the Crocketts' Appaloosa Pass Ranch. When no one had come forward to claim her, Jax's parents had adopted her and raised her as their own along with their four sons: Jax, Jericho, Chase and Levi.

"As fraternal twins, Cord was the same age as Addie when he was abandoned, and he doesn't remember anything, either," she went on.

Something Paige had in common with Addie and Cord since she, too, had been left at the hospital when she was a baby. Of course, she hadn't been abandoned by a serial killer.

He got quiet again, but not for long. "Did you see the Moonlight Strangler's face when he tried to kill you?" Jax asked.

This was one of the other questions she'd expected, but Paige had to shake her head and hope she could say the words without having flashbacks or a panic attack.

"He hit me with a stun gun when I was getting into my car in the parking lot of the CSI office in San Antonio," she said. Her words rushed together, spilling out with her breath. "He was wearing a mask so I never saw his face. He said some things to me…cut me and strangled me until I lost consciousness."

Jax pressed his lips together for a moment. "What things did he say?"

That required her to take a moment. Things that were hard to repeat aloud, though they repeated in her head all the time.

And in her nightmares.

"He said if he hadn't managed to get to me, then he would have kidnapped Matthew to draw me out." There. That was the worst of it. The absolute worst. "The next thing I remember after that was waking up with a San Antonio cop leaning over me."

"The cop who helped you fake your death," he mumbled. "Along with Cord." Jax took the venom in his voice up a notch.

Probably because Cord was obsessed with finding and stopping the Moonlight Strangler. But Paige thought maybe she heard something else in Jax's voice. Perhaps a little jealousy. She recognized it because she felt that same ugly emotion when Jax said Belinda's name.

"It's not like that between Cord and me," she volunteered.

His glare didn't soften any. "Then how is it exactly? Why don't you tell me?"

Well, this was a can of worms that she'd hoped to delay opening. The emotions of it were still too raw, and Paige wasn't sure she could tell him without choking on the words. But Jax had to know. Because it was hearing this that would hopefully get him to cooperate with her dangerous plan.

"When the killer was strangling me," she said, but then had to stop to fight back the images of that nightmare. Always the images. "He told me my birth mother was one of his first victims and that he was killing me to make sure her *spawn* didn't live another second."

Judging from the way his eyes widened, Jax hadn't expected that. "And you believed him?"

"No. But the DNA test I took later proved otherwise." That required another deep breath. "According to the test, my birth mother was Mary Madison. Her body was found just a few days after I was abandoned in the hospital. I didn't learn any of this until after I'd faked my death."

"His victim's daughter," Jax said. He did some deep breathing, too, and she could almost see the wheels turning in his head. "That's why he came after you?" But he didn't wait for her to answer. "Then why hasn't he gone after the children of his other victims?"

She had to shake her head. "Maybe my birth mother's murder was more personal to him? Or he could believe I know something about him that the others don't."

"Do you?" he asked, and it sounded like some kind of accusation.

With good reason.

Cord wasn't the only one who'd become obsessed with finding the Moonlight Strangler. She had as well, and even though Paige had dismissed it as part of her job as a crime scene investigator, it'd been more than that. She'd felt it bone deep.

And she'd been right.

She wasn't just searching for a killer who had eluded the cops for nearly thirty years. Now she knew that she'd been looking for the man who'd murdered her mother so she could stop him from killing again. Of course, the obsession had come back to haunt her and just might cost her everything.

"I don't know anything about his identity," she continued, "but I do know how to stop him."

However, it would cost her big-time. The trick was not to have that cost spread to Matthew and Jax.

Paige checked the time. The minutes were ticking away. "I heard you tell Belinda that you were going to the sheriff's office, so she'll be expecting you to leave soon. I suspect you were going to analyze the voice mail I left you."

Jax nodded. "I thought maybe it was a hoax."

Of course he had. Because he hadn't thought she was capable of doing something like faking her own death. "I left the message because I thought it would lessen the blow of you seeing me."

He looked her straight in the eyes. "Nothing could have done that."

True. But she'd had to try. Just as she had to try now.

"So, your plan is to…what?" he asked. "Go to the Appaloosa Creek Bridge and meet a killer who's hellbent on finishing you off?"

Hearing it spelled out like that didn't help, but Paige tried to push her fear aside. "I'm sure he'd like to finish you off, too. I can't think of another reason he would say I could bring you along."

Jax stayed quiet a moment. "But you're thinking I can kill him before he can get to me?"

Bingo.

He gave her a flat stare. "Of course, the only way I'd

get a chance to do that is for him to get close enough to murder you."

Yes. There was no way around that.

"He's never shot anyone before." Not that Paige knew of, anyway. "He'll want an up-close-and-personal kill, like the others." Something that tightened the knot in her stomach. A knot that'd been there for nearly a year since the Moonlight Strangler attacked her.

Jax's next round of profanity was even worse than the others. Before he could tell her a flat-out no, that there was no chance this was going to happen, Paige interrupted him.

"If I could think of another way out, one that didn't involve you, I'd take it. But I can't risk him coming after Matthew. And neither can you."

Jax didn't agree with that. Didn't argue, either.

"He said we're to leave our guns by the side of the road before we approach the bridge," Paige explained. "He has to know that you'll be carrying some kind of backup weapon. That's why I believe he'll use a thermal scan."

"He wouldn't be able to see a gun on thermal scan." Jax closed his eyes for a second, shook his head. "But he would be able to see the outline of one."

"That's why it can't look like something he'd recognize as a weapon." She took the plastic syringe from her pocket. "Hopefully, it'll look like an ink pen, but it's filled with enough sodium thiopental to incapacitate him in less than thirty seconds."

"Sodium thiopental," he repeated, no doubt knowing that it was a powerful drug that would stop the Moonlight Strangler from moving. It could also kill him, since it was the same drug used in lethal injections for those on death row.

"I would just try to use it on him myself," Paige added, "but he left specific instructions that'll prevent me from doing that."

She took her phone from her jeans pocket and handed it to Jax so he could read the text message for himself. Everything was there. The time and place of the meeting. The offer for her to have Jax and no one else to drive her. If anyone else did show up, the meeting was off, and Jax's house would be attacked. There was also the demand for them to leave their weapons on the side of the road twenty yards from the bridge and then walk there.

And one final demand.

"He wants you to strip down to your underwear so he can make sure you don't have a weapon," Jax read.

She nodded. "Obviously, he doesn't trust me."

"He won't trust me, either," Jax reminded her just as quickly.

"No. He might even have a hired thug hiding nearby to try to take you out. That's why you'll need to wear Kevlar. Do you still keep a vest in your truck?"

Jax nodded. "Kevlar won't stop him from killing you, though."

"No, but it'll stop him from killing you. We can take other precautions for me, like using our own thermal scan of the area." She tipped her head to the small equipment bag she'd stashed behind the truck. "There's a handheld one in there so we can see if anyone's lurking nearby before we surrender our guns."

And there it was. All spelled out for him. Paige just waited to see what he was going to do. Part of her wanted him to refuse. That way, he'd be safe.

For tonight, anyway.

But she didn't believe the killer was bluffing. If he

couldn't have her, then he would come after Matthew and Jax and make her suffer a million times more than she would with just her own murder.

Jax looked up at the ceiling as if asking for some divine advice. They needed it. But when his gaze came back to her, he handed Paige her phone and took out his own. He fired off a text and within just a matter of seconds, he got an answer.

"Jericho will be here in five minutes to guard Matthew," he relayed to her.

Jericho's house was less than half a mile away, and she'd hoped he would be able to come right away. Not to try to talk them out of this plan but to help in a way that wouldn't spur an attack at the ranch. Even though Jericho wouldn't be happy to see her, he would do everything humanly possible to protect Matthew. Not just tonight. But forever.

Good thing, too.

This could be the worst mistake of her life. The worst mistake of Jax's life, too. Because this meeting could make their son an orphan.

"Unless we kill the Moonlight Strangler tonight, you'll have to make sure everything here is secure, that he can't get to Matthew," she reminded him.

Of course, they couldn't shut their little boy away for the rest of his life, and that meant one way or another, someone would have to stop the killer.

"Does Cord know about this plan?" Jax asked.

Paige nodded. "He's in one of the trees across the road with a long-range rifle. He's Jericho's backup. He would have gone with me to the bridge, but the Moonlight Strangler said I could only bring you. Anyone else, and Matthew could be hurt."

Jax's teeth came together. "That's not going to happen."

It was the exact reassurance she needed. One that only a father could give. Yes, Cord would fight to the death for her, but Jax would fight to stay alive so he could keep their son safe.

"Once Jericho is here, we'll come up with some additional security measures," Jax insisted. "He might be able to get a deputy to pose as a hunter so we can scan the woods around the creek before we even get there. That way, we'd still be here if he's detected."

It was a risk, but everything was at this point.

"I saw him," she said, her voice cracking on the last word.

Jax's gaze slashed back to hers. "The killer?"

"Matthew. Belinda had him on the back porch earlier." Mercy, just the memory of seeing him nearly brought her to her knees. "They were on the porch swing, and she was reading to him. He's gotten so big."

No longer a baby. He was a toddler now, almost two years old. Walking and talking. Every second seeing him was like a precious gift that Paige had never thought she'd get.

"I've missed so much." She hadn't meant to say that last part aloud, and it caused Jax to mumble something. She didn't catch exactly what he said, but it was clear he believed that "dying" had been a choice she'd made.

It was.

And at the time it had been her only choice.

She saw the slash of headlights coming toward the garage. Jericho, no doubt. But just in case it wasn't, Paige drew her gun from the back waist of her jeans.

A gesture that had Jax doing the same, along with raising an eyebrow.

Paige had never been much for guns, especially after witnessing her adoptive parents' murders when she was just sixteen. The result of a botched robbery attempt. Since then, guns had always made her squeamish.

"You know how to use that?" Jax asked.

She was about to assure him that she'd learned, but her phone dinged, and Paige saw the text from the unknown sender.

"It's from the killer," she said. Paige's heart went to her knees when she glanced through the message.

"'Change of plans,'" she read aloud. "'You and Jax start walking to the end of the road *now*. If you bring anyone with you or don't follow the rules, I'll start shooting. The first bullet will go into the house, and I'll aim it right at your son.'"

Chapter Three

Jax's mind was already spinning. He'd been hit with way too much tonight, but all of those whirlwind thoughts flew right out of his head. He pinpointed his focus on the one place it should be.

His son.

His first instinct was to run into the house and hide Matthew and Belinda, but that could turn out to be a fatal mistake. The killer might see it as a violation of his demand and start firing. If the killer was close enough to be capable of doing that.

Jax just didn't know.

And it was too risky to find out.

"Oh, God," Paige mumbled, and she repeated it several times. "We don't have everything in place yet."

No, and Jax figured that was part of the killer's plan. To keep one step ahead of them; to keep them off balance. But Jax didn't intend to let this snake hurt his little boy.

"Text him back," Jax instructed. "Tell him we need more time and that we want the meeting place moved back to the bridge."

It was a long shot. Really long. And a moment later he realized it was no shot at all. "He's blocked me," Paige said.

Of course he had. The killer had delivered his orders, and he wouldn't have them challenged, because he would have almost certainly known that they'd try to negotiate with him.

Jax sent a text of his own. To Belinda. It would terrify her, but again there wasn't much of a choice. He instructed her to take Matthew into the main bathroom and get in the tub. The room was at the center of the house and would be the safest place for them to wait this out. Jax added that he would explain everything later and hoped he was around to do just that.

"Okay, what's wrong?" he heard Jericho ask before his brother even reached the door to the garage.

"I don't have time to get into a lot of details," Jax said, motioning for him to come inside. "Paige is alive, and the Moonlight Strangler is possibly nearby, ready to attack."

Jericho came in, put his hands on his hips, his gaze volleying from Jax to Paige. Jax could tell his brother had plenty of questions, but he also saw the moment when Jericho pushed all those questions aside and the sheriff part of him kicked in.

"What do you need me to do?" Jericho asked.

Jax wasn't sure just yet, but he soon would be. He looked at Paige. "Where's Cord exactly?"

She pointed to a cluster of trees across the road and on the far right side of one of the pastures.

"Text him," Jax ordered her again. "Let him know what's going on and ask if he can see anyone approaching the house."

While she did that, Jax went to her equipment bag and took out the thermal scanner and handed it to Jericho. "I don't know the range on this thing, but I need you to try to see if we're about to be ambushed. Also, call the others for backup."

By others, he meant their brothers, Levi and Chase. Both were lawmen with lots of experience.

Jax also considered having Addie's husband, Weston, come down, but Jax didn't want to leave his sister alone. They had a baby and would be in a very vulnerable position if the Moonlight Strangler wanted to make Addie a target instead of Paige. It'd be a first, since the serial killer had never gone after Addie, but it was too big of a risk to take.

"Cord doesn't see anyone other than us and the ranch hands near the house," Paige relayed to them after reading the response she'd gotten from him. "He wants to know if you trust all your ranch hands."

Jax nearly snapped at that since he didn't like an outsider like Cord questioning men he'd known all his life. But Cord didn't know them, and it was exactly the kind of question a good lawman should ask.

"I trust them," Jax assured her. "Tell him to text us if he sees anyone or anything out of the ordinary."

While she did that, Jericho stayed just inside the doorway, out of range so he wouldn't be seen, and he started up the scanner.

"The Moonlight Strangler wants Paige and me to walk to the end of the road," Jax explained to his brother. He went to his truck and took out the Kevlar vest, tried to hand it to Paige, but she shook her head.

"He'll still want me to strip down," she argued, "so he can make sure I don't have any weapons. And because it's a way of humiliating me. He might let you keep on your clothes, though, because he doesn't plan to let you get close enough to him to use a gun or anything else. That's why the vest is better on you. Put the syringe in your pocket so you can easily get to it. When he's attacking me, you go after him."

Jericho glanced at them as if they'd lost their minds. "Let me see if I'm understanding this. You two are going out there, with a serial killer? One who's already killed Paige once. Or rather, nearly killed her. And she's going to let him attack her again?"

"We don't have a choice," Jax assured him.

Well, maybe they didn't.

The situation was moving so fast that it was hard to think, but Jax didn't need a totally clear head to know that this could turn out to be a huge mistake—no matter what they did.

"Do you see anything on the scanner?" he asked his brother.

Jericho shook his head. "I don't even see Cord."

"He's wearing some kind of thermal blanket," Paige explained. "The kind hunters use. It'll make it harder to be seen on infrared."

That meant the killer and/or his henchmen could have done the same thing. And probably had. After all, this killer had gotten away with murder for years, so he wasn't an idiot.

But what was he exactly?

Deranged? Obsessed? Or was this more personal for him?

Then it hit him. The Moonlight Strangler had gone after Paige because he considered her a *spawn* of his victim and believed she didn't deserve to live. The killer probably wouldn't want the victim's grandson to live, either. It sickened Jax to think his little boy had any connection to something like that.

"I guess I also don't want to know why Cord was in on this little plan and I wasn't?" Jericho asked.

"Jax didn't know about the plan until a few minutes ago," Paige informed him.

"And yet you're still going along with it," Jericho mumbled. "Yeah, nothing could go wrong with trusting your ex-wife who let you believe she was dead."

Jax ignored his brother's sarcasm and double-checked the Glock in the back waist of his jeans. It'd likely be detected right away, but he might get lucky and be able to keep it.

"You see anyone?" Jax asked him.

"No. But like you said, we don't know the range on this thing. Somebody could still be out there, hiding under a thermal wrap. Somebody who'll kill you. That vest isn't going to protect you from a head shot."

Nor a shot that would incapacitate him in some other way. "I don't think he wants to kill me. Just Paige. And he doesn't want to put a bullet in her."

Damn, that sounded ice-cold. But it was the truth. The Moonlight Strangler would want his hands on her.

Paige went closer to his brother. She was ash pale now, and her hands were trembling. "I know you don't owe me any favors, Jericho, but if something goes wrong, stay here to protect Matthew."

Jericho doled out a glare to her as if he might confirm the no-favors part, but he nodded. "I'll protect him."

Jax knew his brother would. And Jax would do the same for him. "When Levi and Chase get here, tell them what's going on. Don't have them follow us, but if they can position themselves in front of the house and closer to the road, they might be able to give us some backup."

"Cord might be able to do that, too," Paige added. "He's got sniper training."

Good. Jax would take anything he could get at this point, but he really didn't want bullets flying near the house. Too bad he couldn't guarantee that wouldn't happen, and that meant Paige and he needed to put as much distance between them and the house as possible.

"We need to leave now," Paige pressed, already starting out of the garage.

Jax knew she was right, but he still took a moment to look around, to see if there was anything he could do to make this plan safer.

There wasn't.

He could see more headlights coming from the road that led to the main ranch and to his brothers' houses. Chase and Levi, no doubt. Jericho would have to explain to them what was happening and get in the best positions to protect Matthew.

In the meantime, all Jax could do was get moving toward this showdown with a killer.

Since there was no truly safe position for Paige, Jax fell into step beside her. However, he did maneuver her to his right.

"If someone fires shots, drop down into the ditch," he instructed, pointing at the ground. It wouldn't be ideal protection since it was only a few feet deep, but it was better than nothing.

He glanced back at the house to make sure Belinda wasn't at the window. She wasn't. Hopefully, she would stay put with Matthew in the bathroom until she got the okay from him.

Hell.

He hated putting his son through this. Matthew was too young to understand the danger, but he had to sense something was wrong. After all, he should be getting dinner about now, followed by reading time with his daddy. He shouldn't have to be holed up in a bathtub, hiding from a serial killer.

"I'm so sorry," Paige whispered.

"Don't," Jax warned her. Any apology she attempted would be useless right now and might mess with his head. "And keep watch."

Of course, she was already doing that. Her gaze was firing all around them. Jax couldn't be sure, but he thought he heard her mumble a prayer. Good. Because he was certainly saying a few of them, too.

Paige took out her phone, checked the screen. No doubt for an update from Cord or the killer. But there was nothing on the screen. Ditto for his own phone. No word yet from his brothers. Jax decided to believe that was good news, because if they'd spotted someone in the area, Jericho would have certainly let him know about it.

The road wasn't long, less than a quarter of a mile from his house to the highway that led into town. It wasn't a straight shot, though. It'd once been an old ranch trail, and it coiled around massive oaks and other trees that dotted the acres of land. Those deep curves in the road would no doubt prevent Cord or his brothers from being able to see what was going on.

There were no lights out here, but it wasn't pitch dark yet. Soon would be, though.

And there was a moon.

Since the killer had struck only on nights with a visible moon and left the crescent shaped cuts on his victims' cheeks, that's how he'd earned his nickname. Maybe he wouldn't add another victim or two to his list tonight.

"Still no text from him," Paige mumbled, checking her phone again.

No text from his brothers, either, but Jax did spot something. So did Paige because she stopped, and they both stared at the truck ahead. It was parked right where the ranch road met the highway. The lights were off, and it was positioned so that it blocked any vehicle from getting on or off the ranch. Unfortunately, this made it impossible for Jax to read the license plates, although they were probably stolen, anyway.

"You see anyone inside?" Paige asked.

Jax had to shake his head. Too dark, and the windows had a dark tint, too. He fired off a text to Jericho. Try to use the scanner. You might not be able to see it, but there's a truck parked at the end of the road.

Then he turned to Paige to tell her to text Cord and ask him to do the same thing, but Paige was already in the process of taking care of that.

Nothing, Jericho texted back. I got a glimpse of the truck through the trees, but it's too far away for the scanner.

Yeah, that's what Jax figured, and he also figured that's why the killer had parked it in that particular location.

"Cord's not getting anything on his scanner," Paige relayed to Jax when she got a response. "He's too far away to see the truck and is going to try to move closer. He'll be careful," she added.

No doubt. But careful might not be nearly good enough.

Jax didn't draw his gun, but he kept his hand over it, and he started toward the truck again. Still no sign of anyone inside, and Paige and he were still a good fifteen yards away when her phone dinged with a text message.

Not Cord this time.

"It's from the killer," she said, showing him the screen. "'Guns down on the ground,'" she read aloud. "'Paige, you know what to do.'"

That was it, all the instruction they were going to get, but Paige did indeed know what to do. She shucked off her top, dropping it on the ground next to where Jax placed his Glock. He kept the backup gun in the back of his jeans.

Her shoes and jeans came off next, along with her gun.

"Sorry," she repeated.

It took Jax a moment to realize the apology was aimed at him. And another moment to realize why. That's because he was gawking at her in her bra and panties, and she was apologizing for putting him in this awkward situation.

Talk about bad timing, but Paige always had grabbed his attention. A half-naked Paige could grab it even more.

"He must be somewhere in or around the truck," Paige said. She took a deep breath, then another, and started walking.

Jax could only imagine what was going through her head right now. The Moonlight Strangler had nearly killed her, but here she was, ready to face him head-on.

Part of him admired that, especially since she was doing this to save Matthew. But another part of him remembered how they'd gotten to this point in the first place. She'd become the killer's target because she was obsessed with finding him.

As a lawman, it was hard for him to fault her for that.

As a father, he hated that she'd put Matthew on this monster's radar.

Her phone dinged, and she held it up for Jax to see. Good girl, the killer taunted. Put your hands on top of your head and keep walking. Deputy Crockett, you stop where you are. Don't make any sudden moves, or

I'll put bullets in both of you. And if you've got a gun hidden away, the best way to get Paige killed would be to try to use that gun on me.

Not good. They were still five yards away. Not nearly close enough for him to lunge at a killer.

"Why don't you come out so we can talk face-to-face?" Jax called out. He didn't expect a response.

That's why he was shocked when he got one.

"Talking won't help," a man said. Jax didn't recognize his voice because he was using a scrambler device. Didn't see him, either. "Paige, turn around a sec so I can make sure you don't have a gun tucked in those panties. Nice color, by the way. Would you call that pink or peach?"

This wasn't just a killer, but a sick one.

"Pink," she said through clenched teeth when she finished circling around.

"Nice. Now, do what you know you have to do."

She looked at Jax, their gazes holding, and even in the darkness he had no trouble seeing the fear.

And her surrender.

"Just make sure you kill him," she whispered. "He can't walk out of here alive."

Yes, because he would try to hurt Matthew. Jax knew what he had to do.

Paige took another step toward the truck.

"I told you to stay put, Deputy," the man warned him when Jax moved, too. "I want you to watch."

Definitely not good.

That's the reason the killer had allowed him out here, just so he could witness Paige's murder. Jax had to do something, and he had to do it fast.

"I want to tell Paige goodbye," Jax said.

Paige froze, glanced back at him, no doubt questioning what the heck he was doing. What he was doing was trying to bargain with this fool. Or maybe distract him. Anything that would prevent him from getting his hands on Paige again.

With that stunned look still on her face, Jax went to her, positioning himself between the truck and her, and he pulled her into his arms. She was board-stiff and trembling, but that didn't stop Jax from dropping a kiss on her mouth.

While he slipped the syringe into the elastic of her panties. He made sure the protective plastic cap was secure enough so that she wouldn't accidentally stab herself with it.

"I'll get to you as fast as I can," Jax whispered in her ear, hoping it was a promise he could keep.

Paige nodded. Started walking away.

But she'd barely made it a step when Jax heard the rustling sounds to his right.

And to his left.

The dark shadowy figures were wearing ski masks, and they came out of the ditches, fast, barreling right at them. Jax didn't even have time to react. One of them plowed right into him and knocked him to the ground.

Before he could even grab his backup weapon, the man put a gun to Jax's head.

Chapter Four

From the corner of her eye, Paige saw the man go right at Jax.

She screamed for him to look out, or rather that's what she tried to do, but the sound didn't quite make it to her throat. That's because the hulking man crashed right into her, throwing her to the ground and knocking the breath right out of her.

The pain burst through her.

The fear and dread, too.

She'd failed, and these two goons would almost certainly try to kill Jax and her. Was one of them the Moonlight Strangler? Or were these just his henchmen? If so, they would no doubt deliver them to the Moonlight Strangler so he could finish them off and then go after Matthew.

That couldn't happen.

Even though she was fighting to regain her breath, Paige slammed her elbow into the man's stomach. It felt as if she'd hit a brick wall. He didn't even react to the blow, but he did latch on to her hair and yank her to a standing position with her back against his chest. He put a gun to her head.

And that's when she got a good look at Jax.

Her heart went to her knees. No! Jax was being held

at gunpoint, too. She'd prayed that he had managed to get away, but like her he was now a captive.

"Move and your ex dies," the man growled in her ear.

That stopped her, but then Paige realized the other goon had likely told Jax the same thing because Jax wasn't fighting. He was looking at her and shaking his head, no doubt trying to remind her not to do anything stupid. Of course, she'd already done something stupid by allowing the danger to get this close to Matthew and him.

"I'm sorry," she mouthed.

However, that only earned her another one of Jax's glares.

"What now?" Jax asked, and it took her a moment to realize he wasn't talking to her but rather to the thug who had his arm hooked around his neck.

Neither of the men jumped to answer, but Paige did hear some chatter. She glanced back and saw that it was coming through a tiny communicator fitted into the man's ear. No doubt the voice of the Moonlight Strangler, and he was almost certainly doling out instructions.

Instructions on how he wanted them murdered.

She'd been a fool to think she could outsmart him. A fool to involve Jax in this. She should have just come to the meeting alone. Yes, the Moonlight Strangler would have just finished what he'd started all those months ago, but at least Jax would be inside his house where he could hopefully be protecting Matthew.

The chattering sound stopped, but Paige heard something else. Movement to her right, in the direction of the Crockett ranch. Maybe Jericho or Cord. Unfortunately, the hired thug must have heard it, too, because he dragged her back to the ground. Across from her, the guy holding Jax did the same to him.

The road was still hot, though the sun had already set, and the small rocks and debris dug into her skin. So did the syringe. It hadn't cracked when she fell, thank God, but she might have a hard time getting to it now that the goon had her on her stomach. However, she had managed to keep hold of her phone, and while it wasn't an ideal weapon, she might be able to bash him with it.

"Come any closer, and they both get bullets to the heads," the brute holding her called out when she heard the sound of more movement.

She doubted Jericho or Cord would just come charging in there, but maybe one or both of them could get into a position to have a clean shot.

More chatter came from the earpiece, and this time Paige caught three words. Her own name and a simple sentence that chilled her from head to toe.

She's mine.

Paige knew exactly what he meant by that. He wanted to do the job himself.

"Shoot the deputy if anyone fires at us or tries to come closer," the hired gun told his comrade. "Hear that?" he said in a much louder voice, no doubt to Cord, Jericho or whoever else was approaching. "Jax Crockett pays the price if you try to save her."

The man hauled her back to her feet, and he shoved the gun even harder against her temple. Even in the darkness, Paige managed to make eye contact with Jax. *Brief* eye contact. Enough for her to see his gaze drop to her panties. Or rather to the syringe he'd put there.

"Use it," Jax mouthed. Even though he didn't make any sound when he spoke, his captor must have realized Jax was trying to communicate with her because he tightened the chokehold on Jax.

Paige wasn't even sure she could get the syringe without either of them getting shot, but she had to try. And she didn't have much time, either. The man started moving her toward the truck. Once he had her inside the vehicle, there wouldn't be any reason for them to keep Jax alive. Probably the only reason they hadn't already killed him was to get her to cooperate.

And that's what Paige did—she cooperated.

Or rather that's what she pretended to do. She let the man maneuver her away from Jax, and she looked for her chance to make a move. That chance came when she spotted a rock on the road. It wasn't big, but when they reached it, Paige stumbled, pretending to trip.

She would have fallen if the man hadn't yanked her back by her hair. That hurt, but it was a drop in the bucket compared to the pain that exploded through her head when the man bashed the butt of his gun against her temple.

Paige dropped down again, but there was no faking it this time.

Mercy. She was able to choke back a scream but couldn't stop the groan of pain that tore from her throat.

Jax must have heard the groan because he shouted something. Something she didn't catch because both her head and ears were throbbing. She couldn't hear much of anything, but thankfully her hands worked just fine.

Fueled with the anger from the attack and the fear that Jax would get killed trying to save her, Paige yanked out the syringe and used her thumb to flick off the plastic tip from the needle. In the same motion, she stood, spun around and jammed the syringe right into the man's neck.

The shot blasted through the air. And it took her a moment to realize he hadn't shot her. He'd pulled the trigger all right, but his shot had slammed into the road. Thank God. She didn't want any bullets going anywhere in the direction of the house.

The thug staggered back, reaching for her, but Paige shoved him to the ground. Too bad the drug didn't immediately cause him to lose consciousness, because he tried once again to shoot her. However, Paige grabbed his wrist and held on.

"Paige!" Jax shouted.

She wasn't sure exactly where he was or what he wanted her to do, and Paige didn't have time to find out. The man tried to take aim at her, and even though his hands were as wobbly as the rest of him, she didn't want him to get off another shot. They might not be so lucky this time.

The man cursed her, his words slurred, and his head dropped back a little. Paige took advantage of that and used his own gun to knock him in the head. When that didn't work, she hit him again. And again. Finally, he slumped to the ground, his eyes closing and his body going limp.

One down, at least two to go.

Paige snatched up the gun and glanced in the direction of the truck to make sure the Moonlight Strangler or another attacker wasn't taking aim at her. But she saw no one. However, when her gaze slashed toward Jax, she spotted something that put her heart right back in her throat.

Jax, in a fight for his life.

Both Jax and the goon were on the ground, and the goon still had control of the gun. As she had done, Jax was trying to get control while also trying to keep the guy's aim away from the direction of the house.

"Cord, watch the truck," Paige called out, though she was certain that if he was in position, he was already doing that.

Paige didn't waste a second. She ran toward Jax. She didn't want Jax and her to be ambushed while her back was turned, but he was unarmed and outsized. If she didn't help, this could turn even more dangerous than it already was.

Paige was just a few feet away when she heard a sound she didn't want to hear. Another blast. Her stomach and muscles were already in knots, but that tightened her chest so much that she couldn't breathe. Jax couldn't be hurt. He just couldn't be.

And he wasn't.

It took her a moment to fight through the panic, especially when she saw the blood. Thankfully, it wasn't on Jax. It was on the thug, and spreading across the front of his shirt. Now Jax had the man's gun in his own hand.

Jax cursed, moved away from the man, but he didn't lower the gun. He kept it aimed at him while he volleyed glances between the truck, the other man and her.

"You're hurt," Jax said.

Was she? Paige wasn't sure of anything right now except the relief of seeing Jax unharmed.

"Is one of them the Moonlight Strangler?" someone called out.

Cord.

She didn't spot him right away, but Paige followed the sound of his voice. He was in the pasture, moving toward the truck.

Jax spared Cord a glance, too. And a glare. Before he yanked the ski mask off the man he'd just shot. There was just enough light from the silvery moon for her to see his face.

A stranger.

And he wasn't nearly old enough to be the serial killer. The Moonlight Strangler had been murdering women for three decades, and this man appeared to be in his twenties.

He was also dead.

Paige could tell from his now-lifeless eyes, which were fixed in a permanent blank stare.

"Is the other one alive?" Jax asked.

She shook her head. "I'm not sure." Paige looked back at the guy, but he hadn't moved since she'd bashed him with the gun. "But he's got some kind of communicator in his ear. I think he was talking to the Moonlight Strangler."

Jax hurried toward the man but then almost immediately stopped. Paige did, too, when she heard the sound of the footsteps. She got another slam of adrenaline. Followed by relief when she saw that it was Jericho.

Good. Well, maybe.

It was possible the Moonlight Strangler was in that truck and was ready to gun them all down. Of course, Cord was racing toward it no doubt to try to prevent that from happening.

"Call an ambulance," Jax told his brother.

Probably in case the second thug was still alive. But she rethought that when Jericho looked at her and cursed. And when she felt the blood sliding down the side of her head and face. She wiped it away but felt a new trickle follow right behind it.

God knew how bad she looked right now or even how badly she was hurt. Her head and body were throbbing, but Paige wasn't getting in the ambulance. She had to stop the Moonlight Strangler once and for all.

Jax cursed her, too, when he realized she was trailing after him, and he automatically adjusted his position so that he was in between the truck and her. Protecting her. Despite the bad blood between them, that didn't surprise her. It wasn't just the lawman in him that made him do that. Jax had always had this cowboy code about protecting others.

Even if she probably wasn't someone he wanted to protect.

Jax approached the second man with caution. His gun aimed, his gaze still firing all around them. He reached down, pulled off the mask and put his fingers to the man's neck.

"He's alive," Jax relayed. "Barely."

Paige leaned in, hoping this would be the Moonlight Strangler. But he wasn't. Like the other man, he was much too young. And that meant the killer could indeed be in the truck or nearby.

"Be careful," she called out to Cord.

Whether he'd listen was anyone's guess. Unlike Jax, Cord didn't have that whole protection code. He had one goal. Just one.

To catch his biological father, no matter what the cost. That included sacrificing his own life.

Paige had been driven by that kind of justice after her parents had been murdered. That was the reason she'd become a CSI. But justice didn't drive her now. She only wanted to keep Jax and her son safe. That might finally happen if the Moonlight Strangler was in the truck so they could catch him.

But if he was there, why hadn't he driven off when he'd seen that his thugs had failed?

A possible answer popped into her head. An answer she didn't like one bit.

This could be a trap.

Jax must have realized the same thing because his attention went straight to the truck. And to Cord.

"Watch out!" Jax shouted.

However, the words had hardly left his mouth when the blast thundered through the air. And the truck burst into a ball of fire.

Chapter Five

Jax cursed when he read Jericho's latest text message. More bad news. Just what he didn't need right now since he'd already had enough of that tonight.

Both men who'd attacked Paige and him couldn't be interrogated. One had died at the scene from the gunshot wound Jax delivered to the guy's chest. The other one, the man Paige had injected with the syringe, was in the hospital but hadn't regained consciousness. Until he did, he couldn't give Jax answers about the snake who'd hired them.

The only good thing to come out of this was that Matthew was safe and only the one hired gun was dead. Of course, not everyone had come out of it unscathed. He had proof of that right in front of him. Both Cord and Paige were side by side on examining tables in the ER while nurses stitched them up.

Plus, the ER looked like a top-secret facility, what with two security guards standing in the doorway of the room. Anyone coming into the building was being searched for weapons, and everyone was on alert to make sure more hired guns didn't try to come after Paige and him.

"What's wrong?" Paige asked, no doubt because she'd heard his mumbled profanity over the text. No doubt, too, because she was watching him so closely. But then, he was watching her, too.

Paige was alive.

And now that the dust had partially settled from the attack, Jax would need to deal with that. He'd have to deal with a lot of things, and he started with Matthew.

His brothers Chase and Levi were at Jax's house standing guard. The ranch hands were patrolling the grounds and had already searched the perimeter for snipers. Added to that, the road leading to the ranch was a crime scene now and was crawling with Texas Rangers, CSIs, the bomb squad, firefighters and even two of Appaloosa Pass's own reserve deputies. With all those people on the grounds, Jax's house was on lock-down and would stay that way until he could get home and move Matthew to a safer location.

Wherever that would be.

Belinda certainly wanted to know that, too, because she'd called twice and then left a voice mail when Jax hadn't answered her third call. He knew the nanny was worried, as well she should be, but right now he wouldn't be able to do much to calm any of her fears.

Jax walked closer, though he already had Paige's attention. Cord's as well because he ended his latest phone call and stared at Jax.

"There wasn't a body in the truck," Jax explained. "The bomb guys have cleared the CSI team to go in and start gathering evidence, but the explosive device inside the truck appears to have been on a timer."

Paige released the breath she'd obviously been holding, and despite the fact that she was getting stitches near her hairline, she shook her head. "They didn't find the Moonlight Strangler," she said. Not a question. Probably because she knew Jax wouldn't be scowling if they'd managed to nail the SOB.

"Somebody drove that truck to the ranch," Cord snapped. He had two nurses working on him, and they were stitching up his head, arms and even his left leg. They'd cut his jeans to get to the wound. "That means he escaped."

Jax nodded. Then shrugged. "But we don't know for sure the Moonlight Strangler was even there. Do we?" And he made sure there was displeasure in his tone. Plenty of it. Because Jax was still riled to the core that he hadn't been included in this stupid plan before it'd turned deadly.

"He wants to kill me," Paige stated. "He would have been close enough to make sure he could do that."

No displeasure in her voice, but there was plenty of frustration and pain, both physical and otherwise. She winced when the nurse added another stitch.

"Sorry, Paige," the nurse apologized. She was Misty Carlton, someone Jax and Paige had known their entire lives. Ditto for the other nurses working on Cord. With all the other folks coming in and out of the ER, Cord figured it was already all over town that Paige was alive.

He'd have to deal with that, too.

The other members of his family would have to be told. And Matthew, of course. His son was too young to remember Paige, but Jax doubted he could keep Paige from Matthew. Well, not forever, anyway. But for now, he pushed that problem aside and went with the most obvious one.

Jax shifted his attention to Cord. "You couldn't talk Paige out of going through with this plan to meet with your birth father?"

Cord's jaw muscles flickered and tensed. No doubt

because of the birth father reference. Yeah, it was a petty dig, but Jax was pissed off that a trained DEA agent—supposedly a top-notch one, too—had allowed a victim to arrange a showdown with a serial killer.

"Have you ever been able to talk Paige out of anything?" Cord countered.

That was a petty dig, as well. But it was the truth. To say that Paige was hardheaded was like saying the sky had a little bit of blue in it.

"Don't blame Cord for this," Paige spoke up. "If he hadn't come with me, I would have done it alone."

Jax was certain that tightened some of his own jaw muscles. "Of course you would have, and look where it got you." His gaze went back to Cord. "Have you tried to find a personal link between Paige's biological mother, Mary, and the Moonlight Strangler?" Especially since Mary was one of the Moonlight Strangler's first known victims.

"Of course," Cord snapped, clearly insulted that Jax had asked the obvious. "I haven't found one yet. And yes, I did alert the FBI when Paige's DNA test came back as a match to Mary's."

"Any reason you didn't tell me?" Jax pressed.

"Because I asked him not to," Paige volunteered before Cord could say anything. "I thought if too many people were trying to make the connection between Mary and me that the Moonlight Strangler would suspect I was alive."

Jax was already riled six ways to Sunday, and that didn't help. "I'm not 'too many people.'" He nearly added he was her husband.

But he wasn't. Not anymore.

However, he was still a lawman and the father of her

son. That alone should have earned him a place in the inner circle of information.

"The FBI decided to keep it secret, too," Cord went on. "Until they can look for a possible link. The lead investigator said there were already too many hands in this particular case."

No surprise there. The FBI had been keeping lots of things about this close to the vest. Not that it'd helped. The Moonlight Strangler always seemed to be in the know.

Especially when it came to Paige.

Jax was on the verge of questioning her about that, but his phone buzzed before he could say anything. Not Jericho this time, but it was another family member. Or rather a soon-to-be family member. Levi's fiancée.

"It's Alexa," Jax relayed to Paige.

That didn't help Paige's already pale color, and Jax didn't have to guess why. Alexa Dearborn and Paige had been best friends, and Paige had even worked for Alexa's security company when Alexa had been investigating the Moonlight Strangler. It was Paige's involvement that led to her nearly being killed.

Jax answered the call but didn't put it on speaker. "Is it true?" Alexa asked right off. "Is Paige really alive?"

Even though Paige couldn't have heard her old friend's voice, she no doubt guessed what Alexa had asked. "Tell her I'll call her first chance I get," Paige said.

"She's alive," Jax told the woman. "And she'll call you later."

Silence. For several long moments. Followed by a hoarse sob from Alexa. No doubt a sob of relief. Later, she'd have questions, but for now Alexa was likely glad that the past months had been just a nightmare and that her friend was alive.

Jax ended the call and slipped his phone into his pocket. "Alexa's engaged to Levi now."

More surprise went through her eyes. Then approval. Alexa and Levi had always had a thing for each other, but until recently Levi—and Jax—hadn't been able to get past Alexa's connection to what'd happened to Paige.

Or rather what they had thought had happened to her.

"Alexa's been beating herself up about your 'death.'" Jax hadn't said that to make Paige feel any guiltier about what she'd done.

All right, maybe he had.

Hell. This sliced into him like a knife, and Jax wasn't sure where to aim these old and new feelings. Old because he remembered the obsession that'd torn them apart. An obsession in part because of Alexa's investigation into the Moonlight Strangler.

The old attraction was still there between Paige and him, too. Jax had gotten a reminder of that when she'd stripped down on the road. Thankfully, she was dressed now in the jeans and shirt she'd been wearing when she had first arrived at the ranch.

And she was also sporting that pained look on her face.

That's where the new feelings played into this. He'd never seen Paige afraid and in pain. But she was now.

Their gazes held, and things passed between them. Unspoken things that only former lovers could share.

"I need to see Matthew," Paige said.

Well, that took care of any reminders of the old attraction. "It's not safe."

"Make it safe." Her voice broke. Tears sprang to her eyes. "Please."

Until she'd added that *please* and he'd seen the tears, Jax had been ready to flat-out refuse. He still might. But the trouble was, Paige had a legal right to see their son. Well, unless he could force Paige into protective custody with the marshals. Or he could whisk Matthew away to a safe house out of her reach. Either or both of those things might happen, but Jax was a long way from making that decision.

Since Jax couldn't figure out what to do right now, he turned back to Cord.

But Cord didn't appear to be in a conversing kind of mood. Even though he was still getting stitched up, he stood when his phone rang. He only glanced at the screen but didn't answer the call.

"I have to go," Cord insisted. He looked at Paige and added, "I'll be in touch. And remember, don't do anything stupid."

The nurses and Paige looked at him as if he'd lost his mind. "We're not finished," one of the nurses pointed out, but she was talking to the air because Cord started for the door. He would have just walked out if Jax hadn't stepped in front of him.

"You might want to take this drive for justice down a notch," Jax advised him.

Cord met his gaze head-on with eyes that Jax recognized because they were a genetic copy of Addie. It was strange to see Addie's usually loving eyes stare back at him with this raw intensity.

"My birth father's a serial killer who's targeted your wife," Cord said like a warning. And Jax doubted Cord was stating the obvious to hear himself talk. This was a reminder that Jax had no say in this as far as Cord was concerned.

"Ex-wife," Jax automatically corrected, and hated that it was nitpicking.

Cord continued to stare at him. "He's targeted Paige and God knows who else. I want him stopped."

Jax did his own stating the obvious. "Everyone wants him stopped. But you need to take some precautions. You nearly got yourself killed tonight."

"Nearly is good enough. I'm walking out of here alive, and I *will* find him." With that, Cord pushed past Jax. Past Jericho, too, who was coming in as Cord was going out.

"Mr. Sunshine," Jericho grumbled, upping Cord's scowl with one of his own.

That was a little like the pot calling the kettle black, since Jericho wasn't exactly a cheerful sort of guy. The nurses must have thought so as well because the one working on Paige quickly finished up, and she eased out of the room along with the other two who'd stitched up Cord.

Jericho's attention, however, didn't remain focused on Cord. He turned toward Paige. Or rather glared at her. "Do I want to know why you faked your own death?" Jericho asked.

She took a moment, probably because she needed it. It'd been a helluva long night, and it was just starting. "At the time, I thought it was the only option I had. Don't say I told you so," she added.

Jericho didn't say the words, but his shrug and flat look conveyed it. Jax agreed. Paige had had other options, but she hadn't taken them. She could have let him know she was alive so he could have arranged protective custody for her. For Matthew, too.

"Please tell me you found the Moonlight Strangler," Paige said.

"Afraid not." And Jericho glanced at a note he'd made on his phone. "Do the names Luca Paulino and Brady Loveland mean anything to you?"

Paige repeated them and shook her head. "No. Who are they?"

"They're the men who attacked Jax and you. Paulino's the dead one. Loveland's still out cold. Both had mile-long rap sheets so we were able to match their prints, but neither has an obvious connection to the Moonlight Strangler."

Jax didn't bother to groan, because it was news that he'd expected. The Moonlight Strangler had avoided capture for over thirty years, and he wouldn't have left a paper trail or any loose ends to lead back to him. And Loveland was definitely a loose end.

"You have a guard on Loveland?" Jax asked his brother.

Jericho nodded. "Dexter and Mack."

Both deputies. Good. Because if the Moonlight Strangler tried to silence Loveland forever, then Dexter and Mack would be there to stop him.

"The Moonlight Strangler's never used hired guns before," Paige said. It sounded as if she was thinking aloud.

Both Jericho and Jax made a sound of agreement. This particular serial killer was usually a loner. Yes, he frequently texted, wrote or even called people connected to the investigation, but to the best of Jax's knowledge, tonight was the first time the Moonlight Strangler had hired thugs to help him.

Why?

"He probably knew we wouldn't just hand Paige over without a fight, so he could have come prepared." Jax was thinking out loud, too.

Except he clearly hadn't given it enough thought because he'd made it sound personal. It was, in a way. But Jax wouldn't have handed over anyone to the Moonlight Strangler. Paige included.

"You believe someone else was behind the attack?" Jericho asked, studying him.

"Maybe." The Moonlight Strangler was still his top suspect, but Jax wanted to add another possibility to the list. "Darrin Pittman could have put this plan together."

Jax could tell that Paige was startled just by the mention of the man's name. She opened her mouth and looked ready to dismiss it, but then it must have sunk in that he could be right.

"Pittman," she repeated in a hoarse whisper.

Paige was no doubt reliving a different set of memories. Not as nightmarish as those the Moonlight Strangler had given her, but Pittman hated Paige enough to do something like this.

"That's the rich college football player who accused you of planting false evidence at a crime scene," Jericho said to her.

She nodded. "I gathered his DNA from a rape scene. A frat party gone terribly wrong. He said I put the DNA there. I didn't." Paige pushed her hair from her face and then winced when she brushed her fingers over the stitches. "Anyway, Pittman threatened and harassed me." Her gaze slid to Jax. "Please tell me he was convicted of those rape charges and is in jail."

Jax knew she wasn't going to like his answer. "No. He got off on a legal technicality. Nothing to do with the evidence you gathered, but a goof-up in his interrogation with the cops. He didn't get any jail time, but he lost his scholarship and was kicked out of school."

Paige groaned. "He's dangerous and shouldn't be on the street."

Jax agreed. He wouldn't mention that he'd nearly punched Pittman in the face when he'd shown up at the sheriff's office after Paige's "death" to gloat about Paige "getting what she deserved." Jericho had had to hold Jax back. But even Jax's threats for Pittman to back off hadn't stopped the man. Pittman had continued to demonstrate his hatred for Paige by posting slurs about her on social media.

"And you think he could want Paige dead?" Jericho pressed.

"Oh, yeah. He'd love to see her dead." No doubt about that in Jax's mind. "Pittman sent party balloons to Paige's funeral, and the headstone on her grave's been vandalized a few times. I'm sure he's the one who did it."

Paige shuddered, maybe at the realization of how much Pittman hated her. Maybe at the reminder that she easily could have been in that grave.

"I'll arrange to have Pittman brought in for a little chat," Jericho offered. "Is there any way Pittman could have found out you're alive and orchestrated this botched showdown?"

"No." But she quickly shook her head. "Maybe. If Pittman suspected I was alive, he has the money to have hired plenty of PIs to locate me. But those first three texts I got weren't from him. Pittman couldn't have known those details of my attack. Those were from the Moonlight Strangler, and I'm not sure how he found me. It's possible though Pittman learned through him or through someone else."

"Someone else?" Jericho questioned.

She dodged his gaze. Not a good sign.

"Leland Fountain," she finally said. "He's the sergeant at SAPD who found me after the attack and reported me dead."

"He's the one who helped you fake your death?" Jax cursed. "I know him."

Paige nodded. "Leland and I dated for a while right after high school."

Yeah. Jax didn't need to be reminded of that. Paige and he had broken up for a few months right before she started college, and she'd met Leland. Jax didn't think it'd gotten too serious between Paige and Leland, mainly because she'd come back to Appaloosa Pass and him. But maybe the relationship had been more serious than he'd originally thought.

"And you think Leland could have told Pittman you were alive?" Jericho pressed.

No gaze dodging or hesitation this time. "No. Not intentionally, anyway. But it's possible he let something slip."

Jax thought there was something else she wasn't saying. Something he wasn't going to want to hear, but he didn't get a chance to press her on it because Paige's phone made a dinging sound to indicate she had a text message.

She dug her phone from her pocket, her face bunching up with every little move. Probably because she was sore and bruised from the fall she'd taken during the attack. However, her forehead bunched up even more when she saw the screen.

"Unknown caller." Paige's voice had little sound. "It's from the Moonlight Strangler. He's the only person other than Cord and Leland who sends me messages."

Her gaze skimmed over the screen, and with her hands shaking, she gave the phone to Jax so he could see it for himself. And what he saw was the string of profanity. Really bad curse words. All aimed at Paige. After that was a short warning:

This isn't over.

Jax hadn't thought for one second that it was, but it seemed to shake Paige to the core to see it spelled out like that.

Jericho read through the message, too, and he stared at the phone a moment before looking at Paige. "How do you know this is actually from the Moonlight Strangler?"

The question seemed to throw her for a moment, maybe because she thought Jericho was disputing what she'd told them. "Because the killer's been texting me, and like I told Jax, he knew details about my attack that weren't released to the press. Details that only me, the killer and Leland knew. Pittman certainly didn't know so he couldn't have sent the texts to set this up. Those had to have come from the Moonlight Strangler."

Jericho held up the phone for her to see. "And he used this much name-calling and profanity?"

She studied the message again. "No. He usually just taunts me with that sugary, sick tone. Why? Do you think it means something? Do you think Pittman could have sent this one?"

"Maybe." But Jericho shook his head, groaned. "Then again, the Moonlight Strangler's not exactly predictable. How'd he get your phone number, anyway?"

"I don't know. The account is under the alias I've been using, and I never give out the number. Not even to my doctor. I have a prepaid cell I use for that. I'm guessing the Moonlight Strangler found me somehow and then had someone hack into my computer to get the number from my online account."

It was possible. They didn't know if the Moonlight Strangler had the money and resources to launch a full-scale search, but Jax was betting he did. Plus, that crescent-shaped scar on Paige's face was like a brand. Anyone who saw it might recognize it as the killer's signature, and the Moonlight Strangler had groupies. One of those sickos could have seen it and then gotten word to the killer.

Jericho's attention shifted to Jax. "When you take Paige's statement, compare this text to the others she's gotten. In fact, have everything on her phone analyzed because we need to know if Pittman has inserted himself into this by sending this latest text."

That was already on Jax's to-do list. A list that had gotten way too long. He needed to get started on whittling it down.

There was a soft knock on the door, and both Jericho and Jax automatically reached for their guns. But it was a false alarm. It was Misty Carlton, the nurse.

Misty sucked in her breath, no doubt alarmed by their reaction, and she lifted her hand to show them some papers. "It's Paige's release forms from the doctor. She can go home now."

Misty's info was simple enough, but Jericho, Paige and he just stood there staring at the nurse.

She can go home now.

Yes, but the question was—would Jax let her?

Paige got up from the examining table and took the papers. "Thank you," she told Misty, and then turned to face Jax. "Please, just let me see Matthew."

Jax considered saying no. After all, he could remind her that it wasn't safe, but the truth was, it wasn't safe no matter where Paige was. As long as the Moonlight Strangler was after her, Matthew was in danger, too, because the killer could use Matthew to get to her. Besides, he didn't have a right to keep Paige from their son.

However, he did have a right to make rules for this visit.

"I'll start making arrangements for a safe house for you," Jax informed her. "Come on," he said. "Let's go see Matthew before I change my mind."

Chapter Six

Chaos. That was the one word Paige could think of
when Jax took the final turn toward the Crockett ranch.
A place that'd once been her home.

Well, it sure didn't look like home now.

The cops and CSIs were there. The medical
examiner's van, too. Blue lights whirled, and the yellow crime scene tape snapped and rattled in the hot
summer breeze.

Before the attack a year earlier, she'd been a CSI for
almost a decade, since finishing college, and she'd been
part of situations just like this. Had been in the middle
of one as well when she'd been left for dead. But it was
different now since she'd been the cause of this particular scene. One man was dead and another in the hospital, and Jax and she had barely escaped with their lives.

And it wasn't the end.

No. The text proved that.

This isn't over.

Paige hadn't needed the text to tell her that, though.
She suspected this nightmare was just beginning
and she needed to figure out what was happening.

Jax was no doubt doing the same thing.

Along with dealing with her return from the dead.
Other than a few internet searches, she hadn't kept

tabs on his life. That wasn't only a safety precaution but also to preserve what was left of her heart and sanity. Just that earlier glance of Matthew with Belinda had sent Paige's emotions into a tailspin. She'd lost so much the day she'd nearly lost her life.

Matthew.

And Jax.

Though Jax hadn't been hers to lose. After countless arguments over her refusal to stop investigating the Moonlight Strangler, they'd separated. Paige just hadn't been able to let go of the case, and that thirst for justice had cost her Jax.

They had signed divorce papers the day of the attack. Ironic. Or maybe that'd been the Moonlight Strangler's plan all along, to wait until she was at the lowest point of her life to strike. To squeeze out every last drop of misery before he choked her to death.

Jax didn't stay on the road, though his house was less than a quarter of a mile away. He maneuvered the cruiser through a cattle gate in the pasture and drove onto a ranch trail. No doubt to avoid disturbing the scene that the CSIs were investigating. The truck explosion had likely scattered debris everywhere, and each little fragment could give them clues as to who'd built the bomb and set it.

"You've added more livestock," she remarked.

Small talk. It almost seemed insulting, considering they had some very serious things to discuss, but with her frayed nerves and the pain pounding in her head, it was the best Paige could manage.

He made a grunt of agreement. Clearly no small talk for him, but his jaw muscles were at war against each other. Probably his thoughts, too. Jax didn't want her here, and he might let her stay only a few minutes.

That was okay as long as she got to spend those few minutes with Matthew.

After he'd cleared the crime scene, Jax pulled back onto the private road that led to the ranch, and his house came into view. Of course, she knew exactly what it looked like. The two-story stone and wood house. None of the lights were on, a security precaution no doubt. This way, a sniper wouldn't be able to see anyone inside. She'd already heard Jax arrange to have the area searched to make sure there weren't any other hired guns lurking around.

It wasn't as large as the main house that was just up the road, but it was still big. Six bedrooms. When Jax and she had first married, they'd joked they would fill every one of those rooms with kids.

Once, she'd been welcome here, but there were no welcoming vibes from Jax now. Just the opposite. He didn't want her here. And Paige wasn't sure she wanted to be here, either. Anything she did right now could put her precious little boy in danger.

Or anything she didn't do.

There was just no way of knowing how the Moonlight Strangler would try to come after her next.

"How much time do I have?" she asked when he pulled the cruiser to a stop.

"Not much."

Since he didn't hesitate, he'd obviously been thinking about how all of this would play out, and Paige would have to go along with whatever demands he made. Before she'd faked her death, Jax and she had worked out a split custody agreement, but with the danger and her yearlong absence, she didn't have any claim to custody.

For now, anyway.

Jax parked the cruiser directly in front of the house

in the circular drive. She immediately spotted two ranch hands in the yard. Both armed. One was Teddy McQueen, someone she'd known most of her life, and he gave Paige a semiwelcoming nod. She didn't recognize the other hand, a reminder that some things had indeed changed in the past year.

That thought caused her to freeze for a moment.

Was Jax seeing anyone? Or more, was he in a serious relationship?

She hated the pang of jealousy that coiled inside her. She'd made her bed, and now she had to lie in it. And she wouldn't be lying in it with Jax.

They got out of the cruiser, started up the steps, but the door opened before they even reached it. Yet another familiar face. Levi. And unlike the others she'd encountered tonight, he flashed her a quick smile and hugged her once she was safe inside.

"You both okay?" Levi asked, his attention going to the stitches on her head before he glanced at his brother and then reset the security system.

"We're alive," Jax answered.

Levi nodded and hitched his thumb toward the hall. "Chase is in Matthew's room."

Good. Like all of Jax's brothers, Chase was a lawman. A marshal. And he would put his life on the line to protect Matthew. All of them would.

Later, if there was a later, Paige wanted to catch up with Levi. Alexa, too. For now, she settled for whispering congrats on his engagement to the woman who'd once been Paige's best friend. Paige wasn't sure how Alexa would feel about her now, though, especially since Jax said Alexa had been beating herself up about a death that hadn't even happened.

"One of the hands drove behind Belinda when she

went home," Levi explained as they headed toward the hall. "No one followed them."

Jax made another of those grunts, this one of approval. Paige hadn't been sure what Belinda's living arrangements were, but she obviously didn't live with Jax if she'd been escorted home.

The moment they reached the hall, she saw Chase. He was sitting in the doorway of the nursery. No smile or hug from him. His hard eyes condemned her and dismissed her with a single glance before he turned his attention to Jax.

"Matthew's asleep," Chase whispered.

Paige automatically checked the time on her phone. It was nearly 9:00 p.m., but she wasn't even sure if this was his regular bedtime or not. She prayed he hadn't been afraid when he'd heard those shots and the sirens.

Almost hesitantly, Chase stepped out of the way so she could enter. Just like that, Paige's heart thudded against her chest and her breath became thin with each step that brought her closer to her son. He wasn't sleeping in a crib but rather a bed with railings, another reminder that she'd lost so much time with him.

Paige knelt on the floor so she could get a better look at his face. She didn't dare ask Jax to turn on the light. For one thing, it might not be a safe thing to do, and for another he might not want to be accommodating.

She reached out, touched her fingers to his hair. He still had those baby curls. Still had his daddy's face. But she could see some of herself in him, too. The blond hair and the shape of his mouth.

Paige couldn't stop the tears that sprang to her eyes. Couldn't stop herself from brushing a kiss on Matthew's cheek, either. She kept it soft, but it must not have been soft enough because Matthew stirred, and his eyes popped open.

Jax grumbled something under his breath. Something she didn't catch. But he clearly wasn't happy about this. Matthew, however, didn't seem upset at all. His gaze went from Paige to his dad and uncles before his attention settled on her.

"Mommy," Matthew said.

Paige couldn't have been more shocked, and she looked back at Jax for an explanation.

Jax shrugged. "I've shown him your picture." He glanced at the nightstand, but the only thing there was a lamp and baby monitor. "It's usually right there by his bed." He went closer, searching through the drawer. No picture. "Belinda must have moved it."

Maybe Belinda had taken it with her when she'd moved Matthew into the bathroom during the attack. At least Paige liked to think that Belinda wanted Matthew to know who his mother was.

"Thank you for showing it to him," Paige managed to say, though she wasn't sure how her little boy recognized her from an old picture. Not with this brunette hair.

But Paige didn't waste any time trying to figure that out. She studied her son's face, soaking in every feature and committing it to memory.

"Mommy's here," she whispered to him.

Matthew smiled in that lazy, no-effort kind of way that reminded her of Jax, but his eyelids immediately started to drift back down. She sat there, trying to hang on to each precious moment, but they slipped away so quickly, and it took only a matter of seconds before Matthew was asleep again.

"We need to talk," Jax said, motioning for her to follow him.

She did, but Paige didn't take her eyes off Matthew as she made her way to the door. She continued to look at him until he was no longer in sight. Maybe, just maybe, this wouldn't be the last time she'd ever see him.

Chase took up his guard position by Matthew's door again, and Levi disappeared into another part of the house. No doubt to give Jax and her some time alone so he could deliver whatever bad news he was about to tell her. And it would be bad. Paige could tell by his expression. That was the problem with knowing him so well.

Jax led her to the other side of the house and into the family room. Someone had redecorated it with a fresh coat of soft gold paint and new furniture that looked more kid-proof than the leather set they'd once had in there. The most noticeable change, though, was that their wedding pictures were missing from the mantel.

"I'll take you to the safe house as soon as Jericho has it set up," he said.

No surprise about that. She'd heard Jax talking to Jericho about it on the drive over. Considering how Jericho felt about her, he was probably working at lightning speed to get the house ready so that Jax wouldn't have to be under the same roof as her.

He motioned for her to sit on the sofa. An invitation, of sorts, and yet another reminder that this wasn't her home. Not that she needed such a reminder. It was obvious Jax had erased her. Well, except for that photo he'd been showing Matthew.

"You'll need to stay at the safe house until Jericho and I can find the Moonlight Strangler," Jax added.

Which meant she could be locked away for years. Not

exactly what she wanted. "But what about Matthew? And you? You need a safe house, too."

He nodded. "I'm working on that, as well. My plan is to move Matthew first thing in the morning, and we'll lock down the ranch. Chase, Jericho and Addie all have children now, and I have to make sure none of this danger spills over onto them."

Paige couldn't agree more. However, she didn't want her son living with this dark cloud always following him.

"If we don't get answers from Loveland," she said, "then I need to set some kind of trap for the Moonlight Strangler."

Jax was already shaking his head and mumbling some profanity before she even finished. "That didn't work so well tonight. No, you'll stay put in the safe house while I work this investigation." His eyes narrowed. "And this time, you'll listen."

Paige deserved that last dig. Jax had warned her too many times about involving herself in the Moonlight Strangler investigation, and she hadn't listened. Look where that'd gotten her.

"I'm sure Cord is working on some kind of plan," she continued. "You might want to call him to make sure you two don't get in each other's way."

Of course, Cord would consider anything that Jax did as getting in his way. Still, she didn't want Jax or Cord caught in each other's cross fire if they did manage to trap the killer.

Jax didn't agree to her request to call Cord, but he did ease down in the chair across from her so they would have direct eye contact. "Start from the beginning and tell me everything about who helped you fake your death, who helped you afterward and finish by explaining how the Moonlight Strangler found out you were alive."

Paige took a long, deep breath because she figured she'd need it. "Like I already told you, Leland helped. He was on duty that night, arrived at the scene and got in the ambulance with me. He talked the doctor at the San Antonio hospital into going along with it. The doctor's name is Wesley Nolan. He had me transferred under an alias to a hospital in Houston, and I recovered there."

Well, her body had recovered, anyway.

"So, who did we bury in the family cemetery?" Jax asked.

"A cadaver of a homeless woman. Dr. Nolan told the funeral home to have a closed casket service because my injuries were too severe for a viewing."

"This Dr. Nolan went above and beyond. I'd like to know why. I want to talk to him."

She sighed. "Don't bother looking for him. He died in a car accident a couple of months ago."

That got his attention. "Accident?"

She knew why he was asking. One of the three people who'd helped her was now dead. "Cord checked into it, and he said it didn't look suspicious." Of course, that didn't mean the Moonlight Strangler or even someone else hadn't made it look like an accident.

"How'd Cord get involved?" Jax snapped, sounding like a lawman. Strange, because he usually didn't. He was the lawman Jericho used in interrogations when they wanted to coax out a confession without the criminal even realizing he was being interrogated. Of course, Jax wasn't personally involved with those interrogations.

"I contacted him after I got settled in Houston. I

knew he was investigating his birth father, and I thought he could help me find him before you or Matthew were in any danger."

The flat look he gave her let her know that it'd been a huge mistake on her part. And it had been. She'd tried to exclude Jax from her life so she could protect Matthew and him, but that had obviously backfired.

"So how do you think the Moonlight Strangler found out you were alive?" Jax went on. "You said it was possible that Leland let something slip."

She nodded. "Because at the time, Leland was the only person who knew where I was. I did ask him about it, and he said he'd been careful when he visited me and had made sure no one followed him."

"He *visited* you?" Jax asked.

Paige opened her mouth, closed it and decided to take a moment to figure out what Jax's tone meant. Was he jealous? No. It couldn't be that. This was about her trusting Leland instead of him.

"Leland was the one who helped me move from the hospital to the safe house in the Panhandle where I stayed while I was recovering. Then, when I was well enough to work, he got me a job doing computer background checks for a security agency that vets corporate executives," she explained. "His friend owns the agency, and Leland told him that he was the one doing the work."

"Leland really went out of his way for you," Jax said. His tone was flat, but that wasn't a flat look in his eyes.

"I needed money, and I couldn't very well access my old savings accounts. Anyway, Leland helped me get a fake ID and he found a small apartment for me in Houston. He'd drive over every other week from San Antonio and pay me in cash for the work I did."

There was some part of that explanation Jax obviously didn't like because his mouth tightened, and she got another glare from him. "At any point did it occur to you to call me, or maybe even Chase? He's a marshal and could have gotten you into official protective custody."

"Of course it occurred to me. I've already told you that it did, but I was afraid I'd get Matthew and you killed."

She had to fight the tears again, and she cursed them. Mercy, she already felt so bruised and weak, and she didn't want to be crying in front of Jax. Evidently, he didn't want her crying, either, because he cursed again and leaned closer. For a moment she thought he might lend her a shoulder, but his phone buzzed, and the moment was lost. Which was just as well. The last place she needed to be was in Jax's arms.

Even if her body thought it was a good idea.

"It's Jericho," he said, glancing at the screen, and he put the call on speaker. Probably because he wanted her to hear details of the safe house—a place he likely couldn't wait to take her. Anything to get her out of his house.

"Bad news," Jericho greeted. "And that's bad news on more than one front. Loveland's dead. He never regained consciousness, never uttered a word about who hired him to attack you and Paige."

That didn't help her fight the tears, but Paige blinked them back. It'd been a long shot, anyway. Even if Loveland had lived, he might not have ratted out his boss.

Of course, now she had to live with the fact that she'd killed a man. She'd done that to stop him from hurting Jax and her, but still, it settled like a dead weight in her chest.

"What else is wrong?" Jax asked his brother when Jericho didn't continue.

Jericho's hesitation had her moving to the edge of the seat. Not that she was especially eager to hear another round of bad news, but she didn't want to miss a word of what he had to say.

"The safe house is ready," Jericho finally said, "but you won't be able to take Paige there. Not tonight, anyway. I don't think it's a good idea for you to leave the house with her right now. Not until I've had someone check the area."

Paige met Jax's gaze to see if he knew what this was all about, but he only shook his head. "What's going on, Jericho?" Jax pressed.

"I got a weird text about five minutes ago. I'm sending you a screenshot."

Paige hurried to Jax's side so she could see the message for herself. "'Tell Jax that I'm watching Paige and him. Love how he parked the cop car right in front of his house so that she didn't have to be out in the open. Bet she appreciated Levi opening the door for her, too,'" she read aloud.

Oh, God. Whoever had sent the message, either the Moonlight Strangler or Pittman, was close. Close enough to see their every move.

"'Yeah, I saw it all,'" Jax continued to read. "'And I'll keep on seeing every move Paige makes. Tell her that soon she'll be dead for good.'"

Chapter Seven

The sound woke Jax. Not that he was fully asleep, anyway. But despite the fact that the sound was barely a whisper, it made it through the cobwebs in his head, and he sprang to his feet and grabbed his holster from the nightstand.

Damn it. What was wrong now?

Since it was barely 5:00 a.m., he figured neither Paige nor Matthew should be up yet. Chase should be asleep, too, since he was barely an hour off watch detail. Levi would be up, taking his turn at making sure they were all safe, but he shouldn't be whispering to anyone at this hour unless something had come up.

Jax was already dressed. For the most part, anyway. After he'd pulled a shift to keep watch, he'd changed clothes but not to his usual sleeping boxers. He'd put on fresh jeans and a shirt in case they had to make a quick escape, but his shirt was unbuttoned, and he was barefoot.

"It's Paige," Levi said the moment Jax stepped into the hall. His brother tipped his head in the direction of Matthew's room.

Jax's heartbeat went into overdrive. Not only because Paige was apparently in Matthew's room but because the sound Jax had heard was of someone crying. Matthew maybe.

He ran, skidding to a stop on the hardwood floors, and what Jax saw wasn't anything compared to the worst-case scenario he'd built up in his head. Paige was sitting on the floor. Not near Matthew but on the other side of the nursery. Matthew was still sacked out, and Paige was watching him.

Well, watching him through her tears and soft sobs.

Her head whipped up, her gaze colliding with Jax's, and she waved him off. Maybe her attempt to get him to leave. As if that was going to happen. He holstered his gun, went to her and helped her to her feet.

"I've ruined everything," she said.

Jax didn't argue with her, though he had to admit this wasn't her fault. Most of it, anyway. But she didn't need to hear him say that right now since she was obviously beating herself up.

Judging from the hoarseness of her voice and her red eyes, she'd been crying for a long time. And she likely hadn't slept.

He'd lent her some pj's—a Christmas present that he'd never used—but they looked as wrinkle-free as they had when he'd taken them out of the package and given them to her. There were also dark circles under her eyes. Circles that were nearly the same color as the nasty bruise that was now on her forehead.

So, with all of that, how the hell did she still manage to look so good?

Probably because he was still attracted to her. He always had been, and certain mindless parts of his body just weren't going to let him forget it.

Jax went over and helped her to her feet. "Come on. I'll make you a cup of tea if I can find some." After the divorce, he'd cleared out her stash of the Irish breakfast tea she bought in bulk, but he might have missed some.

Since Paige wasn't too steady on her feet, Jax hooked his arm around her waist and got her moving. Past Levi, who gave him a raised eyebrow. Maybe at the close contact.

Jax gave him a raised eyebrow right back for that hug he'd given Paige the night before. Jax wasn't jealous that his brother had done that, but this situation was already complicated enough without giving Paige the full-court welcome back home.

"It really hit me this morning," she said, wiping away the endless stream of tears. "I've lost so much time with him. Too much."

Yes, she had. Again, Jax didn't voice that. He got her headed in the direction of the kitchen, cursing the fact that the house suddenly seemed gigantic with miles and miles of floor space. That probably had plenty to do with the fact that he didn't want to keep her in his arms any longer than necessary.

"All that time I spent investigating the Moonlight Strangler," she went on. "I kept at it, knowing it was causing a rift between us."

It was an understatement, and at the root of it was that she just couldn't let go of something that Jax had known could be dangerous. It was something she should have trusted him to investigate, but she hadn't.

Lack of trust was his hot button.

Giving up had been an equally hot button for her.

Not a good combination when both were putting in so many hours with the baby and at work that they didn't have time for each other. Jax would accept his blame for part of that, but this whole faked death thing was on Paige's shoulders.

When they finally made it to the kitchen, Jax put her at the breakfast table and went in search of that tea. Nada. He had vague memories of getting drunker than a skunk and tossing everything that would remind her of him.

Everything except that picture he'd put in Matthew's room.

He gave up his search, got a pot of coffee brewing and made a check out the window. Something he'd been doing most of the night. A team of ranch hands was out there, patrolling, and there'd be a team in place until he moved Paige and Matthew. Hopefully, that would happen soon.

When the coffee was finished, he set both a cup and a box of tissues on the table in front of her, but Paige just stared at them. Stared, and then she got to her feet.

"Just please hold me a second," she said.

That was the only warning Jax got before she was in his arms.

Instant jolt of memories. Really strong ones. His body immediately started to prepare itself for Paige. And not a good preparation, either. His body was smacking the foreplay label on this and reminding him that it'd been way too long since he'd had her in his arms.

And in his bed.

Jax didn't push her away, though. Mainly because this wasn't anywhere near foreplay for her. She was falling apart right in front of him, and he felt his arms close around her before he could talk himself out of it.

"I'm sorry," she said.

The latest apology put his teeth on edge. No way could an apology erase what she'd done. For nearly a year he'd grieved for her. Cursed her. Because he'd believed she had caused her own death. Now he was cursing her for lying to him. Cursing her because of this blasted attraction that just wouldn't die.

She eased back, her gaze finding his, and she looked down between them. At his bare chest.

Where she had her hand.

Paige didn't exactly jump back, but she did step away from him and mumbled yet another apology that he didn't want to hear. She also wiped away the tears, and this time they stayed gone. Jax could almost see her steeling herself. Maybe to fight off the attraction. Maybe because she just didn't want him to see her cry.

"I promise I won't go crazy on you," she said. "I just need to get my footing and figure out how to catch the Moonlight Strangler."

Definitely more like the old Paige now. Except this time, he totally understood her obsession to catch this particular killer. Because this time his son was the one in the crosshairs.

"There's nothing new on the investigation," he told her, and Jax got himself a cup of coffee. "But I've been giving some thought to that last text. Why send it to Jericho? We know the Moonlight Strangler has your phone number because he's been texting you, and you said he included details of the attack that only a few people knew."

She stayed quiet a moment and nodded. "You think that text to Jericho was from Darrin Pittman?"

Now it was his turn to nod. "Whoever sent it used a burner cell, one that can't be traced, of course. But even if Darrin wasn't the one behind the attack last night, he's probably heard you're alive."

"One of the Unknown Caller texts could have been from him." She took out her phone from the pocket of the pj's and showed him the cache of calls and texts.

Unknown caller, Cord and Leland.

Jax couldn't help but notice that she had four missed calls from Leland, and they'd all come since she had been back at the ranch.

"I let Leland's calls go to voice mail," she said, putting her phone away. "I wasn't up to talking to him."

There. He heard it again. Something in her tone. It'd been there the night before when the cop's name had come up.

"Is there anything about Leland that you're not telling me?" he came out and asked.

Paige gave a heavy sigh and sank back down into the chair. "We, uh, had a parting of the ways."

"What the heck does that mean?" Jax pressed when she didn't continue.

Another sigh, and she didn't make eye contact. "I told you that Leland had been helping me. Well, he started to develop feelings for me—again. Feelings I could never return, and I told him that."

Jax took a moment to process that. "I'm guessing Leland was upset?"

She made a sound to indicate that that was an understatement. "He didn't say anything to me. He just walked out the same way he did after I broke things off with him years ago." Now her gaze came to his. "All of that happened right before the Moonlight Strangler contacted me to set up the meeting. And no, I don't believe Leland told him."

Maybe. "Then it's a helluva coincidence, especially since Leland was only one of two people who had your phone number at that time."

"That still doesn't mean he gave the number to a killer. Or to Pittman. Yes, Leland was upset and hurt, but I don't think he would have set me up to die."

The jury was still out on that as far as Jax was concerned, and he took out his phone to text Jericho and let him know he should call Leland in for an interview. However, the sound of a car engine stopped him, and Jax hurried to the window. It was a vehicle he recognized.

Belinda's.

And it was indeed the nanny all right. Hard to miss that gold-blond hair when she stepped from the car.

She normally arrived at his place around this time of morning so he could do some ranch work before going into the sheriff's office. However, with everything that'd gone on the night before, Jax had made it clear that she should stay away until he had some things settled.

Jax buttoned his shirt and went to the back door to temporarily disarm the security system. By the time he did that, Belinda was already on the porch.

"I couldn't wait," she said, her breath rushing out. "I had to make sure Matthew and you were all right."

"We're fine." Jax stepped back for her to enter only so he could shut the door and turn the security system back on. That way, if a hired gun did manage to sneak past the hands, at least Jax would know if there was a break-in, since all the doors and windows were wired.

Belinda immediately pulled him into her arms. His second hug of the morning, and Jax didn't want this one any more than he'd wanted the other one. Of course, the one from Paige still had the heat simmering in his body. This one from Belinda had him stepping back.

She noticed.

So did Paige, judging from the way her gaze shifted between Belinda and him. She probably wanted to know if Belinda was more than just Matthew's nanny. She wasn't. But Belinda had made it pretty clear that she wanted to be a whole lot more.

Belinda's attention landed on Paige, specifically the pj's, and because Jax was watching her so closely, he saw the flicker of disapproval go through Belinda's pale blue eyes. Once, Belinda and Paige had been friends. They'd all gone to high school together, but the tension in the air wasn't so friendly right now. Paige stood slowly, adjusting her pj's and looking as uncomfortable about this situation as Jax felt.

"Paige," Belinda said. Not exactly a warm greeting. "How could you have done this to Jax? And how could you come back into his life now after all this time? He'd gotten over you. He was moving on with his life. And now you've brought danger right to his doorstep."

"She didn't have a say in that attack," Jax told Belinda when Paige stayed quiet. But he wanted to groan. Now he was defending Paige. Great. Just great.

Belinda's bottom lip started to tremble and her eyes watered. "I prayed it wasn't you I saw yesterday by the garage."

Jax pulled back his shoulders. "You saw Paige?"

It was a really easy question, but it still took Belinda several long moments to answer. "Yes. I was on the porch swing with Matthew and I got a glimpse of someone. Maybe her, but I also thought maybe it was a friend of Buddy's or one of the other hands."

Paige looked surprised, but Jax figured he had her beat in the surprise department. "And you didn't tell me that you thought you might have seen her?" he snapped.

Belinda blinked. "I was hoping it wasn't her. Not that I wanted her dead," she quickly added. "But I didn't want her to come back. I figured if she was alive, then the Moonlight Strangler would still be after her. I was right, wasn't I?"

Maybe.

Jax didn't doubt for a minute that the Moonlight Strangler would want to finish what he'd started, but Jax wasn't convinced the killer was the only player here.

"Did you break into the house, too?" Belinda asked, looking at Paige.

"W-what?" Paige shook her head and turned to Jax. "You had a break-in?"

Jax's hands went on his hips. "This is the first I'm hearing about it. When did this happen?"

The tension in the room went up a significant notch. "Yesterday afternoon. While you were at work, I took Matthew out to see the new horses. I was only gone for about thirty minutes, but when I came back in, I saw that someone had…damaged Paige's picture, the one you usually keep next to Matthew's bed."

"Damaged?" Paige and he asked in unison.

Belinda didn't jump to answer, but she went to the junk drawer and took out the framed photo. It was indeed the one of Paige, and there was "damage" all right.

The glass had been shattered, and it appeared that either the glass—or someone—had cut Paige's face. Not an ordinary cut, either. There was a gash on the cheek, very similar to the real one the Moonlight Strangler had given her.

Jax cursed, and Paige staggered back a step.

"Why wouldn't you have told me about this?" Jax demanded of Belinda.

More tears sprang to Belinda's eyes. "At first, I thought it had fallen off the table. Or that maybe you'd gotten upset and did it."

"I wasn't here," Jax reminded her. "You knew I was at work."

He tried not to sound furious with her, but he was. This was huge. It could have meant someone had indeed broken in. Or rather just walked in, because he doubted Belinda had locked up to take Matthew to see the horses.

Her tears turned to sobs. "Don't be upset with me. I thought maybe you'd come back home for something, that you saw the picture and decided it was finally time to put Paige out of yours and Matthew's lives."

"I'll always be part of his life," Paige whispered. Not angry but rather hurt. "Even if I'm not here, I'll always be his mother."

Belinda's face turned red, and her nostrils flared. She looked ready to scream or do something Jax was sure they'd all regret. Emotions were running sky high right now, and he needed to diffuse it.

"Was anything else broken or taken?" Jax asked her, not only because he wanted to know but also because he would get them talking about this potential break-in rather than Paige.

Belinda's glare stayed on Paige for a while before she finally shook her head. "Nothing that I found. Nothing else seemed to be out of place."

So, why would someone break in only to destroy a photo of Paige? Jax figured he knew the answer to that, and it was an answer he didn't like one bit.

"You should go home now," he told Belinda.

She frantically shook her head. "But Matthew—"

"Will be fine," he interrupted. Jax hoped that was true, anyway. "I'll call you later when I have some things settled."

Belinda took hold of his arm and opened her mouth as if she might argue about staying. But then she glanced at Paige, the anger returning to Belinda's eyes. "You'd be a fool to get involved with her again. Just remember how she broke your heart and don't let it happen again."

And with that crystal-clear warning, Belinda walked out. Or rather she stormed out.

Jax went back to the window to watch her leave. "She's not usually this, well, emotional." Not the exact word he wanted to use, but at least it didn't include any profanity.

"She's in love with you," Paige provided.

This would have been a really good time for him to deny it. But he couldn't. Because it was almost certainly true.

He was about to assure Paige that he hadn't encouraged Belinda's feelings, but he stopped himself. Saying something like that might only encourage this blasted attraction between Paige and him.

That attraction already had enough steam without his adding more.

"I didn't break in," Paige insisted. "And I certainly wouldn't have done this to my own photo." She paused. "But maybe Belinda did."

Again, it would have been a good time to deny that, but it was indeed possible. Jax hated that he could even consider that Belinda would do something like that. He trusted her with his son's life. His safety. And if Belinda was coming unglued over the prospect of Paige's return, then he didn't want her anywhere near Matthew. Telling her that, though, would go over like a lead balloon.

"Maybe the picture just fell the way Belinda suggested," Paige added. "Maybe." But she didn't sound any more certain about that than Jax.

Since the picture seemed to turn Paige's stomach—it was doing that to him, too—he put it facedown on the counter. "I'll have it checked for prints and traces just in case." Though any evidence had likely already been destroyed.

Paige shuddered and scrubbed her hands down her arms. "If the Moonlight Strangler was really here in the house…" She didn't finish that. No need. Jax was right there with her at that sickening thought.

Was this part of the warped game he'd been playing with Paige?

Jax's phone buzzed, and he was so on edge that the sound startled him. But it was only Jericho. Maybe calling with good news, because heaven help them, they needed it.

"I got another text," Jericho said the moment Jax answered.

Damn. He knew from his brother's tone that this was from the killer. Or else someone pretending to be the killer. Either way, it definitely wouldn't fall into the good-news category.

"Want me to send a screenshot or just read it?" Jericho asked.

"Read it." Jax doubted Paige wanted to see anything else that was stomach-turning. That's also why he didn't put the call on speaker. He could give Paige a sanitized version of the message afterward.

"'Tell Paige that I hope she's enjoying her visit with your son's nanny,'" Jericho read. "'Guess it didn't go well, considering how Belinda sped away.'"

"He's watching us," Jax said on the tail end of a single word of profanity.

"Yeah. And the CSIs used infrared to search the area around your house." Jericho paused. "That means there are probably cameras somewhere. Small ones that the CSIs missed. There shouldn't be any snipers because we set up sensors to alert us if anyone is hiding out in those trees near your house. If the sensors are triggered, the alarm at the main house will sound, and one of the hands will call you right away."

Good. Though it was a precaution that Jax hoped they didn't need. Especially since he'd be moving Paige soon.

Hell, he hoped so, anyway.

"I'm sending the CSIs out there now to check for cameras," Jericho continued. "I'll have them go through the cruiser and the other vehicles as well, but you can have the hands go ahead and start looking, too."

It was something Jax should have already thought to check, especially since it wouldn't have been that hard for someone to attach a camera or tracking device. However, it was possible someone had done that when they broke in.

"I'll need the house checked, too," Jax added. "And I'm bringing in a photo that I need processed for evidence." He was about to explain what had happened, or rather what had possibly happened, but a sound stopped him.

Two cars were approaching.

After the run-in he'd just had with Belinda, at first he thought the woman was returning for another conversation. But these weren't vehicles he recognized. This was a sleek silver sports car and a blue pickup truck.

"I'll call you back," he told Jericho and then glanced at Paige. "Stay away from the window." And Jax drew his gun.

But she didn't stay back. She hurried to the fridge, took the gun that he had stashed there and looked out just as the man stepped from the car.

"Oh, God," Paige said under her breath. "What's he doing here?"

Jax intended to find out. And fast. Because their

tall, blond-haired visitor was none other than Darrin Pittman.

Hell. What now?

Jax also recognized the other much smaller man who threw open the truck door. So did Paige.

"Leland," she grumbled, clearly not happy.

Neither was Jax. This was yet someone else he didn't want near Matthew, Paige or his home.

Leland got out of his truck, and in the same motion, he drew his gun. And he aimed it right at Darrin.

Chapter Eight

Paige wasn't in the mood to deal with either Darrin or Leland, much less both of them at once. And she certainly didn't want to face them while still wearing Jax's pajamas.

"Will Leland shoot Darrin?" Jax asked her.

"Possibly." It was sad that she didn't know for sure. "Leland knows that Darrin harassed and threatened me. And Leland's got somewhat of a short fuse. Stall them. I'll talk to them after I've changed."

Jax looked at her as if she'd sprouted some extra noses. "You're not going out there."

She appreciated his attempt to protect her, but she was going to have to overrule him on this. "I want to find out if Darrin was behind the attack last night, and he's far more likely to say something to me than to you or Leland. Even if what he says is out of anger."

Except it wasn't anger when it came to Darrin. More like blind rage.

"Make sure someone's with Matthew," she said to Jax, maybe insulting him, since it was so obvious.

Still, she didn't want to take any chances with Matthew's safety, especially since there were so many other things about this dangerous situation that they couldn't control.

Paige didn't wait for Jax to respond to or argue with her. She hurried back to the guest room and practically threw on jeans and a top. No change of clothes. She'd cleared all of her personal things out during the divorce, but Jax had washed and dried her things after lending her his pj's.

She kept the gun she'd taken from the fridge and prayed she didn't have to use it. While she was praying, she added that maybe Matthew would sleep through all of this.

"I'm ready," she said, racing back to the kitchen.

But Jax wasn't there. Levi was, though. He was in the back doorway. She huffed when she glanced out the window and spotted Jax in the side yard. He, too, had his gun drawn.

"Jax says I'm supposed to keep you inside," Levi warned her.

The flat look she gave him must have made him realize this was a battle he'd lose, because he cursed and stepped aside. She got another scowl and some unspoken profanity from Jax when she walked out onto the back porch.

"You shouldn't be out here," Leland shouted to her. Other than a glance, he didn't actually look at her. He kept his attention, and gun, nailed to Darrin.

"He's right," Jax agreed, his gaze sweeping all around them. Levi and the ranch hands were doing the same.

Paige didn't go out in the yard. She stayed on the porch and wished that Jax would do the same. No such luck. He was right out there where he could be gunned down.

If Darrin cared one ounce about being held at gunpoint, or being out in the open with a killer loose, he didn't show it, and unlike Leland he kept his gaze on her.

And Darrin smiled.

That sick smile she'd seen him dole out too many times before he issued a veiled threat or called her some vile name. She'd told Jax the truth about Leland having a temper, but it was as cold as ice compared to Darrin's.

It'd been a year since she'd seen Darrin. He certainly hadn't been smiling at her then. He'd been threatening her with yet another lawsuit and with bodily harm. But other than that, he hadn't changed. He was still driving a pricey car. Still wearing those high-end preppy clothes. Probably still living off his trust fund and assaulting women any chance he got. There was a string of women who'd made complaints against him for sexual assault, but the complaints always disappeared when his daddy paid off people in the legal system.

All but one.

The rape charge where Paige had collected the evidence. That was the start of this whole nightmare with Darrin.

"Why are you here?" Paige asked, aiming the question at Darrin, but she also glanced at Leland to let him know she wanted an answer from him, as well.

"Visiting you, of course," Darrin said, that smile still on his face. The morning breeze tossed his fashionably rumpled hair. "Back from the dead, I see, but you're looking a little beat-up there, Paige. What? Did you piss off the wrong person and get smacked around? That bruise and scar look good on you."

"Shut up," Leland warned him. He continued to stand there, his gun aimed at Darrin.

"Both of you shut up," Jax warned Leland and Darrin right back. "Neither of you should be here. This is private property, and you're trespassing."

Leland flinched as if Jax had slugged him. Maybe because he expected cooperation from a brother in blue? But after the attack, Jax wasn't in a trusting mood, and it probably didn't help that Leland was her old flame.

"Just taking a detour," Darrin said. "Your brother, the sheriff, told me to come in for questioning." Now his gaze narrowed when he looked at Paige. "Guess you've been telling lies about me again?"

"No need. The truth will get you in more trouble than any lie I can make up. You raped a woman."

"Not according to the law." Darrin outstretched his arms. "I'm free as a bird."

"Not for long if I have anything to say about it," Leland volunteered. "I was on my way into town to talk to the sheriff, and I spotted this clown heading out here. I figured he was looking for Paige so he could cause some trouble."

"I was looking for her," Darrin readily admitted. "But not to cause trouble. I just wanted to welcome her home. And to let her know that I'm ready to do whatever it takes to clear my name. That involves getting her to tell the truth about that so-called evidence."

Paige couldn't help it. She laughed. Not from humor, but from the absurdity of his threat. "Someone wants me dead. Clearing your name isn't anywhere on my list of things to do. Unless, of course, you're the one who orchestrated the attack against us last night."

Darrin shrugged, but she thought maybe she'd hit a nerve. Of course, Paige had no idea if that was because he was truly innocent of the attack or if he was riled that she'd figured him out so easily.

"Let's end this so that Paige can go inside," Jax said.

He tipped his head to Darrin. "You get back in your car now and leave. Go straight to the sheriff's office so you can be charged with trespassing and any other charge I can come up with."

Paige thought Darrin would argue with that, but he glanced around at the five guns aimed at him and must have considered that staying just wasn't a bright idea.

Darrin threw open his car door, his glare going right to Paige. "This isn't over."

The words went through her like knives. Because it was the exact threat the Moonlight Strangler had made to her.

Or had he?

She'd been so certain that the texts had been from the true serial killer, but maybe it'd all been a hoax set up by none other than Darrin. Of course, it didn't make this situation any less deadly.

Darrin started his car and sped off, gunning the engine so that the tires kicked up some pebbles right at Leland. Leland sidestepped them, but what he didn't do was get in his truck and follow Darrin. Instead, he came closer to the porch.

"I need to talk to Paige," Leland said. His tone wasn't that of a tough cop. Nor was it directed at her. He looked at Jax when he spoke, and he was clearly bargaining with a fellow officer.

"Why don't we all go inside," Leland continued, "so Paige isn't out in the open? There could be snipers in the area."

"The area's been cleared," Jax snapped.

Maybe it would stay that way. Of course, the threat could be standing in front of them. Except Paige wasn't sure she believed it. Darrin clearly wanted to do her harm. Ditto for the Moonlight Strangler. And Belinda probably just wanted her to disappear again. But Leland had actually helped her.

"I'll talk to him," Paige told Jax.

Oh, Jax did not like that, but she tried to silently convey to him that she wanted to question Leland to see if he knew anything about the attack.

The seconds crawled by, and she watched Jax have a debate with himself. She also saw the moment he conceded.

"Holster your gun," Jax ordered Leland. "You've got five minutes, so talk fast. And you're not going inside. Anything you say can be said on the porch."

However, Jax did come onto the porch, and he maneuvered her into the doorway so she'd be more protected. And so that he'd be partially in front of her.

Jax leaned in closer to Levi. "Ask the ranch hands to start searching the cruiser and the other vehicles for cameras or tracking devices," Jax instructed. "I need to make sure they're clean in case we have to leave fast. I also want them to check the exterior of the house."

With that task out of the way, Jax turned back to Leland, but Leland was staring at her now. Maybe glaring, too.

"I'm not here to hurt you," Leland told her. "I want to help you, something I've been doing for months now."

"Yeah, she told me all about that," Jax snapped. "She also told me you two recently had a parting of the ways."

Leland flinched. Clearly hurt that she'd confided in Jax about something that he would see as a personal matter between them. And maybe she'd been wrong to tell Jax. Maybe her newfound concerns about Leland were the product of an adrenaline crash and too little sleep. If that was the case, then she would owe him a huge apology.

But not now.

Not until she was sure.

"You need to be careful of Darrin," Leland said, not to her but rather to Jax. "He's fighting a civil lawsuit filed by the woman he raped. The DNA that Paige gathered at the crime scene is admissible in that particular trial, and Darrin wants Paige to admit she lied and planted evidence."

She'd known about the civil suit, of course, but with everything else going on, she hadn't mentioned it to Jax. Of course, Darrin already had a motive to come after her—revenge—but this only added to it. Maybe he believed if he killed her, or drove her crazy, then she wouldn't be able to testify at the trial. Or be around to try to get him convicted of the original charges.

"Did you come to my house yesterday?" Jax asked Leland. "Did you break in?"

Leland huffed, clearly insulted, and tapped his badge. "I uphold the law. I don't break it." Another huff. "Look, obviously you have a beef with me because Paige turned to me and not to you after she was nearly killed, but I'm not the enemy here. Paige and I have a history together, and she trusted me. Not you."

Now it was Jax who was insulted. Or maybe just riled. "Paige turned to you because she thought that was the only way to save our son. It wasn't."

"Maybe. But the danger's still here, isn't it? Your son is at risk, and that didn't happen until Paige came back."

She hadn't exactly had a choice about that, either. "The Moonlight Strangler found me," she reminded Leland, though there was no way he could have forgotten something as monumental as that.

Still, Leland shook his head. "I went to your apartment in Houston yesterday, looking for you. When you weren't there, I used my key to get in."

Jax jumped right on that. "He has a key?"

Paige nodded. Not her doing, exactly. "The apartment is in Leland's name. He got an extra key when he signed the lease."

Something she hadn't known about until weeks after she'd moved in, and Leland had surprised her one morning. After that, Paige had installed a swinging door bar latch and used it anytime she was inside.

Leland nodded. "When I was there yesterday, I found a listening device in the kitchen. Someone must have broken in and planted it there."

With everything else that had gone on, that shouldn't have chilled her to the bone. But it did. Someone had spied on her. And still was, judging from the texts she'd gotten.

"The bug had been there a while," Leland went on, "because there was some dust on it. My theory is that Darrin found you, broke in and planted the bug."

Jax lifted his shoulder. "If Darrin knew where she was, why not just go after her and confront her?"

Yet another chilling thought.

"Because I think Darrin wants to torment her first," Leland continued. "Over the past months, Paige and I talked a lot. About her life. About the attack. I think that's how Darrin found out the details of the attack that hadn't been released to the press. And I believe he used those details to set up that meeting yesterday. The one that nearly got Paige killed—again."

Paige looked at Jax, but he wasn't dismissing any of this. Neither was she. As sickening as it was to think Darrin might have tried to kill her, it was also somewhat of a relief. Because it would mean the Moonlight Strangler might not be after her.

"Paige's apartment needs to be thoroughly searched," Jax insisted. "Any computers she used, as well."

Leland nodded. "I'm working on it. I've also arranged a safe house for Paige." His gaze shifted back to her. "And I'd like you to go there with me now. Before you say no, just think it through. If you're away from the Crockett ranch, your son will be safe."

If only that were true.

However, Jax might believe that. He might want to send her far, far away. But just the thought of it crushed her heart. She'd barely gotten to spend any time with Matthew, and now she might have to leave.

Or not.

The look Jax shot Leland could have frozen the Sahara. "Paige isn't going anywhere with you."

She hadn't even realized she was holding her breath until it rushed out. But Jax obviously wasn't feeling any relief. It was a mix of anger and frustration. Some of it aimed at Leland. Some at her. The rest, at himself.

"You think that's wise?" Leland pressed. "You said someone had broken into your house. That someone could have planted a bug like the one in her apartment. Paige shouldn't be here until there's been a thorough sweep. She could stay at the safe house until you're sure everything is clean here."

"Paige isn't going with you," Jax said again, without hesitation. "I'm making arrangements for a place for Matthew and her, and I'll be the one to take them there."

Maybe he truly believed Leland could be the bad guy in all of this, or maybe Jax just didn't trust the man because Leland had helped her fake her death. Either way, Leland's safe house was out.

Thank God.

"You need to go to the sheriff's office," Jax reminded Leland. Without holstering his gun, Levi returned from talking to the ranch hands and came onto the porch with Jax and her. And he hurried, too. "My brother needs to ask you some questions."

"Because you Crocketts think I'm dirty," Leland snarled. "I'm not. And I can't help it if you're jealous of me and your ex-wife." He put a lot of emphasis on the words *jealous* and *ex*.

Words that caused Jax's eyes to narrow, but that still didn't stop him from getting to her. "If you're waiting for me to thank you for not telling me that Paige was alive, you'll be waiting an eternity."

Leland stood there, looking at her, no doubt waiting for her to agree to go with him. But Paige only shook her head.

"I'm sorry," she said.

With all the harsh words and glares that'd gone on in the past ten minutes, her generic apology seemed to bother Leland the most. He looked down at the ground a moment and mumbled something she didn't catch before he turned and headed back to his truck.

Jax didn't even wait until Leland had driven away before he turned to Levi. "Get Chase and Matthew out here. We all need to leave right now. Leland was right about one thing. Whoever's behind this could have planted a bug. Or something worse."

"Worse?" Levi asked.

Jax grabbed the keys for the cruiser. "There could be a bomb."

Chapter Nine

Jax wasn't sure if this was the right thing to do, but he didn't want to risk keeping Matthew in their home even a second longer.

He wanted to kick himself for not considering sooner that the killer—or rather the would-be killer—could have set a second bomb. One that would blow up the house and kill them all.

"Are you sure this is a good idea?" Paige asked when Jax pulled the cruiser to a stop in front of the main ranch house. His family's home.

She was eyeing the place as if it were the lion's den. And considering how much his family disliked her, in a way it was. Still, he didn't have a lot of options at the moment. He'd had to move fast to get Matthew, Paige and his brothers away from his house, and he needed to regroup.

"We won't be here long," he assured her.

And hoped that was true.

Since Chase had called ahead with a warning of their arrival and the reason for it, his mother, Iris, was already in the door, frantically motioning for them to come in. Jax got them moving, fast, so they wouldn't be out in the open any longer than necessary. Chase had Matthew bundled in his arms, and they hurried up the steps, his mother maneuvering them all inside. The moment they were all in, she locked the door and set the security alarm.

"Are you all right?" his mother asked, her attention landing on each of them before it settled on Paige. His mom made a face, but Jax didn't think it was solely of disapproval but had more to do with Paige's bruises and stitches.

"We're fine," Jax lied. Paige mumbled something similar.

At least the tension and fear weren't bothering Matthew. He grinned when he saw his grandmother and reached for her. Iris took him into her arms right away and kissed him.

"Paige," his mother said. Sort of a greeting, but there was no welcome-back in her tone. Nor her eyes.

"Iris," Paige answered. And her discomfort came through loud and clear even though her voice was a hoarse whisper. "Thank you for allowing me to be here."

Right. He figured Paige wasn't nearly as thankful as she was just glad to be out of a place that might have a bomb in it.

The silence settled in. Thick and uncomfortable before Jax did something about it. After all, it wasn't as if there weren't things to do.

"I didn't bring any of Matthew's clothes or toys," Jax explained to his mother. "I'll need to change him out of those jammies."

"I'll do it," she offered. "He has plenty of extra clothes here. And I'm sure we can find some toys." She winked at her grandson.

Jax was sure of that, too, since Matthew often stayed the night with his grandmother, Aunt Addie and Addie's husband, Weston, who all lived in the house. Matthew had been especially eager to do that since Addie had given birth to her son, Daniel. Even though Daniel was still way too young to actually play with Matthew, Matthew enjoyed being around him. It also helped that Addie and his mom spoiled him and had a huge playroom filled with every kind of toy a kid could ever want.

"Mommy," Matthew said, and he pointed to Paige. "Her home."

"Yes, I can see that." Iris managed a smile. Not a genuine one, of course, but it seemed to make Matthew happy.

"Cookie?" Matthew asked his grandmother.

Despite the mess they were in, Jax had to smile. His son already knew the perks of coming to Grandma's house.

"It's a little too early for a cookie," Iris explained, "but maybe after I've changed your clothes and you've had your breakfast. Are you hungry?"

Matthew nodded, but his mischievous grin let Jax know that the kid was still hoping for that cookie. And would likely get one.

Iris glanced at Paige, then Jax. "You can get Paige settled into one of the guest rooms. I'll go ahead and take care of Matthew."

Jax wasn't sure they'd be there long enough for Paige to need a guest room, but she might want a place to escape while he was making plans to get them to a safe location.

"I'll have the cruiser searched," Chase volunteered when his mother left with Matthew.

"Thanks. But don't search the house just yet. I want the bomb squad to go through it first."

Chase made a sound of agreement. "I'll call and get

as many people out here as possible to look for those cameras."

Yeah, because until that was cleared up, Jax couldn't take Paige and Matthew to the safe house. It was a call that Jax could have made himself, but after one look at Paige, he figured that the guest room wasn't just optional. She needed it.

"I should have apologized to your mother," she said when Chase stepped away. "Not that it would have done any good."

It wouldn't have. Iris had taken it hard when Paige and he divorced. Had taken it even harder when she thought Paige had been murdered. It would be difficult to undo all that grief and hurt. Still, it would have to happen. He had to believe they'd catch the person behind the attacks and move on with their lives.

Eventually.

And that meant somehow he had to come to terms with the fact that Paige would want partial custody of Matthew. She'd want to be his mother. But that was a worry for a different time.

Jax led her to the first guest room, only to remember it'd once been his room. A room where Paige and he had made out when they'd been in high school. No sex here. That'd happened later after they'd hooked up when she had come home from college. Still, those make-out memories seemed to be still lingering around.

Of course, his body egged those memories on.

Jax wasn't sure if Paige remembered their time together here, mainly because she dodged his gaze when they walked in. However, when the gaze-dodging ended, he saw plenty in the quick glance she gave him.

"I'll just freshen up." She fluttered her fingers toward the bathroom. "And then I can come down and help you with any arrangements that need to be made. I can spend some time with Matthew, too."

He certainly couldn't fault her for wanting to do that. She loved their son as much as Jax did. That's why this hurt so much.

"Am I responsible for that?" she asked. She touched the center of his forehead, which was bunched up.

"Yeah," he admitted. Probably shouldn't have, though. Because his bunched-up forehead was from worry about a subject he should probably wait until later to discuss with her. But his body had a different notion about that, too.

"I'm not used to sharing Matthew," he admitted. Which didn't make sense. Jax shared him all the time with his family. Still, this was different.

"I understand." And that's all Paige said for several moments. "Just know that I won't interfere with the life you've made for him. Or the life you've made for yourself. I'll just figure out a way to fit into it."

The words were right. Heck, they were probably even true. For now, anyway. But soon, once the danger had passed, Paige would want more. She'd want to be a mother to her son.

She stepped away but then stopped, touching her fingers to her stitches. "You think you can get me some aspirin or maybe even something stronger?"

"Sure. How bad is the pain?" Something he should have already asked. Not just for the stitches but for her other scrapes and bruises, as well.

"Not bad."

Probably a lie. Definitely a lie, he amended, when he looked into her eyes. Yep, there it was. The pain, the fear…everything.

Everything.

Including the old attraction.

It was like a dangerous, hot powder keg sitting in the room. Something that should have had him moving away so he could get her some pain meds. But he didn't move. Not away from her, anyway.

Jax moved toward her, and while he was still in mid-step, he slid his hand around the back of her neck and pulled her to him. No resistance. None. In fact, it was Paige who upped the ante by putting her mouth to his. He did something about that, fast.

He kissed right back.

Oh, man. There it was, that powder keg going off in his head.

The heat, fire and taste of her roared through him, and it only took a second for him to want not only this but a whole lot more.

She moved into the kiss when he deepened it and took hold of his arms. Anchoring him. Unless she thought he was about to run off. He wasn't. Jax stayed there, body to body with her, and kissed her until he couldn't stand the ache any more. Only then did he move back.

And he instantly felt his body urging him to return.

Paige's breath was gusting now. His wasn't exactly level, either, and they stood there staring at each other. Maybe waiting for the other to admit that had been a stupid mistake. Playing with fire, and they could both get burned.

Matthew, too.

Because that kind of mistake could cause Jax to lose focus.

"Well, at least I don't need the pain meds now," she said, and before he could think of a smart-ass comeback, she headed to the bathroom. "Let me wash my face, and we'll go back downstairs."

She paused only a second to glance in the direction of the bed. He doubted she was in any shape for sex, but whenever they were near each other, sex came up.

Paige nixed the sex and did indeed go into the bathroom. Jax thought this might be a good time to ram his head against the wall. He might just knock some sense into himself. However, that thought disappeared when he heard something he didn't want to hear. A voice coming from downstairs.

Cord.

Oh, joy. Just what he didn't need, another run-in with what had to be the surliest DEA agent in the country. Of course, it didn't help that Cord had been the one to help Paige keep her death a secret. Soon, Jax wanted to have a discussion about that.

When Paige came out of the bathroom, she must have noticed his change in expression, but she must have also heard Cord's voice because she hurried past him and went downstairs. Cord was still at the door, talking with Chase, but that ended when he spotted Paige.

"I think we have a problem," Cord said, snagging her gaze and moving closer to her.

"He's been analyzing Paige's phone records and text messages," Chase relayed, and he sounded as unhappy as Jax was about having Cord part of his investigation.

Of course, Chase probably didn't have the same motivation as Jax for that particular unhappiness. Chase just wouldn't like having a renegade lawman who operated with plenty of shades of gray. Jax didn't like it that Cord had formed this *bond* with Paige. The last time Paige had teamed up with someone to catch the serial killer, she'd nearly died.

The same could happen this time.

And this time, the danger could pose a threat to Matthew.

Even though he already knew that, Jax let that thought settle in his mind. It didn't settle well. And this time not just because of Matthew but because of Paige herself.

Damn.

This was about that kiss.

He'd known from the start that it was a stupid thing to do, and now it was playing into his mind-set. Not good. Because the only mind-set he needed right now was to protect his little boy.

Chase locked the door, reset the security system, but he continued to keep watch out the side windows.

"I don't think any of those messages yesterday came from the Moonlight Strangler," Cord continued, his attention on Paige. "I've gone through every word, and it's just not the same as the other messages he sent earlier to you. Something's off."

Paige nodded. And groaned softly. "We have suspects. Two of them—Darrin Pittman and Leland Fountain. My money's on Darrin."

So was Jax's. But there was another possibility. "Maybe the Moonlight Strangler purposely altered the wording. He likes to play games. Likes to torment Paige. Maybe he wants her to believe she's got more than one person gunning for her."

"Cord," someone said before he had a chance to respond to that.

Addie, Jax's sister. Cord's sister, too, Jax had to remind himself. His parents had adopted Addie when she was three, the same age Jax had been at the time, and to him she'd always be his sister.

Addie went to Cord, hugged him and then turned to Paige to do the same thing. Paige went a little stiff, no doubt from surprise, but she stiffened even more when Levi's fiancée, Alexa Dearborn, came into the foyer.

The tension suddenly got a whole lot thicker.

Jax braced himself for Alexa to lash out at Paige. After all, they'd been best friends, and Alexa had blamed herself for getting Paige killed. But Paige wasn't dead, and that meant Alexa had grieved for nothing.

But there was no lashing out.

The breath Alexa took was one of relief, and she hurried to Paige to hug her, too. No relief for Paige, though. Jax was watching her and saw the guilt in her eyes. The fear, too. Because while Alexa and the rest of them had lived with Paige's so-called death, her return had put them all in danger.

"I wish I'd been able to let you know," Paige said.

"I'm just glad you're home," Alexa assured her. She volleyed some glances between Paige and him. "Are you two back together?"

"No," Paige blurted out. It was certainly a fast enough response. Adamant enough, too. But it didn't exactly ring true.

That kiss again.

It'd screwed up a lot of things, but mainly Jax's head. He wanted to believe it wouldn't happen again, but he didn't even try to lie to himself about it. That attraction wasn't going away, so the best solution was to try to keep some distance between Paige and him. That wasn't going to happen, though, either, until this danger had passed.

Alexa lightly touched her fingers to the crescent-shaped scar on Paige's cheek. It wasn't as pronounced as the recent bruises and stitches, but it would be a lifelong reminder of just how close she had really come to dying.

"We need to catch that monster." Alexa's voice was barely a whisper, but it came through loud and clear.

Cord was the first to nod, though they all agreed. "We have to figure out for sure if there are any other players in this," Cord added. "I personally don't think the Moonlight Strangler would have partnered with anyone else to go after Paige. He's had no trouble killing women on his own."

Like the scar, it was yet another brutal reminder. And the truth.

"Also, the Moonlight Strangler's never used explosives at any of his crime scenes," Jax added. "My bet's on Darrin, too. He's got the money and motive to pull off something like this."

"Come on." Addie slipped her arm around Paige's waist. "You can take a quick break from the investigation so we can catch up. I want you to meet my husband and our son, and you can have breakfast with Matthew."

Jax gave his sister a *thank-you* look. Paige did need time to catch her breath. Needed time with Matthew, too. However, Paige had barely managed a step when Jax's phone buzzed.

"Jericho," he said, looking at the screen.

That stopped Paige, of course. It stopped everyone, because Jericho was interviewing both their suspects right about now, and he might have gotten a break in the case.

"Good news, I hope," Jax said when he answered the call and put it on speaker.

"I'm not sure what kind of news it is right now. A package arrived for Paige here at the sheriff's office.

A courier service delivered it, and I had it checked for explosives. There aren't any."

That got Jax's attention. Paige's, too. "A package?" she repeated. "Who sent it and what's in it?"

"Don't know who sent it, but there were just two things inside. A cell phone and a typed note telling Paige to call the number programmed into it. Only Paige. The note said if anyone else called, there'd be no answer."

Jericho blew out a long breath that was audible even from the other end of the line. "Jax, I think you should bring Paige in right away. Not just to deal with the phone. But I think she should talk to the courier. He says he's got orders to speak to only her."

Chapter Ten

Paige tried to steady her heart rate. Tried not to think the worst. But since the *worst* seemed to be the norm for her, it was hard not to wonder if this package was some kind of ruse to draw her out.

Still, she didn't have a lot of options—also the norm for her lately—because she hadn't wanted Jericho to bring the courier to the ranch, yet she wanted any answers the man might be able to give.

"Please tell me Matthew will be all right," she said when Jax pulled the cruiser not in the parking lot of the sheriff's office but directly in front of it. Of course, she knew what he would say.

Matthew was safe.

And it was as true as it could be. Chase, Levi and Weston were all there. Cord, too. Plus, there were at least a half dozen armed ranch hands. In addition to that, both Chase and Levi had searched the cruiser to make sure it wasn't bugged or that a tracking device hadn't been attached. It was clear. However, that didn't mean someone wasn't in town watching the sheriff's office and waiting for them to arrive.

"It's not Matthew I'm worried about right now." Jax glanced around the area as if he expected them to be attacked again.

And they very well could be.

Because this could be a ruse not to go after Matthew, but rather to go after Jax and her.

Jericho must have thought it was possible, too, because he had suggested that Levi or Chase drive in with them so they'd have backup. But Jax and she had wanted that backup at the ranch. Something they'd easily agreed on. At least they were on the same page when it came to their son's safety.

Paige mentally shrugged.

Apparently on the same page when it came to that kiss, too. Jax had hardly looked at her since then, and that was a good thing. Kissing was a distraction, and it muddied waters that she needed to be clear right now. All their focus had to be on protecting Matthew.

Jax drew his gun, and with his body practically wrapped around her, he hurried her into the building. Her hair was still damp from the shower she'd hurriedly taken. Not exactly a luxury. She hadn't managed to take one the night before, and she had to wash off some of the scents from the attack. Also, she'd needed all the help she could get loosening up her tight muscles. So tight that her neck was stiff.

The moment they got inside the sheriff's office, Paige spotted Mack, Jericho and a tall, thin man with dark hair. The courier, no doubt. He looked even more nervous about this than Paige did. His Adam's apple was bobbing, and his eyes were darting all around.

There was no sign of Leland or Darrin, so maybe that meant Jericho had finished with them. Or maybe they were still being interviewed by one of the deputies.

"His name is Chad Farmer," Jericho supplied, tipping his head to the man.

Jax's brother was seated at a desk, leaning back in

the chair. Almost casually. But there was nothing casual about that dangerous look Jericho was giving their visitor.

"Does he have a record?" Jax asked.

"Not yet. But he knows he's going to jail after he talks to you. I'm charging him with obstruction of justice for not answering my questions. Oh, and for having a broken taillight on his car. And I'll tack on anything else I can think to charge him with."

Evidently, Jericho wasn't pleased with this courier. Well, neither was Paige.

She went closer to the desk and looked in the box that was next to Jericho. Only the typed note and the phone, just as Jericho had said.

"No prints," Jericho told her. "Well, other than the prints belonging to this clown, and his are the only ones on the outside of the box."

"The man who hired me said he'd kill me if I talked to anyone but you," Chad volunteered, his attention on her.

"Well, I'm here now, so talk," she demanded. "Who was he?"

Chad immediately shook his head. "He didn't say, and I didn't get a good look at him. He was in the backseat of my car when I got in it and put a gun to my head. He said I was to bring the box here and ask to speak to you. Only you. And if I said anything else to anyone I was a dead man."

Paige had no idea if any of this was true, but she could practically smell the fear on Chad. See it in his eyes, too.

"Did this man have an accent?" Paige pressed. "Was there anything about him that stood out?"

He shook his head to both questions. "He just said

he'd know if I talked to anyone but you and that he'd make sure I was dead by morning if I did." Chad swallowed hard when he glanced at Jericho. "Will you ask the sheriff if he's really going to arrest me?"

"You bet I am." Jericho motioned to Mack. "Lock him up and hold him until I can find out if he's telling the truth. If he's not, I can add another charge to the ones I already have."

Chad opened his mouth and seemed ready to argue about that, but he looked at the window, his gaze shifting over the sidewalk and buildings. "He could be watching," Chad said to Paige. "Tell the sheriff to go ahead and put me in jail. Just make sure someone's guarding me so he can't get to me."

Well, that worked in Chad's favor. He was willing to be in jail rather than speak to anyone else. Either he was truly innocent or else he was playing them for some reason she couldn't figure out. Either way, Paige was glad when Mack led the man toward the holding cell.

"It's been a busy morning for all of us," Jericho said, pushing the box closer for her to see. "I still have Darrin in the interview room. Last I checked he was playing a game on his phone, but I've been too tied up with this to talk to him. Dexter's in there with him now."

"I'm surprised Darrin didn't bring one of his attorneys with him," Jax remarked.

"Oh, he called them all right. They're on the way. A whole team of them, apparently. And they're going to sue me for harassment. I don't think Darrin liked it much when I wasn't bothered about that."

No, he wouldn't have liked that. Darrin loved to intimidate people. That didn't work so well on the Crocketts, though. They had just as much money as he did—possibly more. And they had badges. Darrin wasn't big on dealing with authority figures.

"What about Leland?" she asked.

Jericho shook his head. "He hasn't come in. If he's not here by the time we've figured out exactly what this box means, I'll give him a call. Or better yet, call his lieutenant."

That wouldn't please Leland, but Paige couldn't worry about hurting his feelings. She had to get the truth.

The truth that might be in that box.

She took out the note, trying not to touch anything but the edges. Jericho had already said it didn't have prints on it, but touching it seemed like touching the killer. Because she figured whoever wanted her dead had to be behind this.

"'Paige,'" she read aloud from the note, "'this phone and mine are burners, and if I don't hear your sweet voice when it rings, then I hang up, and you'll lose your chance to speak to me. Wouldn't want that, would you? Call me right now. The number's programmed in already.'"

"It's a burner," Jericho verified. "No way to trace it."

Exactly what she'd expected. And Paige knew what she had to do next. She had to talk to this monster and figure out who he was and how to stop him.

"Ready?" Jericho asked her. He took out a recorder, and when she nodded, he pressed the button.

Her hands were shaking, but she didn't realize how much until Jax reached over and touched the number in the contacts. It rang. And rang. By the fourth ring, her heart was in her throat, and she was afraid all of this had been a sick hoax.

But then someone answered. Whoever it was didn't say a word, no doubt waiting to hear her "sweet voice."

"It's me," she said, trying to sound strong. She failed.

"Paige," the man answered. "Good girl, following orders. I knew you wouldn't want to miss this chance for us to chat."

The chill went through her, head to toe, and if she hadn't sat down in the chair, she would have fallen.

"It's him." She had to clear her throat and repeat it for her words to have any sound. "It's the Moonlight Strangler. I recognize the voice."

"Well, of course you do, sweetheart," he purred. "We had some time to talk last year."

That gave her some steel that she seriously needed. "Yes, while you were cutting my face."

"Yes, that. A nasty obsession of mine. We bad boys do have our bad ways, don't we?"

Because Jax's hand was on her shoulder—she wasn't even sure when he'd put it there, though—she could feel his muscles tense. See Jericho's doing the same. Paige could tell they both wanted to speak up, badly, to blast this monster to smithereens, but if they said anything, the killer might end the call.

That couldn't happen.

Just talking to him made her want to throw up, but she had to do this.

"How did you find out I was alive?" she asked.

"I have my ways, but I will say, you had me fooled. I really thought you were number thirty-one."

The FBI didn't have a confirmed number of bodies they could attribute to the Moonlight Strangler, so she didn't know if that was true or not.

"How did you know I was alive?" she pressed. She prayed her voice wouldn't freeze up and that she could get through this without breaking down. God, she could feel his knife cutting into her.

"I heard about the attack at the Crockett ranch," he said. "That's when I found out."

She jumped right on that. "It wasn't you behind that attack?"

"No way." He sounded insulted. "That's not my style. Too sloppy. Too many working parts. But someone wanted to make you think it was me. Someone using my name and reputation. I don't like that. I kill people who pretend to be me."

That time, he sounded dangerous. Not that she'd needed to hear it to know it. The proof was on her face. Plus, he'd actually murdered another man when he had tried to make everyone believe that the Moonlight Strangler was after Alexa.

"So, if it wasn't you last night," she continued, "who was it?"

"That sounds like a personal problem. Yours, not mine. Use all those cowboy cops you surround yourself with to figure it out. I just don't want to be blamed for something I haven't done. Yet."

The *yet* felt like a punch to the gut.

"Are you going to try to come after me again?" Paige wasn't sure, though, that she actually wanted to hear the answer.

"All in due time. I've always wanted to do this mother-daughter thing, and you're my chance to make that happen. But I have someone else in my sights right now. Oh, she's such a sweet little thing. A blonde, like you. I'll bet she begs for mercy when I cut her. I like it when they beg."

That was it. He ended the call before Paige could scream for him to stop. The flashbacks came at her full force. All of them at once. The sounds. The pain. His voice. And now he was going to do that to someone else.

"You have to stop him," she begged, though she knew there was nothing they could do. The only way she could save her sanity was to believe it'd been all talk, that he wasn't about to add another victim to his list.

But she knew in her heart that soon, very soon, they'd hear the news of another murder. Another one that she hadn't been able to stop.

"I would ask if you're okay," Jericho grumbled when he hit the button to end the recording, "but I know you're not." He went to the water cooler, got her a cup and brought it back to her.

Even though she wasn't much of a drinker, Paige wished it was something stronger. She downed the whole cup, but her throat was still bone dry.

Mack came back into the room, and even though he looked at her, he didn't ask what'd happened. Good thing. Because Paige wasn't sure she could tell him that it felt as if she'd just been crushed by an avalanche.

Jericho eased away from her so that Jax could step in. Not exactly a subtle move, and the brothers exchanged a long glance before Jericho went to another desk to make a call.

"He'll kill this woman," she managed to say, "and come after me again."

"No, he won't, because we'll stop him."

Jax sounded so sure of that, but Paige didn't actually feel that certainty, that promise, until he pulled her into his arms. Just the simple gesture gave her a lot more comfort than it should.

"Come on," Jax said, helping her to her feet. "I'll take you back to the ranch. Holding Matthew should help."

It would, but she shook her head. "I don't want to lead the Moonlight Strangler to the ranch."

"He already knows where the ranch is. He knows someone you care about will be there. And we've got people in place to make sure he doesn't come anywhere near you."

Paige knew that no measures of security were foolproof. Especially when it came to this particular killer. But Jax was right about one thing—holding Matthew would make her feel better.

However, they hadn't even moved toward the door when Jericho held up his finger in a wait-a-minute gesture. "Don't touch it. Have Levi bag it and bring it in," he told the person he was speaking to, and he finished the call.

"Bag what?" Jax immediately asked.

"There don't appear to be any bombs at your place, but one of the ranch hands found a camera. It was attached to the bottom of the porch swing, and it appears to have some kind of listening device connected to it."

Jax cursed, shook his head. "That would have given the person a view of the yard, driveway and anyone coming in and out of the house. And the person would have been able to hear whatever we said when we were out there."

Yes, and as sickening as that was, at least it was better than a bomb. "When it's analyzed, we might be able to tell who was on the receiving end of the camera feed. Might." It was a long shot, though.

"There appears to be a print on the camera," Jericho added. "That's why I didn't want him to touch it."

She hated to get up her hopes, but this could be the break they were looking for. Well, unless it was just the prints of another hired gun. Still, that particular lackey might still be alive so they could question him.

Paige heard the sound of the front door opening, but she didn't actually get to see who was coming in. That's because Jax hooked his arm around her, maneuvering her behind him. Only then did she get a glimpse of their visitor.

Leland.

He'd finally arrived for his interview. And he wasn't alone. He was holding on to a very distraught-looking Belinda. She was sobbing and leaning against him. She didn't appear to be hurt, but her face was sweaty and red, and her hair was disheveled.

What had happened now?

And why were those two together?

Belinda immediately left Leland and made a beeline for Jax. She flung herself at him, landing in his arms.

"Someone broke into my house," she said through the sobs. Her words rushed together. "I didn't know he was there, but he must have been watching me."

"Slow down," Jax told her. He helped her to one of the chairs and had her sit. Jericho did water duty again and got her a cup.

While Belinda was drinking that, Paige turned to Leland. "What happened?"

He lifted his shoulder. "I don't know. I pulled into the parking lot and I saw her crying and stumbling. I helped her in." Leland didn't actually look at Belinda. He kept his attention on Paige. "She's your son's nanny, right?"

Paige nodded. Matthew's nanny and Jax's friend. A friend who wanted to be a lot more. Paige got a reminder of that when Belinda lunged at Jax and went right back into his arms.

"You have to help me," Belinda begged.

"I will. Now tell me what happened."

Belinda's tears didn't exactly dry up when she looked at Paige, but she frowned as if she didn't want Paige around for this.

"I could wait in one of the interview rooms while you talk to her," Paige suggested, not to Belinda but to Jax.

He nixed that right away with a head shake and moved out of Belinda's arms again. "Darrin's back there. Stay here where I can keep an eye on you."

Oh, Belinda did not like that, and Paige got a nasty glare from the woman. That alone was enough reason for Paige to stay put. Plus, she really didn't want to be any closer to Darrin.

"Did you see the person who broke in?" Jax asked Belinda. His tone wasn't impatient exactly, but it was close. Probably because it was still morning and they'd already been through the wringer a couple of times.

Belinda took her time gathering her breath. "I didn't see him, but I heard his phone ring. And then I heard him talking. I ran straight here."

Jax and she exchanged glances with Jericho. It was Jericho who continued. "How long ago did this happen?"

"Fifteen or so minutes."

Mercy. That was about the same time Paige had called the Moonlight Strangler. Was it possible he'd been there in Belinda's house?

"Did you hear anything the intruder said?" Paige pressed.

Belinda shook her head, then she stopped. "I did. I didn't remember it until now, but I did hear something." She looked at Paige, her eyes suddenly narrowing. "He said your name."

Oh, God. That's the first thing the killer had said

when he answered the phone. *Paige*. And that could only mean one thing.

Belinda was the Moonlight Strangler's next target.

Chapter Eleven

Hell.

Jax wanted to dismiss all this as a really bad coincidence. But he couldn't. The Moonlight Strangler had admitted he had another woman on his radar. A blonde.

Like Belinda.

And Jax wouldn't put it past the killer to go after yet someone else close to his family.

"What is it?" Belinda asked, obviously picking up on the bad vibes.

Jax wasn't sure how much he should tell her. This could all be part of the killer's sick game, a ruse. Or Belinda could be lying to get some attention from him. But he couldn't take that chance.

"The Moonlight Strangler could have been the person in your house."

Belinda's breath rushed out, and she looked ready to keel over. All right. That reaction looked pretty darn genuine.

"You're responsible for this," Belinda muttered several moments later. And she was looking at Paige when she said it.

"How is Paige responsible?" Jax asked, huffing. But Paige wasn't huffing. She was a little thunderstruck.

"She drew him here." Belinda made it seem as if

the answer was obvious. Her anger was plenty obvious, as well. "He knew Paige was alive. He must have seen her like I did."

Belinda froze, and her hand flew to her mouth. Jax got a really bad feeling that Belinda wasn't talking about having seen Paige the day before.

"How long have you known I was alive?" Paige demanded, and it was a demand. Jax wanted to know the same thing.

Belinda glanced around, swallowed hard. "Two weeks. But I wasn't sure it was her. I only suspected."

Jax had to get his teeth unclenched. "And you didn't tell me?"

"I said I didn't know for sure, and I didn't want you to, well, get your hopes up or anything." Belinda looked everywhere but at him. Her attention finally settled on Paige. "I bought this facial recognition software. I had a feeling in my gut you were still alive, so I started doing internet searches. The software matched your face to a photo that someone had taken at a store opening in Houston."

Jax turned to Paige to see if that could have happened. And she nodded. "A toy store. But I didn't know they'd taken my picture. I arrived there just as they were doing the ribbon cutting, and I guess I got in the shot."

"Why were you there?" Leland asked.

"To buy Matthew something. I was going to have Cord give it to him, but Cord wasn't going to say it was from me."

A toy.

Damn.

"I wasn't sure it was her," Belinda repeated.

Yeah, she had been. Jax could see it in her eyes. Belinda hadn't wanted him to know that Paige was alive because he would have gone after her and found her so she could give him answers.

Now he had those answers, but they weren't ones that Jax liked.

"I know this is a lot to take in," Leland said, "but it sounds as if Belinda could be in real danger."

Jax could add another "yeah" to that, too.

"Belinda can't go back to your place," Paige insisted at the same moment Jericho turned to Mack.

"Why don't you take Belinda to the break room and have her give you a statement. I'll have Dexter go out to her house and look around."

"Someone needs to go with Dexter," Paige blurted out. "He might need backup."

Jericho nodded, but since he was taking out his phone, he'd already considered that possibility. "I'll call in one of the reserve deputies."

"Find that man," Belinda said. To Jericho. "And arrest him."

"If he's still there, Dexter will find him," Jax told her. But he seriously doubted the Moonlight Strangler would be hanging around waiting for the cops to show up.

Belinda caught on to Jax's hand when Mack tried to lead her to the break room. "Jax, I want you to take my statement. I want you to wait with me. Please."

Jax wasn't immune to the fear she was no doubt feeling, but he had to shake his head. "I can't stay." It wasn't safe for Paige to be here, and he didn't want to be away from Matthew any longer. "But Mack will take good care of you."

Belinda looked as if he'd slapped her. And then Jax saw the shock morph to hurt. Then, a glare. Maybe even hatred.

The hatred wasn't aimed at him but at Paige.

Okay, that helped with the guilt he was feeling over not staying there with her. What was going on? Was this just a case of jealousy or something more? He hoped like the devil that Belinda hadn't made some kind of contact with the Moonlight Strangler so that the killer would go after Paige.

"I've been good to you," Belinda added, still sounding more angry than hurt.

He didn't respond, though Belinda was obviously waiting for something. But Jax wasn't sure what to say. He was emotionally spent right now, and he needed to focus his mind and energies elsewhere. Later, if it turned out that Belinda was completely innocent in all of this, then he would owe her an apology.

Belinda didn't put up a fuss when Mack led her up the hall, but she managed to work in one last hard look at Paige.

Jax immediately turned to Leland. "You were supposed to come in a couple of hours ago. Where were you?"

Yet another glare, and it was Jax who got a dose of it this time. "I had work to do." He tapped his badge that was clipped to his belt. "I'm a cop, remember."

"You're also a suspect in the attack last night."

Judging from the sound of surprise Paige made, she hadn't expected Jax to spell it out in no uncertain terms, but there it was. Jax didn't have time to sugarcoat it. And Leland didn't care for it one bit.

"The Moonlight Strangler was behind that," Leland insisted.

"Not according to him. Paige just got off the phone with him, and he said someone else is responsible. He's not very happy about someone using his name, either. He murdered the last person who tried to do that."

Leland had no doubt heard all about it, but it still took a moment for it to sink in. Or maybe it just took him some time to realize that Jax had just told him that he might be on the killer's list, too.

However, Leland didn't respond to Jax. He turned to Paige. "Your ex has already turned you against me." It wasn't a question, and he didn't wait for Paige to say anything. He looked at Jericho. "Are you ready to do that interview?"

Jericho didn't usually look stressed, but he sure did now. He huffed, then hitched his thumb to the hall. "Wait in the second interview room on the right."

Jax waited until Leland was in the room before he said anything to his brother. "I don't think Belinda has the resources to hire gunmen, but I'll check. I'll check on Leland, too."

Jericho nodded. "It doesn't always take money to hire thugs. Both of those gunmen had records. It's possible they owed favors to Leland or someone else." He paused, groaned softly as if very uncomfortable as to what he was about to say. "You didn't know Belinda was in love with you?"

Paige decided it was a good time to go to the water cooler and get another drink, but Jax didn't lower his voice. Because this was something she probably should hear.

"I knew," Jax admitted. "But I never led Belinda to believe she could be anything more than a friend and Matthew's nanny."

Jericho made a sound of agreement. "It's that pretty face of yours. Women just can't resist you." Jericho probably meant that as a joke, to help with the raw tension in the room. It didn't. But Jax was thankful for it, anyway.

"I don't think Belinda would have tried to hurt me," Jax went on. Hurting Paige, though, might be a different matter. Belinda could have been so distraught over hearing Paige was alive that she did something stupid.

Like convincing two men to scare Paige away by making her believe that the Moonlight Strangler was after her again and that her presence at the ranch put Matthew in danger.

However, the huge problem with that was the same warning he'd given Leland. The Moonlight Strangler didn't care much for being used.

Jax was ready to try to get Paige out of there again, but he'd barely got her moving when he heard a door open in the hall. At first he thought he was going to have to go another round with Belinda.

But it was Darrin.

"Good news," he said. "You don't get sued today. We have to reschedule this little chat because my chief lawyer just called, and he's been involved in a car accident in San Antonio. He can't make it."

"You don't look broken up about that," Jericho remarked.

"I'm not. I fired him, of course, which means I'll need to get a new lawyer before you can grill me with your lies. Or rather *her* lies." He shot a glance at Paige before turning to Jax. "Besides, you don't have any grounds to hold me."

"Not yet," Jax warned him. "We're waiting on some lab results."

Maybe it was Jax's expression or his tone, but Darrin actually seemed to take notice.

"Lab results?" Darrin questioned. "Ones that Paige faked?"

"Paige had nothing to do with this. A cop found the

evidence, and the crime lab is processing it." At least it soon would be once Levi brought it in. "Paige hasn't been near the lab."

Darrin's jaw tightened. "What did you find? Or what is it you *think* you found?"

No way would Jax tell him about the print on the camera, but it would make all this so much easier if the print turned out to be Darrin's. Or if a money trail for those hired guns led right back to him.

"You can go," Jericho said, not answering Darrin's question, either. "I'll call your lawyer when the lab results are back."

Darrin suddenly didn't seem to be in such a hurry to leave. He stood there, volleying glances at the three of them before he cursed and headed out. Jax went to the window to make sure he did indeed leave and that he didn't try to tamper with the cruiser.

"Don't let Belinda go back to her place," Jax said to Jericho. "I know we have a lot of manpower tied up, but—"

"Already taken care of," Jericho interrupted. "The other reserve deputy will put her in protective custody."

Good. He doubted Belinda would try to go back, anyway. Heck, she might never go back, but he didn't want to risk it. The Moonlight Strangler might have targeted Belinda simply because of her connection to Jax.

Jax waited until Darrin had driven away and his car was out of sight before he motioned for Paige to get moving. Every second outside was a huge risk, and he tried to minimize that by going out ahead of her to open the door. He practically stuffed her into the cruiser and then hurried to get behind the wheel. He drove off as fast as he could. However, he'd hardly pulled away from the station when his phone buzzed.

Chase.

Jax couldn't answer it fast enough.

"Matthew's fine," Chase said the moment he came on the line. "We all are. But a ranch hand spotted someone climbing over one of the fences." Chase paused. "The guy's armed with a rifle."

Even though he hadn't put the call on speaker, Paige must have heard what Chase said because she gasped. "Hurry," she told Jax, but he was already doing that.

"We've moved Mom and the others into the playroom, and Levi and the ranch hands are going after the guy."

"Paige and I are on our way back to the ranch," Jax let him know.

"Just be careful when you get here. The ranch hand said the rifle had a scope on it."

Which meant the shooter could go into sniper mode. He could set up cover behind one of the barns or trees and start shooting. Of course, the question was—who was his target? Someone inside the house? Or was it Paige and him?

"I'll call you when the situation's contained," Chase added before he hung up.

"The playroom?" Paige questioned the moment Jax was off the phone.

"It's safe, in the center of the house. We set it up a few months back after there was some trouble at the ranch."

It wasn't a panic room exactly, but there were no windows, and if someone did start shooting, the bullets would have to make it through multiple walls to hit anyone. Still, Jax wanted to be there to make sure this guy with the rifle didn't get inside. He didn't want a gunfight right on his family's doorstep.

Jax was already going well over the speed limit, but he pushed the accelerator even harder. Each minute felt like hours.

"We have to move Matthew to the safe house," Paige said.

No argument from him, and as soon as Jax was certain he could get them there safely, he would do it.

"Our security measures at the ranch worked. The ranch hand spotted the gunman," he reminded her. Reminded himself, too. But then Jax saw something he didn't want to see.

Smoke.

Not a small amount, either. It was thick and black and oozing over the road.

At first he thought someone had set a fire on the asphalt, and it took him a moment to realize it was coming from a house. Hell. It was the old Dawson place. A small house just off the road.

"Call the fire department," Jax said, tossing Paige his phone.

He eased up on the gas, not only because of the wall of smoke in front of him but because he needed to see if Herman Dawson had gotten out. The man was eighty if he was a day and a smoker. He could have set the place on fire.

But Jax knew this could be more than just an accidental fire. That's why he kept watch, or rather he tried to do that, when he slowed the cruiser to a crawl so he could have a better look. He prayed he'd see Herman in the yard, unharmed.

He didn't.

However, Jax did get a glimpse of a man near the blazing house. Not Herman, either. The man lifted a rifle and shot right into the cruiser.

SINCE PAIGE HAD her attention on the phone call she was making, she didn't see the shooter before the bullet blasted into the side window right next to her. The glass cracked and webbed, but the bullet didn't go through.

Thank God.

She didn't even have time to react to it before Jax took hold of her arm, unlatched her seat belt and pushed her down onto the floor. He didn't get down, though. He drew his gun, and in the same motion, he got them moving again.

Or at least that's what he tried to do.

But the shots started coming nonstop. Not just from the side. They came in front of them, too, directly from that wall of smoke.

Paige made the call to the fire department. Then she made one to Jericho and asked him to send someone immediately, but to approach with caution because of the shots being fired. Jax and she were only about ten minutes away from town, but it might take longer than that for Jericho to be able to make a safe approach.

And then Paige had a horrible thought.

What if there was an attack like this going on at the ranch?

She couldn't press Chase's number fast enough. But her heart crashed against her chest when he didn't answer.

Paige tried to assure herself that it was because he was in pursuit of that rifleman, but that person could have been a ruse to lure Levi and Chase out of the house so that someone could go after Matthew.

"Stay down," Jax warned her.

He didn't go forward, probably because he didn't know who was on the other side of the smoke. Maybe an entire team of hired killers. Instead, he threw the cruiser into reverse.

She did stay on the seat, but Paige also threw open the glove compartment and took out the gun that Jax had put there earlier before they'd started their drive to the sheriff's office. When he'd done that, he'd mumbled something about it just being a precaution.

Now she might have to use it to help save their lives and get them out of there so they could hurry to the ranch to protect their son.

Even though they were in the middle of cross fire, Paige felt the panic attack threaten. Not solely from this attack, though that was a huge part of it, but also just because she had a gun in her hand.

The flashbacks came.

Not of the Moonlight Strangler's attack. He hadn't used a gun. But from the attack that had left her parents dead. She'd witnessed it. Had been there to watch them both die, and even though it'd happened a long time ago, just holding the gun made those memories fresh and raw.

"Level your breathing," Jax said to her.

Only then did Paige realize her breaths were coming way too fast, and she was trembling. *Get a grip.* She'd worked her way through the panic attacks and didn't have time to deal with her old baggage. If she wanted to stay alive, she had to focus on the here and now.

Just as Jax was doing.

With his gaze volleying from the rear to the front of the cruiser, he kept them moving. Away from the fire and the gunmen. Paige only prayed they didn't have a wreck with any oncoming traffic. This was a farm road, but there were houses and other ranches all along it.

"Damn," Jax spat out.

She didn't have the time to ask why he'd said that. Paige quickly found out. When a bullet slammed into the back window of the cruiser. It was quickly followed by another one. Then, another.

Mercy.

They were being attacked on three sides, and while the cruiser was bullet resistant, it didn't mean those shots soon wouldn't get through. Plus, it seemed as if the gunmen were trying to shoot out the engine. If they managed that, Jax and she would be sitting ducks.

There was only one place for Jax to go. To the left. And that's the way he went. He jerked the steering wheel to the left, gunned the engine and the cruiser barreled off the road, crashing through a white wood fence and into a massive cornfield.

The cruiser bobbled and bounced on the uneven surface, the high stalks and the corn slapping against the car. The noise was practically deafening, but it didn't drown out the shots that continued to come at them.

The gunmen were either in pursuit or they had some of their buddies stashed in this cornfield. All in all, it wasn't a bad place to hide since she couldn't see anything except for corn stalks and the shattered glass in the windows.

Jax cursed when he hit a bad bump, and Paige's head collided with the dash. Right in the very spot where she had stitches. The pain shot through her so bad that she nearly lost her breath, but she had a huge incentive to regain it when the phone buzzed and she saw Chase's name on the screen.

"Is Matthew okay?" she asked, her words running together.

"Yes." Chase paused a heartbeat. "I didn't answer because I was on the line with Jericho. He's on his way out to you. Two of the hands are coming from the ranch."

"No, I want all the hands and you there with Matthew. This could be a trap."

"Maybe, but if so it didn't work. One of the hands shot the guy with the rifle, and there aren't any signs of another gunman."

Despite the nightmarish situation Jax and she were in, the relief came. She'd experience a thousand attacks aimed at her if these goons just kept her son out of it.

"Give him our location," Jax instructed.

She did. Well, as best she could. She'd driven by this cornfield hundreds of times over the years, but she had no idea just how much acreage was involved or what was even on the back side of it. There were plenty of ranch trails out here. Plus, there were no doubt rocks and such that could cause them to have a blowout.

"They're following us," she heard Jax say.

Paige stayed down, but she levered herself up just enough to see out the side window. She spotted the black SUV tearing through the cornfield behind them. The gunmen weren't leaning out of the windows. It wouldn't be safe enough for them to do that, but they'd no doubt be ready to resume this attack when they were out of the field.

Which happened a lot sooner than Paige expected.

The cruiser shot through the last row of corn, skidding onto what felt like gravel. Jax fought with the steering wheel, trying to regain control.

And Paige soon saw why he needed to do that.

There was a creek just to their right, and even though she couldn't see exactly where the water began, they seemed to be only a few inches from it.

It seemed to take an eternity for Jax to get control,

and he managed to maneuver the cruiser away from the water. Barely in time. They likely wouldn't have drowned if the cruiser had gone in the creek, but it would have made it easy for the gunmen to kill them.

Once he was centered on the trail, Jax gunned the engine again, and Paige braced herself for more gunfire.

It didn't happen.

No shots at all. And that's why she wasn't sure why Jax cursed.

Paige looked in the mirror to see what was going on. The SUV wasn't following them. The driver was now on another trail, headed away from them.

She blew out a breath of relief. But it didn't last.

"Where does that trail lead?" she asked Jax. "Where are they going?"

A muscle flickered in his jaw. "To the ranch."

Chapter Twelve

It was hard to speed down a dirt and gravel trail that wasn't much wider than the cruiser, but that's exactly what Jax did. He'd never been on this particular part of Herman Dawson's acreage, but he wasn't far from the ranch. Probably only a couple of miles.

The trick would be to make it there ahead of the gunmen.

"Call Chase again," Jax told Paige. "Let him know what's going on."

She did that while Jax continued to maneuver his way around the winding trail. It wasn't meant for vehicles like his but rather as a way for tractors and utility vehicles to get to remote parts of the property. This one clearly hadn't been used in a while because in places there were bushes and weeds several feet high.

"Chase said there's no sign of the gunmen so far," Paige relayed.

Good. Maybe it'd stay that way. In fact, maybe they weren't headed to the ranch but rather the highway so they could escape and regroup. Jax prayed that was the case, anyway.

The minutes and the miles crawled by while Paige and he kept watch around them. She kept glancing at the phone, too. If it rang, it could be bad news, but thankfully there was no call from Chase by the time Jax reached the road. The second he was on the asphalt again, he gunned the engine.

Jax spotted some armed ranch hands when he made the final turn and drove past his house. The CSI van was parked in the driveway. They had no doubt still been searching for any other cameras or bugs when the gunman had climbed over the fence. Now they'd be processing the scene of a shooting. But Jax couldn't feel bad about a dead gunman. He would have shot the man himself to stop him from getting near his family.

There were ranch hands at the main house, too, and Chase and Levi were waiting for them just inside the door. Thankfully, there were no signs of the gunmen who'd just attacked them.

"Everyone's fine," Chase said right off. "Matthew's having fun with all the attention he's getting."

Good. That was something at least.

As he'd done since this whole mess had started, Jax got Paige inside the house. And that's when he noticed the blood. There was a streak of it running down the side of her head.

Damn.

It'd probably happened when her head hit the dash. But Paige obviously hadn't noticed, and she would have rushed to find Matthew if Jax hadn't stopped her.

"Matthew shouldn't see you like that," he told her.

The words obviously didn't get through to her. Even though Paige was still struggling to get away from him, Jax led her into the nearby powder room, and she froze when she caught a glimpse of herself in the mirror.

"Oh, God." She leaned in, examining it while Jax took a hand towel and wet it.

"I think you might have popped a stitch," he said,

dabbing at the wound. "And it looks as if you have a new cut, too. I'll need to get the medic out here."

He reached for his phone, only to realize Paige still had it. And she wasn't just holding it; she had a death grip on it. Her hands were shaking, and she was fighting back tears.

"I'm not going to cry," she insisted. She practically dropped the phone on the vanity. "I don't want Matthew or your family to see me crying."

Jax was sure he didn't want to see it, either, but he was surprised she hadn't broken down by now. "Just take a minute," he said, because he didn't know what else to say. He shut the door to give her a little privacy while she pulled herself together.

Paige gulped in several long breaths, blinked hard against those threatening tears. "I might need a year to steady my nerves."

Yeah. He might need longer. And while he wasn't a fix for raw nerves, Jax eased her into his arms for a hug. She melted right against him, as if she'd never been away from him. That was the trouble with hugs. With being close to her like this. And yet Jax needed it as much as he thought she did.

They stood there, several moments, and when Jax's lungs started to ache, he realized he was holding his breath. He inched back, meeting her gaze. No tears. And the bleeding had stopped. That should have been his cue to move away from her.

He didn't, though.

Jax didn't see the kiss coming. But he sure as hell felt it. The moment Paige put her mouth to his, he hooked his arm around her, dragging her closer. The frustration was there. She didn't want to be doing this. She didn't want to want him.

But she did.

Jax was right there with her. In regard to both the frustration and the want. Except his was more of a need. Always was when it came to Paige.

She was the one who moved back. "Wow," she said, her voice silky soft. "Your kisses always did pack a punch."

But for some reason he didn't think a punch was nearly enough. He hauled her back to him, and he kissed her again. Now, here was the cure for the nightmarish images in his head. The taste of her kicked out all of the bad stuff, and he was suddenly lost in the heat.

Paige made that sound of pleasure. One he knew all too well. Because he'd heard that sound a lot when they were having sex. Of course, just the reminder of it made his body start suggesting that sex might be just what they needed right now.

Of course, his body was wrong.

But that didn't stop him. Didn't stop Paige, either. It was as if they were pouring every bit of their fears and frustrations into that kiss. Her arms tightened around him again, but Jax did his own share of holding her. Keeping her right against him. Body to body.

Yeah.

This was what he wanted.

And even though he knew it was wrong, he deepened the kiss and touched her. His hand sliding over her breasts. His hands wanted to go a whole lot lower than that, though.

That was the problem with Paige being his ex. They knew all the right spots to drive each other crazy. Paige took her mouth to his neck. Jax dropped his hands to her lower back, aligning them just right so that his erection was in the right place, too.

She made that silky sound of pleasure again. The one that made him want to push this even further. Something that couldn't happen.

At least not in a powder room with his family in the house. Besides, there were plenty of other things he needed to be doing, and Paige wasn't exactly in any shape to be making out with him. That didn't stop him, but it slowed him down so he could come to his senses.

Jax gave her one last kiss and moved back.

This was probably a good time for him to admit that the kissing had been a mistake, but he didn't have a chance to say anything because there was a soft knock at the door.

"You two okay?" Chase asked.

That moved them even farther apart. Not that there was a ton of room for them to separate. They were still way too close. Jax gave her a second. Gave himself one, too, before he opened the door.

"We're fine," he said to Chase.

Chase eyed him, then Paige, and grumbled something under his breath that Jax didn't catch. A reminder that his family, or at least Chase, wasn't on board with his getting involved with Paige again. It wouldn't do any good to tell Chase that it was the attraction and not anything that Paige and he had consciously decided to do. But Chase likely already knew that, anyway.

"I called for a medic," Chase explained. "He should be here soon to check those stitches."

Paige looked ready to argue about that, but she must have realized it'd be a lost cause. She was seeing a medic.

"Is the house locked up?" Jax asked.

Chase nodded. "I reset the security system, too.

Levi's standing guard by the front door. Weston is at the back."

"And what about Cord?" Paige pressed.

"He left right before you got here. He's dropping off that camera for Jericho before he heads out to look for those gunmen who attacked you."

Jax welcomed any and all help, though he figured those men were long gone since they hadn't shown up by now.

"Come on." Jax put his hand on Paige's back to get her moving. "I'll take you to the playroom so you can see Matthew."

"What about going to a safe house?" Chase asked, following them.

Paige immediately shook her head. "It isn't a good idea for Matthew to be out there right now. There could be more of those thugs waiting to attack, and this time we might not get so lucky."

Jax agreed. Having their son at the ranch house wasn't ideal, but with all their layers of security, Matthew was safer here than he was out on the road. At least until they could track down those gunmen.

When they made it to the playroom, Matthew spotted them the second they stepped into the doorway, and he raced out of his grandmother's arms toward them. "Mommy, Daddy," he said, hurrying to them.

Jax scooped him up and kissed him before he moved him closer to Paige so she could do the same. Matthew's attention went straight to the wound on Paige's head.

"Boo boo," he said, but it didn't hold his attention for long. Matthew reached for Jax's badge, and Jax unclipped it so he could play with it.

Not that he needed any playthings.

The room was filled with all kinds of toys to accommodate his mom's grandchildren. Jericho's son. Chase's daughter. Matthew. And now Addie's son, who was sleeping in the playpen.

Jax handed off Matthew to Paige, and he could practically see some of the tension fade from her face. She kissed Matthew again and joined Alexa and Addie on the sofa. Jax stepped out into the hall with Chase.

"What about Herman Dawson?" Jax asked. "Did the fire department make it to his place?"

Chase nodded. "Herman wasn't there. No one was. The house was totaled, though."

Herman's home was gone, and all because somebody wanted to use the smoke to help set a trap.

"There could be a problem with Belinda," Chase said a moment later, getting Jax's attention. "While Paige and you were…in the bathroom, Jericho called, and he said Belinda left."

"What do you mean she left?" Jax snapped.

"She had a short chat with Jericho and told him her prints might be on the camera that was found under the porch swing. After that, she excused herself, saying she needed to lie down in the break room, and she sneaked out the back."

That got his attention, too, and not in a good way. Jax would address the part about her leaving, but first he wanted to hear about that camera. "Did she have a good reason as to why her prints would be on it?"

"No. But she had a bad one. She said she dropped something while she was on the porch, saw it beneath the swing but thought it was some kind of hardware to hold the swing in place."

"And she touched it?" Jax didn't bother to take the skepticism out of his voice.

"You think she could have really been the one to put that camera in place?" Chase went on.

"Maybe." But for him to believe that, he would also have to accept that she might indeed want Paige dead.

Except there was a problem with that.

Those gunmen had been trying to kill both Paige and him, so that would mean Belinda could want him dead, too. It put a huge knot in his stomach to even consider it. This was the woman he'd trusted with his son. Trusted with nearly every aspect of his life. Could she have betrayed him because she was jealous?

Or was she innocent in all of this?

Even though Paige couldn't hear their conversation, she looked at them, the concern in her eyes again. Probably because she saw the concern on his own face. He'd have to tell her about this, but it could wait for now so she could have some moments with Matthew.

"Belinda could be in grave danger," Jax admitted. "If she was telling the truth about not setting up that camera and the truth about the intruder being in her house, she could have a killer after her. So, would she just sneak out of the sheriff's office?"

Chase shrugged. "Giving her the benefit of the doubt, she could have panicked. Unlike the rest of us, she's never had anyone gunning for her before. Added to that, she might feel a little, well, betrayed by you." He immediately held up his hands in defense. "Hey, I didn't say it was true. I was just looking at this from her perspective."

Yeah. And Jax tried to do that, too. Maybe Belinda sensed the attraction still there between Paige and him. Jax took out his phone and pressed Belinda's number. If she answered, maybe he could talk some sense into her. But she didn't answer. His call went straight to her voice mail.

"Anyway, Dexter's out looking for Belinda," Chase went on. "He can't force her to agree to protective custody, but he'll try to talk her into it."

Maybe he could. Belinda wasn't an idiot. And that reminder didn't help the niggling feeling in his gut. If she truly thought she was in danger, why would she have left the group of people who could protect her?

"Belinda could have lied about having an intruder," Chase tossed out there. "Not because she's behind the plot to kill Paige but because she wanted to get some attention from you. When that failed, she could have decided to cut her losses and get out of there."

Sadly, that was the best-case scenario in all of this. Belinda was innocent, and no one wanted her dead.

"Where's this thing leading with Paige and you, anyway?" Chase asked a moment later.

Normally, he wouldn't have minded his brother prying into his private life, but this wasn't exactly a private thing. Being around Paige put them all in danger. "I'm not sure," Jax confessed. "I kissed her. Twice."

Chase made an *hmmp* sound. "I figured you'd already done more than that."

"Not yet," he mumbled.

And he wished that was a joke. It wasn't. Because while his brain was telling him it'd be a mistake, Jax could feel himself on a collision course. One that would land him in bed with Paige.

His phone buzzed, and Jax expected it to be an update from Jericho. It wasn't. "Unknown caller" was on the screen.

His heart slammed against his chest, and Paige must have noticed his reaction because she left Matthew playing on the floor and hurried over to him. When Jax showed her the screen, she jerked in her breath and held it.

Jax didn't want to answer the call. Didn't want to hear the killer, or rather someone pretending to be the Moonlight Strangler, taunt Paige again. But he didn't have a choice here. Every conversation was a chance to figure out who this person was. And Paige must have realized that, too, because she led Jax away from the playroom door. No doubt so their son wouldn't be able to hear any part of this. She motioned for Jax to hit the answer button, and he put the call on speaker.

"Jax," the caller immediately said. "Don't bother to trace this. I'm using another burner."

Hell. It was the same person who'd talked to Paige earlier at the sheriff's office. The real Moonlight Strangler.

"Paige, are you there?" he asked. "Of course you are. You're not leaving Jax's side. Well, unless I can entice you with an offer."

"What do you want?" she asked. Not much emotion in her voice, but it was all over her face, and every muscle in her body had gone stiff.

"You want these attacks on Jax and you to stop? Do you want to know who's behind them? Then meet with me."

Jax wanted to curse. Of course this monster would want that.

"You want to meet with me so you can kill me," Paige said. Not a question.

"Now, now." Unlike Paige's, there was emotion in the killer's voice. Sugary sweet and sickening. "I said I wasn't ready to do that yet, and I'm not. Have I ever lied to you before?"

"No," she admitted after several moments.

"But that doesn't mean she'll trust you," Jax snapped. "If you really know who's trying to kill us, just tell us. I'm sure you want us to stop the person pretending to be you."

"Oh, then I'd miss the chance to see Paige up close and personal again, wouldn't I?" he taunted.

Jax couldn't hold back the profanity. Profanity that caused this snake to laugh. This was all a game to him.

"Now, about that meeting," the killer went on. "Here's your chance to end the danger, to keep your little boy safe. Meet me at the location I'm about to text you. Oh, and you can bring Jax. One of his brothers, too, if you like, but I'd advise against trying to set a trap. Because, you see, I'll have a hostage. One I hadn't planned on killing, but I will if you don't show up."

"Who did you take?" Jax snapped.

Hell. Had he taken Belinda? Or maybe the Moonlight Strangler had managed to get to someone in his family. Jax motioned for Chase to start checking, and his brother stepped away, already taking out his phone.

"The hostage will be in touch with you, too," the killer added. "I'm thinking a call like that might convince you to come. Look for that text, Paige." He ended the call, leaving Paige and Jax standing there, staring at the phone.

"You're not meeting with him," Jax said just in case Paige had some stupid notion about doing that.

And apparently, she did. "You heard him. He has a hostage."

"He's a killer," Jax fired back, but the words had no sooner left his mouth when his phone dinged, indicating he had a text message.

"'Meet me by your grave, Paige,'" Jax read aloud.

"'I'm giving you one hour, but I wouldn't wait too long. The hostage seems to be having trouble breathing. As I said, bring Jax, his brother. Hell, bring anybody you want. Just show up, let me see your pretty face and I'll give you both the hostage and the information.'"

Jax had to curse again. This SOB really wanted to twist the knife into Paige. Maybe literally.

"My grave is in the cemetery at the church near here?" she asked.

He nodded. It was where other family members had been buried, and even though Paige had been his ex-wife, Jax had figured that one day he would want to show Matthew her headstone.

"But the old church isn't there any longer," Jax explained. "Long story but someone blew it up a couple of months back. They're rebuilding it, but it's just a construction site right now."

Which, of course, meant there were plenty of places for a killer to lie in wait.

Jax got right in Paige's face so she could see that he wasn't going to let this meeting happen. "You know what he's trying to do. He wants you dead."

She lifted her shoulder. "He was right about never having lied to me. And we both know he hates people using him to take the blame for these attacks. He might be planning on turning the person over to us."

"And he might just gun you down the second you get there!" he huffed, ready to gear up for more of that, but the phone rang.

Not his cell but Chase's. Since it could be one of the ranch hands calling about another intruder, Jax went to him. And judging from his brother's concerned expression, something had indeed gone wrong.

"It's Cord," Chase said, holding out his phone while he pressed the speaker function.

"Don't come here to save me," Cord immediately said. He didn't sound right. Not his usual iceman self. He grunted and gulped in his breath. Cord was in pain. "No matter what he says to you or does to me, don't come."

"Where are you?" Paige asked, though Jax was certain she already knew the answer.

It took Cord several seconds to respond, and there were more of those sounds that Jax didn't want to hear. "At the church. I'm the hostage."

Chapter Thirteen

"I have to do this," Paige said, something she'd been repeating to Jax for the past thirty minutes. "And we don't have much time. Cord could be dying."

She knew that wasn't an argument Jax wanted to hear. He wasn't fond of Cord, but Jax was a lawman and he wouldn't want the Moonlight Strangler to claim another victim.

Including Cord.

God, she hated to think of what that monster had done to him. And all because of her. Cord had been good to her, he'd tried to help her and now he could be dying.

"Jericho and Dexter just arrived at the road near the church," Chase told them when he finished his latest call. At least Chase was cooperating with her plans to go to the meeting and had scrambled to start getting security in place, not just at the church but here at the ranch, too.

"She's not changing her mind about this," Chase added to Jax. "Would you stay put if you knew you could save a man's life?"

"I would if it meant saving hers," Jax fired back. He cursed right after that outburst, something he'd been doing a lot in the past couple of minutes.

Chase stepped away from them. Maybe to give her time to win Jax over to what could turn out to be a deadly plan. Or maybe Chase was just tired of hearing them argue, especially since he'd already told them that he'd be going to this meeting with her.

"I don't want you to do this." Jax slipped his hand around the back of her neck, holding her in place to make eye contact with her.

"I don't want to do it, either, but I don't have a choice. I couldn't live with myself if he murdered Cord, or anyone else, just because I didn't have the guts to show up and face him. And you wouldn't be able to live with yourself, either."

She stepped away from him to let that sink in, and Paige went into the playroom to kiss Matthew—twice. He had fallen asleep on the sofa, obviously worn-out from his play session.

"We'll take good care of him," Addie offered. "Just be careful." And she kissed Paige on the cheek.

Somehow, Paige managed to thank her despite the lump in her throat, and when she went back into the hall, Chase and Jax were there. Chase handed her a Kevlar vest. Both Chase and Jax already had one on.

"You're wearing it," Jax snarled, the muscles in his jaw at war with each other. He took her hand and put a gun in it. "And you'll be behind me the whole time. If anything, and I mean anything, goes wrong, you'll get down and stay down."

She wasn't sure if her last argument had won him over or if it was something Chase had said. Either way, this meeting was going to happen. And Paige prayed they all survived it.

"Move fast," Jax told her, and the three of them got

moving out the door. Not to the cruiser. It was too shot up. But rather into one of the family's SUVs.

Levi locked up the house as soon as they were out, and he no doubt set the security system. She counted eight ranch hands outside the house. All armed. All looking ready in case there was another attack. With Levi and Weston inside the house, maybe that would be enough to keep everyone safe.

"Jericho let the hospital know that Cord might need an ambulance," Chase explained once Jax got them moving away from the house. "But obviously the paramedics can't just go driving in there."

No. Because they might be shot. Still, maybe they'd be close by and able to respond if all of this came to a quick end.

"Maybe Cord isn't hurt as bad as he sounded," she said, thinking out loud now. "He carries a backup weapon in his boot, and maybe he still has it. Maybe he'll get a chance to use it."

"Too many *maybes*," Jax commented under his breath. "And Cord didn't want you to do this. No lawman would."

But thankfully Jax kept driving, the SUV eating up the distance between the ranch and the church. Which wasn't much distance at all. Just a couple of miles. However, it was more than enough time for the flashbacks to come.

God.

Would they never go away?

Would there ever be a time when she didn't feel this paralyzing fear? It was yet another *maybe*, but perhaps if she faced down this monster, the flashbacks would stop. Of course, he might just give her a new set of memories. A new reason to have flashbacks.

First, though, she had to survive. Cord, too. And somehow she had to keep Jax and Chase out of harm's way.

Jax turned off the road, and she immediately spotted the cruiser, and Jax pulled up along beside it. Jericho was behind the wheel, and Dexter was in the passenger's seat. Both were wearing Kevlar, too.

"Any sign of them?" Jax asked his brother.

Jericho shook his head. "Not yet. But I figure the Moonlight Strangler was in place before he even called you."

Paige figured the same thing. Whatever he'd set up—either a meeting or a trap—the killer had everything just as he wanted it.

"Two Texas Rangers are on the way," Jericho explained. "And an FBI agent out of the San Antonio office. They should be here soon, and I told them to do a silent approach."

Six lawmen. Paige hoped that would be enough to put an end to this once and for all.

But certainly the Moonlight Strangler had known this would happen. Every law enforcement agency in the country was looking for him, and he'd invited her to bring them along.

That didn't help with the acid churning in her stomach.

What was this sick fool planning?

"Follow me," Jax told his brother. "Keep watch behind us."

Jericho nodded, and they all got moving again. It was only about a hundred yards before Jax rounded a curve and she saw the church. Or rather where the church had once stood. Paige was very familiar with it since it was where she and Jax had gotten married. But it was now indeed a construction site.

She didn't see any workers. In fact, she didn't see anyone at all, but there were three huge piles of building materials, all covered with black tarp. The killer could be hiding beneath any one of those.

Or in the cemetery.

Jax pulled to a stop about fifty yards away. But he didn't turn off the engine. They just sat there and waited.

They didn't have to wait long.

Jax's phone buzzed, and she saw "Unknown caller" on the screen. Jax answered it without taking his attention off their surroundings.

"Paige," the killer said, his voice oozing from the other end of the line. It was the Moonlight Strangler all right. "You came."

She cleared her throat before she even attempted to answer. "Of course I came. You didn't give me much of a choice. Now, where's Cord? And where are you?"

The silence dragged on for so long that Paige thought for a moment that he'd hung up. But he hadn't.

"I'm here," he answered.

There was some movement. Not near the church or cemetery, but way back. Hundreds of yards away in a cluster of trees.

It was cloudy, there was a storm moving in, and what thread of sunlight there was didn't help much. All she could see was a silhouette. But it was a man all right, and he was holding a phone to his ear. Even though she hadn't gotten a good look at the man who left her for dead, she'd gotten a sense of his height and weight.

"Oh, God," Paige whispered. She couldn't stop herself from gasping. "It's him. It's really the Moonlight Strangler."

"OF COURSE IT's really me, sweetheart," the man said.

And it was. Jax had no doubts about it when he heard the man speak. It was the same voice from the earlier calls.

Jax took out binoculars from the glove compartment for a closer look. The guy was about six feet tall, medium build and had brown hair. He was wearing jeans and a gray shirt. The description that came to mind was average-looking.

But this guy was far from average.

Nor did he stay in their line of sight for long. He ducked back behind one of the trees.

Paige swallowed hard, but Jax had to give it to her. She wasn't panicking, and she hiked up her chin, trying to look a whole lot stronger than she probably felt at the moment.

"You're not at my grave where you told me to meet you," Paige reminded the man.

"No. I thought it best if I stayed back at bit. Those cowboys do like to shoot people, don't they?"

"They do," Jax assured him. And that's exactly what he would do if he got the chance. But the snake was out of range, and that's almost certainly why he'd taken up position there.

That, and he might have some backup in the woods behind him. In the past, the Moonlight Strangler had acted alone—or at least there'd never been any evidence of him teaming up with anyone—but this wasn't just an ordinary situation for him. He wanted to get another shot at killing Paige.

"All right, here's how this will work," the killer continued. "Paige, I want you to step out of the SUV. You can hide behind any lawman of your choosing. Just one, though. I want to see your face, and I can't do that if there's a wall of badges in front of you."

"Release Cord first," she spoke up before Jax could say anything. "I want to make sure he's alive."

"Oh, he's alive all right. Maybe not all in one piece, exactly. But he will live if you do what I tell you and don't dawdle. He's bleeding out."

Her breath caught, and her bottom lip trembled. "I still want to see him before I get out."

Her gaze connected with Jax's for just a second, and he knew what she was aiming for here. She didn't just want to see Cord, though that was critical. She wanted to try to get Cord to safety so he'd be out of the line of fire.

The moments crawled by with no word from the killer. Then Jax saw the movement in the same area where the Moonlight Strangler had disappeared.

Cord.

Using the binoculars again, Jax could see the blood. On Cord's face. On the front of his clothes. Cord glanced up at them and shook his head.

Damn.

Was that some kind of signal?

Jax didn't have time to find out. Cord stumbled, falling about five yards in front of where the Moonlight Strangler had been earlier.

"Don't worry," the killer said. "He's alive. For now."

Maybe so, but he also appeared to have been drugged. He tried to get up but collapsed.

"What did you do to him?" Paige snapped.

"Oh, he's not hurt that bad. But I did have to medicate him a little so he wouldn't try to escape. Or kill. The boy's a real fighter. The meds will wear off in an hour or two."

They didn't have that long. The killer hadn't lied about Cord's condition. He appeared to be bleeding out.

"Now it's your turn, Paige. Step out, let me see you and I'll tell you the name of the real person who's been trying to murder you."

Paige stared at Cord, no doubt praying that he would move farther away from his captor. Jax adjusted the binoculars and spotted the reason Cord wasn't trying to do just that.

"There's a rope tied around his leg," Jax explained. "And the other end of the rope is around a tree. That's as far as Cord can go."

"Time's a-wasting, Paige," the killer snarled. Not so much of a taunt now. His temper was coming through.

Jax was about to remind her of the dangers again and that this might all be for nothing. The Moonlight Strangler could gun Cord down at any time. Plus, this piece of dirt might not even know who was behind the attacks.

But Jax stayed quiet. There was nothing he could say that would talk her out of this. Paige might have a boatload of emotional baggage, but she wasn't a coward. Never had been. In hindsight, it was one of the reasons he'd first been attracted to her.

And this was a hell of a time for him to realize that.

"I'll be in front of you," Jax insisted. He would take the killer up on that particular offer.

She didn't argue. Probably because she knew it was the only way he'd let her out there. "If something goes wrong—"

"Don't," he interrupted. It sounded like the start of a goodbye. Something he didn't want to hear.

Jax put the SUV in gear, maneuvering it so that the driver's side was facing the killer. Or at least facing where the killer had been earlier. It was possible the guy had moved.

And Jax opened the door.

Though he was still out of range, he already had his gun drawn, and he slipped his phone into his pocket to free his hands and stepped from the SUV.

No shots.

That was a surprise and somewhat of a relief. Jax had half expected this moron to start shooting. Or maybe he was just waiting for Paige before he pulled the trigger.

Paige's grip on her gun had caused her knuckles to go white. She was still shaking, too. That didn't stop her from getting out behind him. Thankfully, she didn't move to Jax's side. She stayed behind him.

"Can't see your face," the killer complained, though his voice was muffled now because Jax's phone was in his pocket. "At least stand on your tippy-toes so I can get a good look at you. I wouldn't put it past your ex to try to bring in a ringer."

"It's me," she assured him. "And you'll see me when I see you."

Jax mentally groaned. Yeah, courage all right. But this was one time when he wished she'd just shown her face and ducked back in the SUV. Maybe she was hoping Jericho, Chase or Dexter would have a shot.

They didn't.

And even if they did, Jax was betting this coward would just slink behind one of those trees and escape. Because there's no way the Moonlight Strangler would have come out here without an escape plan.

"Awww, you want to see me?" the killer purred. "How sweet. All right. Just one little look-see, though I'm not sure how much you can see without those binoculars."

"I'll see enough," she snapped.

Even though Jax kept his attention and gun aimed at those trees, he felt Paige move, coming up on tiptoes so that the killer could see her.

"There she is," the killer said. No more temper. It was the tone one might use with an old lover. "And my mark looks so good on you. One day we'll meet again, and I'll get to finish it."

Her muscles tensed even more. "Now it's your turn. I've done everything you asked. Tell me who's behind the attacks so we can get Cord to the hospital."

Jax wasn't sure he saw the man move. Or maybe he just sensed it. But it seemed to take only the blink of an eye for the killer to whip out a rifle.

Hell.

He was going to shoot her.

Jax moved as fast as he could to push Paige back into the SUV. But the killer and he weren't the only ones moving. From the corner of his eye, he saw Cord.

Cord reached for his boot. He no longer seemed drugged. He pulled out his backup weapon, turned and fired. And he just kept firing.

Each of the bullets slamming into the killer.

The Moonlight Strangler clutched his chest and collapsed onto the ground.

Chapter Fourteen

Paige couldn't stop shaking. Or pacing in the ER waiting room. Her heartbeat was going a mile a minute. Her thoughts, too. Especially the bad thoughts.

Cord might be dead, or dying.

So she paced and waited for news. Oh, and she prayed, as well. She'd been doing a lot of that in the past half hour since they'd arrived at the Appaloosa Pass Hospital.

The medic had already suggested to Jax that she might be going into shock and that she should be checked out by a doctor. But Paige didn't want a checkup. She didn't want to stop moving in case she fell completely apart. As long as she was on her feet and moving, she could expend some of that raw adrenaline and energy boiling inside her.

Jax finished his latest call and went to her, slipping his arm around her and trying to get her into one of the many empty chairs. But she didn't budge, and as he'd done on his other attempts, Jax pulled her to him for a hug.

That helped.

But knowing that Cord was all right would help even more.

The ambulance had been there within minutes after

the shooting, and they'd whisked Cord away to the hospital. Jax and she had left to follow it, but she hadn't even managed to get a glimpse of Cord before he'd been taken into surgery for the multiple stab wounds to his chest.

Jax pulled her even closer, and she felt the tension in his muscles then. Of course, they were both tense, but this was different. She pulled back, met his gaze and saw the worry, or something, in his eyes.

"What's wrong?" Oh, God. "Is it Matthew—"

"He's fine. Everyone at the ranch is fine, and Addie is on her way here to see Cord."

Addie would want to be here, of course. Cord was her biological twin brother.

"It's the Moonlight Strangler," Jax continued a moment later. He paused, for a long time. "He's alive."

Of all the things she thought he might say, that wasn't one of them. "How? We saw him fall."

Jax nodded. "I just got off the phone with Jericho, and he said when he checked, the killer had a pulse, so he called another ambulance. They're bringing him here to the hospital right now."

Her heart skipped several beats, and she had no choice but to fall back into Jax's arms. He was there to catch her.

"You won't see him. The paramedics have been instructed to bring him in through a side entrance."

Paige was shaking her head before he even finished, and not because she was worried about seeing him. "He's dangerous. He could kill someone here."

Jax was shaking his head, too. "He's not even conscious. And he might not survive the ambulance ride. Jericho said he lost a lot of blood."

She wanted him dead, not clinging to life.

Paige groaned and finally sat down, only because her legs were wobbly and she was dizzy. But then she considered something else.

"Maybe he can tell us who orchestrated the attacks." Yes, it was wishful thinking, and she wasn't sure she wanted him to draw another breath, much less to have to speak to him again. Still, if he could just tell them.

"He could have been lying about what he knew anyway," Jax reminded her. "He clearly set all of this up to kill you. That's why he had that rifle."

Yes, that. She'd gotten a glimpse of it. Of Cord, too, as he'd shot the man. His own father. But Cord didn't think of him that way, only that he was a monster who needed to be stopped. He'd devoted the last year of his life to catching him, and in a roundabout way, he'd succeeded.

Paige couldn't help but think of the similarities between Cord and her. She'd been obsessed with the Moonlight Strangler, too. And she'd found him. Of course, he'd found her as well and had come within a breath of making her number thirty-one.

Well, at least now there wouldn't be more bodies to add to his count.

"He had a wallet in his pocket," Jax went on. "According to his driver's license, his name is Willie Lee Samuels. Does that sound familiar?"

It was stupid, but she didn't even want to repeat it. Didn't want to have his name come out of her mouth. But Paige forced herself to think, to dig through her memories and see if there was a connection. Was it familiar?

No.

"I don't know that name, and I didn't recognize his face, either. Only his voice and the overall size of his body. I could be mistaken about the body size, of course, but that was his voice, Jax. I swear, it was him."

Paige hadn't realized she was starting to sound a little hysterical until Jax sat down beside her and pulled her back into his arms.

"His face matches his DMV photo," Jax went on. "But his DNA will be sent for testing even though they're almost positive he's the Moonlight Strangler."

So was she. No way could Paige forget that voice. It would almost certainly be added to the flashbacks of the previous attacks. Along with that blood on Cord's face and chest.

"Jericho checked, and he doesn't have a police record. Not even a parking ticket," Jax added.

Ironic. Since he'd murdered so many women. And would have murdered her if Cord hadn't stopped him.

Paige heard the hurried footsteps, and she automatically tensed. So did Jax, and he put his hand over his Glock. But it was a false alarm. Addie came rushing into the ER.

"How's Cord?" Addie asked, her breath mixed with her words.

"He's in surgery." Paige stood and pulled Addie into her arms. "We'll know something soon." She hoped.

"How bad was he hurt?" Addie pressed. A sister's love, and worry, were all over her face.

"He was bleeding," Paige settled for saying, "but he was strong enough to shoot the Moonlight Strangler. He saved us. He saved all of us."

And despite the fact that tears were the last thing she needed, they watered her eyes, anyway. Addie's, too.

"Addie insisted on coming," Levi said. He trailed in right behind her, and just his mere presence gave Paige another jolt.

"Who's at the ranch with Matthew?" Paige snapped.

"Weston and a whole bunch of ranch hands armed with rifles and automatics. The two reserve deputies should be there by now, too."

Good. She knew that the sheriff's office had to be stretched for manpower, but she didn't care. Paige wanted Matthew and the rest of Jax's family to be safe.

Addie pulled back from the hug and met Paige's gaze. "Did you see *him*?" Addie asked.

It took Paige a moment to realize Addie was talking about the killer and not Cord. Paige nodded. "From a distance."

She wasn't sure what Addie wanted to know about the monster who'd fathered her. Maybe nothing that could be said in words, anyway, because Addie just held on to her, and they stayed that way until Paige heard yet more footsteps.

This time both Levi and Jax put their hands over their guns. And it wasn't family who came rushing in.

It was Leland.

His face was beaded with sweat, and his attention zoomed around the room until it landed on her. "Thank God. You're all right. I heard about the attack."

Leland moved toward her, but Jax stepped in front of him, blocking his path.

"Hell." Leland mumbled even more profanity, too. "You can't still think I want to hurt Paige. It was the Moonlight Strangler all along. Can't you see that?"

Paige wanted to *see* it. To believe it. But the attack was still way too fresh in her mind for her to trust anyone except family.

But she immediately rethought that.

Jax's family. They weren't her in-laws any longer, but this had certainly brought them closer. Well, at least they weren't scowling at her, and maybe they were beginning to understand that she'd stayed away to protect them.

Maybe.

Leland continued to stare at her. Mixing in a glare, too. Likely waiting for her to say he was innocent. She didn't, but Paige did go closer to him.

"You shouldn't be here," she said.

The glare vanished, but she saw the hurt again. The same hurt look he'd gotten a few days earlier when she told him that she could never have feelings beyond friendship for him. The rejection still stung.

He glanced around as if trying to compose himself, and then hitched his thumb toward the parking lot. "There are reporters outside. Darrin was out there, too, but I told him if he tried to come in that I'd arrest him."

Both Jax and she groaned. She definitely didn't need a run-in with Darrin right now, and she doubted Jericho would be able to interrogate him anytime soon. Not after the hellish ordeal they'd all just been through.

"Do you need anything?" Leland asked. "Tea?" He glanced at her top. "A change of clothes?"

She hadn't realized there was blood on her shirt. Cord's blood. She'd hurried to him after he'd shot the Moonlight Strangler and had tried to help him before the ambulance arrived. Jax had done the same, and there was blood on his shirt, too, on the places that their Kevlar vests hadn't covered. The vests had blood on them as well, but they'd left them in the SUV.

"If Paige needs anything," Jax said, staring at the man, "I'll get it for her."

This wasn't a jealousy, man-contest kind of thing going on between them. Jax was just worried about her safety. But Leland clearly didn't like it. No surprise there. He hadn't liked much of anything Jax had said to him. For Leland, it was indeed jealousy.

Leland started to step away, but Jax stopped him. "Any idea where Belinda went after she sneaked out of the sheriff's office?"

"None," Leland snapped. "Are you accusing me of trying to hurt her?"

"Just asking." But it certainly wasn't a friendly sounding question.

"If you're worried about her, find her yourself," Leland snarled before he walked out.

"You want me to follow him and make sure he leaves?" Levi asked.

Jax seemed to be still considering that when Jericho came in. Not from the ER entrance but rather from one of the halls that fed off the waiting area. He, too, had some blood on his shirt, and he was carrying an evidence bag.

"Willie Lee Samuels is in a coma," Jericho immediately volunteered.

In a coma. But not dead. For Paige, that wasn't good news. "He could be faking it," she suggested.

"I thought so, too, but the doc who just checked him said it was the real deal. So are the three bullets that Cord put in his chest. Don't worry. I'll have a guard posted outside surgery just in case, and the FBI is sending a protection detail from the San Antonio office. They should be here within the half hour."

Good. She prayed they didn't let the Moonlight Strangler out of their sight.

Jericho lifted the evidence bag, and since it was clear plastic, Paige saw the one item inside it. A driver's license.

"Yeah, it belongs to Willie Lee Samuels," Jericho

confirmed. "Either of you recognize him from the photo?"

Addie took the bag as if it might explode in her hands. Paige looked as well, and while she didn't recognize the man, she did see something familiar about him. Addie must have, as well.

"He looks like Cord and me. We have his eyes." Addie's hand was shaking when she handed the bag back to Jericho. "I'd hoped..."

But she didn't finish that. No need. Because Paige knew what she'd hoped—that she didn't share any DNA with this sick man. That it had all been a big mistake.

Willie Lee Samuels's face proved otherwise.

"So, it's really over," Addie whispered. She blew out a long breath of relief.

But it was relief that Jericho didn't share. His forehead was bunched up, and he took out a notepad from his pocket. "Dexter took Willie Lee's phone to the office so the lab could pick it up for processing, but I looked through the numbers he'd called. Just two. There was the call he made to Paige, and then he called this number."

As he'd done with the driver's license, Jericho held it up for them to see.

Both Addie and Paige shook their heads, but Jax didn't. He took one look at the number and cursed.

Chapter Fifteen

Belinda.

Jax had no idea why the Moonlight Strangler had called her earlier in the day, and he was no closer to finding that out. Because Belinda was nowhere to be found. Since it was already dark and a storm had moved in, there wouldn't be much more searching done for her tonight.

There wouldn't be much sleep for Paige, either.

With all the pacing she'd done at the hospital, Jax was surprised that her legs hadn't given out on her. Surprised, too, that she hadn't just broken down and cried. The adrenaline crash had come and gone—for him, too—leaving them both looking past the exhausted stage.

"Cord will be all right," he reminded her, hoping that would help get that weary look off her face.

And it was true. Despite his blood loss, he'd come out of surgery just fine, and there'd been no major damage to any of his organs. Of course, Paige knew that. She'd been there for the surgeon's update and even to see Cord when he'd been allowed visitors.

That was the good news.

The bad news was that the Moonlight Strangler was still alive and in a coma.

Paige looked at Jax. Only for a second. Before her attention went back to the road. Or rather their surroundings. Something that both of them had been doing since they'd started the drive from the hospital back to the ranch.

They were in a cruiser now, not the SUV they'd used to go to the hospital. But what they were missing was backup. There just hadn't been anyone available what with the investigation and the security at both the hospital and the ranch. Plus, Jericho had the courier still in lockup and was having to deal with that. And the search for Belinda. While trying to keep an eye on both Leland and Darrin.

Definitely a full plate.

Neither Jax nor Paige had wanted to wait any longer to go home now that Cord was out of the woods. Still, the memories of the other attacks were very fresh, and Jax knew he wouldn't be able to let down his guard until he had Paige safe.

"He's a coward," Paige said.

It took him a moment to realize she was likely talking about the Moonlight Strangler. And yep, Jax agreed. The snake had broken into Cord's vehicle and had ambushed Cord with a stun gun. Then, he'd drugged and stabbed him while Cord hadn't been able to fight back. Of course, Jax hadn't expected a vicious serial killer like that to do anything aboveboard.

Jax took the final turn toward the ranch, checking each side of the road. The ditches, too. Hard to see, though, with the wipers slashing away the rain. Maybe the weather alone would deter another attack. He could hope so, anyway.

And maybe the attacks were over.

It was possible that the Moonlight Strangler had been behind them all along.

"I don't want Matthew to see me like this." Paige motioned to the blood on her clothes and then his.

It was 8:00 p.m., and while it was possible Matthew was already asleep, he might indeed be up and see them. Jax considered calling ahead, but then he spotted the familiar blue truck parked in front of his house. It belonged to his ranch hand Buddy, so Jax pulled up alongside the truck and lowered the passenger's-side window just enough for him to see that Buddy was inside, and armed.

"Jericho asked me to make sure no one got onto the ranch who wasn't supposed to be here," Buddy explained after he put down his window, as well. He pointed to another truck parked just up the road. "Hank's up there."

Hank was a hand, too, one Jax trusted. Jax hated that the men had to do this, but unfortunately it might be necessary.

"Paige and I need to get a change of clothes," Jax said. "Then we'll be heading to the main house for the night."

Buddy nodded. "There are hands guarding up there, too, and we'll stay put until we hear otherwise." He paused. "Some reporters drove up earlier. They had one of those vans with the TV logo on the side and a little satellite dish on top of it. I stopped them, told them to turn around, that it wasn't a good time for a visit."

It was the right thing to do. Nobody in his family was in the mood to deal with reporters right now, though he figured the news frenzy would continue for a while. Especially since the media would be looking to score an interview with Addie, the serial killer's daughter. However, Addie was still at the hospital with Cord, Levi, a reserve deputy and the protection detail from the FBI assigned to guard the Moonlight Strangler.

Jax thanked Buddy, made a mental note to thank all the hands and give them big bonus checks and pulled into the back, parking on the side of the porch next to the porch swing where they'd found that camera and listening device. There was no need to tell Paige to move fast. She knew the drill all too well since running and hiding were all they'd been doing since she'd returned to the ranch.

Jax didn't bother with an umbrella since they'd be changing their clothes, anyway. He got out ahead of her, unlocked the door and disarmed the security system only long enough to get Paige inside. Even though they weren't going to be there long, he reset it and locked the door, too, behind him.

He didn't turn on the lights, just in case someone was indeed watching the house, but he could see that the place was a mess. The CSIs had apparently left no stone unturned when they'd searched for cameras and bugs. Thankfully, other than the one on the porch, they hadn't found anything.

"I'll have to get you one of my shirts," he told her. There were probably some of Belinda's things around, but he doubted she'd want to wear those.

Jax stripped off his shirt and tossed it into the laundry room just off the kitchen. Only then did he realize being shirtless probably wasn't a good idea with Paige in the room.

Or maybe it was.

She looked at him. Looked at his bare chest. And everything inside her finally seemed to go still. She definitely didn't seem ready to start pacing again.

The rain was coming down harder now, slapping

against the window. The lightning streaked through the sky, the flashes enough for him to get glimpses of Paige even without the overhead lights.

"I'm a mess," she whispered. Maybe she was talking about her bloody clothes, but it could be a whole lot more.

She turned, the streaks of rain and lighting hitting just right so that it looked as if tears were sliding down her face. Maybe they were. If anyone deserved a good cry, it was her.

But he didn't want her to cry.

He wanted to do something about that stark look on her face. Wanted to do something about her uneven breathing, too. And the nerves. So close to the surface that he could feel them.

He took off his waist holster, laying it on the counter, and went to her. And he kissed her before he could change his mind. All in all, it was a good decision. Paige didn't back away, and she slipped right into his arms. Right into the kiss, as well.

The soft sound she made was one of pleasure. Mostly. Mixed with some doubts that he had no trouble hearing, either. But Jax didn't want doubts. They'd have enough of those later. For now, he just wanted her.

He knew the fix for that. Jax deepened the kiss, bringing her closer to him, and he put his hand at the base of her throat and slid his palm down to her breasts.

Oh, yeah. Familiar territory. But the doubts were still there.

On her part, not his.

"I don't want you to see me naked," she whispered. Her breath shivered. She did, too. "The Moonlight Strangler cut me, and I have scars."

Not an easy thing to hear, but Jax was determined to

take some of those old nightmares and put a new light on them. Or at least he'd try. Even if this was probably a bad idea.

He kept kissing her. Kept touching her, too. But Paige did her own share of touching, and like all the other times they'd been together, it didn't take long for the fire to ignite.

Just how long was he going to let that fire burn?

Apparently, pretty damn long, he decided, when her hand landed on his bare chest. Then his stomach.

He turned her, pressing her against the edge of the counter so he could rid her of that bloody top. Jax didn't want any more reminders of the day. What he wanted was her bare skin against his. He took off her bra and lowered the kisses to her breasts.

One of the scars was there. On her left breast. There was another just below it on her rib cage. He kissed both, lingering long enough to make sure she felt only pleasure and not the old memories.

That upped the urgency in him. Upped those silky sounds she was making, too, and she latched on to him and let him add some fuel to the fire. He kissed her stomach, all the while unzipping her jeans, sliding them off her along with her shoes and panties.

Then he kissed her exactly where he wanted.

Her breath broke, and Paige fisted her hand in his hair, and she gave in to the heat for several moments before it must have become too much for her. She dropped down, pulling him to the floor with her, and in the same motion, she went after the zipper on his jeans.

Jax figured he should ask her if she was ready for this, but judging from her nonverbal cues, that answer was yes. She kissed him, shoved off his jeans and boxers, and then straddled him. He could have sworn his head exploded when she took him inside her.

Oh, yeah. He remembered this. Remembered just how good it could be. Of course, sex had never been an issue for them. Apparently, it still wasn't.

She moved, shoving her body against his. Creating the rhythm and the friction needed to make that fire rage out of control. She looked like a woman on a mission.

Maybe she was using this to take out some of her frustrations or to burn off some of that restless energy. Or maybe this was just about them.

Either way, it worked.

She made another sound. Not one of pleasure this time. But release. Jax felt the climax ripple through her. And thanks to a bolt of lightning, he got to see it on her face, as well.

The moment was perfect despite all the imperfections.

And Jax pulled her to him and let himself go with her.

PAIGE COULDN'T MOVE. But she could certainly feel, and that feeling went up a notch when Jax lifted his hips and she got a nice little aftershock from the climax.

Wow.

She hadn't seen this coming, but she didn't have to think long and hard to know it was needed. Jax wasn't just the cure for her headache and tight muscles; he was the cure for other things, too. For the first time in over a year, her mind settled down just enough for her to see and feel something other than the nightmare she'd been living.

Later, she'd decide if that was a good thing.

For now, Paige just savored the moment of her body still joined with Jax's. The feel of his body beneath hers. His scent. That scent alone could stir all sorts of hot thoughts, but it calmed her, too.

Or maybe just the great sex had done that.

However, it didn't last. Jax eased her off him and got up to get his gun and phone. For a second she thought he might just walk away, but he scooped her up, too, and with both of them buck naked, he carried her to the master bathroom. Yet another place she knew well, because she'd come up with the remodel design.

Including the massive stone and tile shower.

Which was exactly where he took her.

Other than a night-light by the vanity, the room was dark, and he kept it that way as he put aside his gun and phone so he could turn on the water. The moment it was hot and steamy, he took her inside, setting her on her feet. Slowly. While her body slid down his.

"Foreplay," he said a split second before he kissed her mouth. Then her neck. "We sort of skipped that in the kitchen."

They'd skipped a lot of things. Like finesse and conversation. But that was okay even if Paige knew that later they were going to have to talk about all of this.

But not now.

For now, she just let him kiss away all the worries. All the pain. And even all the doubts.

Despite the fact that she'd just had him, Paige felt the heat return. Slow and easy like those kisses he was delivering. But he stopped, looking down at her forehead and frowning.

"I don't think you're supposed to be getting those stitches wet," Jax said.

Paige was sure she frowned, too, because it was true, and it caused him to turn off the shower.

"We should be getting dressed, anyway," he added.

Now the doubts came. Not only hers but his. She could practically feel them. But he was also right. They shouldn't be standing around naked even if that was exactly what she wanted to do. Except the sooner they dressed and left, the sooner she'd get to see Matthew.

Jax handed her a towel when they got out of the shower, and after grabbing a towel for himself, he went into the bedroom. Several minutes later he returned, fully dressed in jeans and a black T-shirt. And he handed her not only the clothes she'd taken off in the kitchen, but one of his clean shirts, as well.

Since it felt awkward for her to be standing around naked when he was dressed, Paige hurried to put on the clothes, but she didn't even manage to get her jeans on before Jax's phone buzzed. Considering all the bad news they'd gotten, she immediately thought the worst.

And it likely was.

Because Jax frowned when he glanced at the screen.

"Darrin," he said, showing her the caller ID.

Great. She definitely didn't want to chat with him tonight. Jax must have felt the same way because he let it go to voice mail. Then he listened to the message that Darrin left. He didn't put it on speaker, but judging from the way his teeth came together, it wasn't well wishes.

"Do I want to hear the message for myself?" she asked.

"No," he said without hesitation. "But it wasn't one of his usual threats. He sounded, well, desperate. He said he needed to see you right away. You're not meeting with him."

"No," she agreed. "Did he say why he wanted to meet?"

Jax shook his head. "But I'm betting it wouldn't be to have a nice conversation. He probably wants you to get Jericho to back off on that interrogation that's scheduled for tomorrow."

An interrogation that might not happen since Jericho was up to his eyeballs with all the stuff going on.

"Sometime soon I should start the process to get a restraining order on Darrin." She paused. Met his gaze. "Or maybe I should wait to see if we'll be moving to that safe house?"

Or better yet, staying in Appaloosa Pass.

Near Matthew and Jax.

Jax didn't answer her. Probably because he heard a sound that caught his attention. Paige heard it, too.

A car engine.

She hoped that it was just Buddy or one of the other hands, but when Jax's phone buzzed and Paige saw Buddy's name on the screen, she figured they had a visitor.

"Put it on speaker so I can hear," she insisted. She wanted to know if they were about to come under attack.

"Anything wrong?" Jax asked when he answered, and he hurried to the living room where there were windows facing the road.

Paige went, too, though Jax motioned for her to stay back. She did, but she still saw the headlights of the vehicle making its way toward them.

"It's another one of those reporter vans," Buddy explained. "You want me to send them packing like the other one?"

"Yeah. And as soon as they're gone, Paige and I'll be leaving to go to the main house."

Suddenly, there was no other place Paige wanted to be. She inched closer and caught a glimpse of the van. It was indeed one that reporters used, and it was from a local station out of San Antonio.

The rain was still heavy, making it hard to see, and the only light came from the van's headlights. Buddy didn't get out of his truck. As he'd done with Jax and her, he lowered the window. The passenger's window on the van lowered, too.

And that's when Paige saw the gun.

Chapter Sixteen

"Get down!" Jax shouted to Buddy.

He did see Buddy duck down on his truck's seat, but Jax had no idea if it was in time. Because a split second later, there was another sound that Jax didn't want to hear.

A shot rang out.

Damn.

The shot hadn't come from Buddy, either, but whoever was inside that reporter's van. Jax seriously doubted it was reporters, and it sure as heck wasn't the Moonlight Strangler.

So who was it?

"Oh, God," Paige said, moving closer to the window. "Was Buddy hit?"

But Jax didn't have the answer to that. Not yet. However, he couldn't just stand here while Buddy was killed right in front of him.

He texted Buddy. And waited. The seconds crawled by with no answer. So Jax tried Hank next. He got an answer right away, but it wasn't an answer he liked.

What the devil's going on down there? Hank wanted to know.

I'll let you know when I know, Jax texted back.

"Get the gun from the closet in the bedroom," Jax

instructed Paige. She'd know exactly where it was since it was where she'd left it before she moved out. "When you get back, I want you to stay inside and stay down."

She started to move, then stopped and frantically shook her head. "You can't be thinking about going out there."

Jax didn't have time to argue. "Just get the gun, and we'll go from there."

Thankfully, she hurried off to do that while Jax kept watching out the window. No more shots. And he couldn't see either Buddy or the shooter. Buddy was smart, so maybe he was playing dead, hoping the shooter would get out so that Buddy could return fire.

Because of the van's blinding headlights and the rain, Jax couldn't see through the windshields of either vehicle. However, there was likely at least two people in the van because the shot had come from the passenger's-side window.

Without taking his attention off the vehicles, Jax pressed in Jericho's number. There were ranch hands nearby, but Jax might need Jericho to coordinate the communication so that no one was hurt from friendly fire.

"There's trouble," Jax said the moment Jericho answered. "A van just pulled up in front of my house, and someone inside fired a shot at Buddy." He rattled off the license plate number to Jericho. "We might need an ambulance."

Jericho cursed. "Where are you and Paige now?"

"Inside my house, but I'm about to go outside and see if I can sneak up on the people inside the van. Just let everyone know what's going on so the main house is all locked up. Text me if you need to tell me anything and make sure I have some backup ASAP."

"I will. Don't guess it'd do any good to tell you to wait. No, I'll save my breath," Jericho added before Jax could say anything. "Just be careful."

"I will. Hank's nearby, too, so you should probably call him first. I don't want him coming down here into the middle of this. Not until I figure out what *this* is, anyway. But if he spots me, I want him to cover me."

Just as Jax was finishing up the call with Jericho, Paige came running back into the room with not just one gun but with two. And she had some extra magazines of ammo, as well.

"Any sign of Buddy yet?" she asked. She tried to peer out the window, but Jax moved her back behind him.

He shook his head and tried to figure out the best way to do this. If he waited, Buddy could die. And if he didn't wait, the same might happen.

Jax made brief eye contact with her. Just enough to let her see that this was not a negotiable situation. "I'm going outside to get a better look at what's going on. Once I'm out the door, I want you to arm the security system. The code is 4031. Then I want you to hide and not come out until I tell you it's safe."

"No," Paige repeated several times during his instructions.

But Jax didn't even try to bargain with her. He dropped a kiss on her mouth and hurried to the back door, grabbing his black Stetson along the way. He turned off the alarm and shot her a glance to remind her of what she needed to do.

"I'll be right back," he said, giving her another kiss.

Jax ignored the pleading look in her eyes, and he stepped out the door and onto the back porch. He didn't move, though, until he heard her press in the code to set the alarm.

Good.

At least if anyone tried to break through any of the windows or doors, the alarm would go off.

He went to the side of the porch by the swing where they'd found the camera and jumped down to the ground. It'd been raining long enough that the ground was soggy, and the water and mud oozed over his boots. The rain wouldn't help with visibility, but it could give him an advantage.

If he couldn't see them, then maybe they wouldn't be able to see him, either.

Ducking down and using the cruiser for cover, Jax looked around. He still didn't have a good view of the van because of Buddy's truck, so he hurried closer, sandwiching himself between the house and the cruiser. At least this way, no would sneak up on him from behind, but that left sides he had to cover.

He checked the cruiser door. Locked, of course. And he cursed himself for not grabbing the keys from the kitchen counter. That could turn out to be a bad mistake. Maybe, though, when Jericho arrived, he could open it using a remote. That would give Jax a bullet-resistant shield in case this turned into a gunfight.

There was no sign of Hank, but that didn't mean the ranch hand wasn't out there somewhere. And he wouldn't be alone. Soon, Jericho would have others around. He hoped Weston and Chase would stay in the main house with Matthew. Jax didn't want backup if it meant putting his son at risk.

Since the angle was still wrong for Jax to see what was going on, he crawled beneath the cruiser. The ground was wet here, too, and the rain soaked straight through his clothes. However, when he came out on the other side, he finally had the viewpoint he needed.

And his heart slammed against his chest.

No. This couldn't be happening. The back door of the van was wide open.

Hell.

There was no telling how many gunmen could have gotten out of there by now. They could have used the ditches or even Buddy's truck for cover so they could get closer to the houses.

He texted Buddy again, hoping the man would respond so he could tell Jax just how bad this threat was. But still no answer. Jax prayed that was because Buddy was still playing dead and not because he actually was.

Jax's phone dinged before he could put it away, and he saw Jericho's name on the screen. Hank's behind the center barn but can't see you. I'm on the way.

Hurry, Jax texted back, because he was certain he was going to need help. And soon.

"Jax?" someone called out. "Don't shoot. It's me." And it was a voice he instantly recognized.

Belinda.

A dozen thoughts went through his head. There was no reason for her to be here. No good one, anyway. But there was one bad reason.

Was Belinda the person who'd been trying to kill Paige and him?

It sickened him to think it was her, someone who'd been so close to him and his family. But Jax pushed all of that aside so he could deal with this.

"Come out so I can see you," Jax demanded.

He didn't expect her to obey that order. And that's why he was surprised when she did.

With the rain sheeting down in front of the van's headlights, he saw the movement. Then the person stepped out, not from the back but rather from the driver's seat.

It was Belinda all right.

And she started walking straight toward him.

PAIGE HAD FOLLOWED Jax's orders to a tee. Except for one thing. One thing he wasn't going to like.

She hadn't hidden as he'd wanted. She couldn't. Not with him out there facing heaven knew what.

One of the first things she'd done after faking her death was to take firearms training. It had meant overcoming a lot of old fears, but she'd managed it, and that training might be needed now to help Jax.

She kept to the side of the window in the living room, and she continued to glance out. Nothing.

Well, not at first.

Then she'd heard Belinda call out to Jax, and Paige had known that this situation was about to take an ugly turn.

Paige readied her gun when Belinda came out from behind the wheel of the van. Belinda was wearing a light-colored dress that stood out in the darkness, and when she came out in full view and started walking toward the cruiser, Paige realized something was missing.

Belinda wasn't carrying a gun.

And with the way the rain was making her dress cling to her body, it would be next to impossible for her to have a concealed weapon.

Still, why was she here? And why had she been driving that van?

And where was Jax?

Paige was sure he was out there somewhere, but she'd lost sight of him after he'd jumped off the porch.

Judging from the sound of his voice when he'd called

out to Belinda, he was still somewhere near the house. Paige prayed he had taken cover, because while Belinda might not be armed, someone in that van certainly was. And that person had shot at Buddy.

"Jax?" Belinda said again. She kept walking, her hands stiff as boards by her sides, her focus on the cruiser. If she felt the rain whipping at her, she didn't have any reaction to it.

"Did you shoot Buddy?" Jax asked. "Did you hurt him?" Definitely near the cruiser. Or maybe under it.

Belinda shook her head, but there was no outcry of innocence. She seemed dazed, or else she was pretending to be. This could all still be her doing. Some kind of ruse to draw Jax out, but if so, why wasn't Belinda trying to do the same to Paige? The woman hated her, not Jax.

Didn't she?

Maybe Belinda wanted Jax to suffer because he'd allowed his ex-wife back in his life. Except he hadn't really done that—despite what'd happened earlier in the kitchen. There'd been no reconciliation. But perhaps Belinda didn't know that.

Belinda stopped when she was still about five yards from the cruiser, and since she was still in the path of those van headlights, it was easier for Paige to see her. Easier for Paige to take aim at her, too.

And that's what Paige did.

"Buddy's hurt, I think," Belinda finally said. She sounded as woozy as she looked, and she wobbled a little. She made an uneasy glance over her shoulder. "You don't have much time. You have to do this before Jericho and the others get here."

"What do we have to do?" Jax challenged.

"I'm supposed to give you a message." The woman

made yet another glance over her shoulder. "If Paige comes out right now and surrenders, then no more bullets will be fired."

Everything inside Paige went still. *Surrender.* Somehow, she'd known it would come down to this. Whoever was in that van wanted her dead.

Darrin or Leland.

Of course, Belinda could be faking this, too. That way, she could pretend someone else was behind it so she could get Paige out of the picture while allowing herself to get back in Jax's good graces one day.

"Who told you to give me that message?" Jax asked.

Belinda shook her head again. "I'm not sure." Her gaze darted around again. "He was wearing a mask. All four of them were wearing masks, and only one did all the talking. I didn't recognize his voice."

Oh, mercy. If Belinda was telling the truth, then there were four hired killers practically on their doorstep. Except one of them might have been the person doing the hiring, if Belinda hadn't.

"Buddy needs medical attention," Belinda went on. "I'm supposed to tell you that an ambulance can come right away as soon as Paige gets in the van."

"That's not going to happen," Jax shouted. Not to Belinda. The message was no doubt meant for the men in the van. "And what about you? What happens to you in this so-called plan?" Jax added. Now, that was addressed to Belinda.

Belinda appeared to be fighting back tears. "They said I could stay here, that I'd be all right." The fight against the tears—whether real or pretend—was a fight that Belinda lost, and she started to sob.

"Hurry up!" someone yelled. "Quit your crying and

tell him the rest now." A man. And he wasn't inside the van. It sounded as if he was much closer to the house.

Paige's breath stalled in her throat. Was someone about to break in?

The security alarm would go off if a window broke or if someone came in through the door, but it'd be too late by then. She'd find herself in the middle of a gunfight.

"I don't want them to hurt Matthew," Belinda sobbed.

"Tell him the rest now," the man repeated.

It took Belinda a couple of seconds to speak, and even then she continued to sob. "If Paige doesn't come out now and surrender, there's a gunman near the main house. He climbed out through the back of the van and made his way there on foot. He's got a rifle, and he has orders to start shooting."

Paige's breath didn't just stall. It vanished.

No.

This couldn't be happening.

"Paige?" the man called out.

He sounded even closer than before. Maybe on the front porch, though she hadn't seen him move from the van to there.

"I'm not giving you any more time," the man yelled. "If you're not out of that house in five seconds, your son will pay for it."

Paige had no doubts, none, that he was telling the truth. Her little boy was in danger. Jax, too. And the only chance she had of stopping it was to go out there.

"Paige, no!" Jax shouted. "Don't do it."

But she was already on the move.

She disarmed the system so the alarm wouldn't sound. Paige wanted to be able to hear the monster who was responsible for this. She wanted to try to kill him before he did any damage.

With her gun gripped in her hand, Paige threw open the door and stepped out onto the front porch.

Chapter Seventeen

This was not what Jax wanted. He wanted Paige in the house, out of the line of fire, but here she was out in the open. Worse, judging from the sound of the hired gun's voice, he was somewhere in the front yard.

No doubt waiting to grab her. Or kill her.

Jax had to do something to stop that.

He scrambled out from the cruiser, keeping close to the house, and ran to the front porch as fast as he could. He didn't call out for Paige because he didn't want the gunman or anyone inside that van to try to take him out before Jax got to her.

The moment he reached the porch, he grabbed hold of Paige and pulled her to the ground. He wasn't able to break her fall, which meant he'd probably hurt her, but it was better than her being out in the open and gunned down.

Someone fired a shot, and it blasted into the house right behind them. Another inch, and it would have hit Jax in the head. Jax pushed Paige even lower, until she was flat against the ground, and he lay across her, trying to protect her. He prayed it would be enough.

"I had to come out here," Paige insisted. "To protect Matthew. Belinda said there was a shooter in place."

"I'm pretty sure that was a bluff. There are a dozen

men patrolling the grounds around the house. They wouldn't let a shooter get that close."

He hoped.

And while he was hoping, Jax added that if shots were indeed fired there, Matthew and the others would be safe in the playroom at the center of the house. Certainly, Jericho had alerted the family to trouble, and they would go in there.

Paige shook her head. "I just panicked."

Heck, so had he. Hearing his son threatened like that had made him want to tear these fools limb from limb. And he still might do that before the night was over. But for now, Jax needed to do some damage control.

First, he checked to see if Belinda had gotten down on the ground. She had. If she was innocent in all of this, he didn't want her caught in the cross fire, and if she was guilty, he didn't want her in a good position to try to shoot at them or call out orders to those thugs.

Of course, Jax hadn't seen a gun anywhere on her, and she didn't appear to be wearing any kind of communicator. That still didn't mean she wasn't calling the shots for this fiasco.

"Without lifting your head," Jax whispered to Paige, "try to keep an eye on Belinda."

Paige nodded and maneuvered beneath him just enough so she could do that. "Is Jericho coming?"

"He should be here any minute." In fact, maybe he was already there. Jax wasn't sure if his brother was going to do a quiet approach or not.

And it was quiet right now.

Too quiet.

Jax listened, trying to pick through the sounds of the rain and make sure that hired thug wasn't trying to sneak up on them. However, he didn't hear any footsteps, but he heard voices coming from the van.

Someone—two men from the sound of it—seemed to be arguing.

Maybe that would work in their favor. If the shooters were distracted, Jax could maybe do something about that idiot at the front of the house.

Jax moved, trying to keep his body in front of Paige in case the shots started again. He could still hear the two men arguing, and he hoped it was distracting the guy in the front. Jax crawled to the edge of the porch, looked around. But didn't spot him.

Where the hell was he?

And Jax hoped that he wasn't trying to make his way to the main house.

Jax was so focused on looking for the goon that the sound of the gunshot startled him. His heart jumped to his throat.

Paige.

Had the goon shot her?

He couldn't look behind him fast enough. But she was all right and looking as confused and worried as he was. Jax hoped that she would realize the shot hadn't gone anywhere near the main house. This one was much, much closer.

"Got one of them," someone called out. "I'm pretty sure this one's dead. He was trying to sneak up on you from the back porch."

Hank.

Thank God. The last Jax had seen of Hank, he'd been in his truck, but obviously he'd gotten out and moved closer to the house. Good.

One down. Three to go.

Or maybe four if Belinda was involved.

However, Jax was beginning to believe she was a victim in all of this. She was still sobbing, so either she was innocent or she regretted this stupid, dangerous plan that'd been set into motion. A plan that might have already killed Buddy.

"Jericho," Paige said, and she motioned toward the end of the road.

Jax looked in that direction and saw the flash of the blue lights. Obviously his brother had decided not to go with the quiet approach. Maybe it would spur the arguing men to use the van to try to get away.

They wouldn't.

Not while they were sandwiched between Jericho and Jax. Still, it would get them away from Paige, and he wanted her as far from the gunfire as possible. And it was likely that van was loaded with enough firepower to do some serious damage. Not good. Because as long as this fight went on, they were all in danger, and an ambulance wouldn't be able to get to Buddy.

In case the gunmen stayed put and made their stand here, Jax knew he had to get Paige to better cover. He tossed her his phone. "Text Jericho. See if he can open the cruiser."

Paige gave a shaky nod and fired off the text. They waited. Not long. And she shook her head. "He's too far away. But he's going to drive closer."

Maybe that wouldn't take long. Because Jax heard something that put a knot in his stomach.

Silence.

The men were no longer arguing. By now, they must have seen the lights of Jericho's cruiser, and they were no doubt ready to do whatever it was they'd come here to do.

Jax hurried back to Paige. "Stay low and move toward the cruiser. Fast. The second Jericho unlocks it, get inside."

They'd hardly made it a foot when the next shot came. It slammed into the ground way too close to them.

"Keep moving," Jax told Paige, and he turned, hoping to see the shooter.

No such luck, but since he had the extra ammo in his jeans pocket, Jax fired a shot directly into the windshield of the van. The bullet didn't shatter the glass. Didn't stop the shooter, either.

Because the shots started coming, and not just from one angle. All three of the remaining gunmen were shooting, not just at them. Plenty of those shots were going in Jericho's direction.

Thankfully, Paige just crawled, and Jax followed, trying to pinpoint the exact location of at least one of the gunmen so he could try to send a shot his way.

And then Jax heard it.

Not the sound of the shots. Nor of the gunmen. Even with the slap of the rain against his hat, Jax heard the voice coming from the van.

"Daddy."

Hell, no.

It was Matthew.

PAIGE FROZE, THE sound of her baby's voice slamming through her as hard as a bullet. Oh, God.

Had they kidnapped him?

Were they going to hurt him to try to draw her out?

Matthew's voice came again, the sound slicing through her. "Daddy."

She started to scramble toward the van, but Jax caught on to her and pulled her right back to the ground. This time, though, he didn't cover her with his body.

He maneuvered them to the cruiser, and they ducked behind it.

But Paige didn't want to stop there. She had to keep moving. Had to get to her son.

Everything inside her was screaming for her to help Matthew. It didn't help that her little boy's voice kept coming from that van. Repeating that one word.

Daddy.

It sounded like a plea for help.

Were they hurting him?

Jax took hold of her chin, forcing eye contact with her. "It's a recording. It has to be. Think this through. If these men had taken Matthew, someone at the house would have texted me."

Paige had to fight through the panic to let that sink in. Jax was right. Unless, of course, the absolute worst had happened—that these monsters had managed to break into the main house, kill or incapacitate everyone inside and then kidnap Matthew.

"We would have heard gunfire," Jax added, as if he'd known exactly what she was thinking. "The ranch hands wouldn't have let anyone that close to the house without there being gunfire."

True. And she remembered that someone had planted the camera with an eavesdropping device on the porch swing. Paige had seen Belinda out there on that very swing with Matthew. At some point Matthew could have said, "Daddy," and the device could have recorded it.

And these monsters were using it now to torture Jax and her.

It'd almost worked. Paige had nearly bolted out there, and that was almost certainly what this killer wanted her to do.

"Matthew!" Belinda shouted. "You can't hurt him. Please don't hurt him."

Paige couldn't see the woman, but she understood the sheer panic and terror that Belinda was likely feeling. And that didn't sound fake.

"Damn. Belinda's running out there," Jax mumbled.

Belinda screamed when there were more shots, and Paige flattened herself on the ground so she could look beneath the cruiser.

Unlike Jax.

He was no longer down but rather peering over the trunk. Paige wanted to shout for him to get down, but she saw the movement from the corner of her eye.

Someone scrambled toward Belinda, and she hoped it was Hank. No such luck. It was a man dressed all in black, and he was wearing a ski mask. He grabbed hold of Belinda's hair, dragging her to a standing position in front of him, and he hauled her backward until they were against the detached garage.

And the thug put the gun to Belinda's head.

For the first time since this latest nightmare had started, Paige actually hoped that Belinda was part of this. If so, she was safe. Her own hired gun wouldn't shoot her. But if she was innocent, then she was in grave danger. She'd been a loose end that these men might want to tie up by murdering her.

"The boss man says you probably won't care a rat about me holding the nanny at gunpoint," the man behind Belinda shouted. "But I figure a lawman's a lawman to the core, and you aren't going to just hide behind that cop car or your badge and let me put a bullet in her head."

He was calling Jax out. But why? Why did they want Jax dead?

Maybe they didn't.

Perhaps the plan was to separate Jax from her. Either way, he could be hurt or killed, and Paige wasn't going to stay put and let that happen.

"What do you want?" she called out.

That earned her a glare from Jax. "Just stay quiet. Jericho should be close enough soon to unlock the cruiser."

Paige had no idea when that would happen. At least one of the gunmen was still shooting at Jericho, and while his cruiser would be bullet-resistant as well, it wasn't bulletproof, and some of those shots would eventually tear through the cruiser and get through.

Jericho and whoever was inside could be shot.

And all that could happen while Buddy was bleeding out.

"I have to do something to end this fast," Paige told Jax, and even though he was cursing at her, Paige repeated her shouted question. "What do you want?"

Paige had expected the thug holding Belinda to start doling out their demands. Demands that would almost certainly involve her surrender. Not exactly a surprise since they'd already demanded it when she'd been inside the house.

"What do I want?" a man shouted back. "I want *you*."

Not the guy behind Belinda. This voice came from the van, and it was a voice she had no trouble recognizing.

Leland.

Chapter Eighteen

Jax wasn't surprised that Leland was behind these attacks, but he wouldn't have been taken aback if it'd been Darrin, either. Of course, maybe the two were working together.

After all, Darrin could be the one shooting at Jericho. Or even the one calling the shots.

"I'm so sorry," Paige whispered.

"Don't," Jax snapped, and he hated that she even felt the need to apologize. Hated his harsh tone even more.

She probably thought he was blaming her for this, too. The way he'd blamed her for nearly getting killed by the Moonlight Strangler.

But he wasn't.

Jax was blaming himself. He had seen the anger in Leland. Had felt it. And he hadn't been able to do a damn thing to stop it.

"Stop shooting at Jericho," Paige called out to Leland. "And tell me what you want from me."

Jax doubted the shots would stop. But they did. Good. Maybe that meant he could reason with Leland, after all. Or perhaps it would give Jericho a chance to shoot both Leland and the other gunman in the van. Either way, Jax would take it.

"I want you to come out from hiding," Leland said,

his voice a little closer now. Jax glanced around the cruiser and saw why.

Leland was out of the van and had made his way to the front of it. Not out in the open, exactly. He was using the van for cover, but it might make him an easier shot for Jericho or even Hank.

Wherever he was.

Jax hadn't heard a peep from the ranch hand since he'd managed to shoot one of the hired guns.

"I love you, Paige. I never wanted you dead," Leland added, sounding as unhinged as Jax figured he was. He'd always known that Leland was wrapped too tight, and the man had obviously lost it.

"Really? You never wanted me dead?" Paige answered, her voice filled with fear and some sarcasm. "Because it doesn't seem that way. Your hired thugs tried to kill us—twice."

"That wasn't the plan. The plan was only to kill Jax."

So he'd been the target. That felt like a punch to Jax. He was the reason Paige had nearly died. Of course, that reasoning was coming from the mind of a sick man. One in a rage because he was jealous.

"Were you working with the Moonlight Strangler?" Jax tossed out there.

"Hell, no." Leland didn't hesitate even a second, and judging from the venom in his voice, he hated the serial killer as much as Jax did. Something they actually had in common.

Well, along with his feelings for Paige.

But Jax pushed those feelings aside right now. Later, he'd deal with them and what'd happened between them in the kitchen. For now, he couldn't let those thoughts and emotions get in the way.

"Is Belinda part of this?" Jax asked.

"Are you kidding me? She's in love with you, you fool. That bitch has fought me every step of the way, though I'm betting she wouldn't mind if Paige died tonight. That's not gonna happen, though."

"I don't want anyone dead," Belinda shouted. "Please, just stop all of this."

"For once, I agree with her," Leland spat out. "I've done everything I could to win Paige, and it didn't work."

"Did you put that camera there?" Belinda, again. "Because they were trying to accuse me of doing it. I only touched it."

"Yeah, yeah. I put it there so I could hear and see what was going on. I waited until you took the kid out to see the horses, and I just waltzed right in and did it. I figured if anyone found it, they'd blame the Moonlight Strangler."

They had. At first. And with Belinda's print on there, it had definitely put her under suspicion.

"Did you send me the texts, too?" Paige asked.

Jax hated that she'd even spoken to the man. He could practically feel the rage coming off him.

"Yes," Leland finally answered. "I sent those texts to set up a meeting. I thought if I could just get you alone, someplace private, I could talk some sense into you. That's why I had my men set the fire near the road, too. It was all about getting you away from him." The volume of his voice got louder with each word. "I didn't know the real Moonlight Strangler was going to get involved. And not just involved with contacting Paige, but going after Belinda, too."

Jax believed him, about that, anyway. There was no reason for Leland to have the Moonlight Strangler mark Belinda as his next victim. And if Leland really wanted

Paige for himself, he wouldn't have put her in the path of a serial killer. But that's exactly what he'd done, because his attacks had alerted the Moonlight Strangler that Paige was still alive.

"Enough of this. We have a grenade launcher," Leland went on. "And my man's got it aimed at Jericho. Tell your brother to stop moving that cruiser forward, or we'll blast him and his deputy to smithereens. The same will happen if he even tries to shoot us."

Damn.

Jax wanted to believe that was a bluff, but he seriously doubted it. No, Leland would have come prepared, and this was almost certainly the way he planned to escape with Paige.

But Jax wasn't going to let that happen.

She'd nearly died once from an encounter with a violent killer, and Jax hadn't been able to stop it. Somehow, he would stop this one.

"Or maybe you'd rather we aim the grenade launcher at the main house?" Leland went on. "It's not what I want to do, Paige, but I will if you don't cooperate."

Jax had no idea of the range on the launcher, but he doubted it could deliver a grenade all the way to the main house. Still, he didn't want to risk it.

"Since you want me dead," Jax shouted to the man, "why don't I come out instead of Paige. You want to punish her, right? Punish her for coming back to me. Well, here's your chance. You can punish her by killing me and then keeping her alive so she'll have to live with it."

Now it was Paige who glared at him. "You're not sacrificing yourself."

That wasn't what he had in mind, but whatever he

did at this point would carry that risk. A risk that would be worth it.

"I just want to do something to get Leland out of cover so I can shoot him," Jax told her.

That was true. For the most part. He did want to shoot Leland, but Leland was a cop, too, and no doubt had just as good of an aim as Jax.

"I want you dead, all right," Leland answered. "But no deal. Paige is coming with me."

Jax didn't see that with a happy ending. Leland might not kill Paige right off, but it would eventually happen.

"You really think you can just leave here and have a life with Paige?" Jax fired back. "The law would be looking for you."

"Maybe. It wasn't supposed to happen this way." Leland cursed. "I was supposed to be out of here without anyone seeing me, and then Darrin would take the fall."

"Darrin?" Paige and Jax asked at the same time.

"Is he with you right now?" Jax pressed.

"No. He's not here. He's at his place in San Antonio. Darrin's *committing suicide* right about now from a drug overdose. He has a history of drug abuse, and his medical records will prove it. But I guess he'll be dying for nothing. Still, the world won't miss a pig like that."

That was a serous example of the pot calling the kettle black. Yeah, Darrin was a pig, but Leland was a killer. Darrin, maybe Buddy, too, and heaven knew how many others would be dead before this was over.

Unless Jax ended it now.

Jax still didn't have a clean shot, not even close, but it would have to do. He levered himself up just enough so he could see over the trunk of the cruiser. And he took aim.

But before Jax could even pull the trigger, the shot blasted through the air.

PAIGE COULDN'T SEE what was happening, but she had no trouble hearing the shot. Or the one that followed.

Not ones that Jax or Leland had fired, either.

These bullets had come from the direction where that hired gun had hold of Belinda.

Belinda screamed, a blood-curdling sound that cut through even the blasts of gunfire. And for several horrifying moments, Paige thought the thug had shot the woman.

He hadn't.

Someone had shot the thug.

The man dropped like a stone, his gun splatting onto the soggy ground beside him.

That's when Paige saw someone. *Jericho.* He came out from the side of the detached garage, his gun still aimed at the fallen man. Jericho hooked his other arm around Belinda and dragged her back behind the garage.

But how had Jericho gotten there? No one had come out of the cruiser. No one that she'd seen, anyway. Of course, it was dark and raining, and it was hard to see much of anything.

Or maybe he'd never even been in the cruiser.

He could have sneaked out at the end of the road and had the deputy drive it closer. If so, it was a smart plan, and it had likely saved Belinda's life.

However, Leland clearly wasn't happy about it.

"No!" Leland shouted. "You can't do this to me. Launch the grenade now."

Oh, God. Paige hadn't forgotten about that particular threat, but she hadn't realized Leland would use it so quickly. She didn't even have time to say a word, not that it would have stopped Leland anyway, before the cracking sound came from the opened back doors of the van.

Followed by the blast.

Much, much louder than a gunshot, and the cruiser exploded into a fireball. It lit up the night sky and sent fiery debris falling down all over the road and yard.

Paige's heart stopped. Whoever was inside there had to be dead. And Leland wasn't finished.

Yelling at the top of his lungs, Leland turned, taking aim at Belinda and Jericho. He fired four shots, nonstop. Just as Jericho pulled Belinda to the ground.

Paige had no idea if Jericho had gotten Belinda, or himself, out of the path of those bullets in time, but it was possible there were four injured or dead people: Buddy, Jericho, Belinda and the deputy in the cruiser.

"Stay down," Jax warned her when she moved to try to see Jericho.

Jax came up again and fired his Glock right at Leland. Judging from the profanity that Jax mumbled, he missed.

But Leland kept shooting, and so did the hired gun who had launched that grenade into the cruiser.

"Wait here," Jax said. "And I mean it. I need to get a better angle so I can stop Leland."

She caught on to his arm when he started to move. Paige wanted to beg him not to go out there, but time wasn't on their side here. They needed to end this fast so the ambulance could get onto the grounds. Still, it crushed her to think that Jax might be hurt or worse.

"Be careful," was all she managed to say.

That was it. And Jax was gone.

He lowered himself to the ground, crawling toward the front porch. Away from cover and directly toward Leland. Leland had finally stopped firing at Jericho, but a few seconds later, she realized that was probably because he was reloading. The shots soon picked up again.

"We've got one more grenade," Leland shouted. "Paige, this is your last chance. I know you're behind the police car by the house. And that's exactly where the next grenade would go. It'll take out both Jax and you."

Her breath stalled in her throat, and the panic started to rise again. The grenade could do that. As big as that other blast had been, it'd take out them and the house, and maybe hurt Jericho and Belinda, too.

But maybe she could save Jax.

Maybe.

She wasn't just going to give up. She'd done that once when the Moonlight Strangler had left her for dead, and she wasn't doing that again. If she had to die, she wanted to at least die fighting.

Paige came up off the ground, ready to try to shoot Leland. But there was another shot. Not one that Jax had fired, either. She saw Jericho, and he was no longer by the garage with Belinda. He was closer to the road where the cruiser was still blazing. And Jericho had shot into the van.

Hopefully, he'd killed the man about to launch that grenade at them.

But there was no time for Paige to figure that out now. Leland was alive, and he could still do plenty of damage.

Paige took aim at Leland, but Leland saw her and pivoted in her direction. Ready to kill her.

And Paige pulled the trigger first.

She missed.

But Jax didn't.

Jax was already in place, and he sent two shots straight into Leland's chest. Everything seemed to stop. Including Leland. He stood there, frozen, his blank gaze connecting with hers for what seemed an eternity before he collapsed.

"Stay here," Jax warned her.

Not that she could move, anyway. Paige wasn't sure she had enough breath for that, and her legs were shaking. The rest of her body, too.

Jax hurried to Leland, kicking aside the man's gun and checking for any signs of life. "He's dead," Jax called out.

On the back side of the van, Jericho did the same thing to the thug he'd shot. "This one, too."

Jax didn't stay near Leland. He ran to Buddy's truck and looked inside. "Get an ambulance here *now*!"

Chapter Nineteen

Lucky.

That was the one word that kept going through Jax's mind.

They'd gotten damn lucky tonight. And while he hated to rely on something as fragile as luck, he'd take it. Things had gotten bad, but they could have been a whole lot worse.

The proof of that was right in front of him.

Paige was sitting on the floor of the playroom at the main house, and she was holding Matthew. Their son was sacked out, but Paige kept holding him, anyway. Probably because it helped settle her nerves. Well, as much as anything could settle them after the ordeal they'd been through.

Jax looked up the hall when he heard the footsteps. Jericho was making his way toward him, and his brother was finishing up yet another phone call. Something that Jax had been doing on and off as well for the past two hours since all hell had broken loose. Those two hours hadn't done much to take that stark look out of Paige's eyes, but maybe nothing could do that.

Paige and Matthew weren't alone in the room. Alexa and his mom were still there. Both were pretending to watch a movie they'd put on before Matthew fell asleep.

Before the other kids dozed off, too. But Alexa and his mother looked more shell-shocked than anything else.

There'd been several good things that had come out of this mess. Good things other than just them all being in one piece. Leland and his hired guns were dead.

All of them.

And as Jax had learned later, there'd been no one in the cruiser that Leland's thug had blown up. Jericho had gotten out at the end of the road and walked up. Before the explostion, Dexter had slipped out through the back and into a ditch. Hank was all right, as well. Not a scratch on him.

Jax couldn't say the same for Buddy, though.

"Anything from the hospital yet?" Jax asked when Jericho was closer.

Jericho nodded. "Buddy's out of surgery. The bullet collapsed his lung, and he'll be out of commission for a couple of weeks. Buddy said to let you know that it'll only be a couple of days."

It would be weeks. Jax would make sure of it, though it would be hard to make the ranch hand stick to resting.

"What about Belinda?" Jericho asked.

"She's shaken up but on the way to her sister's in San Antonio. She'll come back tomorrow to give her statement, but she said Leland kidnapped her."

Jericho made a sound of agreement. "That's what she told me, too, when I had her by the side of the garage. I figure Leland was using her as a decoy, but he would have killed Belinda if he'd managed to get his hands on Paige."

Definitely.

They'd gotten lucky all right.

"I don't think Belinda will be coming back to the ranch, or even to her house for that matter," Jax added a moment later. And he couldn't blame her. Besides, Belinda had to know that Paige would be staying around.

At least Jax hoped that was Paige's plan.

He frowned.

What was her plan, anyway?

"I asked about Cord when I was talking to the doctor," Jericho went on, snaring Jax's attention. "No change, but Cord's already complaining about having to stay in the hospital. I figure he'll sneak out first chance he gets."

Cord wouldn't if Addie had anything to say about it. And she would. It was obvious that she loved Cord like a brother. Because he was just that. Still, it stung a little, and Jax wasn't even sure why. It wasn't as if he'd had his only sister to himself over the years. He'd always shared her with his other brothers. Adding one more to the mix didn't seem like a big deal, but it was.

It was something he was definitely going to have to get over.

"No change in the Moonlight Strangler's condition, either," Jericho went on. "The doc said that's not good, that the longer he's in the coma, then the chances are that he'll stay that way for the rest of his miserable life."

Which meant they'd never be able to question him. They'd never be able to ask him why he'd murdered all those women.

Of course, he probably wouldn't have told them, anyway. Killers rarely spoke the truth, and the bottom line was the Moonlight Strangler might be just an ordinary sociopath with no real motive for murder. Not a motive that would make sense to anyone else, anyway.

Paige glanced up at Jax, maybe because she'd heard him mention the killer, but she didn't get up and join Jericho and him in the conversation. Which was good.

She didn't need to hear any more details about the man who'd made her life a living hell.

"How long will the Moonlight Strangler be at the hospital?" Jax asked. Because it was only about fifteen miles from the ranch.

Too damn close.

Of course, a million miles was too close. Jax wanted the killer as far away as possible from Paige and the rest of his family, and he wanted that to happen yesterday.

"The doc thinks they can transfer him to the prison hospital as early as tomorrow," Jericho answered. "His condition is stable, and they can better guard him there than in Appaloosa Pass."

Agreed. A monster like that needed to be behind layers and layers of bars and security.

"What about Darrin?" Jax continued.

Jericho shook his head. "He didn't make it. By the time the ambulance got to his house, he'd been dead for a half hour or longer."

Another of Leland's victims. It was hard for Jax to feel sorry for the man who'd caused Paige so much pain, but Darrin didn't deserve to be murdered.

Jericho tipped his head to Paige. Her attention was still fixed on Matthew. "How's she holding up?"

Jax was about to put that *shaken up* label on her the way he had Belinda. And she was indeed shaken to the core. But she was also tough as nails. She'd gone straight from nearly being killed by a crazy cop to the main house to see Matthew. Paige had even managed to give their son a smile and make this seem like playtime.

"How are you holding up?" Jericho pressed. "And how are you *holding up* with Paige?"

There it was. Jericho's famous ESP. Jericho's tone

let him know that he was certain that Jax and she had become lovers again.

Jax lifted his shoulder. "I'm not sure." And sadly it was true. Yeah, they had indeed become lovers again, but Jax wasn't sure if that was because of their feelings for each other or because it'd been just sex and a good release for tension.

Paige glanced at him again.

Jax knew what he wanted it to be—much more than just sex, that was for sure—but it was hard to undo all the arguments that had torn them apart. And there was her lie about being dead.

That suddenly didn't seem so big in the grand scheme of things.

"Want my advice?" Jericho asked, but he didn't wait for Jax to answer. "You should have sex with her again."

Jax gave him a flat look.

But Jericho only flashed him that all-knowing brotherly half smile. "I know people say that sex messes with your head, but sometimes it can make things a whole lot clearer."

Yes. It could.

And it had for him.

However, this wasn't something Jax intended to keep discussing with Jericho. Even if it was good advice.

"I don't expect the family just to welcome Paige back with open arms," Jax said, speaking more to himself than Jericho now.

"Well, you sure as hell should, considering how you feel about her." With that, Jericho gave him a pat on the back and strolled away.

Now Paige got to her feet. She kissed Matthew on his cheek, eased him onto the quilt that had been stretched on the floor and made her way to Jax.

"Is everything okay?" she asked.

Jax considered giving her a summary of all the up-dates he'd just gotten from Jericho, but that could wait. Because he thought they could both use it, he slipped his arm around her waist, eased her to him. And he kissed her.

Man, he wasn't sure how she managed, but every kiss with Paige felt like the first one. Even though there'd been a ton of them in between the first one and now.

The kiss went on a little longer than Jax had planned. Mainly because she tasted so good and because Paige slipped right into the kiss, and his arms, as if she could spend the rest of the night doing just this.

And maybe they could.

He stopped the kiss only because he heard his mother clear her throat. Jax looked into the playroom, expecting to have to dole out a lukewarm apology for carrying on in front of her. He darn sure wasn't about to apologize for the kiss itself, though.

But his mother was smiling. Alexa, too.

Jax hadn't especially needed the green light from either of them, but he'd take it, and he moved Paige out of the doorway and into the hall so they could have some privacy.

He kissed her again. And again.

His plan was to make her mind a little cloudy and to remind her of this heat between them. Of course, in doing that, he also reminded himself.

"You saved my life tonight," she whispered against his mouth. "Today, too," she added. And just like that, she shuddered, the flashbacks no doubt getting through the haze of the kiss.

Jax pulled her back to him. "I'm a cop. It's my job." He tried for it to sound like a joke, and she managed a little smile. But the smile didn't quite make it all the way to her eyes.

But the tears did, and she started blinking them back. "I'm so sorry—"

No way did he want to hear this, so he gave her one more kiss. Jax made it long and deep, and he pressed her against the wall, body to body, so that she'd remember some other things that didn't have to do with killers and bullets.

He kissed her so long that he thought maybe his lungs were about to burst. They broke apart, both of them gasping for air.

"I don't need an apology," he assured her. "None of this was your fault. Or mine. Let's pin this right on Leland and leave the blame there, agreed?"

"But I was a fool to let him get so close to me."

Ah, hell. This was going to take more than just a kiss. "You're not a fool," he assured her.

Jax let go of her just long enough to step back to the playroom. "Could you watch Matthew for a while?" he asked his mom. "I need to…chat with Paige."

He hadn't meant to pause in the middle of that, and it made it sound as if he had something sexual on his mind.

Which he did.

"Of course," his mother said, smiling. "Take your time."

Jax went back to Paige, taking hold of her hand and leading her up the stairs. To the guest room. He got her inside, shut the door and kissed her before she could ask any questions or attempt another apology.

"Is that to convince me I'm not a fool?" she asked, breathless again.

"More or less. Less," he settled on saying. He lowered the kiss to her neck.

Then to her breasts.

Finally, he got the results he wanted. That silky sound. Her face flushed, and he could see her pulse on her throat. All good signs. So was the fact that she latched on to him and dragged him back for another kiss.

And then she dragged him to the floor.

He was mindful of all her bruises and scrapes, but she wasn't. Paige pulled him on top of her.

There it was again. That raging fire. The timing for it sucked since she was probably dealing with a bad adrenaline crash, but maybe there was no bad time for sex when it came to them.

She reached between them and unhooked his holster, dropping it on the floor next to them, and she went after his shirt. He wanted this. Wanted her naked, too.

But then Jax froze.

But he also wanted a heck of a lot more.

"I'm in love with you," he said, but then shook his head. "I'm *still* in love with you."

Considering she had him half naked and looked like sex on a silver platter, he was surprised at the soft smile she managed. Not a trace of lust in it. Well, just a little trace. There was always some heat whenever they looked at each other.

"Good, because I'm still in love with you, too." She paused. "And I want to move back home with Matthew and you. I want to make up for all the time I lost with both of you."

He nodded in approval. That was the best news he'd heard all day. Maybe in his entire life. "You'll have to marry me again, though. Just so I can make an honest woman out of you."

She smiled, too, at his lame joke. "And I can make an honest man out of you."

Judging from her next kiss, it wasn't that kind of honesty she had on her mind. It wasn't on Jax's, either. But when they were done here, he was getting Paige back to the altar ASAP.

"Oh, and I want more kids," she added, breaking the kiss only long enough for her to speak those few but very important words.

"Agreed." He wanted more, too, and at the rate they were going, they'd have one in under a year. Heck, they might be starting one tonight. "Anything else on your wish list?"

She smiled. "Just you, Jax. Just you."

That was his cue to kiss her like he meant it. Which he did. Jax also worked on getting her naked, and he kissed all those places he was uncovering.

"One day we're going to actually make it to the bed," Paige whispered, unzipping him.

"We'll work our way there together." And Jax kissed her again so they could get started on their new-old life together.

* * * * *

The words seemed final somehow. As if Josh had accepted something was about to happen and there was no going back.

He removed her hands and crossed his arms across his chest, tilting his head to stare at the top of hers because she was frightened to meet his hazel eyes. Frightened of the desperation she might see there.

"I made you the guardian of the twins last year."

"Without asking me?"

"Yeah. I was afraid you'd say no." Josh shrugged and lifted the corner of his mouth in a little smile. "You asked what I was willing to do. They're my kids, Tracey. I'll do anything for them, including prison time."

"Just tell me what to do."

"Nothing. You can't be involved in this. It has to be me." She believed him. She had to. But she couldn't promise to stay out of his way. She meant what she'd said about doing anything for Jackson and Sage. And if that meant *she* was the one who went to jail. . .so be it.

HARD CORE LAW

BY
ANGI MORGAN

First Published in Great Britain 2016
By Mills & Boon, an imprint of HarperCollins*Publishers*
1 London Bridge Street, London, SE1 9GF

© 2016 Angela Platt

ISBN: 978-0-263-91912-7

46-0816

Our policy is to use papers that are natural, renewable and recyclable products and made from wood grown in sustainable forests. The logging and manufacturing processes conform to the legal environmental regulations of the country of origin.

Printed and bound in Spain
by CPI, Barcelona

Angi Morgan writes Mills & Boon Intrigue novels where honor and danger collide with love. Her work is a multiple contest finalist, RWA Golden Heart® Award winner and *Publishers Weekly* bestseller. When not fostering Labradors, she drags her dogs—and husband—around Texas for research road trips so she can write off her camera. See her photos on bit.ly/aPicADay. Somehow, every detour makes it into a book. She loves to hear from fans at www.angimorgan.com or on Facebook at Angi Morgan Books.

There is never a book without my pals Jan, Robin, Jen, Lizbeth and Janie. Lena Diaz, thanks for the brilliant ideas and personal information you shared about raising a child with diabetes. Tim. . .I love you, man!

Prologue

"It was great to meet you. Night." The last of the birthday guests waved from their cars.

Tracey Cassidy stood at the front door waving goodbye to another couple she barely knew. Two sets of little arms stretched around her thighs, squeezing with an appropriate four-and-a-half-year-old grunt.

"What are you two doing up? I tucked you in three hours ago."

"Happy birthday," they said in unison.

Jackson and Sage giggled until the sound of a dish breaking in the kitchen jerked them from their merriment. Their faces, so similar but different, held the same surprise and knowledge that their daddy was in super big trouble.

"Daddy's going to get it now." Sage nodded until her auburn curls bounced.

"Hurry." Tracey patted them on the backsides and pointed them in the right direction. "Back upstairs before the Major has to scoop you up there himself. You know you'll have extra chores if he catches you down here."

The twins took each stair with a giant tiptoeing motion. It would have been hilarious to watch them, but their dad was getting a bit louder and might come looking for her to help.

"Scoot, and there's sprinkles on Friday's ice-cream cone."

Bribery worked. They ran as fast as their short legs could carry them up the carpeted staircase. Tracey was sure their dad heard the bedroom door close. Then again, he was making enough noise to wake the barn cats.

"Tracey!" he finally yelled, seeking help. "Where's the dustpan?"

Hurrying to the back of the house, she found Major Josh Parker holding several pieces of broken glass in one hand and the broom in the other. A juggler holding his act. Yep, that's what he looked like. He was still completely out of his element in the kitchen. Or the laundry. Good thing he had a maid.

"It should have been in the closet with the broom. Here, let me take these." She reached for the pieces of crystal covered in the remnants of spinach artichoke dip.

"I'm good." He raised the mess out of her reach. "Sorry about the bowl. I thought I was actually helping for once. Damn thing slipped right out of my hand."

"Here, just put it in this." She pulled the covered trash can over to the mess and popped the lid open.

"Hell, Tracey, you don't have your shoes on. This thing splintered into a thousand pieces."

Two forbidden words in one conversation? She'd never seen Josh even the little tiniest bit tipsy. But the group had toasted a lot tonight. First her birthday, then an engagement, then to another couple who'd looked at each other like lovebirds. Then to her birthday again.

"Are you a little drunk?" She ignored his warning

and crossed the kitchen to look for the dustpan, which was hanging on the wall of the pantry exactly where it should have been. She turned to tell Josh and walked straight into his chest.

"Well, would you look at that." He cocked his head to the side emphasizing his boyish dimple. "If it had been a snake it would have bitten me."

"Bitten a big chunk right out of your shoulder." She tapped him with the corner for emphasis, but he still didn't back up out of the doorway.

Josh leaned his forehead against the wood and exhaled a long "whew" sound. The smell of whiskey was strong. He had definitely drunk a little more than she'd ever witnessed. Maybe a little more than he should have. But he'd also been enjoying the company of his friends. Something long overdue. Most of his free time was spent with the twins.

"We need a cardboard box or something. This stuff—" He brought the glass from his side to his chest. "It'll bust through plastic."

His head dropped to the door frame and he closed his eyes. This time he relinquished the broken glass to her and backed up with some guidance. She helped him to the table, set a cold bottle of water in front of him and went about cleaning the floor.

Technically, it wasn't her job. She was officially off duty because Josh was home. But she couldn't leave him with his head on the kitchen table and glass all over the place. The kids would get up at their normal time, even if it was a Saturday. And the maid service wouldn't stop back around until Tuesday.

"The way you look right now, this mess might still be here after school Monday."

She moved around the edge of the tiled kitchen

avoiding as much of the mess as she could. He was right about one thing, glass was everywhere. She retrieved her sandals from the living room next to the couch. She'd kicked them off while watching the men in Josh's company interact with one another.

The wives hadn't meant to exclude her, but she wasn't one of them. She was the hired help. The nanny. She detested that word and told those who needed to know that she was the child care provider. In between a few bits of conversation, she silently celebrated in the corner. Not just her birthday, but also the achievement of receiving her PhD.

I need to tell him.

She pulled her sandals from where they'd crept under the couch and slipped them on her feet.

"They weren't very…approachable tonight, were they." A statement. Josh didn't seem to need an answer. One hand scrubbed at his face, while the other held a depleted water bottle. "Sorry 'bout this."

"Hey, nothing to be sorry for. The cake was out of this world."

"Vivian ordered it."

"Yeah, I was sorry she couldn't stay." Josh's receptionist had done her best to keep Tracey involved in the conversations. "Would you sit down before you fall down?"

"I'm not drunk. Just real tired. We've been working a lot, you know."

"I do. I've been spending way too many nights here. The neighbors are going to start talking."

"Let 'em." He grinned and let his head drop to the back of the couch cushions. "They can whinny all they want. And moo. Or just howl at the moon. I might even join 'em."

"I think you need a dog to howl."

Josh's closest neighbor was about three miles away. He did have several horses, three barn cats and let Jim-Bob Watts run cattle on their adjoining field. No one was really going to know if she was there all night or not.

No one but them.

They'd become lax about it recently. Whatever case the Texas Rangers were working on had been keeping him at Company F Headquarters in Waco. The case would soon be over—at least their part in it. She'd gathered that info from one or two of those whiskey toasts.

Tracey looked around the room. Plastic cups, paper plates with icing, napkins, forks. How could ten people make such a mess? A couple of the women had tried to offer their help, but everyone had seemed to leave at the same time.

Of course, the man now asleep on the couch, might have mentioned it was late. And if she worked in his office, she might misinterpret that as an order to get out. Tracey sighed and picked up a trash bag. What did one more late night matter?

Not like she had any reason to rush back to her campus apartment. She dropped two plastic cups into the bag and continued making her way around the room. She might as well clean up a little. It was mostly throwaway stuff and it wasn't fair to make the twins help their dad.

After all, it had been *her* birthday party.

Josh had his hands full just keeping up with the twins. The floor would be horrible by Tuesday if she didn't pass a mop across it. So she cleaned the floors and stored the cake—not to mention put the whiskey bottle above the refrigerator. On the second pass through the living room, she took a throw from the storage ottoman and covered her boss.

It might be triple-digit weather outside, but Josh kept the downstairs like a freezer. She draped the light blanket across him and his hand latched on to hers.

JOSH SHOULD BE ashamed of himself for letting Tracey clean up while he faked sleep. *Should be*. He wasn't drunk. Far from it. He was hyperaware of every one of Tracey's movements.

"Tonight didn't go exactly like I planned."

"Oh shoot. I don't know why you scared me, but I thought you were asleep. It was fun. A total surprise." She placed her hand on top of his, patting it as if she was ready to be let loose. She also didn't have a mean bone in her body. She'd never intentionally hurt his feelings.

But Josh had to hold on. If he let her go, he might not ever get the courage again. "You're lying. You were miserable. I should have invited your friends."

"It was great. Really." She patted his hand again. "I better head out."

"No." He stood, letting her hand go but trapping her shoulders under his grip. He lightened up. "I mean. Can you stay a couple of minutes? I didn't give you your present."

"But you threw the party and everything."

Was it his hopeful imagination that her words were a little breathier when he touched her? Touching was a rare occurrence now that the twins walked themselves up to bed and didn't need to be carried. Not his imagination. Her chest under the sleeveless summer shirt was rising and falling faster.

One wayward strand of dark red hair that she tried so hard to keep in place was curled in the middle of her forehead. Most of the time she shoved it back in with the rest, but he practically had her hands pinned at her sides. This time, he followed through on a simple pleasure. He took the curl between his fingers and gently tucked it away.

Josh allowed the side of his hand to caress the soft skin of Tracey's cheek. His fingertips whispered across her lips and her eyes closed. It was time. Now. A conscious decision. No spur-of-the-moment accident.

He leaned down as he tilted her chin up. Their lips connected and his hands wrapped around her, smashing her body into his. They molded together and all the dormant parts of his soul ignited.

Four years since he'd really held a woman in his arms. The last lips he'd tasted had been a sweet goodbye. It had been a long time since he'd thought about passion.

Tracey's eyes opened when he hesitated for a split second. He didn't see fear or surprise—only passion waiting for him. He kissed her again, not allowing them time to think or reconsider.

Her lips tasted like the coconut-flavored lip balm she recently began using. But her mouth tasted of the butter-flavored icing from her birthday cake. Lips soft and rich. Her body was toned, yet pliant against him.

Yes, he analyzed it all. Every part of her. He wanted to remember just in case he never got another chance.

Intimacy hadn't been his since… Since… He couldn't allow himself to go in that direction. Tracey was in his arms. Tracey's body was responding to his caresses.

Their lips parted. He wanted to race forward, but they needed a beginning first. He'd worked it all out a hundred times in his head. This was logical. Start with a kiss, let her know he wanted more.

"Okay, that was…surprising for a birthday present."

No doubt about it, her voice was shaking with breath-lessness.

"Sorry, that wasn't it. I kept the box at the office so the kids couldn't say anything. It's in the truck." He slipped his hands into his jeans pockets to stop them from pointing to one more thing. One step away from her and he wondered if she was breathless or so sur-prised she didn't know how to react.

"Josh?"

No.

"It'll just take a sec."

Tracey caught up with him and followed him onto the porch. "Maybe I should go home?" She smiled and rubbed his arm like a pal.

"Right." He slipped his thumbs inside his front pock-ets. He lifted his chin when he realized it was tucked to his chest.

"It's just… Well, you've been drinking and I don't want…" Her voice trailed off the same way it did when she was sharing something negative about the twins' behavior. She didn't want to disappoint him. Ever.

"Got it." He marched to her car and forced himself not to yank the door off the hinges.

"Don't be mad. It's not that I didn't—"

"Tracey. I got it."

And he did. All he knew about Tracey was that she'd been there for him and the kids. Assuming she felt the same when— Dammit, he didn't know anything about her life outside their small world here.

"I'm going to head out." Purse over her shoulder, she waved from the front door of her car. "Night." She waved and gently shut the door behind her.

Change is a mistake. Nah, he'd had this debate with

himself for weeks. It was time to move on. He couldn't be afraid of what might or might not happen.

Tracey's tires spun a little in the gravel as she pulled away. He hoped like hell that he hadn't scared her away. From him, maybe. But she wouldn't leave the twins, right? She was the only mother they'd ever had in their lives.

For a while, he'd thought he admired her for that. But this wasn't all about the kids. He needed her to say that she felt something for him. Because four years was long enough.

He was ready to love again.

Chapter One

Nothing. Two weeks since Josh Parker had kissed her, and then avoided her like the plague. Two weeks and she'd barely seen him. Adding insult to injury, he'd even hired a teenager to watch the kids a couple of nights.

Tracey tilted the rearview mirror to get a better view of Jackson and Sage. They were too quiet. Smiling at each other in twin language. It was ice cream Friday and they'd behaved at school, so that had meant sprinkles. And they'd enjoyed every single colored speck.

The intersection was busier than usual. The car in front of her turned and Tracey finally saw the holdup. The hood was up on a small moving van at the stop sign. She was making her way around, pulling to the side, when another car parked next to the van.

"Tracey, we're hungry," Sage said.

"I know, sweetheart. I'm doing my best." She put her Mazda in Reverse trying to turn around in the street. "Can you reach your crackers, Jackson?"

"Yep, yep, yep," he answered like the dinosaur on the old DVDs he'd been watching. She watched him tug his little backpack between the car seats and snag a cracker, then share a second with Sage.

"Just one, little man. You just had ice cream."

Two men left the moving van and waved at her to

back up. She was awfully close to the other van, but she trusted their directions. Right up until she felt her car hit. She hadn't been going fast enough for damage, but the guy seemed to get pretty steamed and stomped toward her door.

Great what a way to begin her weekend.

The men split to either side of her car, where one gave her the signal to roll down her window. She lowered it enough to allow him to hear her, then she unbuckled and leaned to the glove compartment for her insurance card.

"Sorry about that, but your friend—" Tracey looked up and froze.

Now in a ski mask, the man next to her window shouted, pulling on the door handle, tapping on the window with the butt of a handgun before pushing the barrel inside. "Open the door!"

She hit the horn repeatedly and put the car back into gear, willing to smash it to bits in order to get away. But it was wedged in tight. Once she'd backed up, they'd quickly used two vehicles to block her, parking in front and behind, pinning her car between the three.

Would they really shoot her to carjack an old junker of a Mazda?

"You can have the car. If you want money, it'll take a little while, but I can get that, too. You don't have to do this." She kept careful control of her voice. "Just let me unsnap the twins and take them with me."

"Get out! Now!" A second gunman shouted through the glass at the passenger door.

Where were all the cars now? Why had she lowered the window an inch to answer this man's question? What if they didn't let her get the kids out? Her mind was racing with questions.

They shouted at her, banging on the windows. The twins knew something was wrong and began to cry. Tracey gripped the steering wheel with one hand and blared the horn with the other. Someone had to hear them. Someone would come by and see what was happening.

"Lady, you get out of the car or I'll blow you away through the window." Gunman One pointed the gun at her head.

"You don't want these kids. Their dad's the head of the Texas Rangers in this area."

With a gun stuck in her face, Tracey didn't know how she was speaking—especially with any intelligence. Her hands were locked, determined to stay where they were. That's when she had the horrible feeling it wasn't a random carjacking.

"You're wrong, sweetheart. That's exactly why we want them," Gunman Two said.

"Shut up, Mack!" Gunman One screamed, hitting the top of the car. "You!" he yelled at her again. "Stop blabbing and get your butt out here before I blow your brains all over those kids."

One of the drivers got out of his box truck with a bent pole. Not a pole. It looked like it had a climbing spike on the end.

"No!" She leaned toward the middle, attempting to block what she knew was coming.

The new guy swung, hitting the window, and it shattered into pebble-size glass rocks. The kids screamed louder. She tried to climbing into the backseat. The locks popped open and three doors flew wide.

Gunman One latched on to her ankles and yanked. Her chin bounced against the top of the seat. Jarring pain jolted across her face. Before she could grab anything or brace herself, her body tumbled out of the car. Twisted, her side and shoulder took most of the fall to the street.

She prayed someone would drive by and see what was happening. She looked everywhere for help. Wasn't there anyone who could intervene or call the police? Her small purse was still strapped across her chest, hidden at her hip. Her cell phone was still inside so maybe she could—

Gunman One flipped open a knife and sliced the strap, nicking her neck in the process. "We wouldn't want you to call Daddy too soon. You got that tape, Mack?" He jerked her to her feet, hitting the side of her head with his elbow. "You just had to play the hero."

"Here ya go, Mack." Gunman Two, already in the car, tossed him duct tape.

Gunman One smashed her face into the backseat window, winding the tape around her wrists. Both of the children were screaming her name. They knew something wasn't right. Both were trapped in their car seats, clawing at the straps then stretching their arms toward her.

"It's okay, guys. No one's going to hurt you." She tried to calm them through the glass. "Please don't do this. Jackson has diabetes. He's on a restricted diet and his insulin level has to be closely—"

Gunman One rolled her to her back and shoved her along the metal edge of the Mazda to the trunk.

Oh my God. They knew. She could tell by his reactions. She was right. It wasn't a carjacking. This was a planned kidnapping of Josh Parker's twins. Gunman One knocked her to the ground. The other men cut the seat belts holding the kids, took them from the car in their car seats, grabbing their tiny backpacks at the last minute.

How could men in ski masks be assaulting her in broad daylight and no one else see them?

"Please take me. I won't give you any trouble. I swear I won't. I...I can look after Jackson. Make sure he doesn't go into shock."

Gunman One pulled her hands. "You won't do, sister. It's gotta be somebody he loves."

"Let him have crackers. Okay? He has to eat every three or four hours. Something," she pleaded. "Sage, watch your brother!"

When this had all started, Tracey hadn't paid attention to what the man coming to her window had looked like. An average guy that she couldn't swear was youngish or even in his thirties. They were all decked out in college gear. She searched this man's eyes that were bright and excited behind the green ski mask, memorizing everything about their brown darkness.

The tiny scar woven into his right eyebrow would be his downfall. He raised the butt of the gun in the air. She closed her eyes, anticipating the blow. The impact hurt, stunning her. Vision blurred, she watched them carry the twins, running to the back of the moving van. Her legs collapsed from the pain, and she hit the concrete without warning.

I'm so sorry, Josh.

Chapter Two

How were you supposed to tell someone you'd allowed their kids to be kidnapped? Tracey would have a doctorate in nutrition soon, but none of the courses she'd taken prepared her to face Josh. Or the future.

When someone found Tracey unconscious on the sidewalk and the paramedics revived her, she'd cried out his name. She could never articulate why she was calling to him. Once fully awake and by the time anyone would listen, the twins had been missing for almost an hour. Tracey hadn't been able to explain to Josh what had happened. The police did that.

"He's going to hate me," she mumbled.

"I don't think he will. I've dealt with a lot of kidnappings. This isn't your fault. Major Parker will realize that faster than most." Special Agent George Lanning had answered her with an intelligent response.

The problem was...

"Intelligence has nothing to do with emotional, gut-wrenching pain. I lost his kids. He'll never trust me again and I don't blame him."

After she awoke in the hospital, she'd only been allowed to talk with one police officer, her nurse and a doctor. The door had been left open a couple of inches. She'd recognized rangers passing by, even heard them asking about her. But the officer had refused her any visitors. At least until this FBI agent showed up.

Two hours later she was sitting in a car on her way to the Parker home to face Josh for the first time. Where else was she supposed to go? She'd refused to return to her apartment as they'd suggested. "How bad is my face?"

"As in? What context do you mean?"

She flipped down the passenger mirror to see for herself. "Well, I don't think makeup—even if I had any—would help this." She gently touched her cheekbone that felt ten times bigger than it should. "I don't want to look like…"

"Tracey. Four men yanked you from a car and hit you so hard they gave you a concussion. They kidnapped Jackson and Sage. No matter what you think you could have done differently, those men would still have the Parker twins."

She wiped another tear falling down her cheek. Agent Lanning might be correct. But nothing anyone said would ever make her feel okay about what had happened.

Nothing.

The road to the house was lined with extra cars and the yard—where they needed to park—filled with men standing around. The police escort in front of them flipped on the squad car lights with a siren burst to get people out of the way. Tracey covered her ears.

Everything hurt. Her head pounded in spite of the pain medication the doctor had given her. But she was prepared to jump out of the car as soon as it slowed down. First she needed to beg for Josh's forgiveness. And then find out what the authorities had discovered.

"You really took a wallop," he said. "You should probably get some rest as soon as possible."

She had rested at the hospital, where so much had been thrown at her. Part of the argument for her going home was to sleep and meet with a forensic artist as soon as one arrived. She'd refused, telling Agent Lanning it was useless to draw a face hidden with a ski mask. Then they'd finally agreed to take her directly to Josh.

The sea of people parted and the agent parked next to cars nearer to the front porch. She didn't wait for the engine to stop running. She jumped out, needing to explain while she still had the courage.

Moving quickly across the fading grass of the lawn, she slowed as friends stared at her running inside. She completely froze in the entryway, looking for the straight dark hair that should have towered over most of the heads in the living room. But Josh wasn't towering anywhere. She pushed forward and someone grabbed her arm. A ranger waved him off.

Everyone directly involved in Josh's life knew who she was. The ranger who had spotted her was Bryce Johnson. He put his hand at her back and pushed the crowd of men out of her way.

"You doing okay?" he asked, guiding her through probably every ranger who worked in or near Waco. "Need anything? Maybe some water?"

She nodded. There was already a knot in her throat preventing her from speaking. She'd assumed a lot of people would be here, but why so many? "Why aren't you guys out looking for the twins?"

Everyone turned their attention to a man near the window seat. But she focused on the twins' dad. Josh looked the way he did the day Gwen had died. From day one, neither of Josh or Gwen had felt like employers. They were her friends. She wanted to be there for him again, but didn't know if he'd let her. He glanced at her, and then covered his eyes as though he were afraid to look at her.

The guy in the suit near the window jerked his head to the side and they left. All of them. Except for a woman and Josh, both seated at the opposite end of the breakfast table. They were joined by Agent Lanning, who pulled out a chair and gestured for Tracey to sit.

It was a typical waiting-on-a-ransom-demand scene from a movie. The three professionals looked the parts of FBI agents. The woman sat at something electronic that looked as if it monitored phone calls. Agent Lanning moved to the back door and turned politely to face the window. The other man, who they both seemed to defer to, uncrossed his arms and tapped Josh on the shoulder.

Josh's head was bent, almost protected between his arms resting on the table. He hadn't acknowledged the fact that nearly everyone had left. He hadn't acknowledged anything.

"I don't know what to say. I'm sorry doesn't seem like enough," she began.

Josh's head jerked up along with the rest of him as he stood, tipping the chair backward to the floor. She winced at the noise. She assumed he'd be disappointed and furious and might even scream at her to get out. But feeling it, seeing it, experiencing the paralyzing fear that they might not get the kids back…

"This might sound stupid, but we need to verify that Jackson was wearing his insulin pump," he whispered without a note of anger.

"Yes. I checked it when I picked him up."

"Thank God. I knew you would. You always do."

The woman opened her mouth but the agent at the window raised a finger. She immediately smashed her lips together instead. Josh covered his face with his hands again. What had she expected? That he'd be—*oh, everything's going to be okay, Tracey. Don't worry about it Tracey. We'll find them together, Tracey.*

"Has anyone seen anything? Said anything?" she asked no one in particular.

"Let's step into the bedroom, Miss Cassidy." The agent by the window took a step toward her.

"She stays," Josh ordered, holding up a hand to halt him. "I want to hear everything firsthand. Same for anything you have to say to me. She can hear it, so she stays."

"All right. I'm Special Agent in Charge Leo McCaffrey and this is Agent Kendall Barlow. No, the kidnappers haven't called. There's been no ransom demand." He pointed to the woman at the table and crossed his arms. "Have you remembered anything else that might help?"

"Not really. A van was broken down. Two men came to my car to help me back up. It seems like one purposely let me reverse into the rental van. Then one came to the passenger window and tapped. I thought they needed my insurance or license or something. They looked like college students until they pulled the masks over their faces. I have to admit that I didn't pay any attention to their faces when they were uncovered." Tracey latched her fingers around the edge of the kitchen chair, hoping she wouldn't fall off as the world spun a little on its side.

"You didn't think that was unusual?" the woman asked.

"Not really. Students walk a lot around here. That part of Waco isn't far from downtown."

It was weird what she noticed about Agent McCaffrey. Average height, but nice looking. His short hair had a dent around the middle like Josh's did when he wore his Stetson. Or after an afternoon with his ball cap on. She glanced at his feet. Sure enough, he wore a pair of nice dress boots. And then she remembered the men abducting her had worn work boots.

"Wait. The men who got out of the moving truck. They both wore an older Baylor shirt from about five years ago. And they all wore the same type of work boots. I could almost swear that they were new and the same brand. The man who...who pulled me from the car..." Everyone looked at her, waiting. "He had dark brown eyes and thick eyebrows. Not thick enough to hide a scar across the right one."

"That's good, Miss Cassidy. Anytime something comes to you, just make sure to tell Agent Lanning. Anything special about the others?"

"I wasn't close to the other two. It all happened so fast that I didn't know what to do." She choked on the last word. She hadn't known. Still didn't.

"When you were questioned at the hospital, you had a hard time remembering the small details, but they'll probably come back." The woman spoke again, pushing a pad toward the center of the table. "You should keep a notebook handy."

"I...uh...couldn't get to the hospital," Josh said loudly. He swallowed hard and shook his head, looking a little lost.

Tracey had never seen that look on his face before. "I didn't expect you to."

"It's just... I haven't been there since Gwen..." Josh

looked at her asking her to understand without making him say the words. "I guess I had to have been there once with Jackson." He pushed his hand through his short hair. "But I can't remember when for some reason."

"I know. It's okay," she whispered, wanting to reach out and grab his hand. "You needed to be here."

Major Parker was her employer, but she couldn't stand it. Someone needed to help him. To be on his side like no other person would be. This time she shoved back from the table and her chair was the one that hit the floor. She pushed past Agent McCaffrey and covered Josh with her arms. He buried his face against her, wrapping his arms around her waist as if she were the only thing keeping him from falling off a cliff.

Until two weeks ago, they hadn't hugged since Gwen had died. Had rarely touched each other except for an accidental brush when handing the kids to each other. Then there'd been that kiss.

An unexpected kiss after an impromptu surprise birthday party with several of his friends. A kiss that had thrown her into so many loop-de-loops, she'd been dizzy for days. But it must have thrown Josh for a loop he didn't want. He hadn't spoken to her except in passing. Which was the reason she'd accepted the out-of-state position.

She held him, feeling the rapid beating of his heart through the hospital scrubs they'd given her. They had so much to face and right now he needed to be comforted as much as she did.

Someone at the hospital had said she was just the nanny. She didn't feel like *just* the hired help. She'd avoided that particular title and thought it demeaning when Josh's friends referred to her that way. Months when the rent was hard to come by, her friends asked her why she didn't move in to take care of the twins.

At first it had been because she thought it was a temporary job. Eventually Josh would hire a real nanny. Then she'd been certain Josh would eventually date and remarry, so she hadn't wanted to complicate the situation. And this past year it had been because she was falling in love with him.

Now the word *nanny* didn't seem complex enough for their situation. She'd been a part of the twins' lives from infancy. She'd been told to go home and stay there with a protection detail so she could be easily reached if needed. She was *just* the nanny.

Just the person who provided day care—and any other time of the day care when Josh was on a case. But his lost look was the reason she hadn't obeyed the order.

Technically, Tracey knew she *was* just the nanny. Yet, her heart had been ripped from her body—twice. Once for each child.

She held Josh tight until Agent McCaffrey cleared his throat. She sat in the chair next to Josh. Bryce brought the bottle of water he'd offered when she first arrived and dropped back to the living room doorway.

"Is this a vendetta or revenge for one of the men you've put away?" Tracey asked Josh, who finally looked her in the eyes. "I tried to convince them to take me instead. They said it needed to be someone you loved."

Chapter Three

Someone you loved...

Did she know? Josh searched her face, seeing nothing but concern for his kids. It was on the tip of his tongue to tell her they would have gotten it right if she'd been taken.

That sounds ridiculous.

He didn't want her abducted any more than he wanted the twins to be gone. He reached out, touching her swollen cheek.

"They hurt you." Stupid statement. It was obvious, but he didn't know what else to say. "Of course they did. They took you to the hospital."

He noticed what she was wearing, the streak of blood still on her neck, the bandage at her hairline. Hospital scrubs because her clothes had been ruined.

Time to shed the shaking figure of a lost father. Tenoreno had hit his family—the only place he considered himself vulnerable. But he was stronger than this. He needed to show everyone—including himself. Gathering some courage, he straightened his backbone and placed both palms flat on the table to keep himself there.

He knew what McCaffrey was thinking. The agent had repeated his questions about Tracey's possible motives more than once. Agent Kendall Barlow had been ordered to run a thorough background check on "the nanny." If Tracey heard them call her that she'd let them know she was a child care provider and personal nutritionist.

Definitely not the nanny.

The FBI might have doubts about Tracey—he didn't. First and foremost, she had no motive. They might need to rule her out as a suspect. No one in the room had mentioned Tenoreno by name. But Josh knew who was responsible.

Drawing air deep into his lungs, he readied himself to get started. Ready to fight Tenoreno or whoever he'd hired to take his kids.

"The agents need to know how long Jackson's insulin will be okay. Can you give them more details?" All the extra chatter around him died. He took Tracey's hand in his. "I took a guess, but you know a lot more about it than I do. These guys need an accurate estimate. I couldn't think straight earlier."

"It depends." She drew in a deep breath and blew it out, puffing her cheeks. "There are stress factors I can't estimate. A lot will be determined by what they give the twins to eat, of course. The cartridge can last three days, but he might be in trouble for numerous reasons. They could give him the wrong food or the tube might get clogged. The battery should be fine."

"Hear that everybody? My son has forty-eight hours that we can count on. Seventy-two before he slips into a diabetic coma. Why are you still here?" He used his I'm-the-ranger-in-charge voice.

It worked. All the rangers, cops and friends left the house.

"I'm more worried that Sage might try to imitate

what I do with the bolus when he eats. She knows not to touch it. But she also knows that when Jackson eats, I calculate how much extra insulin to give him. She's a little mother hen and might try since I'm not there."

"What's a bolus?" George Lanning asked.

"An extra shot of insulin from his pump. You calculate, it injects." The female agent shrugged. "I read and prepare for my cases."

Josh hated diabetes.

Bryce stayed by the kitchen door. He'd driven Josh and wouldn't leave until he had confirmation of orders that the two of them had already discussed. Unofficial orders when no one had been listening. Ranger headquarters had someone on the way to relieve him as Company F commander. Whoever was now in charge would make certain every rule was followed to the letter and that personnel kept their actions impeccable.

"Everyone is working off the assumption that the Tenoreno family is behind this. Right?" he asked McCaffrey, finally stating what everyone thought.

The FBI agents' reactions were about what he expected. No one would confirm. They zipped their lips tight and avoided eye contact. But their actions were all the confirmation he needed.

The Mafia family connection was the reason the FBI had been called as soon as Josh had received the news. He'd rather have his Company in charge, but the conflict of interest was too great.

Bryce stood in the doorway and shook his head, warning him not to push the issue. They'd talked through the short list of pros and cons about confronting anyone called in to handle the kidnapping.

The more they forced the issue, the less likely the FBI would be inclined to share information. It could all blow up in his face. But it was like a big bright red button with a flashing neon sign that said Do Not Push.

The longer the agents avoided answering, the brighter the button blinked, tempting him to hit it.

"The Tenoreno family?"

Tracey was the only one left who didn't know who they were. She needed to know what faced them because she was certain to be used by the Mafia-like family. No one wanted to explain so it was up to him to bring her up to speed.

Two hours and thirty-eight minutes after Tracey was found unconscious on a sidewalk, his phone rang. Brooks & Dunn's "Put a Girl in It" blasted through the kitchen.

"That's my ringtone for Tracey. They're using her phone. It's the kidnappers."

EVERYONE STARED AT the phone. Only one person moved. Agent Barlow pulled a headset onto her ears, clicked or pushed buttons, then pointed to Agent McCaffrey. It really was like being a part of a scripted movie. Tracey could only watch.

"You know what to do, Josh. Try to keep them on the line as long as possible," Agent McCaffrey said.

Tracey cupped her hands over her mouth to stop the words she wanted to scream. They would only antagonize the kidnappers and would probably get her dragged from the room. She needed to hear what those masked men were about to say.

Agent Barlow clicked on Josh's cell.

"This is Parker." Josh's fingers curled into fists.

"You won't hear from us again as long as you're working with the FBI." The line went dead.

"No. Wait!" Josh hammered his hand against the

wood tabletop. But his face told her he knew it was no use.

"What just happened? Shouldn't they let us know how to get in touch with them?" Tracey looked around the room, wanting answers. What did this mean? "You do have a plan, right?"

Agent McCaffrey clasped Josh's shoulder, then patted it—while staring into Tracey's eyes. "That's what we expected."

Everyone's stare turned to Agent Barlow, who shook her head. "Nothing. We've been monitoring for Miss Cassidy's phone, they fired it up, made the call and probably pulled the battery again."

"So we're back to square one." Agent Lanning tapped on the window, silently bringing attention to the suits monitoring the outside of the house.

"We have instructions." Josh stared at the only other ranger left in the house—Bryce.

Tracey was confused. It was as if they were speaking in some sort of code. Or maybe they were stating something obvious and the concussion was keeping her from recognizing it. The others shook their heads.

"You don't want to do that, Josh." Agent McCaffrey kept his cool. He clearly didn't want whatever Josh had just silently communicated to Bryce. "This case is going to be difficult—"

"It's not a case. They're my kids." Josh hit his chest with his fist. "Mine."

"You need our resources." Barlow dropped the headphones on the table.

"I *need* you to leave. I've told you that from the beginning." Josh stood. Calmly this time, without tipping the chair to the floor. "I've played along for the past couple of hours hoping it's not what we thought, but it is. These guys aren't going to play games. They either get what they want or they kill—"

"You can't do this," Barlow said.

The agent seemed a little dramatic, but what did Tracey know?

"Yes, I can. It's my right to refuse your help." Josh gestured for Tracey to lead the way to the back staircase.

"Look…" Agent McCaffrey lowered his voice. "We'll admit that the kidnapping involves Tenoreno. We assume these men are going to ask you to do something illegal. You're better off if we stay."

"I haven't done anything illegal. You need to go." Josh took the Texas Ranger Star he was so proud of and dropped it in the agent's open palm. "Bryce. You know what to do."

Josh caught Tracey under her elbow and led her up the staircase. They went to the kids' bedroom, where he shut the door.

"What is Bryce going to do?"

"First thing is to get my badge back. I shouldn't have given it to McCaffrey. But the agent wanted it for show in case the kidnappers are watching. I'll surrender it to the new Company commander if they ask me to resign, not before. Then he'll get everyone out of the house. Before the FBI arrived, we assumed we knew who was behind the kidnapping. There's really no other motive. It's not like I have a ton of money to pay a ransom."

Tracey winced, but Josh was looking out the window and couldn't have seen. The twins' kidnapping didn't have anything to do with her. The man said it has to be someone he loves. *He meant someone Josh loves. Right?*

"What if…" She hesitated to ask, to broach the subject that this entire incident might be her fault. She cleared her throat. "What are you going to do without the FBI's help?"

"Get things done. Bryce has already arranged for friends in the Waco PD to watch the agents who will be watching us." He quirked a brow at his cleverness, sitting on the footstool between the twin beds.

His wife's parents had chosen that stool to match a rocker Gwen had never gotten to hold her children in. She'd been too weak. It's where Josh refused to sit. The stool was as close as he'd get. The chair was where Tracey had rocked the babies to sleep.

"Have you told Gwen's parents?"

"There's nothing they could do. McCaffrey thinks it's better to wait."

"The FBI will be following us when we leave the house." He stood again, wiping his palms on his jeans. "They'll wait for me to issue an order to my men. I'd be breaking the law since I've been asked to step away from my command. Then they'll swoop back in like vultures and take control of things."

"Will you?"

"What? Leave? Don't worry." He straightened books on the shelf. "When I do, I'll make sure someone's here with you. Bryce will be close. I won't leave you alone."

"No. That's not what I'm talking about. Will you break the law?"

He gawked at her with a blank look of incredulousness. Either surprised that she'd asked, insulting his ranger integrity. Or surprised that she questioned...

"What are you willing to do to save Jackson and Sage?" She tried not to move the rocker. She was serious and needed to know how far he'd go. "For the record, I'm willing to do anything. And I mean anything, including breaking the law."

Did he look a little insulted as he bent and picked up Jackson's pj's from the floor? Well, she didn't care. It was something she needed to hear him say out loud.

"Don't look so surprised. I've heard about the integrity of the Texas Rangers since the first day I met you. How could I not after listening to the countless kitchen table conversations on the subject? Not to mention this past year when three of your company men might have been straddling the integrity fence, but managed to come out squeaky clean heroes."

"You act like having integrity is a bad thing." He clutched the pajamas and moved to the window instead of placing them back in the dresser.

"Not at all." She stood and joined him, wishing she could blink and make this all go away.

All she could do was wrap her palms around his upper arm, offering the comfort of a friend. Even though they'd been raising his children together for four years, she couldn't make the decisions he'd soon be faced with.

"Are you going to tell me about the Tenoreno family? At least more than what I've heard about them in the news? Are you in charge of the case?"

Josh didn't shrug her away. They stood shoulder to shoulder at the pastel curtains sprinkled with baby farm animals. He stared at something in the far distance past the lake. Tracey just stared at him.

"In charge of the case? No. Company F has prepared Paul Tenoreno's transportation route from Huntsville to Austin. I finalized the details this morning. Now that this…the kidnapping, your injuries…" He paused and took a couple of shallow breaths. "Tenoreno's transport to trial has to be what this is all about. Thing is, state authorities are sure to change everything. It's why they brought the FBI onto the case so quickly."

"Is Tenoreno mixed up in the Mafia like the news insinuates?"

"Tenoreno *is* the Mafia in Texas."

A chill scurried up her spine. The words seemed final somehow. As if Josh had accepted something was about to happen and there was no going back. He hadn't answered her question about how far he'd go. But he wouldn't let the Mafia take his kids. He just wouldn't.

"You need to make me a promise, Tracey."

"Anything."

He removed her hands and crossed his arms over his chest, tilting his head to stare at the top of hers because he was frightened to meet her hazel eyes. Frightened of the desperation she might see in his face.

"Hear me out before you give me what for. I made you the guardian of the twins last year."

"Without asking me?"

"Yeah. I was afraid you'd say no." Josh shrugged and lifted the corner of his mouth in a little smile.

It was Tracey's turn to look incredulous. "Seriously? When have I ever told you that I wouldn't do something for those kids?"

He nodded, agreeing. "I need you to promise that no matter what happens to me…"

"I promise, but nothing's going to happen to you."

Of course, she didn't know that. This afternoon when she'd headed to the day care to pick up the twins, she wouldn't have believed anything could have happened to any of them. It has been an ordinary day. She'd finally made up her mind to talk with Josh about finding a permanent nanny to take her place.

"You asked what I was willing to do. They're my

kids, Tracey. I'll do anything for them, including prison time." Josh still had the pj's wrapped in his hand. "Believe me, that's not my intention, but you have to know it's a possibility."

Was he aware that she was willing to join him? She meant what she'd said about doing anything for Jackson and Sage. And if that meant *she* was the one who went to jail—so be it. And if it came down to it, she'd do anything to keep them with their father.

"Just tell me what to do, Josh."

"Nothing. If Tenoreno's people contact you, tell me. You can't be involved in this. It has to be me." He gripped her shoulders and then framed her cheeks. One of his thumbs skated across the bruised area and settled at her temple. "You got that? *I'm* the one who's going to rescue my kids and pay the consequences."

She believed him. She had to. But she couldn't promise to stay out of his way. She might have the answer. What if money could solve their problem? Even if it wouldn't, now wasn't the time to tell him she'd never let him be separated from the twins.

Chapter Four

Josh pulled Tracey to his chest, wrapping his arms around her, keeping someone he cared about safe. He stared at the green pajamas decorated with pictures of yellow trucks—dump trucks, earthmovers, cranes and he didn't know what else. He used to know.

How long had it been since he'd played in the sand-box with the kids? Since he'd been there for dinner and their bath time?

Mixed feelings fired through his brain. He couldn't start down the regret road. He needed to concentrate on the twins' safety. The overpowering urge to protect Tracey wasn't just because she was an unofficial member of the family.

Tenoreno had hired someone to assault her and steal his children. Her cuts and bruises—dammit, he should have been there to protect her. To protect all of them.

"There has to be something we can do to make this go faster." She pressed her face against his chest and cried.

It was the first time to cry since she'd entered the house today. He fought the urge to join her, but once a day was his limit. If he broke down again, he wouldn't be able to function. Or act like the guy who might know what he was doing.

A knock at the door broke them apart. Tracey went to the corner table and pulled a couple of Kleenex from the box.

"Yeah?" It could only be one of two people on the other side. Bryce or Agent McCaffrey.

"You fill her in yet?" McCaffrey stepped inside, closing the door behind him.

Tracey looked up after politely blowing her nose; a questioning look crinkled her forehead.

"We were just getting there."

"Here's the phone you can use to contact us. We won't be far away."

"But far enough no one's going to notice." Josh took the phone and slid it into his back pocket.

"Anyone following you will see the obvious cars. They'll lose you after a couple of miles, but George and I will be there."

"Josh?" Tracey said his name with all the confusion she should be experiencing. After all, he'd just demanded the FBI and police leave him alone, get out of his house and off the case.

"It's okay, Tracey. All part of the plan. We need the kidnappers to think I'm in this on my own. No help from anyone. Hopefully that'll limit what they ask me to do."

When he left the house he'd have a line of cars following and hoped it didn't look like a convoy. A bad feeling smothered any comfort he had that law enforcement would be close by.

"So everything you just said—"

"Was the truth. Every word." He shot her a look asking her to keep that info to herself.

He knew that stubborn look, the compressed lips, the crossed arms. It would soon be followed by a long exhale after holding her breath. Sometimes he wanted to squeeze the air from her lungs because she held on to it so long. Each time he knew she wasn't just controlling her breathing. She was also controlling her tongue because she disagreed with what he was saying or doing.

Mainly about the kids.

Lately, it had been about how often he worked late or how he had avoided necessary conversations. Like the one congratulating her on finishing her thesis. Yeah, he'd avoided that because it would open the door to her resignation. What they needed to talk about was serious. She'd most likely accepted a position somewhere—other than Waco. If he could, he'd also like to avoid a conversation about what happened two weeks ago when they'd kissed.

This time, he could see that she didn't believe the lines he was spouting to the FBI. He just hoped that Special Agent McCaffrey couldn't read her like a book, too. Then he might suspect Josh had his own agenda.

"I don't think they'll wait very long to make contact after I leave." The agent unbuttoned his jacket and stuck his hands in his pockets. "My belief is that they knew about Jackson's diabetes and believe it will scare you into following their orders faster. If they didn't, they've seen the pump by now and are scared something might happen to him. Either way, I don't think they're really out to hurt the kids."

Agent McCaffrey stood straight—without emotion—in his official suit and tie. Just how official—they'd find out if he kept their deal to let Josh work the case from the inside.

"But you can't be sure of that," Tracey said. "How can anyone predict what will happen."

Tracey was right about part of Josh's inner core. He

was a Texas Ranger through and through. He'd try it the legal way. But if that didn't work, they'd see a part of him he rarely drew upon.

"George said you held up at the hospital exceptionally well, Miss Cassidy."

McCaffrey had a complimentary approach, where George looked like a laid-back lanky cowboy leaning on a fence post. Josh had met George several times on cases. He trusted him. George had given his word that McCaffrey would be on board. But Tracey didn't know any of that history. She had no reason to trust any of them.

"Don't I get a phone for you to keep track of my location?" Tracey asked.

"Actually, yes." McCaffrey handed her an identical cheap phone to what they'd given him. "By accepting this, you're allowing us to monitor it."

The man just didn't have the most winning personality. Josh saw the indignation building within Tracey and couldn't stop her.

"Were you really going to wait for my permission? That seems rather silly to ask. Just do it." Her words seemed more like a dare. She was ready to go toe to toe with someone.

"Tracey. That's not the way things are." Standing up for the FBI wasn't his best choice at this precise moment. Tracey looked like she needed to vent.

"Have you ruled me out as a suspect?" she asked.

Why was she holding her breath this time? Did she have something to hide? Josh opened his mouth to reason with her, but McCaffrey waved him off.

"I have a lot of experience with kidnappings, Tracey. I imagine you're familiar with the statistics that most children are abducted by someone in their immediate family or life. My people ran our standard background check on you first thing. We would have been reckless not to." He leaned against the doorjamb not seeming rushed for time or bothered by her hostility. "A reference phone call cleared you."

Tracey stiffened. She drew her arms close across her chest, hugging herself, rubbing her biceps like she was cold. Her hand slipped higher, one finger covering her lips, then her eyes darted toward the window. She was hiding something and McCaffrey had just threatened to expose whatever it was.

"Tracey, what's going on?"

"We're good, Josh." The agent looked at Tracey.

She nodded her head. "I don't know why I said anything. I was never going to keep you from tracking this phone." Tracey sank to the footstool. "I already told you I'd cooperate and do anything for Jackson and Sage."

The special agent in charge crossed the room and patted Tracey's shoulder. He'd done the same thing to Josh earlier, but it didn't seem to ease Tracey. There was nothing insincere in his gesture. But it seemed a more calculated action, as though McCaffrey knew it was effective. Not because it was real comfort.

Josh wanted to throw the agent out of his kids' room and be done with the FBI. "Do you need anything else?" he asked instead.

"I can't help you if you keep me out of the loop, Josh." McCaffrey quirked an eyebrow at Josh's lack of a reaction. "You've got to work with my people to get the children back. We stick with the plan."

"That's all nice and reasonable, but we both know that there's nothing logical about a kidnapping. You can never predict what's going to happen."

"The quicker you pick up that phone and let us know what they want the better."

"The quicker you clear out of here, the faster they'll contact us." Josh's hands were tied. He had to work with the FBI, use their resources, find the kidnappers. Or at least act like he was being cooperative. He sighed in relief when the agent left and softly closed the door behind him.

What the hell was wrong with him?

His twins had been kidnapped. It was natural to want to bash some heads together. But for a split second there, he'd wanted to just do whatever Tenoreno's men wanted and hold his kids again.

Tracey was visibly shaken by whatever McCaffrey's team had uncovered. His background check five years ago when he'd hired her hadn't uncovered it. And in the time that she'd been around his family, she'd never shared it. He had his own five years of character reference. No one else's mattered.

"I don't know what that was about." He jerked his thumb toward the closed door. *Should he ask?* "Right now I don't care."

"I swear I was never… It's just something I keep private. But I can fill you in. I mean, unless it's going to distract you. This shouldn't be about me."

"Will it make a difference to what's going to happen?" Sure, he was curious, but what if she was right and it did distract him? The FBI didn't think it was relevant. He could wait until his family was back where they belonged. "You know, we have more important things to worry about, so save it."

"Okay." Tracey sat straight, ready to get started. "So how is this going to work? Do you think the kidnappers will use my phone to call yours again? Wait!" She popped to her feet. "We don't have your phone. It's downstairs."

Josh blocked her with an outstretched arm. "If it rings, Bryce will let us know. He'll come up here before he leaves and that won't be until everyone else is out of the house."

They stared a second or two at each other. He wanted to know what she was hiding from him. She bit her lip, held her breath, and then couldn't look him in the eyes.

"Tracey, we have to trust each other. If you don't want to go through with this…"

"Of course I want to help. It's my fault they're missing. I don't know how you're being kind to me at all or even staying alone in the same room. I'm not sure I could do it."

"I don't blame you for what's happened. How can I?" He kept a hand on her shoulder. She didn't fight to get away. "I'm beating myself up that I didn't put a security detail on all of you. If anyone's to blame, it's me. Tenoreno has come after three of my men and their families. Why did I think you or the kids weren't vulnerable?"

"We have to stop blaming ourselves," she said softly. "If you have a plan, now might be the time to share it with me."

"It's not so much a plan as backup. What I said before McCaffrey came in, I meant it. But if I can keep the FBI on my side…we're all better off."

A gentle knock stopped the conversation again. "They've cleared out, Major. I've secured all the windows and doors. Here's your phone." Ranger Johnson said through the door.

Josh turned the knob and stuck out his hand. "Thanks, Bryce. You guys know what to do. My temporary replacement's going to have a tough time. The other men are going to resent that he's there. They're also going to want to help with the kidnapping. You've got to make the men understand that none of you can get involved and that those orders come from me."

"Good luck. And sir—" Bryce shook his hand, clasping his left on top of it "—let's make sure it's just a temporary replacement. You know we're all here when you need us."

"We appreciate that."

"I think this is one time that One Riot, One Ranger shouldn't apply. I'll take care of things." Bryce walked downstairs.

Tracey gently pushed past Josh, nudging herself into the hall. "I can't stay in their room any longer. And I really think I need a drink."

Josh followed her. "But you don't drink. And probably shouldn't, with a concussion."

"Don't you have some Wild Turkey or Jim Beam? Something's on top of the refrigerator, right? It's the perfect time to start."

"Yeah, but you might not want to start with that." How did she know where he kept his only bottle of whiskey?

"Actually, Josh, I went to college. Just because you've never seen me drink doesn't mean it's never happened. A shot of whiskey isn't going to impair my judgment."

She was in the kitchen, pulling a chair over to reach the high cabinet before he could think twice about helping or stopping. He sort of stared while she pulled two highball glasses reserved for poker night that had been collecting dust awhile. A finger's width—his, not her tiny fingers—was in the glass and she frowned before sliding it toward him across the breakfast bar.

"Drink up. You need it worse than I do."

He stared at it. And at her.

She suddenly didn't look like a college student. He noticed the little laugh lines at the corner of her eyes and how deep a green they were. It took him all this time to realize she was wearing a Waco Fire Department T-shirt under the baggy scrub top. Something he'd never seen her wear before.

She threw the whiskey back and poured herself another. "Am I drinking alone?"

He swirled the liquid, took a whiff. That was enough for him. Clearheaded. Ready to get on the road. That's what he needed more than the sting and momentary warmth the shot would provide.

Tracey threw the second shot back, closing her eyes and letting the glass tip on its side. Her eyes popped open as if she'd been startled. Then they dropped to the phone that was resting next to his hand, vibrating.

Her hand covered the cell.

His hand covered hers.

"Wait. Three rings. It'll allow the FBI time to get their game face on."

Ring three he uncovered her hand and slid through the password, then pushed Speaker.

"Time for round one, Ranger Parker. You get a new phone from a store in Richland Mall. We'll contact you there in half an hour. Bring the woman."

The line disconnected.

"Do they really think that no one is listening to those instructions he just gave us?" Tracey asked.

"We follow everything he says. He'll try to get us clear of everyone. We get the phone, but the next time he makes contact—before we do anything else—we get proof of life." Josh dropped the phone in his shirt pocket realizing that the kidnappers had just made Tracey a vital part of their plan. "I hoped they'd leave you out of this. We just need to know both kids are okay before I argue to take you out of the equation."

"Of course." She hurried around the end of the breakfast bar, grabbing the counter as she passed.

"You look a little wobbly. You up for this?"

"You probably should have stopped me from drinking alcohol when I have a head injury and they gave me pain meds." Tracey touched her swollen cheek and the side of her head, then winced.

Josh held up a finger, delaying their departure. He walked around her and pulled an ice pack from the freezer, tossing her an emergency compress. "This should help a little." Then he pulled insulin cartridges from the fridge, stuffing them inside Jackson's travel and emergency supplies bag.

Instead of her cheekbone, Tracey dropped the cold compress on her forehead and slid it over her eyes. "You're right." She took off to the front door. "You should definitely drive."

Proof of life. That's what they needed. He looked around his home. Different from the madhouse an hour ago. Different because the housekeeper had come by this morning. Different because Gwen was no longer a part of it.

Different because Tracey was.

Chapter Five

Josh wandered through Richland Mall with the fingers of one hand interlocked with Tracey's. With the other he held the new phone securely in its sack. No one had the number so the kidnappers couldn't use it for a conversation. He expected someone to bump into him. Or drop a note. Maybe catch their line of sight, giving them an envelope.

"Hell, I don't know what they plan on doing. The dang thing isn't even charged."

"You've said that a couple of times now," Tracey acknowledged. "My head is absolutely killing me and I'm starting to see two of everything. Can we get a bottle of water?"

"Sure."

He kept his eyes open and wouldn't let go of Tracey as he paid for the water at a candy store. She looked like a hospital volunteer in the navy blue scrub top.

"Josh, you are making my hand hurt as much as my head." She tugged a little at his thumb.

"Sorry. I just can't—"

"I know. You're afraid they'll grab me. I get it. But my hand needs circulation. Come on. Let's park it on that bench."

He looked in every direction for something suspicious or a charging station for the phone. Whatever or whoever was coming for them could be any of the people resting on another bench or walking by.

"Here, I'm done. Drink the rest." She capped the bottle and tried to hand it to him.

"No thanks."

"If I drink it, I'll have to leave your side for a few and head into the restroom all alone. I know you don't want that."

"Then throw it away. No one's telling you to drink it." He watched the young man with the baby stroller until he moved in the opposite direction.

"Lighten up, Mack," a voice said directly behind them. "Don't turn around."

Tracey stiffened next to him, the bottle of water hitting the floor. A clear indication that she recognized the voice. The guy behind him tapped on Josh's shoulder with a phone.

"Pass me the one you just bought."

Josh forced himself not to look at the man. No mirrored surfaces were nearby. The guy even covered the phone before it got close enough to see his face in the black reflection of the screen.

"That's good, Major. You're doing good. Now, I know you're concerned about your kids. You can see them when you play the video in about twenty seconds. Just let me get through this service hallway. Yeah, you've got a choice—let me go or follow and lose any chance of ever seeing your brats." The kidnapper tapped the top of Josh's head. "Count to twenty. Talk to ya soon."

Josh had his hands ready to push up from the bench and tackle the guy to the ground.

"No." Tracey pulled him back to the bench. "You

heard him. He means it. We have to stay here and let him walk away. You promised to do whatever it took. Remember? So please just turn the phone on and get their instructions."

He listened to Tracey and stayed put. The phone had been handed to them with gloves. Most likely no prints, so he turned it on. He clicked through the menu, finding the gallery.

There were several pictures of the twins playing in a room—sort of like a day care crowded with toys. The video shattered his already-broken heart. Sage was crying. Jackson was "vroom vrooming" a car across his leg and through the air.

A voice off camera—the same as behind them—told them to say hi to their daddy.

"I want to go home." Sage threw a plush toy toward the person holding the phone. "Is Trace Trace picking us up?"

Tracey covered her mouth, holding her breath again.

"Can you remember what you're supposed to say? You can go home after you tell your daddy," the kidnapper lied.

The twins nodded their heads, tucking their chins to their chests and sticking out their bottom lips. They might be fraternal, but they did almost everything together.

"Daddy, Mack says to go to…I don't remember." Jackson turned to his sister, scratching his head with the truck. "Do you remember?"

"Why can't you tell him?" Sage pouted.

"Come on, it has a giant bull." Another voice piped in.

"We've been there, Jacks. It's got that big bridge, 'member?" Sage poked him.

"Can you come there and pick us up, Daddy?" Jackson cried.

"Maybe Trace Trace can?" Sage's tears ran full stream down her cheeks.

"You have twenty minutes to be waiting in the middle of the bridge. Both of you. No cops," a voice said on top of the twins cries.

The video ended. All Josh wanted was to rush to the Chisholm Trail Bridge and pick them up. But they wouldn't be there. Instructions would be there. The guy who'd dropped the phone off would be watching them to make certain they weren't followed.

"Let's go." He wrapped his hand around Tracey's. It killed him to hear his kids like that.

"Are they going to keep us running from one spot to another? What's the point of that? And why have us buy a new phone only to replace it with this one?"

While they were leaving the mall in a hurry would be the ideal time for a kidnapper to try to grab one or both of them. He locked their fingers and tugged Tracey closer to his side.

"Before we get to the car…" He lowered his voice and stopped them behind a pillar at the candy store. He leaned in close to her ear, not wanting to be overheard. "We need to look closely where he touched us. He might have planted a microphone."

He dipped his head and turned around to let Tracey check. She smoothed the cloth of his shirt across his shoulders.

"I don't see anything, Josh." She shook her head and turned for him to do the same.

He pushed his fingers through his short hair. Found nothing. Then ran them through Tracey's short wavy strands and over her tense shoulders.

"If I were them, I'd use this time to plant a listening device. I'd want to know if we were really cooperating or playing along with the Feds."

"Who *are you* playing along with?" She looked and sounded exasperated.

"I'm on team Jackson and Sage. Whoever I have to play along with to get them back home. That's the only thing that's important to me."

"All right. So you think they're planting something in the car?"

"Got to be. Or this phone is already rigged for them to listen. Stand at the back of this store and keep an eye out while I call McCaffrey on his phone." Josh took a last look around the open mall area to see if they were in sight of security cameras or if anyone watched them from the sidelines.

Tracey smothered the kidnapper's phone with the bottom of her shirt. "I hope you know what you're doing."

"So do I." He waited for her to get ten feet away from him then took the FBI-issued phone and dialed the only number logged.

As soon as he was connected he blurted, "They have a new phone listed in my name. Bought it prepaid at a kiosk. No idea what the number is. Handed us another and told us to head to the Brazos Suspension Bridge."

"You can cross that on foot. Right?" McCaffrey was asking someone on his staff. "You know they'll be waiting on the other side."

Tracey kept watch, walking back and forth along the wall. She'd look out the storefront window, then make the horseshoe along the outside walls again to look out the other side.

Josh kept his head and his voice down. "I can't contact you on this again. It'll be in the car."

"We'll have men on the north side of the bridge waiting," McCaffrey stated. "Trust me, Josh."

"For as long as possible." He pocketed the phone, waved to Tracey.

"Josh, the kidnapper called you Mack. I remember that they all called each other Mack."

"It kept them from using their real names. Helped hide their identities." He didn't speak his next thought—hoping that they kept their masks on in front of his kids.

They both walked quickly from the mall toward the car.

"We just used five of our twenty minutes. Aren't you going to call Bryce and let him know where we're headed?"

"No need. If the Rangers are doing their job, they'll already know."

Josh pointed to a moving van that matched the description Tracey had regarding the vehicle blocking the intersection. If law enforcement spotted it, they'd be instructed to watch and not detain.

The truck pulled away from the end of the aisle as soon as they reached the car. He was tempted to use the phone, but he'd just proved to himself that they were being watched. He couldn't risk it.

Josh didn't wait around to spot any other vehicles keeping an eye on them. He didn't care if any of them kept up. "Flip down the visor, Tracey." He turned on the flashing lights and let traffic get out of his way. "We're not going to be late."

Tracey braced herself with a foot on the dashboard. "I'm rich. That's my secret."

He slowed for an intersection and looked at her while

checking for vehicles. She cleared her throat, waiting. Josh drove. If that was all the FBI could dig up on her, how could that be leverage?

The flashing lights on his car made it easy to get to the bridge and park. He left them on when they got out. Tracey reached under the seat and retrieved a second Jackson emergency kit. He snagged the one he'd brought from the house.

Armed with only a phone and his son's emergency kit, they walked quickly across the bridge to wait in the middle of the river.

"Not many people here on a Friday night." Tracey walked to the steel beams and looked through. "I hope they don't make us jump."

"That could be a possibility." One that he hadn't considered.

"I don't swim well. So just push me over the edge."

"You don't have to go." Josh stayed in the middle, his senses heightened from the awareness of how vulnerable they were in this spot. "How's your head?"

"Spinning. You grabbed extra insulin cartridges and needles. That's what I saw, right? I think I should take a couple, too."

It made sense. He opened the kit. She reached for a cartridge and needle. If the kidnappers took only one of them, they'd each have a way to keep Jackson healthy.

TRACEY WAS SCARED. Out-of-her-mind scared. If today hadn't happened, she would have felt safe standing on a suspension bridge above the Brazos River in the early moonlight with Josh.

But today *had* happened and she was scared for them all.

"What kind of a secret is being rich?" Josh walked

a few feet one direction and then back again. "I don't get it. Why is being rich a secret McCaffrey would threaten you with?"

"You really want me to explain right now?"

"You're the one who brought it up." He shrugged, but kept walking. "It'll pass the time."

"My last name isn't Cassidy. I mean, it wasn't. I changed it."

That stopped him. There was a lot of light on the bridge and she could see Josh's confused expression pretty well. He was in jeans and a long-sleeve brick-red shirt that had three buttons at the collar. She'd given it to him on his birthday because she wanted to brighten up his wardrobe. The hat he normally wore was still at home. They'd left without it or it would have been on his head.

"I ran a background check on you. Tracey Cassidy exists."

"It's amazing what you can do when you have money. In fact, I could hire men to help you. My uncle would know the best in the business."

"Let's go back to the part that you aren't who you say you are." The phone in his palm rang. He answered and held it to his ear. "We're here."

Josh looked around the area. His eyes landed on the far side of the bridge, opposite where they'd left the car. Tracey joined him.

"Whatever you want me to do, you don't need my babysitter."

"No, you need me. I can take care of the twins, change Jackson's cartridge." She held up the emergency pack.

"I don't need any extra motivation. Leave her out of—" He pocketed the phone.

"I'm sorry for getting you into this mess." He hugged her to him before they continued across the bridge then on the river walk under the trees. The sidewalk curved and Josh paused, looking for something.

Another couple passed. Josh tugged on Tracey's arm and got her running across the grass toward the road. If the couple were cops, he didn't acknowledge them. Their shoes hit the sidewalk again and a white van pulled up illegally onto the sidewalk next to Martin Luther King Jr. Boulevard.

The door slid open. That's where they needed to go.

The blackness inside the van seemed final. But she could do this. She'd do whatever it took. Whatever they wanted.

Out of the corner of her eye she saw a man approaching. Then another. The more the two men tried to look as if they weren't heading toward them, the more apparent it was that their paths would. Maybe they were the cops that Bryce had arranged to follow them. If they got any closer, the men inside the van would see them, too.

"What are those guys doing?"

Josh looked in their direction, but yelled at her. "Run. I think they're trying to stop us."

"But—"

"Just run."

It wasn't far. Maybe fifty or sixty feet. The men split apart. Josh dropped her hand. She ran. The van slowly moved forward—away from her. One of the men shot at the van. Then she was grabbed from behind and tripped over a tangle of feet. The man latched on to her waist, keeping her next to him.

"Let me go. I have to get— You don't understand what you're doing."

Another shot was fired. This time from the van. The

man's partner fell to the grass. The guy holding her covered her with his body. These men weren't police. The real police raced after the van in an unmarked car, sirens echoing off the buildings across the water.

The man on top of her didn't move and wasn't concerned about his injured partner. She was pounding with her fists on a Kevlar vest trying to get the man off her when a loud crash momentarily replaced the police sirens.

"Oh my God! What have you done?"

Chapter Six

Fire trucks. An ambulance. At least three police cars—maybe more—with strobe lights dancing around in circles. College students edging their way closer in a growing crowd. An angry FBI agent in her face. And a bodyguard who kept insisting that she was too open as she sat on a park bench.

The lights, the voices, the desperation—all made her head swim. Of course it might have been a little remnant of the whiskey. Or possibly the head injury from the kidnappers this afternoon. Maybe both.

Whatever it was, she didn't like it. It was the reason she rarely drank at any point in her life. She simply didn't like being under the influence of anything. Including her uncle Carl, who had taken it upon himself to dispatch bodyguards to protect her. They'd destroyed any chance of getting insulin to Jackson.

The van lay on its side. The driver had escaped before anyone could reach the crash site. Both the guard and Josh had run to the scene, but he was gone. Vanished.

"Miss Cassidy, if you're ready to go. Your uncle instructed us to bring you back to Fort Worth as soon as possible. We've cleared it with the police to pull out." The guard spoke to her with no remorse for what he and his partner had caused. As if she was the most important person in the entire group.

She hated that. She always had.

"How can you stand there and talk as if nothing's happened? Your partner may have shot someone in that van. The driver's disappeared along with the instructions to rescue the twins. What if the kids had been inside? If anything happens to Josh's son—"

"We were just doing our job." He stood in front of her with his hands crossed over each other, no emotion, no whining—and apparently no regrets. His partner had his breath back—which had been knocked out of him by the bullets hitting him in the chest or him hitting the ground.

Jackson and Sage were missing and now the kidnappers would be angry. What would happen now? She needed these men gone. There was only one way to do that. One man. One man could make it happen.

"Let me have your phone."

"Ma'am?"

"I don't have a phone. I need to borrow yours."

He reached inside his jacket pocket, turned on his phone and handed it to her. She searched the call history and found the number she'd almost forgotten. The phone rang and rang some more, going to voice mail, which surprised her. Unless he was with someone— then nothing would disturb him. Not even the fact that he thought her life was at risk.

Hadn't he sent the guards because he was worried?

A more likely story was that he thought the kidnappers would find out who she was and try to extort money from him. Just the possibility of the family being out any cash would send him into a frenzy to get her safely back inside a gilded cage.

Should she leave a message? She hung up before the beep. What she had to say didn't need to be recorded.

"Where's Josh?" The men standing close to her shrugged in answer. "You do know which man I was with when all this began? The father of the children you just placed in more danger."

The big bulky bodyguard looked like he didn't have a clue. He didn't search the crowd. She followed his gaze to the edge of the people, then across the river where another line of people formed, then back to just behind her where the emergency vehicles were parked.

"Hey. Don't play dumb. I ask. You answer," she instructed, using the power that came with her family name. "And don't think I can't stop your paycheck."

"They moved him to a more secure facility," he finally answered.

"You mean we're trying," Agent McCaffrey corrected as he approached. "I was just coming for you, Tracey. We're heading back to Josh's house. He insists on driving himself but would like to speak with you first."

The agent and bodyguard parted like doors when Josh barreled through them.

"My car's been brought to this side of the river. I'm heading back to my place. You ready?" He extended a hand and she took it.

What would she say to him this time? "Sorry. I should have told you about my powerfully rich uncle who might send bodyguards." Those words didn't roll off her tongue and she'd had no idea he'd send anyone to protect her. Actually, it seemed surreal that he'd found her so quickly.

Josh put his hand on her lower back and guided her through the crowds. Her silent guard followed. The one

who hadn't been hit by two bullets in his chest ran toward the road, presumably to get their vehicle.

Josh stopped and did an about-face. "I need to talk
with Tracey. Then she's all yours."

"What?" *What did he mean? He was turning her
over to her uncle?* She'd been right. Josh wouldn't forgive her this time, but she had something to say about
where she went and with whom.

"I can't let her out of my sight, sir." The bodyguard
stood more at attention, looking ready to attack. Had
he just issued a challenge to a Texas Ranger?

"I don't have time for this. I need to know how you
found her." Josh responded by placing his hands on his
hips and looping his thumbs through his belt loops. Either to keep from dragging her the rest of the way to
his car, or to keep himself from throwing a punch at
the bodyguard. She would prefer that he not restrain
himself from the latter.

"We tracked her phone. We're assuming it was in
the van."

"How did you get the number?" she asked. "I didn't
give it to my uncle."

"I have a job to do. And I don't work for either of
you."

Josh's hands were pulling the guard's collar together
before the man could nod at them both. The guard's
hands latched on to Josh's wrists to keep from being
choked. Agents who had been watching them closely
as they approached the car began running.

If any of them were afraid of what Josh might do,
they didn't shout for him to stop. Tracey couldn't bring
herself to call out to him, either. After all, it was this
man's actions that caused them to lose their main lead

to the twins. It was this guy—she didn't even know his name—who had flubbed everything up.

"If you lift one finger…" she said to the guard. But she couldn't blame him or let Josh take out his frustration on the hired help. She'd lost the kids on her watch. She should have been more careful. She laid her hand on Josh's arm, trying to gain his attention. "It's not his fault."

Josh's strong jaw ticked as he ground his teeth. His wide eyes shifted to hers in a crazy gaze, but his muscles relaxed under her fingers.

"Earlier I asked how being rich could be an awful secret." He released the guard shoving him away when two FBI agents were within reaching distance. "I think I have my answer."

"You don't, but I'd rather talk about it in private."

Josh turned and stomped toward his car—the agents close behind.

"Whatever my uncle is paying you, I'll give you the same to stop following me," she said to the bodyguard.

Tracey fell into step next to Agent Barlow, who held up her hand for the guard to stop and not follow. It didn't work. Josh spun around so fast Agent Lanning nearly collided with him.

"No! I need to be alone. That means all of you." He waved everyone away from him. He shook his head, chin hanging to his chest. Then he looked only at her. "They might need you around, but I can't do it. And I don't have to."

"He doesn't mean that," the agent said.

Tracey stopped. Exhausted from everything but really rocked by Josh's words. Her words had been similar when she'd walked away from her uncle when she was twenty-one. She'd left him, the man designated by her parents and grandparents as her guardian, about the same way Josh had disappeared in his car.

Tracey hadn't only meant every word back then, she'd changed her name and began working for the Parkers. Oh yeah, some hurts just couldn't be fixed with "I'm sorry."

JOSH DROVE, HEADING for the long way home. Flashing lights to warn the cars ahead of him that he was going fast. He was angry. More than angry—he was back to being scared that he'd never see his kids again.

Different than Gwen's last days. That was something he'd prepared for, something he'd known was possible even though he couldn't control it. If those men hadn't shown up, the kidnappers would have given him more instructions. He'd know what he needed to do. Or at least his son would have another insulin cartridge.

There was a blood sugar time bomb ticking away for Jackson, and at the moment Josh had no way to defuse it.

He sped under Lake Shore Drive and realized where his subconscious was taking him—the Rescue Center. He slowed the car to a nonlethal speed and switched off the lights. The phone he'd been given from the kidnappers was still in his back pocket. McCaffrey knew it was there but hadn't obtained the number yet. A true burner that wouldn't lead anyone to his location.

Josh could wait for the kidnapper's next call and instructions. They wanted him to take care of their problem. Right? They had to call back.

Whatever they demanded, he'd do. Alone. No more plans behind the plans or counterespionage. He was on his own and would stay here so no one would find him.

With that decided, Josh parked close to the back door

and rang the buzzer. At this time of night there would only be a couple of people on duty. The door opened to a familiar face.

"Hey, Josh. You haven't been around in a while. What's it been, about six or seven months?" Bernie Dawes stepped to the side, holding the door open and inviting him inside.

Six or seven months ago he'd been thinking about asking Tracey on a date. He'd chickened out. Funny how he could be the tough Texas Ranger ninety percent of the time, making decisions instantly that saved lives. But the possibility of asking a girl on a date caused his brain to malfunction.

"Got any dogs that need to be walked?"

"One of those kinds of nights?" Bernie asked.

"Yeah. I'm waiting on a phone call." Josh stuck his hands in his back pockets, willing the phone to ring. Nothing happened.

"Well, I just took 'em all out about half an hour ago. How about I set you up with an abandoned litter of pups? They've had a pretty rough start."

"That'll do the trick."

Bernie led the way to the kennels and pulled a chair into a small room with a box of four or five black fur bundles. Five. They were all cuddled on top of each other.

"What's on their heads? Are those dots of paint?"

"We've got a Lab that just whelped, so we rotate these dudes in. But they're black, too." Bernie laughed and scooped up one of the pups. "We have a chart with their different colors. It's the only way to tell if they've all been fed. These guys are all full. They just need a little TLC."

"I shouldn't stay long. I might not have much time."

"Whatever you give them is more than they have."
He leaned against the wall.

Loving on the puppies was easy. Seeing the other
animals—the strays, the injured, the unwanted... The
tough guy he appeared to be suddenly needed to know
how this man survived day after day. "How do you do
this, Bernie?"

He shrugged. "I like animals."

Bernie turned to go, but hesitated. He might have
realized that Josh was back because there was a problem. It was like he was the bartender, wiping down the
counter a little more often in front of the man sipping
his third whiskey.

"I got in trouble today," Bernie said, picking up a
puppy. "I didn't mention my wife's hair. She told me
to find my own dinner because I didn't notice she had
highlights. She's always doing something. I didn't think
I had to say anything about it. Sometimes it's the little
things that cause you all sorts of big problems. Catch
what I'm throwin' at ya?"

Josh nodded. He could still see Tracey as she walked
into the kitchen. He'd wanted to look into her eyes and
reassure her that everything would be okay, but she'd
been staring at the floor. He could only see her thick
red hair, messed up as if someone had placed angry
hands on her. Seeing her hair like that, he knew she'd
been hurt and it killed him.

"Tracey doesn't think I notice that she dyes her hair
red." He picked up the first puppy and stroked the entire length of its body. He wasn't completely sure why
Tracey's hair color was important, but he could breathe
again. "She started about three years ago, getting a little
redder every couple of months. Further away from the
brown it used to be."

The room was quiet. No barking or whining. Bernie kept wiping down that metaphorical bar's counter. Josh felt…relief. There weren't too many people Josh could just talk to. He was the commander of the Company. Being a single dad, he didn't go for a drink with the guys after a case very often. It had been a long time since he'd had friends.

"I should have told her I liked it," he admitted.

"Probably," Bernie agreed. "You get that phone call, just make sure the door closes behind you. You come around anytime, man. We understand. Hey, aren't your kiddos old enough to choose a dog? Maybe one of these will do?" He handed the pup with a green dot to Josh. He brushed his hands and gave up waiting on an answer. "Well, I've got a cat who had surgery today and it's having a hard time so I'm going to leave ya to it."

Bernie left in a hurry. Josh figured he must have scowled at the mention of the twins. Poor Bernie thought his visit was about work. Getting a dog? He brought the pup to his face. It was about time. There hadn't been a dog at the house since before he got married.

A whirlwind relationship, elopement and pregnancy that led to Gwen's diagnosis. There hadn't been time to add a dog to the family. Maybe it was part of the reason these types of visits helped. He didn't know who got more out of them—him or the dogs he comforted.

Admit it. The comfort was for him. The idea had come from Company F's receptionist, Vivian. She volunteered for the shelter, trying to place animals and fostering.

The gut-wrenching pain hit him again like it was yesterday. It had been at least a year since he'd felt the loss of his wife so strongly. He put the puppy down and bent forward knowing the pain wasn't physical, but trying to relieve it like a cramp.

When Gwen had been diagnosed with leukemia, every minute of his time had gone to either the job or research or treatment. There had come a time when he'd protected himself so much that he could barely feel.

After the third or fourth late-night trip out here, he'd realized that his unofficial therapy was working. Petting and walking the dogs made him reconnect. He switched puppies and gently stroked, letting the motion replace the fright. It freed his mind. A couple of minutes later he switched again and realized that's why he'd come to the shelter.

It was also a reason he kept the visits to himself. Vivian was the only person in his life that knew he came here to get his head on straight. And he sure needed a minute to think calmly tonight.

The last two pups were smaller than the others. Each had one white paw—one right and one left. He concentrated on those paws and cuddled both of them together. They both almost fit into his palm.

Jackson and Sage had been small. But when they were born they were strong and hadn't needed machines. Trips here to sit with dogs had been fewer when the doctors attacked Gwen's cancer full force. Some days, just taking the time to hold his kids was an effort that made him sleepless with guilt.

The twins were four months old when Gwen realized she was losing the battle. Somehow that had made her stronger. She'd gotten everything in order—with Tracey's help. Gwen fought hard, but in the end, she was at peace that her family would be taken care of.

Removing the phone from his pocket, he replayed the video of his kids. "Ring," he commanded.

He got on his knees next to the box and arranged the blanket where the pups would be secure as they piled on top of each other seeking sleep.

"It can't be over for them. You've got to give me another chance. This can't be the end. She fought so hard to bring these kids into the world," he told the puppies or God or anyone else who might be listening.

The phone rang and he didn't hesitate. "This is Parker."

"You're a very lucky man, Ranger."

"I'm not sure I share your definition of lucky. Does this mean you haven't hurt my kids?"

The insulin cartridges and needles were on the front seat. *Meet me tonight. Ask me to do something right now. I need to make sure my kids are safe.*

"The deal's still moving forward, no matter where you're hiding out."

He heard the uneasiness in the man's voice. Whoever they were, they had no idea that he was at the animal shelter. That might work to his advantage.

"What do you need me to do?"

"You know what we want. Get it. Keep the phone close and wait for instructions."

"Can I talk to Jackson? Is he okay? He has—"

"Diabetes, yeah, we know. We're dealing with it."

"I need to see him, talk to him. His pump and needle will need to be changed. He has to be monitored closely." There wasn't any way he could talk anyone through all the different possibilities that might happen if something went wrong.

"I said we were taking care of it!" the voice yelled. "Don't forget to bring the woman."

"That's not possible."

"Make it possible. Or they'll die."

Chapter Seven

Josh drove to his second home—Company F headquarters. The lights were on and he recognized the vehicles in the parking lot. They were all there. All of his men.

Bryce met him at the door. "We didn't expect to see you, Major. At least not tonight."

"My replacement here?" Josh waited while the ranger secured things, so he could be escorted through the building like a visitor. "I need a minute of his time."

"How you holding up?"

"Can't take time to think about it."

"Captain Oaks is in your office." Bryce led the way through the men.

All of them stood and offered support. They were the best of the best and working the case with or without him as their leader. He entered his office. Nothing had changed. The lifetime he'd been away was actually less than twenty-four hours.

"Aiden." Josh closed the door and dropped the blinds. He didn't want witnesses to the conversation. Nothing that could hinder the case or put his men at risk of something to testify about later.

Aiden left the chair behind the desk and sat next to Josh. The Captain was much older, but barely looked it. Josh only knew because the "old man," as he was referred to, had been eligible for retirement a couple of years ago. He'd proved his mettle earlier that year when he'd been shot defending the witness of the Isabella Tenoreno murder.

Captain Aiden Oaks had been after the Tenoreno and Rosco Mafia families longer than a decade. It was fitting that he'd take Josh's place as head of Company F.

Even if it was temporary.

"I could ask how you're holding up, but it's obvious. What can I do for you?" Aiden kept his voice low. No chance anyone would overhear them. He also leaned forward, seeming anxious to know what was needed.

There was a chance that Aiden Oaks was the only man in a position of authority who would keep his word. Josh needed to make certain that the captain wasn't going to turn him over to the authorities—state or federal. Or call them as soon as he pulled out of the parking lot.

"They want Tenoreno's transportation route."

"Everyone assumed that's where this was headed." Aiden pressed his lips together into a flat line. "Your men filled me in and headquarters gave me a rough outline before booting me this direction."

"I shouldn't be here." Josh started to rise from the chair, but Aiden coaxed him to sit again. "Just talking to me could get you written up, but I don't have any options."

In his years as a Texas Ranger, Josh had never doubted whether he could count on his partner or the men in his company. If this case was just about him, there'd be no doubt about what he'd do. But his kids' lives had never been dependent on that trust.

Until now.

"I guess the strategy to follow and catch these guys

when they weren't looking fell apart when your baby-sitter's bodyguards showed up." Aiden nodded. "Yeah, I'm staying on top of things. But you're here. You obviously have a plan. How can I help put it in action?"

Could he trust this man so intent on helping save his kids?

"I need the route or Jackson dies." Josh watched Aiden's eyes. They never wavered. Never looked away like someone hiding something. "I heard the panic in the kidnapper's voice—both about my son and whatever his original plan was. This character is smart enough to know that he had a short window before everything changed. He's playing it by ear now, just like us."

Aiden nodded again, acting like he understood. "Even if you deliver the route there's no guarantee. Say we give 'em a bit of rope, hoping they might hang themselves, it won't guarantee that your kids will be safely released. Won't mean they'll release you either for that matter."

"But I'll be with them." Josh choked on the words, took a second, then stood. "My kids aren't going to be the victims in this. I know the limits of the Rangers, of the FBI, of the state prosecutors. They're hoping for an easy fix. We both know there isn't one."

Josh stared at the frame hanging above the door. Gwen stitched the Ranger motto when she'd first been confined to bed rest with the twins. It was a reminder every day of what he'd lost, but he kept it there. Over the last year, it had also become a reminder of what he'd gained—the twins. *And Tracey.*

"One Riot, One Ranger," Aiden said.

Strength and truth were in his voice. Josh had to trust him. His plan could only work if he did.

Aiden gripped his shoulder with a firm, steady hand.

"I yanked your company into this mess when I sent Garrison Travis to a dinner party and they witnessed Tenoreno's assassin. I owe you, Josh. So what's the plan?"

Eager to help or eager to learn how to stop him? Aiden might be giving him a long piece of rope to hang himself. It was a risk Josh had to take.

"I need a feasible route, you supply a decoy, we bring these guys down like the rest of the Tenoreno family."

"It's a good start. Are you going to exchange yourself for your kids?"

"That's what I was planning, but I'm not sure it'll work. They're insisting that I bring Tracey."

Aiden rubbed his chin and leaned back in the chair he'd reoccupied. "That does throw a kink in the works. Could possibly mean that they'll keep all three as hostages until you do whatever they want."

"Yeah, that's the most likely scenario."

"It seems that the only way to get your kids back is to tell the kidnappers the truth. We'll need to inform them how and where Tenoreno is really being moved from Huntsville to Austin. Company F will just have to be prepared."

"Are you going to run this through state headquarters?"

"They won't approve it—not even as a hypothetical." He winked. "Just like they wouldn't have approved the last-minute operation that brought Tenoreno down to begin with. Might be one of those situations where it's better to ask forgiveness than permission. Of course, there's nothing at all to stop us from talking hypothetical situations. Your experience would be valuable and much appreciated."

"My experience. Right." Josh's gut told him to go for it. *Trust him.*

His friend pointed to the motto. "This is one time, more than one of us might be required."

No more stalling. This fight was bigger than just one man. He had to trust that Aiden wouldn't turn him in.

"If I were still in charge of Tenoreno's transport, I'd arrange for air travel. It would be limited ground vulnerability. At this point the state prosecutor is probably scrambling to even make that a private jet."

"I'm not disagreeing with you," Aiden said. "Hypothetically."

In other words, Josh was right. They planned to move Tenoreno from the state prison via plane to Austin for the trial.

"Since we're just talking here, you know what's bothered me? Why did the kidnappers go to so much trouble to put your situation in the public eye? I mean, they could have kept the kidnapping quiet, but they drew you to a popular, normally crowded place."

"If I were Tenoreno's son, a plane is the fastest route out of the country. Huntsville's just a hop into the Gulf and then international waters. All he has to do is hijack the plane."

"That's a fairly sound guess of what they're likely to do." Aiden tapped his fingertips together, thinking.

"Dammit. Is that what all of this is about? Make the kidnapping public so the transfer is by plane instead of car? I thought it was just about gaining access to my credentials so the kidnaper could get close enough to free Tenoreno."

"They manipulated the kidnapping to force you to hijack a plane?" Aiden nodded his head, agreeing, not really asking a question.

"It would make it harder to recapture Tenoreno.

Harder for the FBI or Rangers or any law enforcement not to comply since the twins are at risk."

The kidnapping made sense.

"Did you find out why Tracey's uncle sent the guards? Who notified them?"

Josh shook his head, shrugging.

"Too upset? I understand." The older man stood, joining Josh by sitting on the opposite corner of the desk. "We'll be ready. I guarantee that. And if you just happen to let me see the number you're using on that new phone, then I might have a misdial in my future letting you know what plane and airfield."

Josh turned on the cell and Aiden nodded his head.

"Here's something to ponder while we wait." He jotted down the number. "How did Miss Cassidy's entourage get here? On one hand maybe the kidnappers really want her to take care of the kids. Maybe they just made a mistake not abducting her at the same time. On the other, Xander Tenoreno might have alerted her uncle. That means he knows she's from money. Maybe the kidnappers know too and want a piece of that cash cow."

"How rich is rich?" Josh asked.

"Probably need to have a conversation with the source about that."

Aiden was a wise man. Josh stuck out his hand, grabbing the older man's like a lifeline. It was the first hope he'd had since the van had crashed.

"I can't thank you enough, Aiden."

"I haven't done anything yet. A lot of this depends on you."

Josh looked at Gwen's artwork. "I'll do whatever it takes."

"Just remember, you're not alone."

PULLING A LIGHT throw up to her chin, Tracey curled up as small on the couch as she could get. She closed her eyes, pretending to be asleep, wanting everyone in the house to leave her alone. The FBI agent who'd picked her up at the hospital encouraged her to take the up-stairs bedroom.

Josh's room?

George Lanning had no way of knowing she hadn't been in that room since Gwen had gotten very, very ill. It was better to be bothered by people in the living room than to be alone in Josh's bed.

"Miss Cassidy?"

"What?" she answered the bodyguard, who hadn't left her side since coming into her life.

"It's your uncle."

Part of her wanted to tell him to call off these guard dogs and part of her wanted to ignore him—as he'd obviously ignored her for the past several hours. The best thing was to confront the situation and attempt to discover his true motives.

She sat up, tugged her shirt straight and was ready to get to the heart of things. It had been a while since she'd thought of her grandmother's advice when facing a problem. But the words were never truer than at that moment.

Taking the phone, she drew in a deep breath placing the phone next to her ear, ready for an attack.

"Tracey, darling, are you okay?"

"Who is this?" The female voice was a little familiar, but it had been a long time since she'd had contact with her family. She couldn't be sure who it was.

"It's your auntie Vickie, dear. Are you on your way home yet?"

"I don't have an aunt Vickie." At least she hadn't

when she'd gone to court to change her name. There hadn't even been a Vickie in her uncle's life. Then again, there'd always been someone *like* a Vickie.

"I know I've met you, dear. I'll admit—only to you— that it's been much too long."

"Where is my uncle? I was told he was calling." She didn't have time to speak with a secretary or even a new wife. She wanted the confrontation over and the guys in the black suits off her elbow.

"Well," the woman's voice squeaked, "he's not really available, but I thought you needed to know that it's important for you to come home."

"Wait, my uncle didn't tell you to call?"

Vickie began a long, in-depth explanation why she'd taken it upon herself to contact her and explain the complexity of the situation in her childhood home. Tracey tuned her out.

Home? The room surrounding her, keeping her warm and safe, was more of a home than any room had ever been in Fort Worth. That place had been more like a museum or mausoleum. Beautiful, but definitely a do-not-touch world.

As a little girl, she'd had the best interior designers. Everything had been pink. She couldn't stand pink for the longest time. Now she had to bite her tongue whenever Sage wanted a dress in the color.

Realizing the phone was in her lap instead of her hand, she clicked the big red disconnect button and put an end to a stranger's attempt to coax her home. Her new constant companion reached to retrieve it, when it rang again.

Tracey answered herself, more prepared, less surprised. "Yes?"

"Listen to me, you spoiled little brat." Vickie didn't

try to disguise the venom. "Carl wants you back here pronto. Niceties aside, you should do what you're told."

"Vickie…dearest—" she could make the honey drip from her voice, too "—I walked away a long time ago. There is absolutely no road for me that leads back there."

The red button loomed. Tracey clicked. It wasn't hard. Not now.

The phone vibrated in her hand. She tossed it to the opposite end of the couch. Totally content with her decision. Her uncle wasn't calling her back and, whoever Vickie was, she couldn't do anything to help save the children.

"I only have two things for you to do," she said to the guard. "My first is that you both get in that car of yours and leave. Without me. The second is not to interrupt me again unless it's really my uncle calling. Period. No secretaries. No Auntie *Vickies* that haven't celebrated as many birthdays as I have. No one except him. And don't say that you don't work for me."

"Yes, ma'am." He nodded and backed up to the door.

What he was acknowledging, she didn't care. Just as long as he stayed next to the door and let her wonder where Josh had gone or whether he was coming back. If she were him she wondered what she'd be thinking.

Before she could lean back into the cushions, the man answered his phone and held it in her direction.

"Speaker, please."

He mumbled into the phone, pressed a button and…

"Tracey? You there?"

She raised her hand, using her fingers to indicate she'd take the call. She popped it off Speaker and paused long enough to fill her lungs again.

"Hi, Uncle Carl."

"You okay, Tracey?" Her uncle didn't sound upset. He might even sound concerned. "I heard there was an accident and a car fire."

"I'm good. My head hurts from earlier, but I'm sure you already have the hospital records."

"It's been a while. I have to apologize for Vickie. She sometimes gets…overly enthusiastic."

"She sounded like it." He hadn't called to talk about his girlfriend, which was the category she could safely put the woman in. He hadn't said anything about getting married. The man was in his fifties and had avoided a matrimonial state his entire life.

"I assume you don't want to come home."

"I am home. My place is here and the men you sent— You did send them, didn't you?"

"As soon as I heard you were assaulted."

"You should have asked me first." As if that step had ever been part of his trickeries.

"You would have said no."

"Of course I would have said no. I work for a Texas Ranger who has a lot of law enforcement access. Why in the world would I need two bodyguards to muck things up?"

"Muck?"

"Yes, Uncle Carl, muck. They arrived and everything became a big mess. Josh is gone, the kids are still in danger, Jackson doesn't have anyone there that understands diabetes. Yes, everything's pretty *mucked* up."

"Mr. Parker's children are in danger?"

"They were kidnapped. That's the reason the FBI called you."

"The FBI? Did they tell you they spoke with me?"

"No. I just assumed that's how you found me." Wasn't that what Agent McCaffrey had insinuated?

"That's ridiculous. I've never *not* known where you are. Just because you changed your name doesn't stop you from being my niece and my responsibility. I'm your guardian, but more importantly, we're family."

It sounded good. The speech wasn't unlike the words that she'd heard most of her life. It did surprise her that he'd known exactly where she was. Well, then again, it didn't. She hadn't gone far.

Same city, same school—she only lived four blocks from the place he'd been paying for. That all made sense. What didn't was his statement that he hadn't heard from the FBI.

"Concern for me was never a problem."

"Ah, yes, you wanted your freedom. Well, anonymously donating to your university down there, did keep me informed."

Same old, same old. Carl was very good at saying a lot of nothing.

"Can we stop this? Just tell me what it's going to take to call off your bodyguard brigade."

"I think you need to sit the rest of this out. Come back here where I can keep an eye on you. Better yet, you've finished your presentation, so why not take a long overdue vacay to someplace breezy. You always liked the beach."

"You're wrong, and this time you have no control over my life." She caught the upward tilt of lips—mostly smirk—of the man at the door. Right. Her uncle's money would always have influence over her life. Money always did. "Just call off your goons."

"That won't be happening. They're there for your safety. You need them." Carl's voice was more than a little smug. As usual, it was full of confidence that his choice was the only choice.

"That couldn't be farther from the truth."

Her uncle never did anything without proper motivation. So what was motivating him this time?

"No need to argue the point any longer, Tracey. I returned your call, answered your questions and have informed you what your option is. Yes, I'm aware you only have one. I must say good night."

"You aren't going to win." It embarrassed her to feel her face contract with a cringe. She knew the words were a fool's hope as soon as she said them.

"My dear, I already have. Those men are not about to leave your side. They'd never work anywhere again. Ever. And they know it."

The phone disconnected and she was no closer to discovering the truth of why her uncle sent the bodyguards. Man, did that sound conceited. Josh would want to know the entire story and specifically that answer when he returned. *If* he returned.

Part of the discussion in the past couple of hours was that Josh had a new phone and it was taking much too long to discover the number. Something to do with finding the kiosk owner, then a person who actually had keys to obtain the sales records. Followed by getting permission to enter the mall.

In other words, they had no clue where Josh was. No one could find him on the road. Some of their conversation had been that the kidnappers may have already contacted him. If so, then at least he had the Jackson emergency kit with him. Josh could monitor his son, save both of his kids.

The bodyguard silently retrieved his phone. He stepped on the other side of the door to take a phone call, but she mostly heard manly grunts of affirmation.

Tracey wanted to run and lock the door. Of course,

there wasn't a lock, but it didn't stop her from wanting to be completely alone. She could sulk as good as the rest of them. But it felt ridiculous feeling sorry for herself.

What problem did she have? It was Josh's twins who were missing. Josh would have to do whatever it took to get them back. She could sit here and offer support. Be the loyal day care provider. Her role in the family had been made quite clear when Josh had left her behind.

"Your uncle wants you back in Fort Worth in the morning. We'll leave here at eight sharp, giving you time for some rest." He stood with his back to the door as if he were a guard in front of the Tower of London. Eyes front, not influenced by any stimuli around him.

"I'm not a child and you can't force me to get in a vehicle, especially with the FBI here. I'm not going anywhere. I'm waiting here for Josh." At least she hoped he'd return. "And I'm going to help find his kids. Get with this agenda or leave."

The guard didn't answer. He was a good reflection of her uncle, not listening to her. She curled into the corner of the couch again, pulling the blanket over her shoulder. He was right about one thing—she did need some rest. Because when Josh came back, he would need her help.

And she would be here to give it to him.

Chapter Eight

"Where the hell have you been?" McCaffrey burst through the front door, storming across the porch before Josh had the car in Park.

"Not my problem if your guys can't keep up." He didn't care if the agent thought he was a smart-ass. He had barely been thinking when he'd left the river.

During the twenty-minute car ride from Ranger headquarters, he hadn't come up with a way to get him and Tracey out of the house. It didn't help that he lived in the middle of nowhere and there wouldn't be any sneaking off without guards noticing. Men were everywhere again. One of the bodyguards who had stopped Josh from reaching the van sat in a dark sedan parked in front of the barn.

Bodyguards complicated the equation.

What the hell was he going to do?

"Oh thank God! You're all right," Tracey said when his feet hit the porch. "Can we talk? Let me explain?"

Did he want to go there? Then again, when had it mattered what he *wanted*? Life had proven his wants didn't matter. He had to confront Tracey and talk things out. But when? That was the question he decided was relevant. And who else needed to be confronted—the FBI, local PD or Tracey's bodyguards?

Notably absent was the only organization that held the answer he needed. He had to trust Aiden Oaks, but knew the men in Company F had his back. He'd find out the specifics of moving Tenoreno.

He hadn't been able to speak with Bryce. Maybe find out where their tail had been during the bridge incident and why the rangers had been unable to follow the kidnapper from the van.

If they had, Josh would know. First things first. He had to deal with the people back in his house. McCaffrey was standing on the front sidewalk. Looked like he was first, then Tracey.

"You aren't supposed to be here. Pack it up, Agent."

"Did they make contact with you? Is that the reason you returned?"

"I don't know who's out there watching this conversation. Leave." Josh pointed to the empty dark sedans. Then he turned to the cop on his front lawn. "They have two minutes to clear out or arrest them for trespassing."

"I'm not sure I have that authority," he replied.

"Dammit." Josh glared at McCaffrey. "I probably don't have a choice, but I'm begging you for my kids' lives…leave."

"I have my orders."

Josh was dazed to a point that he couldn't speak. No words would form. His mind went to a neon sign that flashed. "Jackson might die."

"Josh, come on inside. You can't do this."

Tracey tugged on his hands. Hands that were twisted in the shirt collar circling McCaffrey's neck. How? When? The blackness. It all ran together until everything sort of blurred.

He released the FBI agent and let Tracey lead him inside. He thought she pointed at a man who took care of emptying the room. "How do we get rid of him and his partner?" he asked once he realized it was the second bodyguard.

"Are you okay?"

"Sure. No. I just… I don't know what happened back there." Josh shook his head in disbelief. "I can't remember going for McCaffrey."

"You're upset, exhausted. The stress that you're under is—"

"Things like this don't happen to me. I don't let them." He shrugged away from the comfort Tracey might offer. He wasn't a pacing man.

When he needed to think he lifted his feet up on the corner of his desk and flipped a pencil between his fingers. He paced so Tracey wouldn't be near him. What if he lost it again?

The television in the far corner of the room was muted. No news bulletins. He hadn't expected any since the FBI was keeping a tight lid on things. There hadn't been any Amber Alerts for his kids. Special circumstances, he'd been told.

That part he agreed with. They all knew who had hired the kidnappers. Now they just had to find them.

"I owe you an explanation," Tracey said softly.

"Not sure I can process anything." He scrubbed his face with his palms, desperately attempting to lift the haze. His mind screamed at him not to. If it did, he'd have to find a way to save his kids.

Too late. He was thinking again.

He dropped onto the cushions, breathing fully and under control. For the moment.

"I don't know how to apologize for what happened." She nervously rubbed her palms up and down her thighs. Gone were the scrubs, replaced by regular clothes.

"Forget that for now. Before the van showed up, I asked why being rich needed to be a secret. Have your family problems put my kids in danger?" He shook his head as if he needed to answer that himself and start over. He didn't want to blame Tracey, but the words slipped across his tongue before he could shut himself up. "If I wasn't certain that Tenoreno's people were behind this… Go ahead—explain to me why I should trust you again."

Tracey snapped to attention, cleared her throat, then shrugged. "I was raised like every normal millionaire's kid."

Josh was too tired to be amused until it hit him that Tracey was serious. She sat on the sofa next to him, knee almost touching his leg, hands twisting the corner of a throw pillow, bodyguard at the door.

"You're serious."

"My family's been wealthy for a couple of generations. West Texas oil fields."

"Let me guess. You wanted to see how the other half lived so you went to work as a nanny?"

"I understand why you're mad, but—"

"I'm not sure you do." Josh burst up from the couch with energy he didn't realize he had. *Pace. Get back under control.* "I looked into your bank accounts, Tracey. There wasn't money there. You drive a crappy car. You've lived in the same off-campus apartment for four years. Why? If you have enough money to buy the state of Texas, why are you slumming it?"

"I didn't lie and *I* don't have all the money. My family does. At first, I thought you knew about all this. I told Gwen when she interviewed me who my uncle was.

I gave you permission to run a background check. Later, when it was obvious you had no idea about the money, it was nice that you didn't want a favor or something from my uncle."

She thought that he'd want something from her family? Second curve... Gwen had kept this from him. He closed his eyes again. The blackness returned along with the thought he had to get moving. He was ready to move past this, leave and find his children. But he had to understand what he was dealing with regarding the bodyguards and Tracey's family.

"Is Tracey Cassidy your real name?"

"Yes. I legally changed it when I was twenty-one. I just dropped the Bass. Not that anyone actually associated me with the Bass family in Fort Worth."

He stared at her after she'd thrown two curveballs at him. She was a Bass? As in Bass Hall and the endowments and three of the wealthiest men in Texas?

"Why now? Why have bodyguards come into your life after you've lived in Waco for this long without them? I know they haven't always been hanging around. I think I would have noticed them."

"My parents divorced when I was six. I went to live with my grandparents. They said it was for my own good. Everyone threw the word *stability* around a lot back then. It might have been better. I'll never know. Both my parents remarried, started new families. By then, I was too old and filled with teenage angst."

He paced until he landed in front of the television screen and the dancing bubbles in the commercial. "Were you hiding from your family?"

"No. My uncle controls the trust fund left to me by my grandfather. With that, he thought it gave him complete control of my life. I decided not to let him dictate who was trailing after me in a bulletproof car, or what I did or when. So I left. I walked away from that life."

He couldn't let the bodyguards or Bass family screw things up the next time he received instructions. "Why didn't Gwen tell me about any of this?"

"I honestly thought she had. Look, Josh, my life changed after I walked away from my uncle. I sold my expensive car and lived on the money for almost a year. I had to keep things simple. I had to find a job. I did that through Gwen. She helped before and after I came to work here."

"I wanted her to hire a nurse. In fact, we argued about it a lot." He swallowed hard, pushing the emotion down. "She was right, of course. It was better to have someone she could be... She needed a friend."

"I told her that—the part about a nurse. But she was insistent that you needed a friend, too. She was a very determined woman."

"Yeah, she was."

"I first came here because a secretary in the department wanted to help me make ends meet. I stayed because Gwen asked for my help."

"Why are you still here? I know about the job offer in Minnesota."

She stared at him. Her lips parted, a little huff escaping before she pulled herself straight. Back on the edge of the couch she shook her head as if she couldn't believe what she'd just heard.

"I've spoken to the men who work for my uncle. They said they work for him and he's the only one who can give them new orders." She ignored his question.

The proverbial elephant was sitting in the middle of the room. Neither of them wanted to talk about her leaving. That's why he hadn't discussed the possibility or their accidental kiss.

He had made it a point to work late to avoid talking to her. "I don't have any control of your life, Tracey."

"Of course you don't. I never thought you did."

"You deserve more."

"I seriously don't believe you. After everything we've been through—are going through." She jumped up from the couch. Her sudden movement caught the attention of her guard at the door. He took a look and didn't react. "More of what, Josh? This is *so* not the time to be thinking about my future. We have to get the twins back before Jackson crashes or worse."

"The kidnappers called me."

"What? Why are we talking about me? Do they want money? I can force my uncle—"

"No. It's not about you." He scraped his fingers through his short hair. "It involves you. I mean, I need your help."

"Anything. I already told you."

"I think they want you to come and take care of Jackson. If they'd known about your family, they would have taken you this afternoon."

"I begged them to."

"It's dangerous. This is possibly one of the hardest things I've ever said, but I don't think you should." *Damn!*

"Why would you even think that? You want me to run to safety while Jackson may be…he might be…"

Control. He needed control. But he wasn't going to get it by ignoring that Tracey needed comfort. Or by pretending she wasn't a part of the situation.

She straightened to the beautiful regal posture he'd

noticed more than once. "I'll do it. I'm not hiding. I'd never be able to live with myself."

He stood, wanting to go to her. To hold her. Take as much comfort as he could, possibly more than he was able to offer her.

"If you said that back at the bridge to hurt me..." she sniffed "...maybe to get me back in some way for messing up the exchange at the bridge...well, it worked. I get it. As soon as Sage and Jackson are okay, I'm leaving for Minnesota."

"Yeah." The resignation in his voice was apparent— at least to him. But he hadn't meant it and didn't want her to go. He needed her.

She walked to the window that opened to the back of the house. Sometime in the hour that he was away, she'd gone by her place and picked up clothes. Now she was in jeans, a long-sleeved gold summer sweater over a black lace top.

The boots Gwen had given her for Christmas years ago were on her feet. He recognized the silver toes. She wore them a lot and every time he thought back to that last gift exchange...

So much about her reminded him of his wife. But the strange thing was he'd actually had a longer relationship with Tracey. God, he was confused. Mixed-up didn't sit well. He wasn't a soft or weak guy.

Not being able to concentrate was killing him or would get him killed. What he wouldn't give for the dependability of his men and a solid plan of action. Give him an hour to be in charge and he should be able to resolve this. But he wasn't going to be in charge. He had to accept that.

Thinking like this wasn't helping. Besides, no one

could have predicted that Tracey's uncle would send bodyguards. Or that they'd arrive at exactly that moment.

Whoever was in charge—he stared at the phone still in his possession—a bastard on the other end was dictating the fates of every person he loved.

All he could do was wait.

Tracey sniffed. Her shoulders jerked a little. She was trying to conceal that she was crying. He'd hurt her and been a… Hell, he didn't want to be a jerk.

"I didn't mean it," he said without making a move toward her. "It's just…everything."

"I know. Everything has to work out somehow."

"I need to be doing something."

"Leave."

Josh looked up from his pity party about to ask her where she wanted him to go. But she'd directed her command at the bodyguard still at the slightly open door.

"If you don't leave, I'm going to encourage this… this Texas Ranger to take your head off. Are we clear?" Tracey wrapped her fingers into fists and snapped them to her hips.

With her short hair whipped up like it had just been blown by a big gust of North Texas wind, she almost looked like Peter Pan. Her shapely bottom would never pass for a boy who'd never grown up. But she did look like she was about to do battle.

The bodyguard backed through the door. Tracey took a step forward and slammed it in his face.

"What was that for?"

She spun around and marched across the room. Her battle stance had been switched to face Josh. "No more tears. You think you need action? So do I. What can we do?"

He sputtered a little. The change in her threw him even more off-kilter than he had been. If he'd had any doubts about her, they flew out the window along with the fictional character he'd been envisioning. Tracey was real and very determined.

"When did they contact you?" she asked, hands still on her hips, unwavering.

"How did you—?"

She came in close, taking his hands. "Let's clear the air and get down to business," she whispered. "I understand that whatever might have been developing between us is gone."

Josh wasn't as certain as her upturned face staring at him seemed to be.

"There's only one reason you would have come back here," she continued. "Me."

He deliberately lifted an eyebrow while he glanced at the closed door and searched for the men who'd been passing in front of the windows.

"The only person I've ever worked for is you, Josh Parker. I want to help." She squeezed his hands.

Clarity returned. Her reassurance seemed genuine when he looked into her eyes. As her strength flowed through her grip, sanity returned.

"Whatever it takes. I mean that." The catch in her voice made him want to draw her into his arms again.

Yet, there was something else hanging there, left unsaid. "But?"

She dropped his hands. "We get through this without doubting each other again. But afterward, I'm really leaving. You need to know that."

"I understand." He didn't. Then again, he did.

After knowing her for five years. After trusting her with his children. Yeah, he'd turned on her with a pittance of circumstantial evidence. She was hurt, but there was no going back. He'd lost her trust and maybe even her respect.

Tracey squeezed his left hand—the one where he'd recently removed his wedding ring. Had she noticed? No one in his life had said anything if they had. Another slight tug encouraged him to look at her.

"Now tell me, what do those bastards want us to do?"

Chapter Nine

Tracey had free run of the house. She'd publicly insisted that Josh shower and change, claiming he smelled like dogs. Fingers crossed it made the men watching him less aware of her. She had her fingers on the back door...

"Where are you heading, Miss Cassidy?" Agent Lanning strolled to the breakfast bar, looking as cold as the granite he leaned on.

"I just realized that no one fed the horses yesterday evening." She pointed toward the barn even though it couldn't be seen from the kitchen.

"I'll go with you. It's been a while since I've set foot in a barn." He continued his laid-back attitude and sauntered to the door as if there were no other explanation for her sneaking outside.

He stepped onto the already-dew-soaked grass, paused, lifted the corner of his slacks and tucked them into his boots. "Like I said, it's been a while, but I've done this once or twice."

Great. Just her luck. He really was going to help her. The bottoms of her jeans would be wet by the time they crossed the yard and opened the gate. The agent who'd sat with her at the hospital stretched his arms wide and waved off the bodyguards who would have followed.

The very men she wanted to follow.

"Did Josh leave in the car or his old truck?"

"I beg your pardon?" She tried to look innocent and knew she'd overacted when George Lanning laughed.

"I may not have kids of my own, but I know what I'd do if they were abducted. And that's anything. I've been through this before with my first partner. Josh came back here for a reason. Has to be that the kidnappers decided they need you to take care of Jackson. So is he leaving using the car or the truck?"

She couldn't look directly at him, but saw that his shoulders sort of shrugged. Right that minute, she could see the tall lanky cowboy who seemed to be her friend. But she wasn't easily fooled. Nor was she going to admit she and Josh had planned an escape.

"We've told all of you several times now. That's what the bridge exchange was all about. Or that's what we assumed. And for the record, Josh completely blames me that it got messed up." She tilted her head toward one of her uncle's bodyguards, who followed them across the yard. "I'm not exactly Major Parker's best friend at the moment."

"So it would appear." He waved a gentlemanly hand indicating for her to precede him down the worn path to the barn.

Feeding the horses was a ruse that he'd seen through immediately. She'd had no intention of feeding them at two in the morning, but now she was stuck. At least an extra scoop wouldn't hurt them. And she wouldn't be there when Mark Tuttle came in the morning to clean up and take care of them before school.

George only thought he'd caught her trying to get free. He'd know for certain in a couple of hours—along with everyone else.

They walked through the barn door and right on cue, the bodyguard followed. Josh had come up with several ways for them to leave. That is, once he'd focused and told her what the kidnappers wanted.

Something had changed for the men who had abducted the children. It might have been the fiasco at the bridge, but their fear was that Jackson's condition had worsened. The faster she got to him, the better.

One thing stood in her way—being confined here at the house. She dipped the scoop into the feed, filling the buckets to carry to each stall. Her hand shook so much that some pieces scattered onto the ground.

"You must be pretty scared." George leaned against the post near the first horse, closely watching her actions.

"Any normal, caring human being would be."

"That's right. So I guess you had to explain your background—or should I call it previous life—to Josh." He rubbed his stubbled chin.

"Is my life as a rich girl pertinent to getting the children back?"

"Isn't it?"

"I don't know what you mean."

He nodded toward the bucket. "The horses only missed one meal, right?"

She'd been intently watching his every move instead of paying attention to what she was doing. The bucket now was overflowing onto the floor, making more cleanup for her. The bodyguard snickered a little at her mistake before he clamped his lips together tight and returned to his stoic expression.

"Let me."

George picked up the bucket, held his hand out for the scoop, then finished putting the right amount into each bucket and then each stall. She let him while she wrapped her hand around the handle of a wooden tail brush. This wasn't the original plan, but it was one of its versions.

Josh had argued against it because they didn't know if the bodyguards would fall in line. She had to risk it. When George bent in front of her to scoop up the spilled feed, she raised her hand and let it fall across the back of his head.

She hadn't rendered him unconscious and hadn't expected to. It wasn't a movie, after all. But he did fall face-first into the dirt. She had seconds. "You! Tie him up. We're leaving."

George grabbed the back of his neck and rolled to his shoulder. The man at the door ran quickly forward, for a man of his size. He stuck a knee in the agent's back, practically flattening one of his hands under him.

"Tracey, stop! You don't want to do this," George called.

She looked around for something, anything to stuff inside his mouth to keep him quiet. The bodyguard yanked George's hands around to his back, looped the lead rope and tied it off. Then he jerked George to a sitting position and tied him to the closest post.

"I don't see anything to keep him quiet."

The guard loosened the tie around George's neck, pulled it up around the man's ears and tightened it enough to quiet any yelling. Then he removed the cell and handgun from under George's jacket.

"Call your partner and tell him to bring the car closer to the gate." She set the cell inside the bucket and stuffed the gun down the back of her pants. That was what everyone always did, right? It didn't seem to want to stay. "Damn." She couldn't run worrying about where the gun would end up and decided to leave it. She grabbed it again and handed it to the guard. "Unload this. Leave the gun, take the magazine."

He followed her instructions. George didn't struggle. In fact, he hadn't put up much of a fight at all. She locked gazes with him and he quirked an eyebrow, then lifted his chin toward the door. "Be careful," was what she could decipher through his muffled speech.

She flipped the barn lights out and waited at the door for her uncle's hired help to make his call. She could see the outline of the car move toward the fence line without its lights. One more look at the agent left behind and she tried not to debate whether George had set her up or helped.

"You know we can take you to a hotel or to your uncle's, but nowhere else." Her guard placed his hand in the small of her back and gently nudged her forward.

Tracey didn't answer him. They silently moved across the paddock to the far fence. Up and over, then a short distance to where the car waited. Part of her wanted to back out and let him take her to the protection waiting in Fort Worth. Just a small part.

The section of her heart seeking to be fixed needed to find those two kids. It was the half of her that won. She ran to the car and stopped at the driver's door.

"Don't say a word," Josh said, getting out of the car holding a gun on the guard who'd been so helpful. "Your partner's in the trunk. You and I are going to ride in the back. Any trouble, Tracey?"

"George Lanning is tied up in the barn."

Even in the starlight, she could see that Josh was surprised. "Turn around." He cuffed the guard, held the gun until the man got into the car and slid in the back, too.

They didn't need to say anything. She drove to the place off Highway 6 where they'd decided to abandon the guards. It was a long walk back to Waco. She doubted her uncle's men would be picked up by a friendly driver after they'd been forced to strip to their underwear.

"Your clothes will be about a mile down the road." Josh merged onto the road and raised the window.

Less than an hour ago she'd been feeling sorry for herself. "I thought you'd left me behind."

"To be honest, Tracey, I would have. I told you coming back wasn't my choice." Josh shifted in his seat. "I don't want to put you in more danger or ask you to do anything illegal."

"Right. Where to now? They didn't call while I was in the barn. Did they?"

"No."

"So do we need to come up with a plan?"

Josh slowed down on the deserted highway. She dropped the clothes that were in her lap to the edge of the gravel shoulder. The bodyguards would be able to find them easily, and they were far enough off the road not to draw attention.

Josh turned in the seat, facing her.

"Shouldn't we be in a hurry to get away from here?" she asked cautiously.

He tossed the phone they'd bought earlier into the seat between them. "They said they'd call."

"So we wait." She slapped her thighs and rubbed. Nervous tension. She looked around, wondering what he really wanted to say.

The car was still in Drive and his foot was on the brake. No reason to ask if they were going to wait on the guards to catch up with them. Josh kept looking at her and she kept looking everywhere but at him.

"I lied."

"About what?"

"I would have come back. I didn't want to bring you with me to the kidnappers, but I would have come back."

Her mouth was in the shape of an O. She said the words silently and rubbed her palms against her jeans again. *He would have come back.* Despite everything happening to them, her heart took off a little. She needed hope.

He let off the brake, steered the car onto the road and placed his palm up on the seat covering the phone. It was an invitation, confirmed by the wiggle of his fingers. She accepted, slipping her hand over his and letting it be wrapped within his warmth.

"I think I know what they want me to do, Tracey. There are some good men out there on our side. The ones at the house can't help. George Lanning realized that. I owe him a debt. In fact, I'm going to owe a lot of people when this is over."

"Not me. I'm the one who lost the kids."

He squeezed her hand. "I should have anticipated a move like this from the Tenoreno organization. They've been threatening Company F all year. I never thought... Hell, I just never thought about it. I'm sorry."

"Do you have any place in mind for us to wait? Or are you just driving?" Her stomach growled loud enough to be heard, jerking Josh's stare to her belly. "Have you eaten anything since breakfast?"

"Sounds like you're the one who hasn't." He chuckled. Things were too serious to really laugh. "I don't feel like eating."

"But you need to eat, right?"

"We need to switch cars first." He pulled into a visitor's parking garage at Baylor and followed the signs to park almost on the top floor. Grabbing a bag she hadn't noticed before from the backseat, he pushed the lock and tossed the keys inside before shutting the door.

"You know...it would lower my anxiety level if you'd let me in on whatever plan you've already formed. And don't tell me you don't have one," she finished. He unlocked an older-looking truck. "Aren't you worried about campus security finding the car? Then Agent McCaffrey will be able to figure out what you're driving."

"I'm only worried about Vivian getting in trouble for leaving it. Of course, it'll take them a little while to discover the connection to me. I have high hopes that this is over by then."

"Whose truck is this?" She grabbed an empty fast-food sack and gathered the trash at her feet.

"Vivian's son's best friend. I'm...uh...renting it."

"Not for much, I hope." The half-eaten taco that emerged from under the seat's edge made her gag. "I don't think I'm hungry anymore."

"We should get something anyway. No telling how long it'll be before we can eat again. Looks like we're on empty. Might be good to get Jackson snacks and juice." Josh exited and swung into a convenience store and handed her three twenties without finishing his sentence. "Better pay cash for the gas."

Even with all the media coverage, neither of their pictures had been flashed on the screen—at least from what she'd seen. If she'd had long hair, she would have dropped her head and let it swing in front of her face. Her hair was the exact opposite. Thick and short and very red, but not very noteworthy.

For Jackson and Sage, she picked up some bottled juice, two very ripe bananas, crackers and animal cookies. Not knowing how much gas Josh was purchasing, she didn't know if she had enough money for a full bottle of honey. She looked in the condiments, but could only pick up grape jelly. That would have to do if—if his blood sugar was too low. She'd have to evaluate him and see.

For them—unfortunately—two overpriced and overcooked hot dogs were in their future. She pointed toward the truck and the teenager behind the counter scanned her items. Josh finished pumping the gas and there was enough cash left for a supersized soft drink for them to share.

The clerk popped her gum and sacked everything. "Want your receipt?"

"No thanks."

Tracey lifted the sack from the counter while the girl continued thumbing through a magazine. It hit her that she'd never experienced that kind of work. Normal young adult work. The only job she'd ever had was helping Gwen and taking care of the kids. It was almost as if she got married her senior year of college, but without all the benefits.

Her life, her classes, her study time were all centered around the Parkers' schedules. That's the reason Josh hadn't known who to invite to her birthday. There wasn't anyone really.

It wasn't his fault. She'd made the choices that had led her to this moment. Josh waved at her to hurry back.

She'd had a very fortunate life. This event didn't seem like it. But they would get the kids back. Josh and the twins would be together again. She took comfort from the way he'd waited to hold her hand. Hopefully that meant there was a place for her in his life, too.

Chapter Ten

"So you have a plan. The Rangers are helping you even though they're not supposed to." Tracey's voice was soft and whispery once the truck engine was off. Josh parked in front of Lake Waco and opened his window.

"The Company isn't involved like you think. I don't have contact with any of them. I won't be sure Aiden is on our side until I get the text with details about the flight. If there is a flight. They might transport Tenoreno some other way."

She rubbed her hands up and down her arms as if she was trying to get warm. Thing was, it had to be ninety degrees outside and he'd cut off the engine quite a while ago. Was she as frightened as he was? Maybe.

He kept his arm across the top of the seat instead of draped over her shoulders where he wanted to put it. Then he extended his hand in an invitation to sit next to him. She took it.

In spite of the trauma and fright, it was a night of firsts. He wanted to hold her because she gave him strength, made him able to face what was coming next. But he couldn't explain that yet. Not while the kids were missing.

He laced his fingers through hers. The tops of her

hands against his palms. His larger hands covered her shaking limbs and she drew them closer around her.

"Want to talk about...anything?" she asked.

"My experience is sort of taking me to the deep end."

"Is that why you're so quiet?"

"I'm quiet?" He never said much. People called him a deep thinker. The Company knew not to interrupt when his feet were up on the corner of his desk. "There's a lot I could tell you. Rain check? It's not the time to think about distractions."

"I look forward to listening and I agree. We need to prepare." She moved their arms as if throwing a punch with each hand.

"Probably. Dammit, Tracey. Do you have any idea how I feel?"

"If your emotions are half as mixed up as mine... Then yes." She squeezed his fingers.

"There's a lot we need to talk about."

"Past, future and present. I know. We've avoided it for quite a while. I understand. I sort of feel disloyal. Then again, I can't help the way I feel."

"You feel disloyal?" he asked, finally looking at Tracey.

"Of course I do, Josh. Gwen was my friend."

He nodded, knowing what she meant. But he also knew that Gwen would want them to be happy...not guilty. When they had the kids back, they'd talk. They'd work it out.

"Do you have any idea what's in store? I know you've worked a couple of missing children cases." She spoke in his direction, but he could only see her in profile.

"Those were more parent abductions. Nothing on this scale."

"But you think they're all right. They wouldn't need

me to take care of Jackson if something had happened."
She sat straighter, talking to the front windshield. "Wait.
You're not sure why they want me, too. Are you?"

"There's a possibility that they've discovered your
family has money. They could want that on top of
what they want from me. I don't think that's the reason, though."

Tracey relaxed against him, pulling his arms around
her like a safety blanket. They shared comfort and intimacy, and the knowledge that they were both scared
without having to admit it.

"So everything's just a big mess. I can never tell you
how sorry I am about my uncle's interference."

"It wasn't your fault. No need to think about it." In
spite of the August heat, she shivered, so Josh hugged
her tighter. "I wish there was time to give you some
training to protect yourself. It's probably better to get
some rest—while you can."

"You think I need self-defense?"

"More like, if you know you're about to be hit—"
He had to clear his throat to say the rest. The thought
of her being hit was tearing him apart. "Yeah, if that
happens, then turn with the…um…the punch. You'll
take less of an impact. But the best-case scenario is to
keep your head down and don't talk back."

"In other words, don't give them a reason to hit me.
I can do that."

"Right." As much as he loved holding her in his
arms, they turned until they could face each other again.
"Dammit, Tracey. You can't do this. It's too dangerous.
When they call I'm going to tell them you refused."

"No. What if it *is* about the money and not just
about Jackson's diabetes? What then? We'll be right
back where we are now." She scooted back to the pas-

senger seat. "I totally get why you don't think I can handle this."

"What? That's not it. I have more confidence in your ability to take care of Jackson than I do in mine. It's dangerous, that's all."

"I haven't forgotten how dangerous it is." She rubbed the side of her face that had been hit during the kidnapping.

Josh took her hand in his again. He wasn't going to let tripping over his own words create a misunderstanding. There was a chance that when they faced the kidnappers they may never have another moment—anxious or tender.

"It's not a lack of confidence. I'm just—"

"Shh. Don't say it out loud. It's okay. I am, too."

Afraid. They were both afraid of what was going to happen to them, to the kids, to their world. Changes were coming.

Dawn was still an hour away as Josh watched Tracey sleep. Her head was balanced on her arm, resting on the door frame, window down with every mosquito at Reynolds Creek Park buzzing its way into the cab.

He swatted them to their deaths in between the catnaps he caught. He hadn't tried to fall asleep. Maybe if he had, he would have been wide-awake. He'd drifted to the sounds of crickets and lake waves splashing against tree stumps.

The lakeside park was quiet during the early morning. On any usual morning, he would get up, feed the horses, make breakfast, dress the twins and drop them off at their day care before heading into the office. Normal for a single dad.

He wanted to believe that their life was just as normal as the next family's. He heard the whining buzz of another mosquito and fanned the paper sack from the convenience store to create a breeze. The everyday stuff might not be that much different for the kids.

Who could say what normal really was in the twenty-first century? Not him. If he got his family back, who was to say it would ever be normal for them again? Tracey waved her hand next to her ear.

"Ring, dammit."

"What's wrong?" Tracey whispered.

"I'm willing the phone to ring."

"Is it working?" she asked with her mouth in the crook of her elbow.

"Nope."

Normal? Since it was Saturday, he should be waking his kids up three or four hours from now, searching their room for shin guards and taking them to a super peewee soccer game. He should be standing on the sidelines, biting his lip to stop himself from yelling at the twins to stay in their positions and not just chase the ball.

She stretched. "I know how to make it ring. Take me to the restrooms and it's sure to buzz while I'm inside. You know, that whole Murphy's law thing."

"You have a point." He moved the truck up the road and around a corner, keeping the headlights off so as not to wake the campers.

Tracey jumped out. He watched a possum by the park's trash area. It had frozen when the truck had approached. Would his kids be afraid after this? Afraid of strangers? Cars? Afraid of being alone? Were they being kept in the dark? Possibly buried alive?

"Anything?" She'd been gone less than five minutes.

He shook his head and took his turn in the restroom. His movements were slowing and his thoughts progressing at the horrors his kids could be facing right at that moment. The hand dryer finished and he heard Tracey yell his name.

"Should I answer it?" She was out of the truck running toward him.

"Do it."

"Hello?" she said, on Speaker.

"That's good. Glad you could join the party, Tracey."

It was the kidnapper. If his ears hadn't confirmed it, then Tracey's look of fright would have. Her hand shook so much that he took both it and the phone between his.

"Put Jackson and Sage on the phone." He sounded a lot more forceful than he felt. Inside he prayed that they'd both be able to talk to him.

"The brats aren't awake yet and you don't want me to send one of the boys in their room to wake them up."

"I need to know—"

"Nothing! You need nothing. You're going to do whatever I want you to do, whenever I want you to do it."

He was right.

Tracey stared at him, nodded. He couldn't say it was okay. He couldn't admit that this man threatening to harm his children could ask him to do anything…and he would do it.

"What do you want us to do?" she asked.

His heart stopped just like it had the day the doctor told him there was no hope for Gwen. He couldn't move. Tracey's free hand joined his, pulling her closer to the phone. Whose hand was shaking now?

"Wherever you're hiding from the cops, you have fifteen minutes to get to Lovers Leap. Don't be late." *Click.*

"Do you know where Lovers Leap is, Josh?" Tracey shook his arm. "Isn't it over by Cameron Park?"

"Yeah. Sure. I know where it's at."

"Then let's get moving." She tugged on his arm.

"I can't seem to move."

"What's wrong?" Even in the low golden light from the public restroom he could see her concern. She moved to his side, tugged his arm around her shoulders. "Come on. Just lean on me and I'll get you to the truck."

It was slow going, but she managed it. It felt like they used all fifteen minutes of their time, but a glance at his watch told him they still had ten.

"Shock. I think you're in shock and I'm not sure what I can do." She turned the engine over.

"Drive. I'll… I'll be okay when we get there."

He needed to see his kids. Needed to get Tracey there to take care of them. Needed to do whatever these crazy bastards wanted him to, so they'd be free.

Whatever the price. Whatever it took.

"Are you having a heart attack?" She split her focus from the dark road to Josh's pale face.

"I'm okay. Just drive. You have to get to the opposite side of Lake Waco." Josh braced himself in the truck. He rubbed his upper arm, kept it across his chest.

And he was scaring her more than the phone call.

"I think I know where I'm going. You really don't look okay."

"I will be by the time you get there. Quit driving like an old lady."

"Quit trying to change the subject. Do you hurt anywhere? Is your arm numb?"

"I told you I'm not having a heart attack." His voice was stronger and he pushed his hand against the ceiling as she took a corner a little too sharply. "Whatever it was it's gone. Your driving has scared the life back into my limbs."

Panic attack. Thinking it was okay. Saying it aloud might just make it begin again. She'd never tell. Josh's men didn't need to know that the major of Company F was human.

"Is there any of that soda left? Maybe you need sugar or something?" They were nearing Cameron Park and she had to change her thoughts to what was going to happen. "What if they take me and the kids?"

"Your first priority is the twins. In fact, that's your only priority. Your only responsibility. No matter what they do to me, say about me, or threaten me." Josh shook his head and swallowed hard.

"The same goes for me, Josh. You do whatever it takes to keep Jackson and Sage alive."

"Remember, they seemed a little scared about dealing with Jackson. If you can convince them to drop him off at a hospital, then do it."

"I will." She gave the keys to Josh. He didn't look as pale as when they were at the last parking lot.

"Why did they all call each other Mack? It's confusing."

"Or smart. They call everyone Mack so no real names are used. They wear masks so we can't identify their faces. Hopefully that gives them the security they need not to kill us. So refer to them by body type or what they do. Like the one that gives the orders. He can be In-Charge Mack."

"Is that what you do with the Rangers?" She nervously looked around the park and raced on before he could answer. "No one's here. I wonder if we should get out."

"They're here. There's no vehicle close by. That means they didn't bring the kids. One's on the back side of the restroom building. Another has a rifle behind the north pillar of the pavilion."

The phone was in the seat between them. It buzzed with a text message for her to get out of the car and go with Mack. The second message told Josh to stay.

She tried to brush it off, but admitted, "Josh I'm... I'm scared."

"So am I. I want you to remember this. I'll insist on a video chat when we make contact. They might force you to say whatever they want. I need to know that you and the kids are really okay. So if it's true, then tell me..."

"Something just we know. It'll have to be short."

"Right."

Tracey was nervous. For her, it would be unusual to say I love you. It was on the tip of her tongue to admit that. Thinking like a criminal wasn't her forte, but she understood that they might force her to say those words.

"Let's keep it as simple as possible. Tell me you think you left the whiskey bottle on the counter if you're okay and still in Waco. If you're not okay, play with your ring. If you don't think you're in Waco, then put the whiskey in a friend's house. Can you remember that? Totally off the wall for them, memorable for us."

"What do I say if you can't see me playing with my ring?"

"Say that you wish we hadn't ditched your bodyguards." He smiled and took her hand in his and tugged her across the seat. "Come on over here to get out. I can always get back inside if they order me to."

He defied their instructions when his feet hit the ground. Turning to help her from the truck, he pulled her into his arms. Their lips meshed and melted together from the heat of the unknown to come. It was a kiss of desperation, representing all the confusion she'd been feeling for months.

Shoes were hitting pavement behind her. Men were running toward them. She'd already experienced how brutal these men could be.

"You need to be in one piece if you're going to rescue us," she whispered to the man she was falling in love with. Before any of the kidnappers could grab her she got her hands on Jackson's emergency kit, juice and snacks inside.

Josh cupped her face with his hands. "You're the bravest woman I've ever known. There's no way to thank you." He gently kissed her again.

This kiss felt like goodbye. Sweet, gentle, not rushed in desperation or as fast as her heart that was pounding like it would explode.

The men pulled them apart, taking Jackson's bag from her. "Stop. Jackson needs that."

"But you don't. We'll give you what you need when you need it." Tracey fell back a step trying to get out of his way. It was the man who'd hit her. The man who'd been talking to them over the phone…In-Charge Mack.

His cruel eyes peeked through the green ski mask. But they weren't looking at her. No, they watched Josh. They scanned him from head to toe, sizing him up just before shoving him into the side of the truck. Hard.

"When I give an order you better follow it. Don't push me, Major Parker," In-Charge Mack screamed. "Take her to the van."

Birds flew overhead as the world began to brighten. She couldn't see the sun yet, but it was that golden moment where you knew the world was about to be brilliant. She also knew—before his hand raised—that

In-Charge Mack intended to hit Josh. It was part of the man's makeup.

The gloved hand moved.

"Stop!" Her hand moved, too. Directly in the path of In-Charge Mack's arm, catching part of the force and slowing him down. "You put me in the hospital. Don't you need Josh without a concussion?"

In-Charge Mack's hand struck as quickly as a snake taking out its prey. The force sent Tracey stumbling into Mack with the rifle. She couldn't see, but she heard the scuffle, the curses, the "don't hurt her" before Josh was restrained by two other men.

"I'm okay. It's okay," she said as quickly as she could force her jaw to move. She looked back at Josh straining at his captors, then at the man who'd hit her. "You need both of us, remember?"

"What I don't need is you talking at all." He gestured with a nod and thrust his chin toward the bike path.

The man who'd grabbed her, slung the rifle over his shoulder and latched on to her arm again. Jerking her toward the park area, she stumbled often from watching Josh instead of the path. When she could no longer see him, she looked in front of her just in time to miss a tree.

The sun was up. Light was forcing the darkness to the shadows. Fairly symbolic for their journey today. She needed good to triumph. She needed hope because they were on their own. Somehow she'd get the twins out of this mire and keep them safe until their dad came home.

THE INSTINCT TO be free was tremendous. The two men holding Josh weren't weaklings by any definition, but he didn't try. He saw the cloth. Then they poured liquid over it. He jerked to the side avoiding their effort to bring him forward.

Chloroform?

Maybe his hunch about the plane wasn't so far off after all. If they felt like they needed him to be out cold for a while, then whatever he was doing wasn't nearby. One of the extras joining the party was digging around the emergency supplies they'd brought. Tracey must have dropped them when she'd been hit.

"Hey! Jackson needs the stuff in that bag."

"Don't worry about your kid. That's why the baby-sitter's here."

"Shut up, Mack," instructed the ringleader. "Put the juice back in the bag and take it to the other Mack."

The guy giving all the orders approached him with the cloth and bottle.

"Look, tell me Jackson's still okay. Is he alert? Talking? How's Sage? Just tell me and I'll behave. No problem. There's no reason to knock me out."

"Your kid is fine."

The guy running the show nodded to the men holding Josh. They planted their feet and tightened their grips. It might be inevitable, but he wouldn't just stand there and inhale peaceably.

Chapter Eleven

Blindfolded. Tracey swore the man driving her to wherever the twins were being held was lost. They had to
be close by. It felt like he literally drove in circles. No
one had mentioned Jackson or Sage. She thought they'd
been joined in the van by a second person back at the
park, but the one who'd escorted her could have been
mumbling to himself.

You're the bravest woman I've ever known.

A lie. Gwen had been that woman. Strong and fear-
less in the face of death. But Tracey wasn't going to
take Josh's words lightly. She couldn't forget that he'd
said them, any more than she could ignore that he was
saying goodbye.

The van stopped and so did her thoughts about Josh.
Now it was about Jackson. Every piece of knowledge
she'd learned and could remember about diabetes would
be important.

They'd kept such a close eye on Jackson before yesterday, that he hadn't had any close calls since his initial
diagnosis. They even monitored Sage regularly to make
certain juvenile diabetes wasn't in her future. There was
no guarantee, but they wouldn't be unprepared.

"Get out."

"Can I take off the—"

"Just scoot to the edge and I'll take you inside."

She did what they said. She didn't hear anything unusual. It was still very early in the morning, but there were few natural sounds. She thought she heard the faint—sort of blurry—noise of cars on I-35. The low hum could be heard from multiple spots—and miles throughout Waco. At least she'd be able to find her way to safety.

The twins...your only priority. Your only responsibility.

The men each held one elbow and led her through a series of hallways. She assumed they were hallways. She heard keys in locks, dead bolts turning, doors opening and shutting. Three to be exact.

Inside there wasn't any noise. It was like the world had turned off. Then the blindfold was removed and she blinked in the bright sun reflecting into a mirror. She was still blinking when the fourth door was opened and she was pushed inside. Jackson's emergency bag was tossed in after her.

Thank goodness.

She expected a dark, dingy place. Maybe full of cobwebs or a couple of mice running around. She'd completely forgotten about the video that showed the kids playing with a room full of toys.

They were everywhere. Plastic kitchens complete with pots and pans. Lawn mowers that blew bubbles. A table where they could build a LEGO kingdom on top. Stuffed animals piled in a corner.

Where were the kids?

Who would buy all these toys for a kidnapping? What would be the purpose? She looked closer at them and noticed they were all clean, but very well-used. They were probably from garage sales or thrift shops.

Wherever they'd been purchased, no one would remember the person.

But where were the kids?

She picked up one of the many stuffed animals and sat in a chair made for children. Two mostly eaten sandwiches were on the table. Two bottles of water, barely touched, sat next to them. She spotted Sage's backpack under a giant bear. Next to it, her gold glitter slipper.

Tracey crossed the room and bent to pick it up. There, huddled under the pile of used stuffed toys, with their eyes squeezed tightly shut, were the twins. Relief washed over her, but she had to remain calm. Even a little excitement might overtax Jackson's blood sugar at this point.

"Hey kidlets, it's Trace Trace," she whispered, afraid to scare them.

Stuffed giraffes, dinosaurs, bears and alligators flew in all directions as the kids scrambled to their feet. Their backpacks were looped around their shoulders, ready to walk through the door. Shoes on the wrong feet meant they'd been off at least once.

Grape jelly was at the corner of Sage's mouth. But the most important thing was that Jackson looked alert and safe.

"Are you okay?"

She opened her arms and they flew into a hug. The relief she felt that they were both alive and okay... She couldn't think of words to describe the emotion.

"Can we go now, Trace Trace?" Jackson asked. "Where's Daddy?"

"I want to go, too," Sage said. "Why didn't Daddy come get us?"

"Have you had breakfast? Are you really okay?" She turned to Jackson again, gauging his eyes, looking for any indicators that his blood sugar was too low. "Do you have a headache or feel nauseous?"

"Nope."

"He's been good." Sage lifted her hand to her mouth, trying to whisper to Tracey—it didn't work. "I hid the candy they gave us in the oven."

"Oh, I knew where you put it. But I didn't want to get sick if there wasn't anybody here to take care of me."

"Sage, hon, run and get that bag with Jackson's medicine stuff."

The little girl skipped over and skipped back. Both children seemed okay on the outside.

"Do we have to stay?" Sage whined, deservingly so.

"For a little while longer." Tracey pulled the materials she needed to test Jackson's blood sugar from the bag.

The little darling was so used to the routine that he sat with his finger extended, ready for the testing. She put a fresh needle into the lancing device, and took a test strip from the container.

Sage tore the alcohol wipe package open and handed it to her. They all lived with this disease. They'd had their share of ups and downs, but they stayed on top of it.

"I love you guys. Do you know that?" She wiped off the extended finger, punched the button, dropped the droplet of blood on the strip and placed it in the meter.

Two little heads bobbed up and down. She hid her anxiousness waiting on the results. He was in the safe zone, ready to eat his breakfast and start his day.

Thank God.

"Have you two been alone all this time?"

"Nu-uh."

"Some guy sits with a mask all over his face. Says

he's hot." Sage was the talker, the observant one, the storyteller. "Then he leaves and comes back sometimes."

"Sometimes he tries to play," Jackson added. "That guy came in with his phone one time. 'Member?"

"Yeah, but he wasn't fun. He was angry and mean."

They sat in the chairs next to her at the table. She put a banana on each little plastic plate. Wiped out the glasses as best as she could and poured a little bit of juice in them. She noticed that one of the juice bottles was missing so she kept a third of the bottle, placing it back in the bag.

"So, eat and I'll get some crackers."

"For breakfast?" they said together.

"There's nothing wrong with bananas and crackers."

"Aren't you eating?" Jackson asked, peeling one section and turning the banana sideways for a bite. He left it there, like a giant smile, then posed until she acknowledged him.

He swallowed his bite and laughed, showing the mashed banana on his tongue. Sage said "yuck," and then they all three laughed, making Tracey want to cry. How could any of this be funny? But if she didn't laugh and act as if it was, then they'd get anxious and stressed.

Stress was bad for blood sugar.

Very bad.

Laughing, playing and maybe casually looking for a way out of this room. That's what their day would be. Maybe the man who was scary and mean would stay away.

Maybe if they were really lucky, Josh would haul all the mean Macks to jail. Then the Parker family could all live happily ever after.

"I want to go home, Trace Trace."

"I know, Jackson. And we will. But while we're here, what do you want to play?"

"Princesses. I thought of something first, so we play my game." Sage darted around looking through the toy pile for princess gear.

"I don't feel like playing." Jackson crawled into her lap and rested his head on her shoulder.

She wasn't going to panic. His level was within normal range. He was outside his routine and would be tired even if he didn't have diabetes. "Okay. Sage, would it be okay if I just told you a story?"

"I can't find any princess hats anyway."

"You know, Sage, you don't have to have a princess hat to be a princess."

"You don't? But isn't it more fun if you do?" She smiled and twirled. "What story are you going to tell?"

"Let's go sit on the mattress so Jackson can take a nap. I mean rest 'cause Prince Jackson doesn't take naps." Then she tickled Sage. "Neither does Princess Sage. Right?"

"Right."

They sat down and Tracey created a story about a prince and a princess who lived with their father, the king. When they asked the king's name she told them King Parker. Sadly, the queen didn't live with them anymore. The story went on and of course the kids recognized that it was about them.

"Then one day a horrible evil dragon swooped down and stole the beautiful princess and handsome prince. The dragon…" The kids held on to her hands tightly and snuggled a little closer. "What should we name the awful dragon?"

"Mack," they said in unison.

"Okay. Mack the dragon was tired of flying around

burning up all the bridges. So he went back to the cave where he held the princess and prince. 'What do you want with us?' said the beautiful princess."

Tracey changed voices for each character in the story. The kids were nodding off. Both rested their heads in her lap when one of the Macks came through the door, bolted it behind him and sat on the bench.

She stopped referring to the dragon as Mack. There was no reason to antagonize one of them. And no reason to continue the story since both of the kids were asleep.

Tracey left them curled where they were and propped another blanket behind her head. She pretended to rest and assessed the room through half-closed lids. There didn't seem to be any other way out. The next time they left her alone, she'd be bold and just look.

All those years growing up a rich kid, she'd been warned to be careful. Super careful. She was never allowed to go anywhere alone. Not until her second semester at Baylor.

She remembered the guy who looked like a college student and had followed her around campus. He even had season tickets to football games. Probably not the section he wanted, but her uncle's money had bought him access to a lot.

It took begging her grandfather and whining that she had no friends to get him to call off the hounds. Promising that she'd be overly careful, she was finally on her own. That's when she realized she didn't really know how to make friends.

Then a bad date had shot her overprotective uncle into warlord status. He declared she didn't have any rights and as long as he was paying the bills—blah blah blah. Poor little rich girl, right?

Who would have thought that the first time she'd be

placed into real danger would be because she worked for a Texas Ranger? What a laugh her grandfather would have had about this mess.

So there she was, thinking about her grandfather, sitting awkwardly with two precious children asleep on her lap, praying that they'd grow up without being frightened of the world. And then more simply, she just prayed that they'd be able to grow up.

"Trace Trace?" Sage said sleepily. "What happened to the king? Did he get his kids back?" She yawned. "Did he get to be happy?"

"Sure, sweetie. He used his strong sword and killed the dragon. And all the Parkers lived happily ever after."

"Trace…is your name Parker, too?"

"No, kidlet. It's not."

Sage drifted back to sleepy land giving Tracey more time to think about it. She wouldn't be a part of the Parker happy-ever-after. It was time for her to ride into the sunset alone.

Chapter Twelve

Josh lost track of how many times they'd covered his face with the sweet-smelling gauze. Enough for him to have a Texas-size headache. Long enough that his body recognized he'd been in one position too long, lying across the metal flooring of a panel van. And long enough that his stomach thought his neck had been cut off.

The skyline through the van window showed only trees and stars. Definitely not the skyscrapers that would indicate a city. They could still be in Waco, but he had a feeling they'd driven closer to the state prison where Tenoreno was being held.

The men surrounding him were unmasked, but it was too dark to make out any of their faces. Now wearing garb like a strike force—military boots, pants, bulletproof vests, gun holsters strapped to their thighs. Tracey was right. The idea of calling each other Mack tended to be confusing. He had to admit that it was effective. But they didn't act like a cohesive team.

Josh's hands were taped behind him. Tightly. The hairs on his wrists pulled with each tug he tried to hide. There must be several layers because it wasn't budging. He wouldn't be getting free unless he had a knife.

For the Macks, it had been a good idea to knock

him out cold while they traveled. His brain was still fuzzy while he attempted to soak up everything about his situation and process it for a way out. If he'd been awake, the problem would be resolved or at least he'd have a working theory.

Someone kicked the back of his thigh. He held himself in check, but a grunt of pain escaped. He tried not to move. He needed time for the cobwebs to clear. But there wasn't any use trying to hide that he was awake. Even if he wasn't alert.

"Masks on. He's awake."

The thought at the forefront of his mind was Jackson's health and his family's safety. He could only estimate how long his captors had been driving. It might still be early afternoon.

One step at a time.

"I need to talk to Tracey."

If only he could get In-Charge Mack and his men to confirm what they had in store for him. As in why did they need him personally? Whatever it was, they felt like they needed hostages to keep him in line. Once they confirmed, he'd know how to proceed.

Or where to proceed.

"It's time to earn your keep, lawman." The guy who'd kicked him laughed.

They had his phone. Aiden must have texted the location information. Good, they also had his bag from the house. He had a few tricks in there that would help get his family back.

"We're talking to the men that are with her in ten minutes. Behave and you might get an update." The In-Charge Mack didn't even glance back from the front seat.

Laughing Mack looked around, saw where they

were, and then pulled a gun to point at Josh's head. "Behave." The gun went under a loose sweatshirt— still aimed at him.

They pulled even with another vehicle, the drivers nodded at each other and separated. He could see the other car lights in the rearview mirror as it did a three-point turn in the road and followed closely behind.

"Where are we?"

"Thanks to you, daddy dearest is scheduled for a private plane ride to get to trial. You're our passport," In-Charge Mack said from up front.

"Daddy? Aren't you a little short to be Xander Tenoreno?"

Laughing Mack kicked out, connecting with Josh's knee.

He'd actually confronted the son of Paul Tenoreno several times. At each encounter he'd looked him straight in the eye. The guy giving the orders here was only about five foot ten. Average height for an above-average criminal.

But he couldn't reject the hunch that these men were regular employees of the Mafia ring in Texas. They were definitely well funded and prepared. The animosity that was associated with their talk about Tenoreno was a bit intense. Why free a man you hated so that he could run the operation again?

"If you'd told me your plans a little earlier, I could have saved you the trouble. They pulled all my authority yesterday when you kidnapped my kids." He wanted to see their reaction. What was their ulterior motive? "I can't get you on that plane."

"Don't be so modest, Major. We have every confidence in your abilities." The one calling the shots turned to show him a picture of Tracey with the kids. "We also have very little confidence that Mack in toy land will keep his cool if you don't get the job done. He's itchy to pull the trigger, don't ya know."

"Isn't it time to stop talking in riddles and tell me what you really want?"

"You haven't figured it out? But you're so good at this. Your Texas Ranger buddies got poor old Mr. Tenoreno moved to the Holliday Transfer Facility. He's waiting to be flown to Austin. We're going to pay him a visit."

"I can't get you inside there, either." Josh attempted to push himself up to a sitting position. His ankles were also taped tightly together. He pushed on a hard-sided case.

"Are you being dense on purpose?" Laughing Mack lashed out with his boot, catching the back of Josh's leg.

"Your kid here is going to make walking anywhere a problem. Call him off. I need my knees." Josh made note of how many guns were in the van.

"Mack, mind your manners." He spoke to the guy still pointing the gun in Josh's direction, but he pointed twice like he was giving directions to the driver.

Josh used the bumps in the road to help shift his position. He was finally upright and could see more of the view. A field, lots of trees, nothing special out the front. But when he glanced out the back, just behind the second vehicle were soccer and baseball fields.

He knew exactly where they were—Huntsville Municipal Airport. He'd assumed that they'd attack here. He'd just expected a little more time to figure out how to throw a kink in their plan.

"Whatever you're planning, I'm not doing a damn thing until I talk to Tracey. And I mean talk, not just see her picture."

"I figured as much. Almost time."

The van started up, speeding down the dirt road, then pulled under a canopy of trees. The second vehicle pulled in next to them.

"They've left the prison. We have six minutes," the Mack next to him said.

"No Tracey. No cooperation."

"Dial the phone. Remember it's face-to-face and you watch," he told Laughing Mack. "Make it quick."

One thing about this outfit, everyone in it obeyed In-Charge Mack without hesitation. Tracey's face was on the phone screen. She reached out toward the phone at her end, looked sharply away and then back at him.

"They won't let me hold the kids so you can see them but they're doing okay. Sage has been watching over her brother, as usual.""

"And how is Jackson?"

"He's doing okay. I'm sure he's going to bounce right back after this."

"Have they hurt you?"

"Nothing that a shot of whiskey wouldn't cure. Did I leave it in the middle of the house?"

"What was that?" In-Charge Mack asked.

"She said she wanted some whiskey," Laughing Mack relayed to him.

"That's enough. Disconnect."

"Josh? I wanted to tell you that I—"

Laughing Mack got a big kick out of cutting her off. *Tell me what?*

He didn't have time to process. They opened the van doors and Josh could see the airfield.

"Out."

He lifted his bound ankles and the Mack nearest the door sliced them free with a knife Josh hadn't seen. He really did need to clear his head and become aware of his surroundings. Think this thing through.

The Macks moved the hard-sided case that had been near his feet to outside and flipped the lid open. Machine pistols.

"You really think those are necessary?"

"Glad you asked, Major. Obviously, this is the backup. If you fail, we're bringing down that plane."

"What exactly do you want me to do? I thought you were here to free Tenoreno." Josh kept his eyes moving. Trying to remember how each of them stood. If they showed any signs of weakness or additional personal weapons.

"Wrong, Major. You're here to kill him."

Chapter Thirteen

Tracey was taking a huge risk. What if they weren't rescued before Jackson needed this cartridge? And what if she *didn't* use the insulin on the sleeping guard? It might be her only opportunity to try to escape. What if Josh didn't—

No! Josh was coming back. He'd never give up and neither would she. She put the kids to sleep on the mattress, leaving their shoes on their feet so they'd be ready. Jackets and bags were by the door. They wouldn't leave without them. It was their routine and no reason to argue.

Taking this risk was necessary, not just a shot in the dark. It would work. She knew what the side effects of too much insulin were. In a healthy person, he'd probably vomit, but he'd eventually pass out. She didn't know how many men were on the other side of the door.

The young man watching them had already complained about how warm it was while wearing the ski mask. The room had its own thermostat. It looked like an old office space. She switched the cool to heat and cranked the temperature up. It was going to be unbearable in a couple of hours. Their guard would get hotter, faster—of course, so would they.

The last thing to do while he was gone from the room

was to prep the needle with insulin and hide it. They'd take the emergency kit back and return it to the other room as soon as a Mack came to keep an eye on them. Their ultimate weapon to keep her in line was taking away the emergency kit for Jackson.

"I bet your boss wouldn't like knowing that you don't stay in here while I check Jackson's blood sugar. Nope. None of this would be possible if you did," she said to herself, capping the needle. She couldn't keep it in her pockets. They'd see it for sure.

So she arranged toys and the kid-sized kitchen station near the bench where the guards sat. It was simple to keep the syringe with the toy utensils. She snagged one and put it on the table so she'd have an excuse to exchange it later.

She could give the injection without the guard feeling more than a small prick on his skin. Insulin didn't need a vein, just fatty tissue. If he was sound asleep it might not bother him at all. But she had a sharp toy ready as an explanation. She also moved the trash can closer to the bench…just in case.

They should be coming back into the room soon. She'd been wondering for far too long about life and what the next stage held for her. When all this was done and over, there wouldn't be any waiting. It was so much better to find out. To know.

Leaving Waco, leaving her friends, leaving Josh wasn't her first choice. Waiting wasn't, either. She had to stop being a scaredy cat and start living life. That meant handing in her resignation to Josh and telling him how she really felt.

Forty-eight hours ago she'd been ready to give her notice and walk away. Even if it broke her heart. Well, there was no doubt her heart would shatter now, but it was a resilient organ and she'd manage. She could walk away if Josh didn't ask her to stay.

The locks on the door turned. She dropped her head into her arms on the tiny table and calmed her breathing. She was physically exhausted from a lack of sleep, food and an abundance of adrenaline pumping constantly. Forcing herself to pretend to be asleep might just slow her physical state to let it happen.

Being bent in half like she was wouldn't let her stay asleep for long.

The same guard came straight to the table to collect the emergency kit. She barely saw him through her lashes, watching his silhouette turn off the lamps in the corners, and then sit on the bench.

First step…check.

Rest, rest, rest. She was going to need it to get to safety.

There wasn't a clock in the room and they'd taken her watch—another way to make her dependent on them for Jackson's care. But her body told her she'd been in the cramped position far too long and she hoped her guard was deep in sleep. She pushed her damp hair away from her face.

It was definitely beyond hot.

She took the toy spatula and stood, trying not to make any noise. She'd cleared her path, thinking this through earlier. No squeaky toys, nothing to trip over.

She kept on her toes, not allowing her boot heels to make noise against the linoleum floor. She exchanged the toy gadget for the syringe and removed the needle cover. Still no peep from the kids or their guard. She looked at him; he'd rolled the ski mask up his face, covering his eyes. The smooth chin meant he'd either just shaved or he didn't need to.

The covered eyes meant it would be easier to follow through on her plan. He'd have to move the mask before he could see where she was. She risked a lot by tugging a little at his black T-shirt, but if she could stick this in his side...

Done.

This Mack, sitting on the bench, turned and grunted. He didn't wake. She replaced the cap, threw the syringe away like all the other supplies from earlier and tiptoed to sit on the mattress with the kids.

It didn't take long before their guard moaned, then held his stomach like he was cramping. Before Mack could reach the door, he detoured for the garbage.

Tracey didn't hesitate. She couldn't let herself think about what would happen to the young man. He was a kidnapper. He'd threatened Jackson's life. She was going to make sure the little boy was safe.

No matter the cost. No matter who she had to knock out with insulin to do it. Even in the dim light she could tell he was sweating and disoriented. He was unsteady on his feet and faintly asked for help.

She wanted to. She had to cover her ears, she wanted to help him so badly.

Instead, she got the kids up and sat them in chairs. Jackson was a little woozy and put his head back onto the table. When the young guard began leaning to one side, she struggled with him to put him on the mattress. Then searched his pockets for a cell phone.

Nothing except the keys to the doors.

Before she scooted the twins out of the room, she checked out the other side of the door. No one was there. She ventured farther, listening before she turned each corner. No signs of the other men. She quietly headed back and saw both of their heads poking around the edge.

Backpacks on, they ran to meet her.

"Are we going home now?" Sage asked.

"First we have to play hide-and-seek. You can't giggle or tell anybody where we're at. Okay?"

Both their heads bobbed. Sage jumped up and down, smiled then got Jackson excited as well. "We get to go home. We get to see Daddy." They said in unison, jumping again.

"Please guys, it's really important for us to be quiet. Shh." She placed a finger across her lips and lowered her voice. "Quiet as church mice. Ready?"

They hurried downstairs, where she used the keys again to get out the front door. Austin Avenue?

They were in downtown Waco? It must be the wee hours of the morning, because this was an area of town that was open until two. She hadn't heard any party or loud music. No wonder they'd filled the room with toys to keep the kids occupied and silent.

Tracey ran. She hoisted Jackson to her hip, holding tight to Sage's little hand. "Come on, baby, I know you're tired, but we've got to run. You can do it."

Where to?

They had to be gone—out of view. Fast. Before someone discovered they'd left their room. She tried the sandwich shop next door.

Locked.

They'd all be locked. Everything closed in this part of town. There was nothing to throw at a window. No alarm she could set off without the kidnappers looking out their window and seeing her.

So close.

They were so close to freedom. If they could just find somebody...

Nothing but parking lots, a closed sandwich shop, more parking lots and the ALICO Building. Maybe there was somebody still there.

It was the dead of night and there were no headlights. No one around to wave down for help. They made it across Austin Avenue and then again across Fifth Street. A door banged open. She dared to look back for a split second. It was them.

"Over there," she heard one of the men say.

"Sage, honey, put your arms around my neck." She'd run for their lives carrying the twins. But where?

The parking garage would be open. She ran between the structures. Garage to her left, fire escape to her right. Fire escape? Then what? Climb twenty-two stories outside the tallest building in Waco with twin four-year-olds?

No. All she had to do was make it up one flight before they saw her. The building was split-level—they could hide on the level that was a parking lot. It was more logical to choose the garage door. She couldn't leave their fate to the off chance someone left their car unlocked and they could hide inside.

What then? Blow the horn until their captors broke the window and carried them back to their downtown dungeon?

It would have to be the fire escape. She set a lethargic Jackson on the stair side of the fire escape, helped Sage over and climbed over herself. They were between buildings where the voices of the men chasing them echoed. She didn't know if it could be done, but it was their only chance.

"Quiet as a mouse, kidlets, we've got to keep quiet.

Go ahead and start climbing, sweetheart." She adjusted Jackson on her back moving as fast as she could behind Sage.

One foot, then another. Four-year-old legs couldn't take stairs two at a time. Neither could a twenty-six-year-old with a four-year-old on her back. If she wasn't scared of falling down, she would pick up Sage and make the climb with both of them.

The shouts changed. No longer echoes from the street, they were directly below them. Tracey stopped Sage and slowly—soundlessly—pulled her to the side of the building. Maybe they'd get lucky. Maybe neither of the men would look up. Maybe they'd take the logical path into the garage.

Maybe luck was on their side. Looking by barely tilting her head, she watched as the men took off into the other building.

"More quietly than ever, baby girl. We can do this."

It took time. The one flight was actually a little more than that. Their luck ran out. Just as they made it to the roof so did the kidnappers. They yelled out to each other or at someone else, she couldn't be certain.

They were on the lower roof. She set the twins next to a door and looked around for something to pry it open. No junk in the corner. Nothing just lying around to pick up and bang against metal. She heard the men taking the metal fire escape two steps at a time.

Running to the Fifth Street side of the roof, she yelled, "Help! Someone help us!" There weren't any headlights, no one walking, nothing.

Then to the parking lot side toward the river. Someone might be hanging out closer to the water, but it was too far away. "Help! Somebody. Anybody."

Chapter Fourteen

The kids were cuddled together. All Tracey could do
was join them. They couldn't tackle the twenty stories
of fire escape stairs. Even if they did, there wasn't a helicopter waiting to whisk them off to safety.

The men chasing them heard her cries for help. She
heard their shoes slam against the metal steps, then
across the roof. She braced herself for punches or kicks.
The repercussions of running away. Maybe now. Maybe
later. But these men would strike out. She'd protect
the kids.

She repeated the promise that they'd be all right as
the men both angrily kicked her legs. These men would
lose. Josh would find them. They *would* lose.

"Stop it! Don't hurt her!" the twins yelled, still
wedged between her and the wall.

Their screams echoed in her ears as they were pulled
from her arms. One of the men jerked her up by her hair
while the other had a hand on each twin. They struggled. She could barely stand.

He dragged her to the edge of the building, threatening to throw her over the side. His hands went around
the back of her neck, pushed her to the ledge. She
dropped to her knees.

"I wish I could get rid of you," he spitefully whispered. "I'd leave you on that sidewalk along with the jerk who let you escape. Did you hit him with a stuffed unicorn?" He shoved her forward into the concrete barrier. "Get up and get hold of one of them brats."

Limping down the fire escape, she wondered if they'd care that their friend might die from the insulin injection. She carried Jackson, and poor Sage was in the arms of the man to her right.

The men constantly looked over their shoulders, but they weren't followed. No one drove by. No police were in sight. They weren't gentle, especially the blond who held a gun instead of a child and shoved her every third step she took.

"He might just kill us for this. If anybody sees, we're dead. We need to get out of here, fast."

"So we don't tell him, right? He'd just get angry," the man carrying Sage answered. "She sure ain't going to tell him. Mack will never know they got loose. Besides, we got 'em back, didn't we? And we still have another twenty before we're supposed to leave and…you know."

Leave?

Yes, he'd cocked his head toward her. So what did he mean? Leave them or leave with them, taking them to a new location? Or maybe they planned to leave them here after killing them?

Once again she wished that she'd been brave or lucky enough to leave earlier, before the bars on the street had closed. Food trucks were normally one of the last things to leave the now-empty parking lot.

"You need to call 911 for your friend," Tracey told the men, trying to gauge their humanity. "He's very ill and needs emergency care"

"So he's sick. He'll get over it." Gun in hand, he shoved her through the outer door.

Would they call 911? If she admitted why he needed help they'd know for certain that she'd planned her escape instead of taking advantage of their guard being sick. Ultimately, she didn't want the weight of his death on her shoulders.

"I injected him with insulin and he's going into hypoglycemic shock." They ignored her as they entered the building they'd just escaped from. "Can't you drop him at the clinic with a note? He may die."

"That's on your head, lady. You're the one that gave it to him and he was stupid enough to let ya."

They pushed her into the toy room, Sage right behind her. The one holding the gun stuck the barrel under her chin and moved close to her face. His minty breath a stark contrast to the threats. "You listen to me, lady. Stay in line or we're getting rid of you no matter what Mack says."

Then bolted the door.

"Oh my!" She cried out before realizing she needed to control herself for the kids.

"What's wrong, Trace Trace?" Sage asked.

Jackson didn't say anything. He went to the mattress, saw it was full with the young man she'd injected and lay down next to the wall using a teddy bear for a pillow.

"When can we go home?"

"Soon, honey. Soon." She pulled the little girl into her arms and rocked her by shifting her weight from foot to foot. Her long hair was tangled again. She'd finger-comb it after breakfast.

"Did Daddy forget about us?"

"Oh no, baby. He loves you and is doing everything he can to get you back to him."

It took only a few minutes to get Sage to drift off to sleep. She adjusted the children on a blanket and used the secondhand animals to make them comfortable and feel safe.

The young guard wasn't comatose. He roused a little, making her heart a little lighter. He was clammy with sweat, so she used the water from the water bottle to dampen a couple of doll dresses and wiped his brow, trying to make him more comfortable. She would never be able to do that again knowing that the outcome might mean somebody would die.

Sitting still in the predawn hours she remembered something odd about their captors…she knew what they looked like. While chasing her, they'd left their masks behind. She could identify them. This development couldn't be good.

It was her fault for trying to escape. But she had been right about telling Josh the whiskey was in the center of the house. At least she knew they were definitely in the heart of Waco. She prayed that he'd be able to find them.

That line was getting old. Of course she'd hope for that. But she couldn't focus on it, either. She'd do her job and think of another way out of this room. Her life wasn't a series of rescues.

She'd walked away from all that when she turned twenty-one. "Heck, I even changed my name to avoid it." *Pick yourself up and get your head on straight, Tracella Sharon Cassidy Bass.* That was her grandmother's voice talking from her overly pink bedroom. Ha! Years ago Grandma Sweetie had declared that her pieces of advice would come in handy. But Tracey bet even Sweetie wouldn't have imagined this scenario.

She looked at the man in the corner. He was just a man now. Not a creep, not an abductor with a gun—just a young man who needed help. No one deserved to die.

And she'd help as best she could. She turned the water bottle upside down and got the last drops onto the cloth.

After she'd cooled their guard's forehead, she decided to talk with the other two guards. She knocked on the door trying not to wake up the kids. Then she knocked a little more forcibly.

"What?" one of them shouted through the wood.

"We need more water."

"Not now."

"Even another bottle for your friend?" She tapped on the door, attempting to get an answer.

"Lady, you need to shut up so we can figure this out."

"There's water in the tan bag you took from me." They'd even taken the kids' backpacks with their toys.

"Yeah, like we're giving that back."

"You have to. It has Jackson's insulin and supplies."

"Isn't that what you stuck in Toby—I mean Mack? One of them insulin needles, right? And you said he could die. So no way. I ain't letting you have it back. Needles are dangerous, man."

There was arguing. Raised voices. Lowered voices.

"Don't matter anyway. We're supposed to head out."

"Are you...are you leaving us? Please unlock the door before—" She tripped backward as the door was pushed open. The gun took her by surprise. When it was pointed at her head, street gangster style, she could only raise her hands and say, "Don't shoot."

"We ain't shooting you, lady. But we don't trust you neither. Get the kids. We're leaving."

"Where are you taking us?"

"Does it matter?" the blond holding the gun in her face said.

"To the airport. He dead yet?" asked the other as he hurried to the corner where the kids were.

"Shut up, you idiot," the blond man insisted. "First you use Toby's name. And dammit, thanks to him," he pointed at the ill man, "she's seen our faces."

She remembered what Josh had said. The kidnappers would feel safe as long as their identities were secret. Would they kill her and the kids now that they weren't? "He, uh, still needs a doctor, but I think he'll be okay."

"That's good I guess."

"No it's not," said the blond, waving the gun like an extension of talking with his hands. "What if somebody finds him? What if he talks?"

"Do we shoot him then?"

"What? You can't— He's unarmed and helpless." Tracey would have pleaded more but the men looked at each other as if she was crazy.

Maybe she was, since they were obviously ready to shoot her and the kids. Now they were going to taking them to a new place? Or could it possibly be…

"Is this an exchange at the airport? Who told you to bring us?"

"We don't do names, lady. We just do what we're told, and then we're gone."

"So there's no reason to kill him." She pointed to the unconscious guy. "You can just leave him here."

"We don't have time, man. If you want to plug him, go ahead. My hands are full." The second man pulled a sleepy Jackson into his arms.

The blond one lifted Sage. She squirmed and pushed at his shoulders. "I want Trace Trace."

Then she began to cry. For real, not a fake cry to get her way. She was genuinely scared of the man who held her and had a gun pressed against her back.

"Here, let me take her." Tracey held out her arms

and Sage threw herself backward, nearly falling between them.

The children were old enough to understand guns. Even at four and a half the twins knew about tension and that guns were dangerous. Their father was a Texas Ranger and had weapons in the house—inside a lockbox and gun cabinet—but they'd already had lectures about how they were weapons and weapons were dangerous.

Sage had watched the gun being waved around. She'd heard the discussion about shooting someone. She could tell things weren't right no matter how many toys were in the room.

"Let's get gone," the blond said. "Mack's expecting us to be there."

Tracey didn't want to draw their attention to the man in the corner, so she grabbed a toy bear for Sage to latch onto and left their backpacks. There were spare crackers and juice in the emergency kit that could tide them over until they received food.

They had almost reached the back door when she asked the blond, "The tan bag with his supplies. Where did it go?"

"Get in the van." He shoved her forward to the back stoop.

"We have to have that bag."

"You ain't jabbin' me with anything."

"No, we can't go without it. Jackson needs it."

"Should have thought 'bout that before you made Toby sick." The second guy put Jackson in her arms after she put Sage in the van.

"Where do I sit?" Sage asked, following with a huge sniff from her tears.

No seats. The panel van had nothing but a smelly old horsehair blanket.

"What an adventure, Sage. You and your new bear friend can help me hold Jackson."

She put the bear on the metal floor and Sage sat cross-legged next to it, then dropped her head onto her hands. Jackson woke up, rubbed his eyes and moved next to the bear, imitating his sister. Sage pursed her lips and Jackson mimicked or answered. Sometimes the twin language was hard to interpret.

The van door closed and they pulled out of the parking lot. It was still before dawn on Sunday morning. Too early for anyone to have noticed them being moved along by gunpoint. A lot of people went to church in Waco, but not *this* early.

Even if someone saw them sitting on the floor of the panel van, no one would think anything suspicious. All they could do was cooperate.

"Trace Trace?" Jackson nudged her leg. "I'm tired and hungry. Where are my snacks?"

"We'll have to wait for breakfast, big boy."

Jackson threw himself backward and stiffened his body. His small fist hit her bruised jaw. She clamped down on the long "ouch" that wanted to escape. It wasn't his fault and she refused to upset him more. When his blood sugar began to get low he became angry and quarrelsome. It was one of the first clues that his levels needed to be adjusted.

"Jackson's always 'posed to have crackers," Sage told her. "He's starting to get a little mean, Trace Trace."

"I know, honey, but they got left with the toys."

Sage leaned closer putting her hand close to her mouth, indicating she didn't want the men to hear her. "Is that man really going to die?"

"No, baby. His sugar's a little low right now, but he's going to be fine."

"That's good."

Tracey held tightly to the sides of the van and the kids held tightly to her. Fortunately, it wasn't a long ride to the Waco Regional Airport. This place wasn't huge by any means. She'd flown home from here several times before she'd turned twenty-one.

Maybe knowing the layout of the airport would be an advantage. If she was given a chance to run, she'd know where to go. But had the Macks hinted at an exchange. Her mind was racing in circles trying to figure it out.

After a few minutes she realized they weren't going to the airport. At least not the one in Waco. The twins fell asleep quickly enough with the rocking motion of the van.

The two men didn't speak to give her additional clues. She couldn't really see scenery out the back window, but it was mainly the black night sky and an occasional streetlamp. She tightened her arms around the kidlets, closed her eyes and concentrated solely on not being scared.

Very scared.

Chapter Fifteen

Kill Tenoreno? Mack wanted him to kill Tenoreno? The person pulling the strings didn't want their leader out of the country? Or who did they bring him here to kill? Less and less about this operation was making sense. He kept coming back to why him and why kidnap his kids? If he could determine the answer to that complicated question, then he might find the solution.

Why tell him to kill the prisoner? Why did they want Tenoreno dead? Why did they bring Josh to pull the trigger? A political nightmare for one. They'd prosecute him and persecute the Texas Rangers. He was thinking too far ahead. The problem was now.

"I'll need a weapon." He was handed a Glock. He fingered the weapon, wanting to pull it on Mack, knowing the man would never hand him a loaded gun. "I prefer my own. It's in the bag you have in the van."

In-Charge Mack shook his head. "Let me say this out loud. Kill me, kill my men, we kill your family. The men holding your kids don't care if they get a call to shoot or get a call to let them go. Understand?"

"Understood."

Thing was, Bryce would be waiting in that hangar, protecting Tenoreno. He wasn't just going to let Josh walk in and shoot anyone. Company F was prepared for an attack to hijack a plane, not massacre everyone. The Mack gang loaded and checked the machine pistols. A lot of men were about to be killed unless he did something.

Or just did what they wanted.

"Your plan doesn't make sense. You can't be certain I won't point this at the wrong person." He aimed the Glock at Mack's head. Three of the leader's men immediately pointed machine pistols at his.

"Hold on, give the Major time to accept the inevitable."

"And what would that be?"

"Mack." In-Charge pointed to the man to his right. "Dial."

Josh aimed his barrel at the night sky. "Point taken."

"You are a useful tool to get us inside the plane...for the moment. Just don't push me again."

Mack waved off the guns and took a step closer to Josh. "Between you and me, I didn't like this plan. Never liked depending on the emotional state of an anxious father. Give me solid logic."

He clapped Josh on the back, took his Glock and removed an empty magazine.

"Then you don't expect me to kill Tenoreno."

"I never depend on anyone with the exception of myself." Mack handed him the gun, nodded to the guy with his phone out and went about his business.

Josh was just a way to get into that hangar. A way to get on that plane. Why? He was tired of asking when the answer was simple—wait and find out.

"They're a couple of minutes out, boss," Laughing Mack said.

In-Charge Mack faced Josh, having to tilt his head up to look at him. "I know what you're thinking. How many of us can you take out if you jump one of the men and take his weapon? But you still have a problem." He folded his arms and looked around him. "Which one of us is supposed to call and check on your girlfriend? Which one of us has the power to tell them to pull the trigger or let them go?"

Damn.

"Now that's all settled. This is where you pull your weight, Major." Mack motioned for his men to come closer. "How many men and where are they located?"

Josh was taller than most of them there. Ten men to be exact. Ten men armed with automatic machine pistols. It didn't matter if they were accurate or not. Just aim close to a human, most likely they'd hit part of him.

Mack waited, his attention on Josh with an expectant look on his face.

"They'll make the prisoner transfer inside the hangar. Less exposure that way. Most likely four men—two rangers, two prison guards. The guards will leave, then the plane. You made this fairly public. They'll be expecting some sort of attack. Additional men might already be waiting."

"So we go in guns blazing and take everybody out," Knife Mack declared.

"Then you don't need me." Josh took a step back toward the van, both hands in the air. He didn't know if any of the guns around him had ammo. But he did know how to use that knife. He just had to get hold of it. "Mind making that phone call before you're all slaughtered?"

"We can get the jump on those guys," one of them said.

Their voices blended together as they spoke over each other. At their backs, Josh could see headlights on the road to the airport. Tenoreno had arrived. But Josh's main focus was on the real Mack. And his focus was on Josh.

The leader lifted a hand. All the conversation stopped.

"Only one person has to fire a weapon. That means only one person needs to get close enough, but we'll take two. Along with the Major."

Tracey had described this man's eyes as frightening. Josh understood why. Black as the dark around them. A color that broke down the walls you thought protected you. Maybe that was a little melodramatic, but true.

The stare was a test. Not just of willpower. It was a test to see who would be giving the orders and who would be taking them. Josh was a leader. It was something that he'd recognized in himself years ago. A skill that mentors had helped him hone. He understood that look. He could also turn his off and allow Mack to believe he'd won.

"I've already told you that I'd do anything to protect my kids. It doesn't matter what happens to me. But what guarantees do I have that my family is going to be okay?"

"You have my word, of course."

"We both know that doesn't mean much to me."

Mack laughed, threw back his head and roared, again halting the conversation of his men. "I knew there was something I liked about you." He turned and waved the men into different directions splitting them into smaller groups that would surround the building on foot. "Put him in the van."

Knife Mack shoved Josh against the bumper. His hand landed on top of his bag, where a smoke grenade and a tracking device were hidden. He just needed to activate the tracker.

"Whoa, whoa, whoa." In-Charge Mack held up his hand. "We still need this guy. Ride up front with me, Major."

Josh was escorted up front, an empty gun tossed in his lap. Empty. The last twenty-four hours had been disturbing to say the least. Sitting here, though, was a bit surreal.

He was in a van with the man who'd kidnapped his family. About to crash through a gate and storm a facility that his friends and coworkers would be defending. When had everything gotten so turned upside down?

"Hopefully this will be really simple," Mack instructed. "We pull up. The Major talks his way to Oaks, Mack takes him out and we take the plane before anyone's the wiser."

"Oaks? Aren't you after Tenoreno?"

"Two for one. We need them both."

Knife had just given him his first piece of useful information. They wanted Oaks and thought he'd be escorting Tenoreno. It sort of made sense now.

"He might not be there, you know. Oaks. There's no guarantee." The gate flew open and their panel van continued toward the hangar. "You could have done all this on your own. You could have taken me out. You didn't need my kids." He was tired of dancing around the truth. "Nothing I do is going to keep you from killing me and...hurting my family."

"You're a sure thing, Major Parker," he said in almost a sad voice. "Smart, too. I always enjoy working with smart people. And I don't think your men are going to just shoot you. You're our element of surprise. Kind of like a flash bang grenade that cops use."

Or maybe that was the answer—he was a sure thing. A sure way to get into the hangar, find Tenoreno and run. Seconds passed in a blur as they screeched to a halt in front of the only open airplane hangar. Handguns were aimed at his chest as he stepped onto the ground.

The other two men stayed in the van with the engine running. It wouldn't be long before eight additional men would be circling the building. They had enough firepower to wipe out everyone on the perimeter before they knew what happened.

"What's the deal, Captain?" Bryce stepped from the back of the hangar. "Trying to make an entrance?"

"I wasn't driving." Josh looked around at his men from Company F. He dropped his handgun—totally worthless anyway—then raised his hands. "There's a couple of guys in this van who want Tenoreno."

"There are a lot of people who want Tenoreno. Sorry."

"They've got the place surrounded, Bryce. Whatever you were planning, it won't work."

"If they're here to hijack the plane they won't get far."

"Change of plans. They say they're here to kill Oaks. Is he on the plane with Tenoreno?" The original plan to overpower Mack's men and discover where Josh's family was being held was a bust.

"Tell the men to drop their weapons," Mack said from the darkness of the van.

"You know they won't do that, but you could lower yours," Bryce answered.

The Rangers were wearing vests. Ready for the shots Josh should have planned to fire with the weapons he had loaded with blanks. But he couldn't. They wouldn't give him his weapon. Knife Mack jumped out of the van next to him, raised his machine pistol, pointing it at Josh's head.

In-Charge Mack left the driver's seat and stood in front of the panel van. When the Rangers made a move, he stopped them by firing a burst into the ceiling. "Hold it! All of you stay where you are."

"You know I don't want to ask this, Bryce, but they've got my kids. Lower your weapons and don't get us all killed."

Bryce led the way, placing his handgun on the concrete and kicking it barely out of his reach. He squinted, questioning Josh as he sank to his knees. This was *not* the plan they'd discussed yesterday. The one that said it was better to ask forgiveness than permission. They were supposed to overpower these guys, not the other way around.

"Up against the wall, on your knees, hands on your head. Where's Oaks? I don't see him," In-Charge Mack demanded.

"Still in Waco. They were afraid he might get caught up in the moment. Maybe shoot the star witness," the pilot told him.

The first to give up his weapon and the first to give them information. Sort of unusual, but Josh didn't want to jump to the conclusion that the pilot was working with the kidnappers. You could never tell how people would react under stress.

"Get on the plane." Knife Mack shoved the pilot, then shoved Josh toward the others getting on their knees.

"Secure them, tell the others we're a go for phase two. No reason to panic. We knew this was a possibility." Mack shot beams of hatred toward the plane.

Them? Phase two?

"Join your men, Major."

"What's phase two? You have Tenoreno. Oaks didn't get in the way. You're done here. Just tell me where my kids are or call for their release."

"You are right not to trust me, Major. Looks like we'll have to hang on to them a while longer." Mack smirked.

"The perimeter is crawling with cops." Knife Mack retreated from a window.

The pilot fired up the engine.

"We'll be out of here in a minute. The others will take care of this mess."

Shotguns against machine pistols. How many would be hurt? Would he watch the men on their knees be slaughtered with a single blast? Whatever playbook Mack or Tenoreno had, it wouldn't be discovered here. His family would still be in trouble.

But maybe there was another way.

Josh's head cleared. He instantly knew what had to be done.

"Take me and let my men go. They get in that van and drive away. I give you my word I won't do anything on the plane. I could convince Oaks to meet us."

"Not a chance," Bryce argued. "Headquarters won't go for that. We're not leaving you."

"Nice play, Major." Mack was twenty feet away giving instructions to his right-hand man, then he boarded, turning once inside. "There's only one problem. As soon as I let your men go, they'll warn Oaks that we're coming. Take out the trash, men."

"This is my choice, Lieutenant." He lowered his voice for Bryce, "You know what to do once that plane is airborne. Take these guys out and warn Waco we're coming. Give the signal."

Knife Mack started toward them with crowd-control handcuffs.

"Now, Bryce. Give the order to attack."

Chapter Sixteen

The Rangers outside the hangar made their move. It might have been the last minute before the Macks reached the building, but they were prepared. Most of the gunfire was outside. Bryce rolled, taking cover farther away from the plane, shouting orders for the others. They took their hidden weapons and attacked.

Josh had extra drive that no one else in the hangar did—his need to save his kids and Tracey. His goal was to get on the plane and Knife Mack was the only person in his way.

Josh pushed the adrenaline he was feeling, channeling it to a rage he'd never experienced. All the while gauging that Knife Mack was raising the barrel of his machine pistol. "Get out of my way!"

In a well-practiced gym move—one he had never used in the field—Josh ran and jumped. Both of his booted feet slammed into the chest of his opponent. Josh was prepared to fall hard to the concrete floor, rolling when he hit, keeping his eyes on his opponent. Knife Mack shot backward.

Relentless fire bursts. Shouts. The engine starting. All the noise added to his rapid heartbeat. He heard or felt Knife Mack's "oomph," slamming hard into the wing of the plane. Still, the man got up quickly and moved toward him again.

Josh reached out, grabbed the man's arm and used his forward momentum to spin him into the fuselage. He banged his elbow hard into the man's chin. Then pounded his fist twice into the man's solar plexus attempting to knock his breath from him. He jerked the machine pistol from the man's shoulder, holding the strap across his neck.

Knife Mack didn't stop. Pushing at Josh's hands, he shoved hard enough to force Josh to stumble backward. Josh drew upon a hidden burst of energy thinking about the smiles of his children. He hit Knife Mack with all his strength. The man fell and slid into the back wall, rattling the metal shelves.

Bryce put a knee in Knife Mack's back and yanked his wrist to his shoulder blade.

Josh took in the surroundings. Three of the Macks were defending the runway for the takeoff but Rangers were flanking and about to overrun. Another couple of Mack men were face down in the dirt next to the taxiway.

Josh's only hope was pulling away from the hangar. The Cessna was a single prop engine so there weren't any blades to get in his way. He ran.

"No!" Bryce yelled behind him.

No choice. Josh was running out of time.

Time? Hell, he had seconds. The plane was turning to line up for takeoff.

One more burst of energy and Josh caught the open door. He grabbed whatever he could and pulled himself through as the plane turned revved its engines.

"Very impressive, Major."

In-Charge Mack sat sideways in the seat, holding his

machine pistol six inches from Josh's nose. The kidnapper could have pulled the door shut. He could have fired the weapon, shooting Josh. Instead he'd allowed a ranger on board.

Now he extended a hand.

Josh ignored the assist and pulled himself into a seat, shutting the door while the engine roared to full life. He was still alive, on the plane and stuck with a half-ass plan for what he should do next.

Keep himself alive. Get his kids and Tracey released. That was the goal...now he needed steps to reach it. "Is the pilot one of your guys?"

"I believe his name is Bart." Tenoreno, sitting in the seat behind the pilot, raised his voice, competing with the engine. "A new employee. Unlike Vince."

Josh had never met Paul Tenoreno in person. He'd seen the file. Photos of crime scenes. Surveillance pictures Oaks had accumulated off and on for over a decade.

"Vince? Deegan?" Josh couldn't remember the list of crimes attributed to this man, just that it was long. As a criminal, it seemed Vince had avoided pictures. It wasn't a good sign when he took off his ski mask, revealing his face. "I think I'll stick with Mack."

Tenoreno shook his chains. "Can we dispense with these?"

Mack tossed the keys across the aisle to Tenoreno's lap. The organized crime leader didn't look as intimidating in his state-issued jumpsuit. But he still behaved like a man used to having his orders followed.

The restraints were quickly unlatched, dropped and Mack transferred them to Josh.

"Gun." Tenoreno held his palm open and Mack dropped a Glock onto it after pulling it from his belt.

The keys flew back, landing against the shell of the plane and sliding to the carpeted floor. Mack left them there, staring at his employer as he transferred to the copilot's seat.

The confidence that the kidnapper had blustered was no longer apparent. His shoulders slumped. His face filled with hatred. His body language suggested he was tired, but he deliberately kept the gun barrel pointed at Tenoreno's seatback much longer than he should have.

"Change of plans, Bart," Tenoreno said, barely loud enough to be heard over the engine noise. "How much fuel did you manage?"

"I have enough to take you to the rendezvous. You didn't buy anything else. That's as far as this baby and I will take you."

"Unsatisfactory. Come up with a new location not far from Waco."

"That's not the deal," the pilot insisted.

"Your deal is whatever I say it is." Tenoreno pulled the slide to verify ammo was in place.

"What the hell are you doing? Are you seriously going to shoot him while we're in the air?" Mack shouted, sitting forward on his seat.

Tenoreno shot him a shut-up look. "Where are we landing, Bart?"

"Hearne."

"Get us there." Keeping his weapon trained on Bart, Tenoreno looked at Mack. "Call your men with the new location."

"That's taking an unnecessary risk. My men can easily bring Oaks to you later. How do you plan—"

"Do it! We'll exchange him and his kids."

Josh crushed his teeth together to keep from interjecting. He'd played right into Tenoreno's plan more than once. Mack removed a satellite phone from the bag at his feet and made the call.

"I want Oaks discredited and dead. He's supposed to be chained back there, not Parker." Tenoreno spoke to Mack who shrugged. "You've gotten sloppy, Vince. There are too many people involved. Too much has been left up to chance."

"I follow orders. It wasn't my plan that went wrong,"

"I suppose it was my idiot son, then. Why didn't kidnapping his kids work? Didn't the Rangers replace him with Oaks?" He pointed to Josh.

"That part of the plan worked fine." Mack smiled as if he'd regained the confidence he'd lost for a moment. "Maybe they thought Oaks would kill you himself if he was on a plane with you."

"Ha." Tenoreno put the headset on and turned to the front of the plane. Mack and Josh sat silently next to each other until Mack leaned forward and added the ankle restraints, locking Josh to the plane.

"I never underestimate the power of emotion. Especially that of a father. I told my employers that, but they insisted on this ridiculous revenge plan. Wouldn't listen to me." Was he bragging that he had predicted Josh's behavior?

"Smart advice for someone dumb enough not to follow it." They could talk without either of the other men hearing. "You know this exchange this isn't going to work. Right?"

"You Rangers are so full of pride that buying you off isn't an option. Fortunately, killing you is."

"You kidnapped my kids so you could kill Oaks?"

"No, Major. We did all this to free Paul. The only way to get Oaks off his back is to kill him." Mack pointed the gun at Josh. He raised and lowered the barrel as if it had just been fired. "You see, you guys just don't stop. We can buy off other agencies, bribe or blackmail some types of guys...like Bart. But Rangers? None of that works."

"So you're telling me that if the Texas Rangers had a history of corruption, my kids would be safe at home?"

"Kind of ironic when you look at it that way." Mack leaned back in his seat, machine pistol in his lap.

There wasn't any reason to keep a close eye on Josh. He wasn't going anywhere cuffed hand and foot. No chance to attempt anything.

"Before I waste my time trying to convince you I'm not important, tell me why you let me board. And don't say it's because you wanted to see if I could make it through the door."

"I've got to say that I admire the way you don't give up. You're here because I can use you for a hostage. Nothing more. Nothing less."

"Use me all you want. Just make the call that will let my kids go." Josh swallowed hard.

"We both saw the mess back at the airport. It won't be long before the Rangers are calling Oaks and the entire state is after us. I have some leverage with you here."

"I'm a nobody. They won't negotiate because of me."

"We'll see." Mack dropped his head back against the headrest and closed his eyes. At this point, Josh shouldn't and didn't trust anyone except himself to save his children. Except Tracey. He trusted Tracey. For one moment, it was nice to imagine what she might have been about to tell him. One moment when he hoped she knew exactly how he felt about her.

Chapter Seventeen

They pulled to a stop and Tracey felt the van settle into a parked position. She kept her eyes down, pretending to be asleep. She sneaked a peek out the windows. It looked the same as the rest of their ride. The sun was just dusting the treetops and highlighting the surrounding fields. Whatever was going to happen, it didn't seem like there was anyplace close to hide.

The two Macks looked at the phone, said things under their breath and got cautiously out of the van. Tracey rose quickly and looked out all the windows. They were at a small airport. One smaller than Waco and not large enough to have a terminal or control tower.

The van was parked a long way from any building or aircraft hangar.

"Listen to me, Sage. There might be a chance that you can run and hide without these men seeing you. If you can, you do it. Don't look back. This is important. Just run as fast as you can. Okay?"

"By myself?"

"Yes, baby." She lifted the little girl to look out the back windows. "You see those hay bales across the road?" She pointed. Sage nodded. "Can you run that far?"

"Is it important?" Sage whispered.

"Yes, baby. Very important. Somebody will find you. Promise."

"I want to go home," Jackson insisted. "I don't feel like running. I want to eat colors 'cause it'll make me run faster."

Tracey looked closely at Jackson's eyes. She hadn't monitored his blood sugar levels in several hours and had none of the necessary tools now. She had to completely rely on her experience of the last year.

Acting out, anger, lethargy, not making sense with his words—those were all sure signs that his blood sugar was dropping. She got up front as quickly as possible. Why hadn't she thought of that first? There weren't any keys in the ignition, but she locked both the doors.

"Sage, lock the back and the side doors. Quick!"

The van rocked back and forth a little when Sage moved. She made it to the side door while Tracey searched for a spare key or food. Nothing but ketchup packets and trash.

The van moved again, but this time it was from the rear door being yanked open.

"I told you she was up to something."

"It didn't matter. I had the keys to get back in." Blond Mack dangled them like candy in front of her.

Tracey huddled with the kids again, not trying to explain herself or reason with them. They were tugged from the vehicle. Tracey held Jackson on her hip and he put his head on her shoulder.

"You sure that's them, man?"

"You think there's more than one plane sitting on this out-of-the-way runway?"

"Then what are they waiting for?"

The men whispered behind her. Maybe they were

using her and the kids as a shield. She didn't know. She held Jackson's forty-four pounds tight against her and wanted to pick up Sage. Instead she held tight to her hand and the little girl held the secondhand bear against her own little chest.

There was no movement from the white Cessna.

"What's going on?" she asked. "Who's in the plane? Do we have to get on board?"

Her thoughts were considering the worst-case scenario. The one where awful things happened in an isolated basement where no one could find them. The bodyguards suddenly seemed like a really good idea.

Neither of the men answered. Neither of the men moved.

"I got a creepy feeling about this, man. You get me?"

Tracey thought it was the blond guy talking, but it didn't matter. They both were armed and the only place close where she could protect the kids was back inside the van.

She'd never make it carrying Jackson, who was more lethargic than just a few minutes ago. He needed food and she didn't know how much.

"What does the text say?"

"I don't care what it says anymore. Get back in the van."

It was definitely the blond Mack giving the orders. She could tell that they faced each other and had a phone between them. She inched Sage toward the corner of the van, ready to make a run for it. She desperately wanted her hunch about this to be right.

A hunch that told her Josh was on that plane waiting to see if she and the kids were released. But that would mean someone—like the FBI or police or Rangers— was here somewhere, waiting.

The men continued to argue behind her and she loosened her hold on Sage. She arched her eyebrows, questioning if she should run, and Tracey nodded. She looked so young and yet so much older than two days ago. Tracey didn't have to guess if she understood the danger—she did. Josh's little girl squeezed her hand, then tiptoed along the length of the back of the van and ran.

The arguing stopped. Tracey turned around, keeping her hand behind her back. Hoping the two Macks would think Sage was hiding there. She stared at the men, one arm cramping from holding Jackson, the other waving his sister to safety.

"Where's the girl?"

"She's right—"

They both took a step in Tracey's direction. Blond Mac's hands were out to take Jackson from her. She turned but only made it a couple of steps. The van doors were still open. Blond had a hold of Jackson; the other guy pushed her inside the van, climbing in on top of her.

She couldn't see if Sage made it across the road. Based on the cursing and slamming fists against the van, then the running to get in the driver's seat, she assumed Sage was out of sight.

Thank God.

THEY HAD LANDED about five or ten minutes earlier. Mack had been surprised and Tenoreno had been rather pleased. Neither had said anything loud enough to let Josh determine what was going on. But it had something to do with meetings and putting them at greater risk.

Tenoreno was in the copilot's chair and Mack was busy sending an in-depth text. Neither paid attention to the activity at the van. The plane was far enough down the runway to make the van visible to Josh. He yanked against the chains when Tracey and the kids had been wrenched from it. He managed to cap his panic when he saw his little girl run. He didn't want to draw attention to her.

"Did your heart stop there for a minute?" Bart the pilot asked. "I know mine sure did. That's this guy's kid. Right? Man, you've got a brave little girl."

Josh nodded. He might have gotten out a yes or confirmation grunt, but he couldn't be certain. As soon as the relief hit that the men weren't following Sage and she might be safe, the anxiety had doubled as Jackson and Tracey were pushed back inside the van. Tracey hadn't run. He'd seen Jackson's form. He was practically limp in Tracey's arms. Something was wrong with his son.

"What are you talking about?" Tenoreno shouted as Sage disappeared behind a hay bale. "Tell them to go get her. Why didn't you say something when she ran?"

"Man, I didn't sign on to hurt any kids. Disengage the transponder, fly the plane, get my payoff. Sure. Hurting kids was not included and won't be."

"If we didn't need a pilot, you'd be dead now." Tenoreno turned an interesting shade of explosive red.

"We don't need the girl. We didn't need additional hostages on the plane. I tried to tell you that."

"This is not a debate. You work for me."

Tenoreno screamed his lack of control. Bart shrank a little more toward the pilot's door. Mack's body stiffened as he deliberately sank back into the leather seat. The muscle in his jaw twitched. He let the machine pistol's barrel drop in line with his boss's head. Accident or deliberate?

Josh didn't want Mack to open fire. Not when he

didn't have a weapon and no control over the men still holding Tracey and Jackson.

"It doesn't matter now. Here they come. Open the door, then tell the men to bring the woman on board."

Josh couldn't see who was inside the darkened windows. Mack did as he was instructed—opened the door and called his men on the phone.

If he made it through this, someone might eventually ask him what he'd hoped to gain by allowing himself to become a hostage. Originally there'd been a lot of adrenaline involved. But it came down to being there for his kids. He couldn't let anyone else make decisions that involved their lives. And if that put his at risk.

So be it.

Chapter Eighteen

"This isn't going to work." George was compelled to voice his thoughts one last time. "There's only one reason they'd want you here, Captain Oaks. Paul Tenoreno wants to kill you."

"We have a sound plan."

"Hardly. It's our only plan. Might be a good one for Tenoreno. You get out of the car, they shoot you. Period. They have no reason to release any of the hostages."

Crouched in the backseat of a small sedan wasn't the most comfortable place George had ever held a conversation. It definitely wasn't the worst, either. At least he wasn't shoved in the trunk like last year. He shook the random thoughts from his mind and concentrated.

Aiden Oaks had parked the car next to the Cessna. His plan to accommodate the kidnappers and escaped prisoner hadn't included the FBI. George was coordinating the teams surrounding the airstrip.

Of course, the entire jumping-in-the-car-at-the-last-minute thing had caught him slightly unprepared. He was only carrying his cell phone and Glock. The ammo he had in the magazine was it. The team was communicating through a series of group texts.

"No one asked you to ride along," Aiden said.

"No, sir, you didn't. I have a lot of experience with

kidnappings and abductions. Did you know that, Captain?"

"I wouldn't say you've had any experience with this kind. Those kids are still in danger because the men who outrank me wouldn't allow me to escort Tenoreno's flight. He's a vindictive son of—"

"I know why we're waiting, but what do you think they're waiting for? Is the van with Tracey and Jackson still sitting on the road? Damn, that was a brave move Tracey made, sending one of the kids to safety."

The cop who picked her up had her safely in his squad car.

"Good thing the Hearne PD picked up Sage as she ran to hide behind the hay. Sweet thing argued that she had to stay there and wait on her daddy." Aiden chuckled. "Van's been creeping up behind us at a snail's pace. Everybody seems to be in a holding pattern. Are the men in place?"

"Three more minutes, sir."

Just before they'd arrived in Hearne to rendezvous with Tenoreno, he'd kicked the rearview mirror off the windshield. It was propped on the backseat headrest so he could see the plane. The door opened but he couldn't make out anything inside.

"Van's speeding up. I'm getting out and leaving the door open for you, Agent Lanning."

"We have eyes on Parker. He's handcuffed and manacled to the seat behind the pilot. Tenoreno is in the co-pilot chair." The team kept him up-to-date with a text. "You have your handcuff key ready?"

"Got it," Oaks said as he swung his legs from the car. He left the door as a bit of protection between him and the plane.

George dialed Kendall's number, ready to get the advance started with his men. He'd pass along information, but his phone was on silent, just in case the perps got close enough to hear him. Then he angled the mirror, attempting to find any guns pointed in their direction. They knew from looking through the windows that at least two hostiles were aboard, maybe three.

The Rangers in Huntsville had stated that only the kidnapper who gave the orders was on board. Bart Temple, the pilot, already had an open investigation about his suspicious activities. The report from the airplane hangar suggested that he had supplied information and had voluntarily gotten on the plane.

"Air traffic has been diverted. We have a helicopter standing by in case we need it."

The van squealed to a stop.

"Where are you going?" a man shouted.

George turned the mirror. "One man, armed with a Glock. Nervous. Anxious. Unpredictable. No eyes on Tracey or the boy."

"Move to the door, Oaks," a voice inside the plane said.

"I ain't no rookie. Release Parker and the other hostages."

"The Major is cozy and staying where he is."

"Then so am I." Oaks sat on the seat.

George knew what the captain was doing. It didn't make it any easier to wait on the kidnappers' next move.

Tracey screamed and George could only imagine what the kidnappers had done to elicit her reaction. Damn, he hated being blind. He whipped the mirror around to see the driver pulling Tracey past the steering wheel. Soon they were joined by his partner, who carried Jackson.

"The kid looks ill. I repeat, the kid looks ill and won't be able to run on his own."

"Hey, you guys in the plane." The driver pushed the barrel of his handgun under Tracey's chin. "Or inside the car. Whoever cares about this woman! You better give us a way out of here or she and the kid are going to get it."

"Yeah," the one cradling Jackson said. "We want our own plane. Or you can kick these bastards out and we'll take this one."

"I can get another plane here. Why don't you give me the kid to show good faith?" Oaks tried to negotiate.

"Oh no. No way! We keep both of them." They argued.

The man holding Jackson started waving his handgun, then smashed it against his own forehead, proving that he was losing it. If he touched the kid, nothing would hold George inside the car.

Everyone on the team hated unpredictable kidnappers. The ones who began to panic. The ones who were sweating buckets, were probably high as a kite and who made everything about his job high risk.

"That's a shame." Oaks raised his voice to be heard over the Cessna's engine. "We have a sweet private jet not too far away. We could have it here in ten minutes."

"Call 'em!"

"Sorry, can't do that until I have a hostage."

"Man, I just want to be gone." He pushed Jackson into Tracey's arms and climbed back into the van.

"Ron, what are you— Hey! Hey!" he screamed into his phone as the door swung halfway shut. "We're getting on that plane no matter what you say!"

He placed his gun at Tracey's throat and started her moving, carrying Jackson toward the plane.

Whether it was their intention or not, they'd parked the van partially in the path of the Cessna. To reach the open door, they had to walk close to the sedan. The men now calling the shots, hidden on the east side of the buildings, sent instructions.

"Captain, if there's an opportunity to rescue Jackson, McCaffrey wants us to take it."

"Are they seeing what we're seeing?" Oaks asked in a low voice. "The kidnappers are panicking. We can't startle these guys."

George wasn't certain if McCaffrey had a good grasp on the situation or not. He could hear the chatter in the background. Hear the arguing over what the best move might be. When the best-case scenario came up, he thought they'd back up his plan.

Jackson looked unconscious and unaware that he was being carried to the plane. Tracey stumbled because the remaining captor's gun was still at her throat and pushing her chin upward. George watched behind him with the help of the mirror. Feeling as helpless as Josh Parker.

The phone buzzed on his chest with another message from his partner. McCaffrey was about to blow a gasket because he hadn't burst out of the car and done anything. George rolled to his side, hiding behind the dark-tinted windows for a better view.

The two men were met at the plane door with a machine pistol. "Send the boy up. Then the woman."

"You dirty rotten son of a bitch! You ain't leaving us here to go to jail." The man holding Tracey turned in circles, always bringing her between him and any of the men who might have a shot.

"Take me." Captain Oaks moved slowly from behind the car door with his hands in the air. "Leave the kid in the car and take me. They'll let you on the plane if you bring me."

George was ready to spring into action. "That is not the plan."

JOSH LOOKED THROUGH the open door and saw Tracey stumble. Whatever was being said outside, he couldn't hear because of the yelling in the small plane.

"Give me the gun so I can shoot him myself." Tenoreno held out his hand, expecting Mack to drop his weapon into it. The older man climbed between the front seats and stuck his hand out again.

"Buckle in, Paul. Bart, get this plane in the air."

"Oaks is standing right there, dammit." Tenoreno pointed. "Shoot him."

"So are the FBI and more Rangers. Even if you can't see them, they have to be here. Oaks isn't stupid. He wouldn't come alone."

Mack was right, but Josh wasn't going to agree with him. He kept his head down and his mouth shut, continuing his search for something he could use to free himself. Unfortunately, the plane had been checked for that sort of material before transporting a prisoner.

"I want him dead. It's the reason we're here."

"I could have taken care of this. I had men in Waco ready to do the job after they got rid of the hostages." Mack explained. "But you had to detour and involve the kids again, making everybody on edge."

"Those incompetent jerks." Tenoreno pointed to the men holding Tracey.

"Someone has confused them." Mack pointedly looked at Tenoreno. "Now they believe they've been double-crossed. Their position is kind of natural."

"Don't take that tone with me, Vince. I know where your kid lives."

Vince, Mack, whatever the hell his name was, didn't like Paul Tenoreno. His knuckles turned a bright white, fisted as they were around the machine pistol grip. The plane shifted slightly to the side as someone climbed up the steps.

The blond guy who had been holding Tracey backed onto the plane—slowly, sticking his foot out behind him while he wrapped one arm around someone's throat. Josh had to pull his legs and feet out of the way. He didn't want the man to fall and choke… Aiden.

A shot of relief hit Josh. He didn't want anyone else on the plane, but knowing Tracey wasn't gave him a little hope she and Jackson might make it out of this situation alive.

"Good to see you alive, son," Aiden said to Josh as the new guy shoved him onto the empty seat.

"Captain Oaks." Tenoreno was halfway between the seats.

"Fancy meeting you here, Paul," Aiden taunted. "You okay, kid?" he asked Josh in a lower voice.

Tenoreno's fists hit both of the seat backs. "Shut up before I shoot you dead. Your blood would be splattered against this white leather in a heartbeat if we didn't need to leave."

"You don't trust that they'll let you?" Aiden taunted.

The result was another beet-red rise in Tenoreno's color. The man definitely didn't have control of his temper. And Aiden definitely knew what buttons to push. Tenoreno slammed Aiden forward.

To Josh it seemed that Aiden sort of threw himself forward, then he knew why. He dropped a handcuff key into his hand. His eyes must have grown wide with surprise because Aiden frowned and shook his head.

Josh recovered and tried to shrink into the seat. Let Aiden have all the attention and he could free his feet and hands pretty quickly. Or at least he thought he could.

The plane dipped slightly again as someone began climbing the steps. The second man was pushing Tracey up, and in her arms she held Jackson.

Escaping was complicated before. Now it was closer to impossible. Was he willing to risk a machine gun blast through the plane with two people he loved occupying seats?

Tenoreno continued to yell. "Get us out of here!"

Bart started the engine. Josh held out his arms to catch his son as Tracey handed him through the opening, before falling to her knees on the carpet as the plane jerked forward.

"Wait! No!" the man on the bottom step fell away.

"Pull the door shut, Tommy, so we can get going," Mack ordered.

Tommy laughed at the man—his partner three minutes ago—being left behind on the runway. He reached for the rope to pull in the steps and the slam of Mack's weapon firing hit Josh's ears. Gunpowder filled his nostrils before he turned his head and caught a glimpse of Tommy falling through the door.

Mack leaned across, fired his weapon again—presumably at the man he'd left behind. Then he pulled the stairs up and secured the door.

"Damn. What now?" Bart yelled.

It seemed like Josh had constantly asked himself the same question again and again for the past forty hours…

Chapter Nineteen

Jackson had barely been noticed by anyone on the plane since they'd tossed him back to Tracey. The sudden firing of the gun had made him scream. She was certain he hadn't seen any part of the cold-blooded murder. She'd had his face buried against her shoulder. His hands had already been over his ears.

"Just stay still and keep your eyes closed," she whispered to him.

She desperately wanted to be next to Josh, or better still not on the plane at all. But they were, and they'd survived another hour.

"Get us in the air, Bart, old buddy." Mack grabbed a pair of handcuffs. He pointed to an older gentleman sitting across from Josh. "Put those on Captain Oaks. And loop the seat belt through them so you can't get up and retrieve a gun."

After he had Aiden's hands locked into place, Mack took the open seat and buckled up. They kept taxiing to the end of the runway. The plane turned around and not only was the van still there, a row of patrol cars and SUVs were side by side, cutting off half the tarmac.

"Same question, second verse," the pilot said. "What now?"

"Can't you run them over with this thing?" the man

sitting up front said, like a minion who didn't really think.

After her time in the van, she realized these men were more like lost boys than criminals. Young men who got used by people like Mack. She couldn't let herself have too much sympathy. If it came down to it, she'd choose the Parkers every time.

"Let's try some diplomacy. Paul, get on the radio." Mack raised his voice to be heard over the prop engine.

She recognized his voice. That was the man who had hit her Friday. It seemed a lifetime ago, but she would never forget. He was the In-Charge Mack, the man who'd given all the orders.

Sitting practically in the tail of the plane, she had a clear view of everyone except the pilot. The fidgets of the men in restraints. The toe tapping of Aiden Oaks. The cavalier words that didn't match the tense, upright stiffness that Mack's body shouted.

And Josh. His glances kept reassuring her that it would work out. He'd come up with a plan. Then he caught her eye and sharply looked at her lap. There was only one seat belt for both her and Jackson. As inconspicuous with her movements as she could be, she buckled the seat belt around her waist.

She'd use her last ounce of strength to hold on to Jackson if something happened with the plane. She was prepared. Tenoreno picked up the microphone to radio the FBI, who was certain to be listening.

"Tell them about our situation. We're taking off or someone's dying. Starting with Daddy Dearest." Mack pointed the gun at the back of the copilot's seat.

"What are you talking about? Is this a joke? You work for me. Or—" Realization hit Tenoreno. "Who hired you? My son will pay you double to escort me to safety."

"Your son is the one who wants you gone. As in forever, never coming back. It would have simplified everything if I could have killed you in Huntsville. Or even right now. But Xander insists on seeing it happen." He kicked the empty seat across from him. "You stupid old man. Did you really think he would forgive you for killing his mother?"

"You've got Special Agent in Charge McCaffrey." A voice boomed through the radio.

"They're threatening to kill me. You have to save me. It's your job! Don't move the vehicles! Don't clear the runway."

"Who is this? What's going on in there? Stop the engine and exit the plane."

Mack placed the barrel next to Tenoreno's temple. The man in the orange jumpsuit tried to squirm aside, but there was no place for him to go. Tracey covered Jackson's ears and eyes.

"Trace Trace, that's too tight."

"That's unacceptable. Didn't you see him shoot one of his own men? He's not bluffing. He won't negotiate." Josh tried to shout loud enough for the agents to hear him.

"He's not going to back down," Aiden shouted at the same time.

Was Josh's fellow ranger talking about Agent McCaffrey or Mack? Josh looked first at her, then in the direction of Mack. She could see the murderer's jaw tighten. The muscles visibly popped.

"If you don't do anything, then you've just killed us." Tenoreno laughed like a crazy man.

"Do you think I'm going to fall for that? If you're

the one holding our people hostage, you won't get far. We have helicopters in the air waiting to follow you to any destination. We know there's not enough fuel on board to get you out of the country. Surrendering now is your only option."

"I don't think he's joking." Tenoreno sat forward looking out the windows.

Aiden seemed more uncomfortable. He'd moved his hands from above his head to closer to the top of his shoulder. "Why set up this elaborate prison break if you just wanted him dead?"

"He's about to pull the trigger." Tenoreno's voice shook into the radio.

Was Mack about to shoot? Tracey couldn't tell. One message had been crystal clear—Josh wanted her wearing the seat belt. And now it looked like they were going to take off.

"To hell with this standoff," the pilot shouted.

He pushed what she assumed was the throttle because the engine roared louder and they moved forward. Fast.

As the plane gained speed, she looked out her window and saw men with guns pointing in their direction. But in a blink they had pointed toward another target. There was gunfire—tiny pops to her ears which drowned in the airplane engine's hum.

The young man she'd dubbed as Simple Mack. The one left alive on the tarmac was firing his weapon. Not at the FBI, he was shooting at the plane. They were dangerously close to the SUVs before dramatically dashing into the air.

The bouncing up and down stopped, but the dipping didn't. Tracey loved roller coasters, but now there were no rails connecting her seat to the earth. It was several seconds before they stabilized in the air. And several more before anyone released their breaths.

Jackson was in her arms. No seat belt. If they crashed, would she be able to hold on to him? *No.* The takeoff was just a couple of bumps and she'd nearly lost the death grip around his waist. She had no more illusions about keeping Jackson safe. He was kicking and crying out and hitting her with his small fists.

"Keep that kid quiet."

"It's the diabetes." She knew that. He didn't realize what he was doing and after his blood sugar stabilized he wouldn't remember his actions. It hadn't happened often, but since it had, the family recognized the signs.

There was a lot of tension surrounding them and a lot of noise, even though she could hear better after popping her ears. Josh and Aiden seemed to be communicating by looks. They were going to do something. She just didn't know what or when.

She quickly rose a little and switched the seat belt from around her waist to tighten around Jackson's. It was a close fit to sit on the edge of the seat next to him pressed against the side of the plane. He didn't like it at all.

"Please, kidlet. We've got to do this to keep you safe," she said next to his ear, scared to death that he'd lift the latch and not be safe at all. She worked with him to get his ears popped and relieve some of the pressure.

"What now, Mack?" Josh asked.

"Don't you mean Vince Deegan?" Aiden smiled. "Yeah, I know who you are. Jobs like this aren't normally your forte. You're more of a...bully. Aren't you?"

From her new position, she could barely see the front of the plane. She heard a jerk on Josh's chains. She could imagine that he wanted to stop Aiden from antagonizing the man holding a machine gun. She hated not knowing what was going on. It made the fright level just that much higher.

"Bart, take us to the landing strip. Somebody's waiting." Mack's attention was on the front of the plane. Maybe on the pilot or Tenoreno.

He seemed to have forgotten that she wasn't tied up or restrained—with the exception that it was a tight fit between the seats. She reached forward, touching Josh's arm. He didn't whip around, but took a look at her slowly around the edge of the seat.

She leaned closer to him and said, "I can do something."

"No," Josh mouthed.

"Daddy! Daddy!" Jackson kicked the seat, and Tracey. "Take me home."

"It's okay, Jack. Everything's okay. I bet you're tired. Maybe try to take a nap." Josh said it loud enough for Jackson to hear. One sincere look from his father and he was leaning his head against the side of the plane.

But the outburst caught Mack's attention, causing him to look and stare at her.

Did he realize she wasn't secured? It was the first time that she hoped she appeared insignificant in someone's mind. And maybe that's how he saw her—insignificant or not a threat—because he turned his attention back to his phone.

Josh looked around the edge of his seat again. He winked. She smiled back in spite of the anxiety speeding up her heartbeat. She wasn't alone. He was there and he was not helpless.

Jackson's breathing evened out. She liked it better when he was awake. Even if the diabetes turned him into a tiny terror, she knew he was awake and not slipping into a deep sleep or diabetic coma. They didn't have long before Jackson was going to be severely ill.

At the risk of Mack noticing her lack of binding, she called out, "Where are you taking us?"

"Yeah, Vince, where are you taking us?' Tenoreno echoed.

"Not far."

"That agent said they're tracking us," the criminal said from the front, his tenor-like voice carrying to the back of the plane.

"We got rid of the transponder. You!" Mack lunged across the short distance between seats.

Tracey heard his fist hit Aiden. She heard him searching through pockets and patting him down. She could see the ranger's hands tighten on the seat belt, heard him release a moan of pain.

"How are they following us?" Tenoreno screamed.

"They don't need much but their eyes. The FBI wasn't bluffing about a helicopter." The pilot pointed to the right side of the plane. All heads looked. Tracey's view was blocked by a compartment of some sort but she could tell the pilot was telling the truth.

"If the FBI knows where we're going and can tell when we land," she said, leaning forward to be heard, "how did you plan on getting away?"

She was genuinely confused.

Mack's dark eyes, which she'd memorized the moment he'd raised his fist to hit her, went dead again. He was filled with blackness that looked so empty... so soulless. "I didn't."

"What the hell does that mean?" Tenoreno asked.

Tracey saw the concerned look on Aiden's face and knew it was mirrored on Josh's. She squeezed back in next to Jackson, dabbing some of the sweat off his forehead. There was nothing for her to give him. No juice, no water—nothing. All she could do was hope.

It wasn't long before the pilot circled an even smaller runway from where they'd left. The engines ebbed and surged as he lined up to set the plane on the ground.

"This isn't going to be pretty, people." The pilot gained everyone's attention. "Those gunshots must have hit something important and the controls aren't handling like they should. So grab something steady. It's going to be a bumpy ride."

Aiden, handcuffed to the seat belt, settled more firmly into his chair and braced a long leg on the seat across the short aisle. Josh couldn't brace himself at all, not manacled to the floor.

"Can't you unlock his feet?"

"Dammit, Mack. Let her have a seat belt."

Tracey's heart raced. Good or bad. It shouldn't matter what side you were on when a plane was about to crash. Mack didn't acknowledge them. He fingered the phone, then put it in his pocket.

There was nothing to grab. She sank between the seats and braced herself between the bulkhead and the closet. As she did, Mack noticed and didn't make a move to stop her or let her move to the open seat in front of him. Jackson was unconscious. None of the shouting woke him up. At least he wouldn't be scared out of his mind like she was.

"I love you," Josh said as the plane dipped and shot back to gain altitude. He didn't have to say anything. She'd known he loved her as soon as he'd held her hand in the bodyguards' rental car. That moment had changed everything for her.

Seconds later the plane bounced against pavement

and was airborne again. She kept her eyes glued to Jackson.

It wouldn't be long. Sage was safe. At least there was that.

"Hold on tight, baby." Only Jackson could have heard her, but she said the words for Josh, too.

Chapter Twenty

Josh braced himself as best he could. Mack was finally
sitting straight in his seat and not watching his every
move. There hadn't been an unobserved moment to retrieve the handcuff key from where he'd hidden it—between his cheek and teeth.

Once on the ground, they'd need the weapons that
should be stored in the small closet next to Tracey. He
couldn't give Mack time to recover from the rough ride
or realize what was happening. He had to be ready. He
had to be fast.

Spitting the handcuff key into his hands, he twisted
his wrists until he could reach the latch. Key inserted,
turned, one hand was free. The plane's power surged,
trying to gain altitude, pressing his body into the seat.
He fought gravity and leaned forward to release his
ankles from the manacles.

"This is it!" Bart shouted, cursing like a sailor.

Josh sat up. There was no time to grab and hold
Tracey like he wanted. Then it was apparent that Bart
didn't have control. The plane was on its way to the
ground. Crashing.

"Hold on, Tracey. We're going to be okay. Just hold
on." He could see her boots in the aisle next to him.

He wanted to comfort his son. There was just no way to be heard.

Nothing was fake about what the plane was doing. There was a radical shimmy when the wheels touched down again.

Noise from every direction assaulted him. At first there were huge vibrations, bounces and slams. He thought that was bad until the plane made a sharp pull to the right, tipped, and he knew they were flipping. His neck felt like it snapped in two from the concussion of hitting the ground.

Stunned. He hung upside down, unable to see around him. Then he realized he couldn't really see his hand heading to his face, either. Stuff was floating in the air. Smoke or steam—he couldn't tell.

"Josh! Josh! You still conscious?" Aiden called.

"Yeah, I'm… I'm okay." His ears were still ringing.

Mack seemed to be unconscious next to him. His arms were hanging about his head.

"Tracey? Jackson?" No sound from either of them.

"The kid's still buckled. The girl looks like she's out cold."

Pulling his heavy arms back to his chest, Josh stretched his legs so he could push his feet against Aiden's seat.

"Hold on, Josh!" Aiden yelled. "I'm pinned in here just as tight as a bean in a burrito. My leg's busted up and caught between these things. Can you get out the door? Or see the machine pistol?"

"Give me a sec."

Bent in half and still a bit disoriented, his mind refused to adjust and accept that the plane was upside down and not just him. He managed to unclip his seat belt. There wasn't room to fall. It was just a jolt. The windows had shattered and the space around him had shrunk.

"Tracey? Jackson? Can you hear me?" He could finally see her, boots pointed toward him, lying on the ceiling. He shook her legs as much as he dared. He couldn't get his shoulders through to the area behind him. His seat was wedged in the way.

"Josh, you need to get the gun, son."

"Yeah." He did *know* that he needed to find the weapon. Logic told him that. But his heart wanted to free Tracey and Jackson first. They were both hurt, or worse.

Mack was hanging from his waist, seat belt still in place, arms swaying with each move that Josh made. He looked around on the ceiling—no weapons.

A pounding at the front of the plane made him jerk around. He hit his head on something fixed to the floor. There was a small triangle of space left where he could see the instrument panel. He carefully got closer, trying not to cause Aiden more pain.

The pilot was strapped in but it looked like his injuries were severe. Tenoreno kicked his door and it was almost open. Josh saw the gun. The strap was caught and it hung just out of his reach near the pilot.

Tenoreno stared at him and followed the direction he was reaching. An evil grin dominated his face. He moved like he was no longer in a rush. He casually lifted the machine pistol, moved the radio cord farther from the opening, then kicked the door a final time.

It sprang open and Tenoreno escaped. Josh pushed on the seat back until beads of sweat stung his eyes. It wasn't budging.

"Josh?" Aiden spoke softly, as if he were in pain. "Try the other door, son."

Crouching, he checked Tracey, giving her a little shake. He reached up and felt a pulse at Mack's throat. Then he checked the door next to his seat. Jammed. Their side of the plane had settled mostly in the field.

His head was beginning to clear a bit. His vision along with it. He checked Aiden, who had passed out. He had lost the handcuff key in the crash, but could get Aiden free with a knife. To get to Tracey and Jackson, he'd need a crowbar or tools to release the seat back. And to get either of those things he needed out of the plane.

"Hello?" a voice from the outside called. Knocks on the outside of the plane. More voices. And light. Lots of light as the door opened.

"Are you all right?"

"I'm fine but there are injured people and a child. Have you got a knife?" Josh asked the man who was at the door on the far side of Mack. Josh's ears were ringing badly and making it difficult to hear. He was catching every other word or so and letting his mind fill in the rest of the answer.

As much as he wanted to sit and let someone else take care of things, his son needed him. Tracey needed him. He wouldn't quit.

"My daughter, Jeannie… Hand me the knife. I think we can get everyone out. Paramedics are on their way."

"Let me get inside here." The man kept the knife.

Without too many words, they worked together and released Mack. The rescuer climbed out and Josh passed Mack through the door to him.

"Make sure you use these." Josh tossed the handcuffs that had been around his wrists a few minutes earlier. "Anchor him to something so he can't get away."

"You can come out," the man helping said. "I can free them."

"Not leaving until they do. You'll need me in here." Josh began moving debris, trying to get to Jackson and Tracey.

The stranger had seen what tools they needed to release the others, retrieved them and they went to work. "Start moving the dirt from the pilot's window," the man instructed someone who had just arrived.

This time another teen jumped in with him, rocking the plane just a bit.

"Where are the rescue crews?" Josh asked.

"We're in the middle of nowhere here," the teenager answered.

"They're probably another fifteen minutes out." The man moved carefully to Aiden. "Your friend has a broken leg, let's get this wreckage off him."

"The boy first," Aiden said.

"Boy?"

"My son's in the back along with Tracey. He has diabetes. They're both unconscious."

The man didn't need more of an explanation. He went to work removing the seat blocking Tracey. It was a tight fit and Josh felt in the way until they got some of the bolts removed and the seat needed to be held in place. His shoulder kept the seat on the ceiling while they finished and moved it in front of the door.

"Tracey?"

Josh needed to be in two places at once. But he let their rescuer check Tracey while he released his son.

"How long have I been out?" Her voice was breathy and tired. "Where's Jackson?"

"He's okay." Josh looked at his watch. "It's been seven minutes since the crash."

"It might be the diabetes keeping him knocked out."

The man called to someone outside the door to come get Jackson. Josh handed him to another stranger and leaned down to get Tracey. Her eyes opened.

"I didn't find anything broken," their rescuer said. "Can you climb out of here?"

"Is it over?" she asked, looking at Josh.

"Tenoreno's out there somewhere," Aiden answered behind him. "Watch yourself."

Josh looked at the Ranger Captain. "I'll be back to help. Just let me check on Jackson."

"You stay with your boy. These guys can handle me."

Josh helped Tracey through the door. She was already at Jackson's side by the time he was halfway out.

"Do you think it's too high or too low?" Agent Barlow asked, running around the tail of the plane.

"He hasn't eaten today, but he's been getting the basal dose so that should—" She turned Jackson on his side, checked where his insulin port should be. "The cannula is still here but no tubing and no insulin pump. So now there's a chance it can be clogged. The ambulance may have one."

Tracey took the information a lot more calmly than he did. He was feeling that intense uncertainty again. But watching Tracey thoroughly check his son brought him stability and reassured him. "He's going to be okay. They've called an ambulance. They'll have what we need."

"Jackson." She shook his shoulder. "Can you hear me? Wake up, baby." Tracey pulled up one eyelid and then the other to check his response. Jackson moaned.

"His skin is clammy to the touch," Josh said, knowing that they didn't have much time. "Where's the ambulance? They can test his level and will have a glucagon shot. That should bounce him back."

"We can't wait on the ambulance. We need honey." Tracey searched the people. "Does anybody have honey in their car!" she called out. "He needs his blood sugar brought up fast."

A woman ran from the other side of the plane. "I have what you need at the house. Our grandson is diabetic. I sent someone to fetch it."

Josh had been absorbed in helping his son and hadn't noticed that there was a small group of buildings about a football field away. Sky High Skydiving was written on the side in big bold letters.

"No! Wait!" Out of breath, a teenager stumbled into Josh. All he could do was shove a bottle of honey and a blood testing kit at Josh's chest. "This will work faster."

Josh popped off the top to open a honey bottle and handed it to Tracey. She squeezed the honey onto the tip of her finger and rubbed Jackson's gums, tongue and the inside of his cheeks.

The people who had gathered around were being moved back. Agent McCaffrey's voice was in the background giving instructions to another agent.

"Don't be too low…don't be too low," Tracey chanted.

Tracey went through all the steps they'd done several times a day in the last year. When this all began Friday afternoon, he couldn't remember the date he'd been to the hospital with Jackson. He knew it had happened, but his mind had just gone blank.

The memories and feelings came rushing back like a jet taking off. His son had looked a lot like he did now. Tracey had held him in her arms. He'd had a hard time talking and staying awake.

Everything a year ago had happened so damn quick. Jackson had gone from a healthy little boy to almost dying. He was an amazing kid who bounced back and took it all in stride. Diabetes was a part of his life—their lives—and he never let it stand in his way.

The details crowded his thoughts, trying to block out everything else. Four days in the ICU while the doctors slowly, carefully brought Jackson's electrolytes, potassium and blood sugar into balance. If they did it too fast, he'd die. If they did it too slow, he'd die.

The memory recreated the raw fright of that drive to the hospital emergency. His heart was pounding faster now than it had throughout the past two days.

He'll be okay. He has to be.

"What's she doing?" an onlooker asked.

"Trying to get his blood sugar up." Kendall Barlow answered for them, then knelt next to Josh and Tracey. "I wanted you to know that Sage is safe. We took her to a hospital near Hearne. She's a brave little girl and is talking up a storm about what happened. If you're uncomfortable with that…"

"You're sure she's okay?" Josh asked.

Agent Barlow patted him on the shoulder. "No reason to worry. Rangers arrived to escort her home. Bryce Johnson said he won't be leaving her side. I'll call and have him bring her to Round Rock."

"Round Rock?"

"It's the closest hospital. Agent McCaffrey gave the order for our helicopter to evacuate you guys." The agent stood and withdrew her weapon. "Can he be moved?"

Josh saw the weapon out of the corner of his eye. He scanned the area around them and saw Mack being loaded and handcuffed into the back of a truck. He didn't want to move Jackson until the digital reading came up, but they were about to be sitting ducks.

"What's going on?" Tracey asked from the ground. "His reading is only at forty. I'd like to see if we could get some juice. I'd hate to be in the air if he doesn't bounce back."

"We should take cover. Tenoreno escaped when we crashed. He grabbed the machine pistol before he got out of the plane."

"Does Jackson need juice or is he stable to make a twenty-minute flight to the hospital?" Kendall asked. "Or do we need to take him to the house?"

"No, we can't risk it. Not unless we can get him to drink something, get his levels a bit higher. This kit doesn't have glucagon." Tracey stood with Jackson in her arms. Josh reached for him but she shook her head. "Tenoreno is out there, isn't he? Do you think he'll try something?"

She'd lowered her voice so none of those watching or helping get Aiden and the pilot out of the plane could hear.

"Agent Barlow, I don't suppose you have an extra weapon for Josh? He's a better shot than I am."

Kendall reached down to her leg, unstrapped her backup pistol and handed it to him.

He nodded his thanks. His mind suddenly became clear, remembering something that had bothered him about their landing. "How did our pilot know where he was heading?"

"What are you saying?" Kendall turned in a defensive circle, keeping her back to Josh. "Like they meant to come here all along? This rough landing strip is a legitimate skydiving school. You sure? Why land at a field with no planes that could get fugitives to Mexico?"

"Dammit. Not Tenoreno. It's Mack who knew where he was heading. He was hired to bring Daddy to the vindictive son. Not set him free."

Josh searched the perimeter of the field again and nodded as they headed toward the buildings to the west. Tenoreno was out there—both father and son. The plane crash had been less than ten minutes ago and a man could get a long way on foot in that length of time. But Josh's gut told him that their escaped prisoner was close.

"So you think Xander Tenoreno wants his father dead?" Kendall seemed as surprised as he'd felt earlier. "And he's here waiting to kill him?"

"Is it such a far-fetched idea that the son would want revenge for his mother's murder? Or even to keep the power he's had since Paul was locked up?" He kept Tracey and his son close between him and the agent leading the way. "Maybe we should see if Mack's awake and find out."

Josh trusted Tracey's judgement about his son. He also trusted his own again. He shook off the insecure blanket he'd draped around his shoulders for letting these events happen. Jackson stirred a little, still displaying symptoms of low sugar, but he was a strong kid. He'd make it.

And Josh was a Texas Ranger because he was good at his job. He'd seen the hatred Mack—or Vince Deegan—had for Paul Tenoreno. It was possible Xander could hate him that much, too.

Chapter Twenty-One

Agent McCaffrey nodded to them, standing guard at the plane as the volunteers continued to free the men. Tracey carried Jackson, protected by Agent Barlow and Josh. Whatever her armed escort was discussing, her only concern was getting Jackson to safety. That meant to get him stable, then on that helicopter to Round Rock.

For the middle of nowhere, there were a lot of people gathered under a shed where Agent Barlow stopped. Parachutes. They were packing parachutes for skydiving.

Tracey could see the FBI helicopter on the opposite side of the road. Mack now sat in the back of the truck next to the helicopter. One of his hands was secured to a rail along the truck bed. The pilot was armed with a shotgun, standing guard.

"Ma'am, you mentioned you had juice?" Josh asked the woman who seemed to be the owner. "Is it in the house?"

"Yes, I've sent someone for it," said the woman who'd arranged for the honey and testing kit. "Do you want to take him inside?"

Tracey sat on a stool, balancing Jackson on her legs. She shook her head not wanting to be out of sight of the helicopter.

"No, thanks. We'll head out as soon as Tracey says." Josh kept turning, searching for something or someone.

She could tell that he was anxious but not just for Jackson's welfare. "I can wait on the juice if you need to talk with that man, especially if they might come back and hurt the kids again."

"The FBI can take care of it."

"Looks like they're a little short-handed. Go on. You can tell the helicopter pilot we'll be ready in five minutes." She was confident it wouldn't be long before Jackson was his normal self. Looking down the hill, they were loading the injured ranger on board. "You need to make sure everything's safe. I can wait on the juice."

"I'll be right back." He kissed Jackson's forehead.

Then he brushed his lips against Tracey's and ran to catch up and interrogate Mack.

Agent Barlow was behind her getting names and asking why each person was there. Jackson kicked out and Tracey almost lost him from her lap.

"You could lay him here. If he's not allergic, this is all fresh hay." A young woman stretched a checkered cloth over a loose bunch. "None of the animals have been near it yet. I just set it out this morning."

"Thank you." Tracey moved to let Jackson stretch out.

"Is he okay?"

"I think he will be. Do you live here?" Tracey wiped Jackson's forehead, now dry and cool. Definitely better.

"Oh no, this is a skydiving school. I'm taking lessons and help out with the animals. They're so adorable."

Tracey didn't normally have bad vibes about people. And after the past two days, she didn't really trust the one she felt from this woman, who seemed to be nice. There shouldn't be anything "bad" about someone trying to help a sick little boy get more comfortable. And yet...

Tracey stood. "You know, he is better. We should probably join Josh." She bent to pick him up, but stopped with a gun barrel in her ribs.

"Wow, you caught on real quick," the woman whispered. "Now, we need to leave the kid and back out the other side of this place. Got it? And if you make a move, then somebody else is going to be hurt."

Where had she come from? No one seemed to be alerted that she was there. It was barely dawn for crying out loud. So why wasn't anyone surprised that she was leaving?

When exactly was this sick nightmare going to end?

"I'll come with you." Only to keep anyone else from getting hurt. Tracey tried to get Agent Barlow's attention. No luck.

The woman holding the gun waited for the agent to walk to the opposite side of the structure. She giggled as they walked around the corner and through another shed with long tables.

The gun continued to jab her ribs as the woman picked up her pace and forced Tracey to the far side of all the buildings. They darted from a huge oak tree to a metal shed. Then another. Then another. This side of the skydiving facility couldn't be seen from the plane crash or where she'd left Jackson.

"They're going to know something's wrong. I wouldn't leave Jackson like that. Not voluntarily."

"We don't care if they come looking for you. The more they look, the more they'll flush Paul from his hiding place," a man in his midthirties answered from behind a stack of hay.

The twentysomething woman, actually about the

same age as Tracey, sidled up next to the man and lifted her lips for a kiss. And, of course, she lifted the gun and pointed it in Tracey's general direction.

"Why in the world do you think you need me to help you find your father? You are Xander Tenoreno. Right?"

It was hard to be scared. Too much had happened in the past two days—she'd barely been conscious half an hour. She'd changed or she was just plain tired. The reason was unimportant, but these two didn't really seem threatening to her.

"You know… I might have a concussion. Even though I feel totally fine." She crossed the lean-to and plopped down on a hay bale. "Or I might be quite confident that Josh won't take long to find me. But I am going to wait. Right here. You can do what you want. I'm waiting."

She was the one who sounded a little scary. Sort of delusional or exhausted. Maybe it was shock. Once she sat, she realized her entire body was shaking and her mouth had gone completely dry.

Xander Tenoreno acted like he was ignoring her, as if she wasn't important. But she'd been watching men and their body language closely for hours. And his was tense, ready to pounce if she moved the wrong direction.

"This is ridiculous," Tracey continued. "Your father is long gone. Probably stole a car and headed out while everyone else was running to the plane crash."

"You can shut up now." The chick—she'd lost the right to be referred to with respect—pulled the rather large gun up to her shoulder again. "Xander knows what he's doing."

Tracey nodded and began looking for a weapon or for something to hide behind when the shooting started.

Wow. She really did feel like help was on the way.

Josh wouldn't let anything happen to her. She was more concerned about both of them being separated from Jackson. He needed juice and was barely coherent enough to swallow.

Xander took out a telescope that fit on top of a rifle. He searched the fields and turned his body in a semicircle. He paused several times but didn't do anything except remove his arm from around the woman.

"Why not just let your father go to jail for the rest of his life?" She was legitimately curious. But it also occurred to her that if he was distracted, Josh would have an easier time taking him by surprise.

"My father wasn't going to jail. He wasn't even going to stand trial." He cocked his head to the side. "He was headed to Austin to make a deal. Screw me and our business over so that he could what? Get away with murdering my mother. That's what. His deal would have put him in witness protection. I have a right to take care of this the way I see fit."

Now she was scared.

"WHERE'S TRACEY?" JOSH SAT Jackson upright and made sure he could swallow some juice. A little dribbled down his chin, but he didn't choke. He'd give him a couple of minutes and then repeat the blood test.

"I thought she followed you. I checked the west side of the house, came back and she wasn't here." Kendall placed her palm on Jackson's cheek. "His color is better. Are you ready to transport now?"

"I..." He looked at his son, looked around for Tracey, then stared at the armed pilot. "Something's wrong. She wouldn't leave him alone like this."

They asked the family members and the instructor if they'd seen anything. Their answers were no.

"Maybe you're overthinking," Kendall said.

"Call it in."

"We only have three agents here, Josh. We can't cover each of these buildings until backup arrives."

"She could be dead or miles away from here by then."

"Ma'am?" He tapped on the shoulder of the home owner. "You said your grandson has diabetes, so you're familiar with it?"

"Oh yes, I'm sorry that we didn't have everything your wife needed."

Josh didn't correct her. Moving forward was more important. "Do you mind sitting with Jackson?"

"No. I'd be glad to."

Josh walked away and caught the end of Kendall's phone conversation.

"He's not going to stay put. Tenoreno's out there, sir. I can at least find out where." She hung up and faced him. "Do people always go out on a limb for you, Josh?"

"Not sure how to answer that, but I am grateful."

"Excuse me, you asked about the woman in the plane." A teenage girl holding a dog waited for an okay to finish. "Shawna's gone, too."

"Shawna?"

"She's taking lessons and wanted to feed the animals this morning."

"Has she ever wanted to do that before?" Kendall pulled out her cell again.

"No. Today's the first time."

"Do you have a picture of Shawna and a last name?" Kendall asked.

He battled with himself over whether he should go. Jackson needed him, but so did Tracey. His son was able to swallow. It wasn't his imagination that Jackson's color was better.

"Kendall, I need you to climb out on another limb for me." Her eyebrows arched, asking what without saying a word. "Five minutes and you take Jackson to the hospital."

"But he's—"

"My gut says yes he's better, but I have to be certain. I can't choose one person I love over the other."

"Better idea. You get on the chopper and I'll do my job and track down where Tracey is. Go. Take care of your kid."

While Kendall got the information necessary for her report or an APB on the missing woman, Josh looked for an exit route. Not because he was trying to ditch the FBI agent. If he could find the best route to leave the shelter, he might be able to find Tracey.

"Can I borrow your phone?" Josh asked and the young man nodded. "That's your mom sitting with my son over there, right? Can you tell her to call this," he shook the phone side to side, "if Jackson's condition changes?" He nodded again.

The boy went to his mother, pointed at Josh. He had to try to take care of them both. He'd track down Tracey. When he was gone, Kendall would take his son to the hospital. He focused.

Where would he... There. To keep out of sight they would have headed toward a tree with a tractor parked under it. It was the only place from that side of the shelter. He ran that direction and sure enough, his line of sight to the helicopter pilot was obscured.

He zigzagged across the property using the same logic. If he couldn't see anyone behind him, they probably didn't see him. Then it wasn't a matter of where he'd come from but what was right in front of him.

Tracey.

Along with Xander Tenoreno.

Tracey didn't seem in immediate danger. He could get Kendall or McCaffrey, surround the man ultimately behind the kidnapping of his kids. He felt the emotion building. He shouldn't burst in there with no plan to rescue the woman he loved.

The lines between logic and emotion blurred as he debated which path to follow. Xander looked through a scope toward the far tree line. Josh moved close enough to hear the conversation.

"Predictable. I knew he'd head for a vehicle after walking away from the plane. A shame I wasn't ready for the crash, but that surprise caught me off guard and I missed."

"It's okay, baby."

The girl, Shawna, who had been at the shed earlier, wrapped her arms around Xander and he shrugged her off, uncovering something on a hay bale. Yeah, it was a rifle. Mack had been telling the truth about Xander wanting to kill his father.

The decision about leaving had been made. The son was scoping the dad like it was deer season. Josh didn't have good positioning, he didn't have backup and he only had a peashooter revolver.

What could go wrong?

"Step away from the rifle. Hands on your heads, then drop to your knees." Josh revealed where he was and stepped from behind an animal feeder.

"Well if it isn't Major Joshua Parker here to save the girl again." Xander fingered the rifle trigger. He was not dropping to his knees with his hands on his head.

The girl got closer to his side. She didn't bother listening to Josh, either.

"Don't be an idiot, Tenoreno. I'm not going to let

you hurt anyone. Even your own father." Josh stepped closer, but not close enough to give Xander any advantage. Swinging the rifle around to point at Tracey or himself would be harder at this range.

"She has a gun," Tracey informed him as she slipped off her seat on the hay.

"And she knows how to use it." Xander shifted and the gun was in his hand. "But I know to use it better."

"Give it up. You're not getting away from here."

"Funny thing about revenge, Josh. I'd rather see my father suffer for what he did. He murdered my mother. All she wanted was to live somewhere else. Someplace where he wasn't. After forty years with him, she probably deserved it."

"So you kidnapped Jackson and Sage, and set up this entire game to get back at your daddy?" Tracey moved another step away from Tenoreno.

Josh could tell she was heading for the back side of the lean-to. All she needed was a distraction. "All this because you have daddy issues."

"Seriously? You think I'm going to fall for a question like that?" Xander aimed the gun at Tracey. "I'll let my girlfriend keep your girlfriend occupied while I take care of my business."

"You know I can't let you pull that trigger."

"You're not on the clock now, Ranger Parker. You can let me do anything you want."

"Thing is…he doesn't want to." Tracey answered for him, her shoulders rising with every frightened breath she took. "It doesn't matter how deviant you are or who your father murdered." She pointed to Josh. "That man is a good man. He'll give his life to protect you both. You'll never understand what makes him decent."

Josh's heart swelled. No two ways about it, she loved

him. His hands steadied. His feet were firm and fixed. He was ready for whatever came next. But she was wrong. He loved her and would protect her before doing anything else.

Xander ignored them and put his eye to the scope again.

"I'll say this one more time. Drop the gun, kneel and put your hands on your head." It was a small backup revolver. "I have six shots. That's three for each of you. No warnings. Center mass. I won't miss."

"Xander? Baby, what do I do?" The weight of the big gun or the nerves of the young woman caused the gun to wobble in her hands. Xander ignored her, too.

Shawna looked from Tracey leaning on the hay, to Josh pointing a gun at her. After he didn't answer or acknowledge her, she didn't look at her boyfriend. The gun dropped from her hands, she fell to her knees and began crying.

For a couple of seconds Josh thought it was over. He wanted to be back with Jackson and Sage. He wanted to talk about everything with Tracey. He wanted all this to become a memory.

Xander Tenoreno pulled the trigger. Josh squeezed his.

Shawna screamed. Tracey fell to the ground.

Josh leaped across the space separating him from Xander. Encouraged by the love he'd heard in Tracey's words and scared to death that something had just happened to her. Shawna was up and running but she was someone else's problem. Tracey needed to find the gun that had dropped from the woman's hands. The man fired and she'd hit the dirt herself, not certain what would happen.

Josh was fighting Xander. She was sure he felt like

he needed to eliminate the threat. The man was crazy. He'd shot his father in front of a Texas Ranger.

Where's the gun? Where's the gun?

Tracey scooted on her hands and knees looking for the silver steel in all the dirt and pieces of hay. Her head was down and she looked up only to see Josh winning the battle.

She got knocked backward when Xander tripped over her. Josh came in to land a powerful blow to the man's abdomen.

"Give it up." Josh watched as his opponent fell backward.

Tracey didn't need to search for the gun anymore. It was over. Xander Tenoreno didn't get up. He was done. Knocked out cold by the time Kendall and the other agent got to the lean-to.

"We heard shots."

"I'm not sure, but Paul Tenoreno might be at the other end of where that rifle is pointed."

"You okay?" Tracey asked. "Can you make it back to the house?"

Josh took a deep breath and stood up straight, wincing. "As long as you're here...I'll be fine. Let's go get our boy."

"TENORENO JUNIOR'S WOUND isn't serious. We'll ride with the emergency unit and transport him and Vince Deegan to Round Rock." Kendall joined them at the helicopter as they watched a now alert Jackson let the pilot settle a headset on his ears.

"And Tenoreno senior?" Josh asked.

"We were too late. Bullet hit the lung."

"I didn't think he'd do it."

"You aren't the murderer, Josh."

"Aiden and Jackson are set and ready. Unfortunately, the pilot didn't make it. There's room on the helicopter for one of you. Who's going?" McCaffrey asked, tapping Josh on the back of his shoulder with whatever papers he had in his hand.

It was his son. His place was beside him. Tracey didn't hesitate, she gently pushed Josh forward. "I'll find Sage and be right behind you, even if I have to steal a car to get there."

Josh stepped on board, watching her, acting as if he was about to say something.

The corners of Tracey's mouth went up and down. She couldn't keep a smile as the door began closing, separating them. She lifted her hand, then covered her mouth to hold back the tears.

"Hold it." Josh pushed the door aside and held out his hand. "She's with me."

They all moved out of his way and an agent got off, not bothering to argue. Once again he showed everyone around them that she wasn't *just* the nanny.

Accidental Baby and some indecipherable scrawl, the pilot didn't risk it. Upon touch on the helicopter's floor, or upon Allie's going, Tracey felt weak, laying back onto a much cushioned chair with whatever strength he had in his hand.

Fred was the first to comprehend his phrase. Tracey didn't understand either what he'd meant. "I'll find you," she admitted. And he had to wait to get there.

Josh and Fred on board—watching the scene laid on

Chapter Twenty-Two

Bouncing back from the low blood sugar levels was a breeze for Jackson. What they hadn't realized was that his right ulna had been cracked in the plane crash. He'd been so out of it at the time that he didn't begin complaining until much later in the day.

Instead of sending them home to sleep in their own beds, the FBI put them in a hotel suite in Waco. They claimed it was easier to protect them there. And since it didn't matter where they slept, Josh agreed. They were all together. Exhausted but very much alive.

"Didn't they catch all the people involved?" she'd asked him once McCaffrey had gone.

Josh had pulled her into his arms and kissed her briefly. "They're playing it safe. Think of it this way, no cooking. No commuting back and forth to your place."

And no talking about how—or if—their relationship had changed. The suite had two bedrooms. She had to admit that room service and not making her bed had huge appeal.

Sage drew pictures that were full of Jackson's favorite things and asked for a roll of tape so she could cover the walls. There were a couple of times where she ran to the bed where Jackson was on forced rest and Tracey thought there might have been a hint of twin talk. Just long looks where they were communicating, but no words were exchanged.

They were back to their regular twin selves.

Whatever happened between Jackson and Sage, they didn't share it with her, but they did involve their dad. Josh had stepped into the hall for several phone calls she assumed were official Ranger business.

Tracey went to bed after watching Josh hold his kids close, tucked up under each arm. A beautiful sight. His look—before he'd fallen asleep—had invited her to join them, but it wasn't time. Not yet.

One day soon, they'd talk about the way they felt. Right now, they all just needed rest and assurance that nothing else would happen.

Day two of their protective custody, under a Ranger escort, Tracey took Sage home to clean up and grab art supplies. She thought Josh would want something clean to wear and headed to his bedroom when she caught Bryce coming from there.

"Oh, hi." He turned sideways in the hall so she could pass. "I was just grabbing him… He asked me to pick up—I even remembered his toothbrush."

He lifted a gym bag. She assumed it was filled with Josh's clothes and she didn't need to worry about picking anything out. But Bryce looked extremely guilty. What was up with that?

"Okay. So I'm just going to grab Sage some snacks, then we'll be ready to head back. Is anything wrong?"

"Nope. Nothing's wrong."

"I got Jackson's stuff." Sage came from their bedroom and Bryce scooped her up to carry her downstairs, making her giggle all the way down.

Everything shouted that the man was lying. She'd let Josh deal with whatever that was about. One short stop by her place and they were ready to head back to the hospital.

"Sage, honey, can you wear your headphones for a little while?"

Bryce waited for the little girl to comply, then her escort took a long breath. "That doesn't bode well for whatever you're going to ask."

"I need to know what's going on. Has something else happened? We're being guarded twenty-four-seven and you're acting very suspicious." Not to mention Josh's compliance with everything Agent McCaffrey suggested.

"Nothing that I know about. It seems that Xander Tenoreno bribed the pilot. They aren't making a big deal about that because he died."

Even with Bryce's assurances, Tracey has a feeling something was being kept from her. Everyone was acting so…different. Bryce drove into the parking lot and she saw the two men who had been her bodyguards standing at the front entrance.

"Oh, that's just great! Just when I thought everything was settling back to normal my uncle strikes again."

"You want me to get rid of them?"

"No. I can do it. Will you take Sage back to Josh?" She walked up to the guard who had at least spoken to her and stuck her palm out. "Your phone, please."

"No need for that, miss. Your uncle's inside. We're waiting for him here."

The demise of the Tenoreno family, the dramatic recovery of the twins. All of it made good television and press for the state and the Rangers. But all of it put the Bass family in the limelight, too. She'd expected a phone call from her uncle, not a visit.

She entered the lobby, expecting an entourage to

be surrounding Carl. He sat in the corner alone, a cup of coffee on the table next to him. He acknowledged her, she overheard some business lingo and expected to have to wait.

"There she is. I've got to go. Call you back later." Carl dropped the phone into his pocket—totally an unusual move for him. "You look tired, darling. Getting enough rest? Do I need to secure the entire floor so you can get a decent night's sleep?"

"I'm fine. It's been pretty hectic lately. So what do you need? If it's about the reporters, my name change is public record—there's nothing I could do about them finding out our family history."

"Same Tracey." He pulled her shoulders, drawing her to his chest for a hug. "But you're all grown-up now, right?"

When he released her, she took a couple of steps back, looking at him. "What's going on?"

"I needed to see that you were okay. Completely okay. And here." Wallet now in hand, he reached inside and took out a check. "Spend it on whatever you need. Buy a new electric fence or a security system or even bodyguards for a while. No, don't argue. You've discovered there are some seriously bad people in the world. Those kids need to be protected. Oh, and I'm here because I was invited."

He wrapped her hand through the crook of his arm and escorted her to as if it was Buckingham Palace. She might actually enjoy being an adult around him, but why would he say he'd been invited? By whom?

Carl stepped aside just before they reached the door to the suite. Bryce handed her a handmade princess hat Sage had decorated that morning. "I think you're supposed to put that on."

She followed instructions and entered. The room was overflowing with friends and relatives. Everyone was wearing either a crown or a princess hat.

"My lady." Carl placed her hand on his and took two steps.

The room was silent, people practically held their breath. Asking what was going on would ruin the entire effect. Carl joined Gwen's parents, who were steadying Sage and Jackson on chairs next to Josh. Both children had towels draped around their shoulders as if they were acting out one of their stories. Sage even had the wand they'd made together months ago.

Josh formally bowed. He raised his eyebrows and carefully took her hand.

"I was hoping for a moment alone before this happened," he whispered, "but I got outvoted." Josh cleared his throat. "Before we have an audience with the Prince and Princess Parkers, you need to know that their father—"

"The king," the twins said together.

"The king, loves you with all his mind, soul and heart. So…Tracey Cassidy…" He dipped his hand in his pocket and knelt on bended knee.

"Would you marry us?" they all said together.

Josh opened his palm where a sparkly diamond solitaire was surrounded by multicolored glitter. She cupped Josh's cheeks and kissed him with her answer as he stood.

Everyone began clapping.

"That means yes!" the twins shouted.

Epilogue

Two weeks later

"Let me get this straight. All you have to do is wait around until you're thirty years old and you get control of your own money. That sounds like a plan. You're already set for life," Bryce told Tracey. He had one arm around the waist of his girlfriend and the other wrapped around a bucket of Bush's chicken strips.

Tracey nodded like the ten other times she'd answered the question for Josh's men. Josh thought she'd lose a gasket if she discovered Bryce was teasing a fellow silver-spooner. She needed rescuing and this time he didn't need a gun.

"Did he tell you that I had to collect that rock and get it to the room before you?" Bryce said, pointing to her ring. "So you really don't have to work—"

"She does if we want to eat." Josh jumped in and stole the chicken from his computer expert. He whisked Tracey away to a corner of the kitchen not occupied by a ranger or significant other. "Sorry."

"You said you wouldn't tell anyone."

"I didn't." He shrugged. "They are investigators, you know. They all worked on different possibilities of who had the kids even when they were told to stand down.

It's just one of those things that happens at my office, Mrs. Parker."

He took a chicken tender from the box. Gone in two large bites. She laughed.

Life still hadn't settled into something resembling normalcy. Maybe it never would. Maybe normal didn't exist. But here they were—husband and wife. Had he been romantic? He couldn't wait that long. He'd asked. She'd replied, "Yes. Let's not wait."

So they hadn't.

Two weeks later, the Company was throwing them a surprise party. Tracey's uncle had flown Gwen's parents in the previous week. They all encouraged them to have the courtroom ceremony while they were visiting.

"Don't you think you should put the chicken on the table with the rest of the food?" Tracey asked, making a lunge for the box.

He plucked another tender and shoved it in his mouth. "We could feed a starving nation with what's on that table. They aren't going to miss this little bit of bird."

"Bryce will. You should have seen his face when you stole it from him."

"Ha. You should see yours now that you can't reach it."

"Oh, I don't want the chicken. I want your hands free. I'm getting kind of used to them touching me. But if you'd rather hold deep-fried chicken, then…" She shrugged and spun out of his arms.

"Okay, okay. You've made your point." He followed Tracey to the table, where she picked up two plates and filled them with munchkin-sized portions.

"I thought Gwen's parents were taking the kids to dinner?"

"They said they'd take them for chicken and since it's here—"

"You feel kind of weird letting them leave the house?" Josh took the plates from her hands and set them on the bar. "I get it. I'll take it up and explain."

"I'll go. They're really nice and I think they'll understand."

"Yep. And you're right." He wrapped his arms around her body and pulled her to him for a kiss.

The door opened and Josh watched from a distance as Aiden Oaks entered. White hat in hand—at least the hand that wasn't holding a crutch, blue jeans ripped up to the knee, leg in a cast, badge over his heart. "May I come in?"

"Sure."

"Need a beer?"

"Here, take this chair." The men of Company F made their commander comfortable.

Aiden swung the crutch like a pro and made himself comfortable. Josh squeezed Tracey's hand and kissed her for luck. That uncertain future might be resolved in the next couple of minutes.

"Hello, Captain."

"Major." He adjusted the crutch to lean on the chair and hung his hat on top. "How are the kids, Tracey?"

"Physically they're great. We're working on the kidnapping slowly. But I think we're all getting back to normal."

Josh threaded his fingers through hers. She knew why Aiden was there. Most of the conversation had stopped. There was the lull of a baseball game in the background. They'd all been expecting a decision on his reprimand at any time. Maybe it was appropriate that they get the news tonight.

They were celebrating the start of a new life.

"A couple of decisions came down the pipe today. Xander Tenoreno's been indicted on racketeering, kidnapping and everything else the attorney general's office could come up with. An operation to free the families of men who worked for him was successful. And before you begin clapping, the thing you've all been wanting to know..." he paused while the crowd came closer. "I'm returning the reins of Company F to Major Parker."

Cries of laughter and relief echoed through the house from the men and women surrounding him. Claps on the back and congratulations should have distracted him, but all he could see was Tracey's joy.

Their relationship had begun with a tragedy, and then adversity had brought them closer. His bride had the right to ask him to walk away from the Rangers after the kidnapping. Her uncle had told them he'd make arrangements for her to access her inheritance. Unlike what he'd told Bryce, neither of them needed to work.

Seemed like all he wanted to do was make up for the time they'd been waiting on each other to make decisions. He knew how much support he had from her. Seeing it now, all he could do was pull her to him and kiss her.

One kiss that turned into a second and a third. It might have gone further, but a couple of fake coughs started behind him.

"Do we have to stay upstairs, Daddy?" Sage crooked her finger several times, then just waved her hands for him to bend down so she could whisper in his ear. "What am I supposed to call Trace Trace now? Grandfather told me she's our stepmother. Is she going to get mean and grow warts like in all the stories?"

Josh laughed and picked up his little girl. "What do you want to call Trace Trace?" he asked, using the kids' nickname.

"Can it just be Mommy?"

His eyes locked with the woman who'd been there with him through the darkest part of his life. Her eyes brimmed with tears ready to fall. "I think she'd like that."

Tracey nodded her head, quickly whisking the tears from her cheeks before letting Sage see her. "Hey, kid-let. That sounds like a perfect name. No one's ever called me that before. You two will be the first."

Cast banging on the rails, Jackson flew down the stairs and into her arms. "They said we needed to ask, but I knew you'd like it."

Tracey kissed both of their cheeks with lots of noise. "I don't just like it. I absolutely adore it." Her eyes locked with Josh's. "Almost as much as I love all of you."

And just like kids that subject was settled and they ran back to their grandparents on the stairs. Their grandmother declared there was enough food to feed all five companies of Rangers. He felt Tracey's sigh of relief as she relaxed within his arms. The kids went up and Gwen's mother came for their dinner.

Before they handed her the plates, she gathered them both close for a hug, then wiped away a tear. "I want you to know how happy we are for you. We had begun to wonder if Josh was ever going to ask you after what he said last Christmas."

Tracey looked confused. "What did he say?"

His mother-in-law pushed forward. "Josh told us how he felt and that he wanted to remarry. You were a bless-ing to our Gwen, Tracey. If she can't be here to raise her children, I know she'd be happy you will be. Welcome to our family."

Tracey looked happy as they watched his mother-in-law return upstairs. "I meant to tell you about that."

"Did you change your mind or something?"

"Obviously not. I thought I should probably ask you on a date first. I intended to on your birthday," Josh whispered.

She twisted around to face him. "Get out of town. Really? What changed your mind? Get a little too tipsy instead?"

"I wasn't tipsy. Just lost my nerve."

"You? The man who ran and jumped into the small door of a plane with machine guns firing all around him?"

"Yeah, I know, hard to believe. But a wise man once told me never to ask a woman a certain question you didn't know the answer to. I thought I did. Only to realize the only thing for certain I knew was that I loved everything about you. But you might not necessarily feel the same."

She swatted at him as if he was totally wrong. He knew better. He'd messed up her birthday and he'd messed up the romance. He'd spend the rest of his uncertain future making it up to her.

Every day was precious. They knew it better than most. And he wouldn't take life for granted.

"Do you think those two will even notice that I've moved in?"

Josh seized the opportunity of her upturned face to kiss her again. Slowly, gaining the notice of their surprise guests and family. He came away with a smile on his face.

Happy. Satisfied that Tracey, Jackson and Sage were the normal he wanted.

Josh whispered his answer so only his wife could hear. "There will be a heck of a lot of sleepovers to explain if they don't."

* * * * *

MILLS & BOON®

The Regency Collection – Part 1

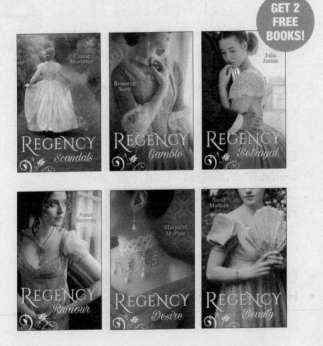

GET 2 FREE BOOKS!

Let these roguish rakes sweep you off to the
Regency period in part 1 of our collection!

Order yours at **www.millsandboon.co.uk/regency1**

MILLS & BOON®

The Regency Collection – Part 2

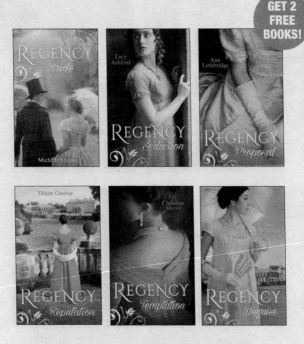

Join the London ton for a Regency season in part 2 of our collection!

Order yours at **www.millsandboon.co.uk/regency2**